HOSPITALITY FINANCIAL MANAGEMENT

CONCEPTS AND CASES

HOSPITALITY FINANCIAL MANAGEMENT

CONCEPTS AND CASES

Editor
Abhinandan Chauhan

DPH
DISCOVERY
PUBLISHING HOUSE

Published by:

DISCOVERY PUBLISHING HOUSE
4383/4B, Ansari Road, Darya Ganj
New Delhi-110 002 (India)
Phone : +91-11-23279245; 23253475; 43596065
Mobile : +91 9811179893 / +91 9871656464
E-mail : discoverybooksindia@gmail.com
orderdphbooks@gmail.com
namitwasan9@gmail.com
web : www.discoverypublishinggroup.com

Hospitality Financial Management: ***Concepts and Cases***
Edited by: **Abhinandan Chauhan**

International Standard Book Number: **978-93-6224-559-5** (Hardback)

Printed at:
Infinity Imaging Systems
Delhi (INDIA)

PREFACE

In the vast expanse of the economic landscape, the hospitality sector stands out as a colossus, marked by its sheer size and remarkable diversity. In hospitality management, however, is not without its trials and tribulations. Business operators frequently grapple with the whims of consumer behavior, which can shift dramatically and without warning. Given the sector's direct engagement with the public, its fortunes are inextricably linked to the fluctuating spending patterns of the populace.

The challenges of adapting to these shifts were starkly illustrated during the global pandemic, a period that saw the hospitality industry face unprecedented hurdles. With countries in lockdown, the flow of patrons to hotels, bars, and restaurants dwindled to a trickle, leading to significant financial strain. Despite governmental aid, the industry struggled to weather the storm, highlighting its vulnerability to external shocks.

Moreover, the competitive nature of the hospitality industry adds another layer of complexity, particularly for newcomers. Success demands not only the ability to deliver exceptional service but also the agility to evolve with the ever-changing tastes and expectations of consumers. Yet, perhaps the most formidable challenge lies in the arena of financial management. It is here, in the meticulous oversight of finances, that the foundation for a thriving hospitality business is laid.

Financial management acts as the linchpin of the hospitality sector, ensuring the smooth operation of businesses within it. Among its key roles, budgeting stands paramount. Effective budget planning enables hospitality ventures to distribute their resources wisely, paving the way for operational efficiency and financial health.

"Hospitality Financial Management" is a comprehensive textbook designed to equip students and professionals in the hospitality industry with essential knowledge and skills in financial management. Spanning eight structured chapters, this book covers a broad spectrum of financial topics relevant to the hospitality sector, offering insights into managing finances effectively to ensure business success and sustainability.

Chapter 1 sets the foundation by introducing the principles of financial management within the context of the hospitality industry. It outlines the significance of financial management for hotels, restaurants, and other hospitality businesses, emphasizing its role in strategic planning, operations, and achieving long-term goals. Chapter 2 covers the components and interpretation of financial statements. It guides readers through the balance sheet, income statement, and cash flow statement, illustrating how these documents can provide valuable insights into a business's financial health and performance.

In Chapter 3, the focus shifts to the development and implementation of effective pricing strategies. This chapter explores various pricing models and techniques that can maximize revenue while considering customer perception and market demand. Chapter 4 addresses the critical issue of cost management. It offers strategies for minimizing costs without compromising service quality, covering areas such as labor, inventory, and operational expenses.

Chapter 5 highlights the importance of revenue management. It discusses the responsibilities of revenue managers, including pricing, demand forecasting, and distribution channel management, to optimize profitability.

Chapter 6 focuses on the techniques and tools for predicting future demand. This chapter is crucial for planning and decision-making, enabling businesses to align their strategies with market trends and customer behavior. Chapter 7 examines the challenges and strategies related to inventory control. It covers stock management, supplier relations, and technology solutions that can enhance efficiency and reduce waste.

Finally, Chapter 8 explores the decision-making process for significant investments. It discusses the evaluation of investment opportunities, risk assessment, and the impact of these decisions on a company's financial future.

Therefore, this book serves as a vital resource for understanding and applying financial management practices in the hospitality industry, blending theoretical knowledge with practical insights to prepare readers for successful financial stewardship in their hospitality ventures.

The textbook "Hospitality Financial Management" is primarily aimed at students pursuing degrees in hospitality management, providing them with a comprehensive understanding of financial principles specific to the industry. It also serves as a valuable resource for professionals within the hospitality sector seeking to deepen their financial management skills. Lastly, it caters to educators and trainers looking for a structured curriculum to guide their instruction in hospitality financial practices.

Editor

CONTENTS

CHAPTER 1

Financial Management in Hospitality Industry: An Overview

INTRODUCTION

Hospitality financial management plays a crucial role in ensuring that the financial aspects of businesses within the hospitality industry, such as hotels and restaurants, are meticulously monitored and organized. This encompasses a broad range of financial concerns, mirroring issues faced by various other sectors. These include, but are not limited to, evaluating the cost-effectiveness and return on investment of marketing initiatives, as well as managing payroll for employees. However, the hospitality sector faces a set of challenges that are somewhat more distinct compared to other industries, notably in areas such as food cost management, which requires vigilant supervision over food-related expenditures.

The essence of hospitality financial management lies in its aim to ensure the judicious handling of a business's financial resources. This objective shares similarities with the financial management practices of companies across different sectors, where the balancing act between revenue inflow and the expenses incurred, including payments to employees and suppliers of the products and services utilized by the business, is a common challenge. Operational costs, such as the leasing or taxation of business premises, particularly in high-demand locations, also represent significant concerns within the realm of hospitality financial oversight.

Moreover, the hospitality industry is confronted with unique financial management issues. Establishments like hotels, bars, and restaurants must regularly procure fresh food supplies for the preparation of dishes, a necessity that underscores the critical nature of managing perishable goods, a concern less pronounced in other sectors. Given that many hospitality businesses are integral to the tourism sector, financial management in this context also entails the strategic allocation of funds towards local tourism initiatives and marketing efforts aimed at both attracting new patrons and retaining existing ones, without causing disenchantment among the latter.

The approach to financial management within the hospitality industry can vary significantly across different entities. For many organizations, particularly large corporations or renowned tourist attractions, financial management might be the sole purview of a dedicated manager tasked with the comprehensive oversight of the company's financial health. This includes managing operational expenses, authorizing additional outlays for various services, and keeping a close watch on the revenue streams generated from customers. On the other hand, smaller businesses may have a single individual, possibly the owner or a hired manager, responsible for both the general operations and the financial management of the establishment. This arrangement is often seen in smaller venues where the manager or owner takes on multiple roles to manage both the day-to-day operations and the broader financial responsibilities of the business, thereby ensuring the sustainability and profitability of the enterprise in the competitive landscape of the hospitality industry.

1.1 FINANCIAL MANAGEMENT

Hospitality managers use financial information to manage activities involving money that is earned and spent in the operation of their business. Financial information that summarizes these activities must be organized and expressed in ways that are meaningful. Analysis and interpretation of data is necessary, and the results must be recorded, summarized, and reported to those needing to know about the economic health of the restaurant. As will be seen, users will be both internal—owners and managers, for example—and external—including lenders and government agencies.

Financial management is not the same as bookkeeping: There is a big difference! Financial management includes organizing, analyzing, interpreting, recording, summarizing, and reporting financial information. By contrast, a bookkeeper's primary task is to analyze and record transactions. In very large restaurants, a bookkeeper may handle only one type of transaction, such as sales, accounts receivable collections, or payroll. The accountant then summarizes the bookkeeper's work and further interprets the results for management.

1.1.1 Meaning of Finance

Finance may be defined as the art and science of managing money. It includes financial service and financial instruments. Finance also is referred as the provision of money at the time when it is needed. Finance function is the procurement of funds and their effective utilization in business concerns.

The concept of finance includes capital, funds, money, and amount. But each word is having unique meaning. Studying and understanding the concept of finance become an important part of the business concern.

According to the researcher, "Finance is the art and science of managing money". Or the word 'finance' connotes 'management of money'.

Another defines finance as "the Science on study of the management of funds' and the management of fund as the system that includes the circulation of money, the granting of credit, the making of investments, and the provision of banking facilities.

1.1.2 Types of Finance

Finance is one of the important and integral part of business concerns, hence, it plays a major role in every part of the business activities. It is used in all the area of the activities under the different names. (See Figure 1.1)

Finance can be classified into two major parts:

- ***Private finance,*** which includes the individual, firms, business or corporate financial activities to meet the requirements.
- ***Public finance*** which concerns with revenue and disbursement of government such as Central Government, State Government and Semi-Government Financial matters.

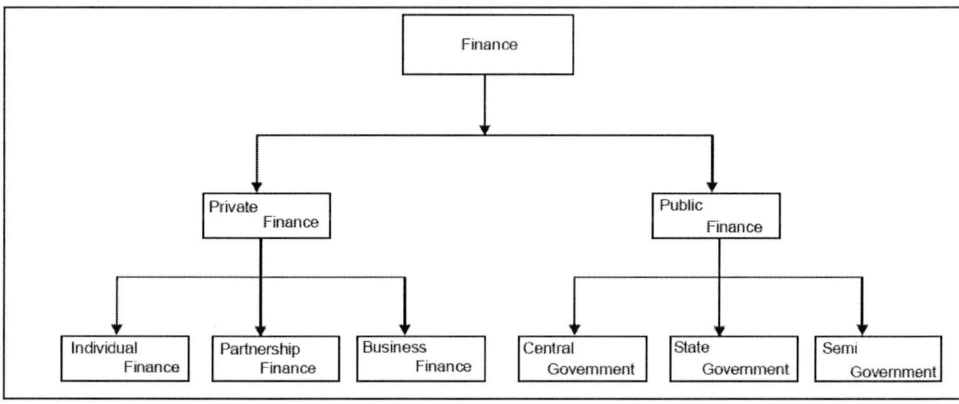

Figure 1.1. *Types of finance.*

1.1.3 Definition of Financial Management

Financial management is an integral part of overall management. It is concerned with the duties of the financial managers in the business firm.

The term financial management has been defined by researcher, "It is concerned with the efficient use of an important economic resource namely, capital funds".

> The most popular and acceptable definition of financial management as "Financial Management deals with procurement of funds and their effective utilization in the business."

Financial management as an application of general managerial principles to the area of financial decision-making.

Another definition financial management "is an area of financial decision-making, harmonizing individual motives and enterprise goals".

Thus, Financial Management is mainly concerned with the effective funds management in the business. In simple words, Financial Management as practiced by business firms can be called as Corporation Finance or Business Finance.

1.1.4 Scope of Financial Management

Financial management is one of the important parts of overall management, which is directly related with various functional departments like personnel, marketing and production.

Financial management covers wide area with multidimensional approaches. The following are the important scope of financial management.

- ***Financial Management and Economics:*** Economic concepts like micro and macroeconomics are directly applied with the financial management approaches. Investment decisions, micro and macro environmental factors are closely associated with the functions of financial manager. Financial management also uses the economic equations like money value discount factor, economic order quantity etc. Financial economics is one of the emerging area, which provides immense opportunities to finance, and economical areas.
- ***Financial Management and Accounting:*** Accounting records includes the financial information of the business concern. Hence, we can easily understand the relationship between the financial management and accounting. In the olden periods, both financial management and accounting are treated as a same discipline and then it has been merged as Management Accounting because this part is very much helpful to finance manager to take decisions. But now a day's financial management and accounting discipline are separate and interrelated.
- ***Financial Management or Mathematics:*** Modern approaches of the financial management applied large number of mathematical and statistical tools and techniques. They are also called as econometrics. Economic order quantity, discount factor, time value of money, present value of money, cost of capital, capital structure theories, dividend theories, ratio analysis and working capital analysis are used as mathematical and statistical tools and techniques in the field of financial management.
- ***Financial Management and Production Management:*** Production management is the operational part of the business concern, which helps to multiple the money into profit. Profit of the concern depends upon the production performance. Production performance needs finance, because production department requires raw material, machinery, wages, operating expenses etc. These expenditures are decided and estimated by the financial department and the finance manager allocates the appropriate finance to production department. The financial

manager must be aware of the operational process and finance required for each process of production activities.

- ***Financial Management and Marketing:*** Produced goods are sold in the market with innovative and modern approaches. For this, the marketing department needs finance to meet their requirements. The financial manager or finance department is responsible to allocate the adequate finance to the marketing department. Hence, marketing and financial management are interrelated and depends on each other.
- ***Financial Management and Human Resource:*** Financial management is also related with human resource department, which provides manpower to all the functional areas of the management. Financial manager should carefully evaluate the requirement of manpower to each department and allocate the finance to the human resource department as wages, salary, remuneration, commission, bonus, pension and other monetary benefits to the human resource department. Hence, financial management is directly related with human resource management.

1.1.5 Importance of Financial Management

Finance is the lifeblood of business organization. It needs to meet the requirement of the business concern. Each and every business concern must maintain adequate amount of finance for their smooth running of the business concern and also maintain the business carefully to achieve the goal of the business concern. The business goal can be achieved only with the help of effective management of finance. We cannot neglect the importance of finance at any time at and at any situation. Some of the importance of the financial management is as follows:

- ***Financial Planning:*** Financial management helps to determine the financial requirement of the business concern and leads to take financial planning of the concern. Financial planning is an important part of the business concern, which helps to promotion of an enterprise.
- ***Acquisition of Funds:*** Financial management involves the acquisition of required finance to the business concern. Acquiring needed funds play a major part of the financial management, which involve possible source of finance at minimum cost.
- ***Proper Use of Funds:*** Proper use and allocation of funds leads to improve the operational efficiency of the business concern. When the finance manager uses the funds properly, they can reduce the cost of capital and increase the value of the firm.
- ***Financial Decision:*** Financial management helps to take sound financial decision in the business concern. Financial decision will affect the entire business operation of the concern. Because there is a direct relationship with various department functions such as marketing, production personnel, etc.
- ***Improve Profitability:*** Profitability of the concern purely depends on the effectiveness and proper utilization of funds by the business concern. Financial management helps to improve the profitability position of the

concern with the help of strong financial control devices such as budgetary control, ratio analysis and cost volume profit analysis.

- ***Increase the Value of the Firm:*** Financial management is very important in the field of increasing the wealth of the investors and the business concern. Ultimate aim of any business concern will achieve the maximum profit and higher profitability leads to maximize the wealth of the investors as well as the nation.
- ***Promoting Savings:*** Savings are possible only when the business concern earns higher profitability and maximizing wealth. Effective financial management helps to promoting and mobilizing individual and corporate savings.

Nowadays financial management is also popularly known as business finance or corporate finances. The business concern or corporate sectors cannot function without the importance of the financial management.

1.1.6 Inter-relation among Financial Decisions

All the major functions or decisions – Investment function, Finance function, Liquidity function and Dividend function, are inter-related and inter-connected. They are inter-related because the goal of all the functions is one and the same. Their ultimate objective is only one – achievement of maximization of shareholders' wealth or maximizing the market value of the shares.

All the decisions are also inter-connected or inter-dependent also. Let us illustrate both these aspects with an example.

Example: If a firm wants to undertake a project requiring funds, this investment decision cannot be taken, in isolation, without considering the availability of finances, which is a finance decision. Both the decisions are inter-connected.

If the firm allocates more funds for fixed assets, lesser amount would be available for current assets. So, financing decision and liquidity decision are inter-connected.

The firm has two options to finance the project, either from internal resources or raising funds, externally, from the market. If the firm decides to meet the total project cost only from internal resources, the profits, otherwise available for distribution in the form of dividend, have to be retained to meet the project cost. Here, the finance decision has influenced the dividend decision.

So, an efficient financial management takes the optimal decision by considering the implications or impact of all the decisions, together, on the market value of the company's shares. The decision has to be taken considering all the angles, simultaneously.

No Function is Superior

All the functions are important. Importance of the function depends on the situation of the firm. If a firm has adequate investment opportunities but experiences difficulty to raise funds, then the finance function is superior to the firm, at that juncture. It does not mean that investment decision is less important compared to finance decision, always.

The essence is no financial function or decision is superior to others. (See Figure 1.2)

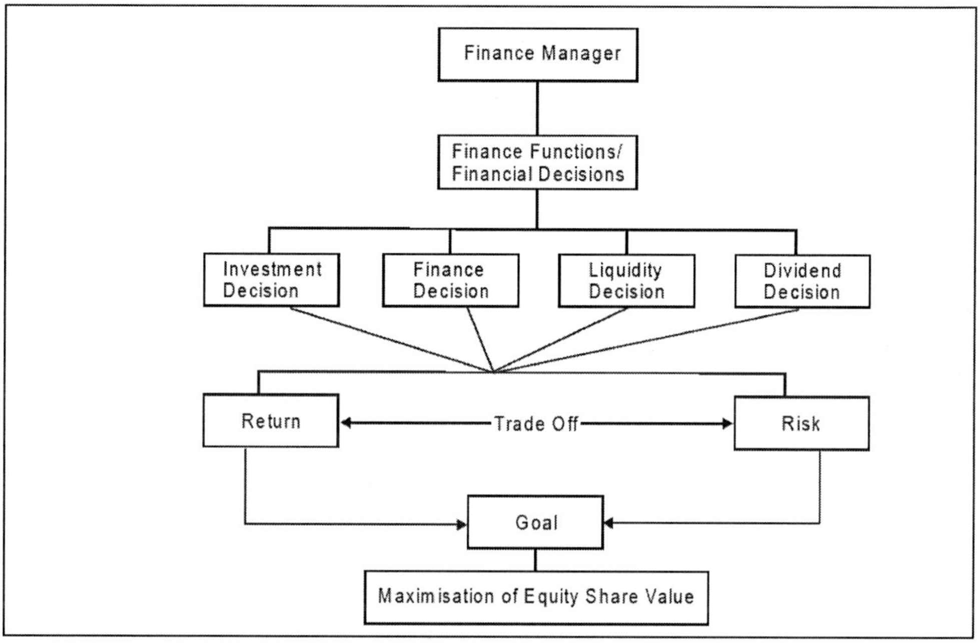

Figure 1.2. *Goal of financial management.*

1.1.7 Nature of Financial Management

The nature of financial management is the relationship with economics and accounting, its functions and its scope. Financial management is the way and the means of making money, the application of the functions of planning and control to the finance function.

The modern approach to financial management is to find out how much money is required by the company in question, and then to source at least that amount. The amount should then be invested to ensure that the objectives of the financial management and the company as a whole are met. To break this down into simple terms, financial management have the responsibility to estimate the funds required, raise the funds and finally to invest the funds.

When raising finance a financial management team should ensure that they strike a balance of owned and borrowed funds. This is simply so the company does not have too big an amount of debt on its hands. Once the funds have been raised it is important to spend them wisely, normally on fixed assets and using the balance as working capital. Fixed assets should only be purchased if they can add value to the business, especially long-term value. Most fixed assets that would be purchased by a company will be expensive so they need to be able to produce work for a considerable period of time.

Working capital will be required for the day-to-day running of the company, and for emergencies. This working capital should not be too large as spare money may gain interest in the bank but it should be cycled back into the company.

An important decision of financial management is how much to pay the shareholders, and how much to retain as working capital for the business. Shareholders expectations and the company performance as whole need to be taken into consideration when making this decision.

1.1.8 Functional Areas of Modern Financial Management

Financial management, at present is not confined to raising and allocating funds. The study of financial institutions like stock exchange, capital, market, etc. is also emphasized because they influenced under writing of securities and corporate promotion. Company finance was considered to be the major domain of financial management. The scope of this subject has widened to cover capital structure, dividend policies, profit planning and control, depreciation policies. Some of the functional areas covered in financial management as:

- ***Determining Financial Needs:*** A finance manager is supposed to meet financial needs of the enterprise. For this purpose, he should determine financial needs of the concern. Funds are needed to meet promotional expenses, fixed and working capital needs. The requirement of fixed assets is related to types of industry. A manufacturing concern will require more investments in fixed assets than a trading concern. The working capital needs depend upon scale of operations. Larger the scale of operations, the higher will be the needs for working capital. A wrong assessment of financial needs may jeopardize the survival of a concern.
- ***Choosing the Sources of Funds:*** A number of sources may be available for raising funds. A concern may be resort to issue of share capital and debentures. Financial institutions may be requested to provide long-term funds. The working capital needs may be met by getting cash credit or overdraft facilities from commercial bands. A finance manager has to be very careful and cautions in approaching different sources.
- ***Financial Analysis and Interpretation:*** The analysis and interpretation of financial statements is an important task of a finance manager. He is expected to know about the profitability, liquidity position, short term and long-term financial position of the concern. For this purpose, a number of ratios have to be calculated. The interpretation of various ratios is also essential to reach certain conclusions financial analysis and interpretation has become an important area of financial management.
- ***Cost-Volume Profit Analysis:*** This is popularly known as "CVP relationship". For this purpose, fixed costs, variable costs and semi variable costs have to be analyzed. Fixed costs are more or less constant for varying sales volumes. Variable costs vary according to the sales volume. Semi-variable costs are either fixed or variable in the short-term. The financial manager has to ensure that the income of the firm will cover its variable costs, for there is no point in being in business, if this is

not accomplished. Moreover, a firm will have to generate an adequate income to cover its fixed costs as well. The financial manager has to find out the break-even point that is, the point at which the total costs are matched by total sales or total revenue.

- ***Working Capital Management:*** Working capital refers to that part of firm's capital which is required for financing short-term or current assets such as cash, receivables and inventories. It is essential to maintain proper level of these assets. Finance manager is required to determine the quantum of such assets.
- ***Dividend Policy:*** Dividend is the reward of the shareholders for investments made by them in the shares of the company. The investors are interested in earning the maximum return on their investments whereas management wants to retain profits for future financing. These contradictory aims will have to be reconciled in the interests of shareholders and the company. Dividend policy is an important area of financial management because the interest of the shareholders and the needs of the company are directly related to it.
- ***Capital Budgeting:*** Capital budgeting is the process of making investment decisions in capital expenditures. It is an expenditure the benefits of which are expected to be received over a period of time exceeding one year. It is expenditure for acquiring or improving the fixed assets, the benefits of which are expected to be received over a number of years in future. **Capital budgeting** decisions are vital to any organization. Any unsound investment decision may prove to be fatal for the very existence of the concern.

1.1.9 Organization of the Finance Functions

Finance functions can be divided into three major decisions, which the firm must make, namely the investment decision, the finance decision, and the dividend decision.

Each of these decisions must be considered in relation to the objective of the firm: an optimal combination of the three decisions will maximize the value of the share to its shareholders. Since, these decisions are interrelated; we must consider their joint impact on the market price of the firm's stock.

Investment Decision

The investment decision is the most important one among the three decisions. It relates to the selection of assets in which funds are invested by the firm. The assets, which can be acquired, fall into two broad groups:

1. Long-term assets which will yield a return over a period of time in future.
2. Short-term current assets which are convertible into cash in the normal course of business usually within a year.

Accordingly, the asset selection decision of a firm is of two types. The first of these involving the first category of assets is popularly known as capital budgeting. The other one, which refers to short-term assets, is designated as liquidity decision.

Capital Budgeting Decision

It is the most crucial financial decision of a firm which relates to the selection of an investment proposal whose benefits are likely to arise in future over the life-time of the project. The first aspect of the capital budgeting decision is the choice of the investment out of the available alternatives. The selection will be always based on the relative benefits and returns associated with it. Therefore, the measurement of the worth of the investment proposal is a major element in the capital budgeting decision. Another aspect of the capital budgeting decision is the analysis of risk and uncertainty. As, the benefits from the proposed investment relate to the future period, their accrual is uncertain. Thus, an element of risk in the sense of uncertainty of future benefits is involved. Investment should be evaluated in relation to the risk associated with it. Finally, this return should be judged with a certain norm, which is referred by several names such as cut-off rate, required rate, hurdle rate, minimum rate of return, etc.

The correct standard to use for this purpose is the company's cost of capital, which is another important aspect of the capital budgeting decision.

Liquidity Decision

The liquidity decision is concerned with the management of the current assets, which is a pre-requisite to long-term success of any business firm. The main objective of the current assets: management is the trade - off between profitability and liquidity.

There is a conflict between these two concepts. If a firm does not have adequate working capital, it may become illiquid and consequently fail to meet its current obligations thus inviting the risk of bankruptcy. On the contrary, if the current assets are too large, the profitability is adversely affected. Hence, the key strategy and the main consideration in ensuring a trade-off between profitability and liquidity is the major objective of the liquidity decision. Besides, the funds should be invested optimally in the individual current assets to avoid inadequacy or excessive locking up of funds in these assets. Thus, the liquidity decision should obtain the basic two ingredients, i.e. overview of working capital management and the efficient allocation of funds on the individual current assets.

Financing Decision

The second major decision of the firm is the financing decision for determining the best financing mix of the firm. After determining the asset-mix, the financial manager must decide the mode of raising the funds to meet the firm's investment requirements. The major issue in decision is to determine the proportion of equity and debt capital. Since the involvement of debt capital affects the return and risk of shareholders, the financial manager should get the optimal capital structure to maximize the shareholders' return with financial management: minimum risk, in other words the cost of capital is the lowest and the market value of An Introduction the share is the highest at that combination of debt and equity. Thus, the financing decision covers two inter-related aspects:

(i) Capital structure theory
(ii) Capital structure decision

Dividend Decision

The third important decision of a firm is its dividend policy. The financial manager must decide whether the firm should distribute all profits or retain it in the firm or distribute part and retain the balance. The dividend decision should be taken in terms of its impact on the shareholders' wealth. The optimum dividend policy is one, which maximizes the market value of share. Thus, if the shareholders are not indifferent to the firm's dividend policy, the financial manager must determine the optimum dividend-payout ratio. Another important aspect of the dividend decision is the factors determining dividend policy of the firm in practice.

The financial management involves the solution of the three decisions of the firm according to the modern approach. The traditional approach with a very narrow perception was devoid of an integrated conceptual and analytical framework.

In contrast the modern approach has broadened the scope of financial management to ensure the optimum decisions by fulfilling the objectives of the business firm.

1.1.10 Objectives of Financial Management

Effective procurement and efficient use of finance lead to proper utilization of the finance by the business concern. It is the essential part of the financial manager. Hence, the financial manager must determine the basic objectives of the financial management. Objectives of financial management may be broadly divided into two parts such as: (See Figure 1.3)

1. Profit maximization
2. Wealth maximization

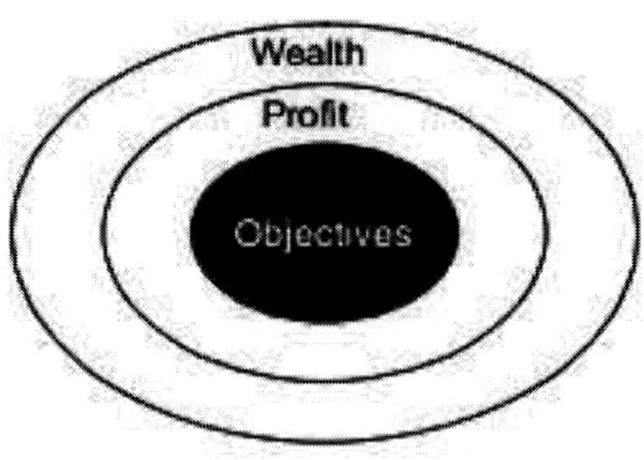

Figure 1.3. *Objectives of financial management.*

Profit Maximization

Main aim of any kind of economic activity is earning profit. A business concern is also functioning mainly for the purpose of earning profit. Profit is the measuring techniques to understand the business efficiency of the concern. Profit maximization is also the traditional and narrow approach, which aims at, maximizes the profit of the concern. Profit maximization consists of the following important features.

1. Profit maximization is also called as cashing per share maximization. It leads to maximize the business operation for profit maximization.
2. Ultimate aim of the business concern is earning profit; hence, it considers all the possible ways to increase the profitability of the concern.
3. Profit is the parameter of measuring the efficiency of the business concern. So it shows the entire position of the business concern.
4. Profit maximization objectives help to reduce the risk of the business.

Favorable Arguments for Profit Maximization

The following important points are in support of the profit maximization objectives of the business concern:

- Main aim is earning profit.
- Profit is the parameter of the business operation.
- Profit reduces risk of the business concern.
- Profit is the main source of finance.
- Profitability meets the social needs also.

Unfavorable Arguments for Profit Maximization

The following important points are against the objectives of profit maximization:

- Profit maximization leads to exploiting workers and consumers.
- Profit maximization creates immoral practices such as corrupt practice, unfair trade practice, etc.
- Profit maximization objectives leads to inequalities among the stake holders such as customers, suppliers, public shareholders, etc.

Drawbacks of Profit Maximization

Profit maximization objective consists of certain drawback also:

- *It is vague:* In this objective, profit is not defined precisely or correctly. It creates some unnecessary opinion regarding earning habits of the business concern.
- *It ignores the time value of money:* Profit maximization does not consider the time value of money or the net present value of the cash inflow. It leads certain differences between the actual cash inflow and net present cash flow during a particular period.
- *It ignores risk:* Profit maximization does not consider risk of the business concern. Risks may be internal or external which will affect the overall operation of the business concern.

Wealth Maximization

Wealth maximization is one of the modern approaches, which involves latest innovations and improvements in the field of the business concern. The term wealth means shareholder wealth or the wealth of the persons those who are involved in the business concern.

Wealth maximization is also known as value maximization or net present worth maximization. This objective is a universally accepted concept in the field of business.

Favorable Arguments for Wealth Maximization

- Wealth maximization is superior to the profit maximization because the main aim of the business concern under this concept is to improve the value or wealth of the shareholders.
- Wealth maximization considers the comparison of the value to cost associated with the business concern. Total value detected from the total cost incurred for the business operation. It provides extract value of the business concern.
- Wealth maximization considers both time and risk of the business concern.
- Wealth maximization provides efficient allocation of resources.
- It ensures the economic interest of the society.

Unfavorable Arguments for Wealth Maximization

- Wealth maximization leads to prescriptive idea of the business concern but it may not be suitable to present day business activities.
- Wealth maximization is nothing, it is also profit maximization, it is the indirect name of the profit maximization.
- Wealth maximization creates ownership-management controversy.
- Management alone enjoys certain benefits.
- The ultimate aim of the wealth maximization objectives is to maximize the profit.
- Wealth maximization can be activated only with the help of the profitable position of the business concern

1.2 FINANCIAL MANAGEMENT IN HOSPITALITY

The hospitality industry is ever-expanding and that's why it needs professional Financial Management. With the right ideas and a true focus on value, you can obtain incredible results. It's a great idea and a wonderful opportunity, one that can bring in outstanding success.

The hospitality industry is a broad category of fields within the service industry that includes lodging, food and beverage service, event planning, theme parks, travel agency, tourism, hotels, restaurants and bars.

1. Budgetary Planning and Control

If you want to have a successful hospitality business, then you need to prepare a budget and manage it properly. You want to have a budget because it will help with the planning process and you can also coordinate operations a lot better. In addition, the idea of participating in the budget is motivating employees and managers alike. It can also help evaluate the managerial performance based on how money are being spent.

2. Create the right pricing strategy

The best way to have a profitable business is to know what pricing strategy works. A good pricing strategy is at the core of financial management and it will help you connect with the customer base. You do need to support your price point with specialized features, so everything will work adequately.

3. Channel Distribution and Management

You will need to boost the online segment and invest in things like exhibitions that give you more exposure. Something like this does bring in front great results and value, and the return on investment can be nothing short of staggering.

4. Forecasting and Capacity Management

It's imperative to know your capacity and figure out just how many people will come to your accommodation service. Preparing for a potential overbooking and finding the right solutions to keep everyone happy is imperative here, and it will definitely help a lot if you know what you are getting into and how to handle the process correctly.

Capacity management is crucial because you want to offer the best services and features for every room, and you always want to make sure that people are happy. You want to have a system that monitors all bookings adequately so there are no problems. Once you have that, the payoff will be great and that's exactly what you need to go for.

5. Segmentation

Segmentation can be performed in a variety of ways. It can be per country for example, or it can be according to the source used. Obviously, it can also be a segmentation by source, where you have conferencing, meetings, leisure groups and individuals.

1.2.1 Dealing with Hotel Finance

Most hotel businesses will have to deal with Value Added Tax once their turnover reaches £61,000. This threshold may change at the end of each year during the budget (according to government policy). Once your hotel business becomes VAT registered your bookkeeping must be completely accurate and up-to-date as you may be liable for financial penalties for failing to declare your VAT return at the end of each quarter. The basic formula for calculating VAT is relatively straightforward to calculate. The output tax is that which is received from your paying hotel guests. The input tax is monies linked to paying out operating expenses (such as trade hotel suppliers). The difference between the two (where your output tax exceeds your input tax) is the amount of VAT paid at the end of the period. Likewise if the input tax is greater than the output tax you can claim back the difference from the VAT man. Be aware that there are different rates of VAT for different product groups and there are also different rules which applied to different geographic areas of the world. You should consult the Inland Revenue and your accountant regarding your bookkeeping process to ensure that all of your invoices and receipts have legally identifiable amounts associated with them.

The main measure of profitability at the end of the year is your profit and loss account. Normally this is generated by your accountant based on all of the bookkeeping activities and receipts. Either you have organized these papers or alternatively you have employed your accountant to do your bookkeeping for you. Your accountant will compare your bank statements for the hotel with all of your bookkeeping records and VAT returns and quiz you on any unidentifiable items of revenue or expense. In simple terms the profit and loss account will formally show the amount of hotel guest revenue received during your annual fiscal period minus all of your allowable expenses to calculate a gross profit figure. Any banking interest is then deducted along with a calculation of corporation tax based on the amount of gross profit to get to a final net profit (out of which shareholder dividends may be allocated). The rates of corporation tax may change every year in line with budget announcements.

By classifying the huge range of expenses into logical categories your piles of receipts and bank statements suddenly become meaningful. Only by organizing a set of accounts can sales and costs become understood and therefore controlled in the future. When running a hotel there are huge range of expense items including advertising, repairs and maintenance, cleaning supplies, hotel insurance, heat and light, food, wages, items, telephone, and stationery. It is recommended that you have a formal system to record all expenses in your hotel business such as a computer software program, ledger system or just a simple accounts book for smaller hotels or bed and breakfasts. Hotels are obviously busy places with lots of cash purchases of sometimes incremental amounts as well as credit card bookings from guests. Time should be allocated in the evening to document all of the day's takings into your system of record keeping. Failure to keep accurate records will inevitably lead to human error, (as receipts get mislaid of not entered) which would provide a nasty surprise to your end of year profit forecast.

Every penny of guests spending must be accounted for no matter how large or small. By entering all items of revenue and expense on a daily basis into some type of system it provides a central record upon which your bank statement can be reconciled. These receipts and records must be stored for at least seven years in case the Inland Revenue decides to undertake an audit to check on the reliability of previous tax returns and current accounting processes.

Your profit and loss account will also become a useful management tool as it will provide a comparative analysis to see how efficiently you are controlling your cost base. Likewise it can be used to check if you are doing a good job of marketing your hotel to attract guests to maximize your occupancy rate. For instance you may agree with your accountant to separate out sales by rooms, food sales, alcoholic beverages sales and room extras. This will help identify areas where margins are under pressure or where opportunities exist to cut costs. Your accountant will also be able to help you break down the average profitability per room and also per person. It is common to use percentages to identify each expense line-item against others to help identify trends over years. Your profit and loss account will also show your break-even point once you have understood more fully your fixed and variable operating expenses. Most hoteliers will have an understanding of the occupancy rate required to break even and the rates at which those rooms must be charged out over a given period. Given that many hotels are highly seasonal, plotting cash flow over a 12 month period also becomes critical.

To account for any petty cash withdrawals from your hotel business, a simple petty cash record log book should be completed at the end of each day outlining the date, the supplier, the amount and the outstanding decreasing balance withdrawn. In other words payment of small suppliers for nominal amounts deducted from the overall petty cash withdrawn. Receipts will need to keep to prove the expense was wholly incurred by the business and is allowable under tax rules.

The balance sheet is the other main statutory document that needs to be submitted in your annual return. It summarizes all of your assets and liabilities of your hotel business at a given point in time and is ordinarily produced by your accountant. Hotel investors will look closely at your balance sheet to understand any outstanding liabilities (such any outstanding business loans, supplier trade creditors and any liquid assets which could be sold off in the event of a resale or liquidation). One area of confusion most hotel owners experience is how to account for depreciation of assets. Your accountant will explain the latest Inland Revenue guidelines regarding the amount which fixed assets can be depreciated (such as kitchen machinery, computers and so on). Depreciation has the impact of reducing profitability and hence corporation tax liability. However large investments in new plant and machinery clearly involves obtaining business loans or utilizing the greater investment during the hotel purchase process. The other area of confusion is the value of goodwill. Goodwill is an intangible asset and it does not appear on the balance sheet. Yet if you ever decide to sell your hotel business you'll overall hotel reputation as quality provider of hotel accommodation in a local area is paramount in charging a premium for your business.

Another important aspect of running a hotel finances is proper budgeting and forecasting. A sales forecast should be both realistic and achievable. While your and operating expense forecast should not degrade the high quality of service you aim to provide your guests via planned excessive cost cutting. Ideally your budget should be calculated on a week by week basis in order to identify guest spending and seasonal trend patterns as actual figures accumulate. For instance your sales forecast budget should identify a number of rooms you have by their respective room rates by week. A simple spreadsheet would allow adjustments based on best and worst case scenarios of occupancy levels throughout the year. By looking at previous years, the actual room occupancy rates are a good basis for future budgeting. On top of a line item for room revenues you should add on sales from dinners and drinks. You will soon understand from your actual figures the proportion of guests that will also order dinner and drinks. By analyzing seasonal trends you can identify where you need to improve your sales figures. Consequently by offering promotional deals in your hotel marketing literature you can hope to plug the gap.

There are specific types of bank charges for various types of transactions which you need to be aware of the hotel owner. These may include charges every time a cheque is paid in, cash is paid out, supplier direct debits, written cheques, automatic paying ins and an authorized and unauthorized overdrafts. Keep a close eye on the volume and types of transactions your hotel has to process in order to build up a picture of the overall bank charges (which collectively can mount up to a significant expense item in your profit and loss account).

Lastly and most importantly hotel guests expect to pay with a credit card (which provides added security and convenience on both sides) for the hotel and as well as the guest. You need to make it clear in your hotel marketing literature which debit or credit cards you accept and which ones you don't. Credit card processing can cost around 5% of the value of the transaction which may vary according to volume so analyze your credit card needs carefully as they can make a significant dent in your net margin.

1.2.2 Importance of Financial Management in hospitality business

Financial management is crucial in the hospitality industry for several reasons. Here are some key points highlighting its importance:

Cost Control: Hospitality businesses have numerous expenses, including labor, inventory, utilities, and maintenance. Effective financial management helps in controlling these costs, ensuring that the business operates efficiently and profitably.

Budgeting and Planning: Financial management enables the creation of budgets and financial plans. This helps in setting financial goals, allocating resources effectively, and planning for future investments or expansions.

Cash Flow Management: Hospitality businesses often have seasonal fluctuations. Effective financial management ensures that there is enough cash to cover day-to-day expenses, preventing liquidity problems.

Profit Maximization: By analyzing financial data, businesses can identify profitable services or products. They can focus on these areas to maximize profits and can also identify and eliminate or modify services that are not financially viable.

Risk Management: Financial management helps in identifying financial risks and developing strategies to mitigate them. It also aids in making informed decisions regarding investments, ensuring a balanced portfolio and reducing financial vulnerabilities.

Compliance and Regulations: Hospitality businesses need to adhere to various financial regulations and tax laws. Proper financial management ensures compliance with these regulations, avoiding legal issues and financial penalties.

Investment Decisions: Hospitality businesses often require substantial investments in infrastructure, technology, and marketing. Financial management helps in evaluating these investment opportunities, determining their feasibility, and estimating the potential returns on investment.

Supplier Negotiations: Effective financial management provides insights into the financial health of the business. This information can be leveraged during negotiations with suppliers, leading to better terms and discounts, thus reducing costs.

Strategic Decision Making: Financial data provides a basis for strategic decision-making. It helps in identifying market trends, customer preferences, and areas where the business can improve. This information is invaluable for making long-term strategic plans.

Performance Evaluation: Financial management allows businesses to compare their financial performance against industry benchmarks and competitors. It helps in assessing the business's strengths and weaknesses, facilitating improvements in various areas.

Financial management in the hospitality industry is essential for ensuring profitability, sustainability, and growth. It provides the necessary tools and insights for making informed decisions, managing risks, and achieving long-term success in a highly competitive market.

Key Fact

The early 20th century saw the establishment of hotel chains and the standardization of services. Financial management became a more critical aspect as businesses expanded. Basic budgeting and accounting methods were introduced.

1.3 FOUNDATIONS OF FINANCIAL ANALYSIS

We present some of the fundamental accounting concepts and methods of financial analysis that will be used throughout the book and also throughout the career of any hospitality manager. These are not only fundamental accounting concepts but important management tools used to operate a business on a daily basis.

1.3.1 Fundamental Methods of Financial Analysis

Analyzing financial reports and statements requires a fundamental understanding of where numbers come from, how they are organized and presented, what they mean, what they measure, and how they are used.

Two Important Tools

First, we will talk about two important ways numbers are used in business. They are used to measure financial performance and to provide a management tool to use in operating the business.

To Measure Financial Performance

Numbers provide a way to determine how a business is performing. Measuring financial performance is historical in nature and uses the actual numbers or results from business operations. It tells us what the business has produced, and it compares and evaluates that performance to specific measures. It is looking back through the rearview mirror at operations. The three main financial statements are all used in measuring financial performance.

The Profit and Loss (P&L) Statement shows the revenues, expenses, and profits for a specified time period. Each month, accounting period, quarter, or year, the numbers produced by an operation are recorded in the P&L statement and tell whether the business revenue and profits are improving, declining, or staying the same.

The Balance Sheet shows the assets, liabilities, and owner equity of a business at a specific time. These numbers tell us whether the business is getting financially stronger by increasing assets or owner equity or if it is struggling and increasing liabilities. The numbers also tell us how the business is capitalized or started—with more debt than owner equity or with more owner equity than debt.

The Statement of Cash Flows shows how much cash is generated by a business and how effectively it is used in operating the business over a specified time period. Cash and liquidity are critical to the success of a business, and the numbers included in the Statement of Cash Flows tells us how cash is being acquired and used.

To Provide a Management Tool

Numbers provide a way for managers to plan for varying levels of business volume. This can take the form of forecasting revenues, scheduling wages, implementing cost controls, expanding business operations, or preparing the annual budget. Numbers give managers feedback on their operations and then assist them in making appropriate changes. This aspect of using numbers is very valuable to a business because it is the process of taking the information numbers provided and applying them back to operating the business.

The Financial Management Cycle

Second is the Financial Management Cycle. It is important to understand this process and how numbers are generated and used in business operations. This cycle deals with the flow and use of numbers in business operations.

1. *Operations produce the numbers.* All the activities involved in the daily operations produce the numbers that measure performance. In a hotel, the daily operations provide products and services to guests, including the rooms department, food and beverage outlets, gift shop, and any other department that produces a sales transaction with a guest. Numbers used in financial analysis have to come from somewhere, and that is the daily operation of the business.

2. *Accounting prepares the numbers and provides financial reports and statements.* At the end of the day, week, or month, the numbers resulting from all operations and activities are collected, summarized, and reported by the accounting

department. These reports describe the operations and activities and are distributed to the appropriate managers for their review and use.

3. *Accounting and operations analyze the numbers.* Operations management and accounting management work together to review and analyze the reports. They look for changes, the cause of the change, and the result of the change to understand operations and determine ways to change and improve. Together they have operational experience and financial analysis experience and can identify any changes or improvements that need to be made to ensure that productive operations continue.

4. *Operations applies the numbers back to the business.* After reviews and discussions, the operations managers make any necessary changes to operations to correct or improve them. The ability to analyze quickly and accurately and then make any necessary changes is an important part of any business operation. It enables the business to constantly improve by being more productive or creating more value in the products and services that it provides.

1.3.2 Comparing Numbers to give them Meaning

Numbers need to be compared to something to have any meaning. A hotel has monthly sales of $1 million. All this tells us is the sales level. How do we know if this is good or bad, up or down, acceptable or not acceptable? A fundamental concept of financial analysis is to compare a number produced by operations to an established number that will tell us if there was an increase or a decrease. The most common comparisons are to (1) last year, (2) budget, (3) forecast, (4) previous month or period, (5) pro forma, or (6) any other established goal.

Last Year

Comparing actual financial results to last year's actual results is a useful comparison. The first evaluation of financial operations is to show if operations are better than the previous year. The best results are if actual operations for the current year are better than last year and the budget. The worst results are if the current year is worse than last year and the budget.

Budget

Actual financial results for a month, quarter, or year are compared to the established budget. The budget is the formal one-year financial operating plan for a company. Budgets include planned increases in revenues and profits, and productivity improvements in costs and expenses. Comparing actual results to the budget shows whether the business is moving in the direction planned and budgeted and how close it is in meeting, exceeding, or missing the budgeted numbers.

Forecast

Forecasts update the budget. Whereas the budget is done once for the entire year, forecasts are done continually to adjust or relate to current business conditions. Forecasts can be weekly, monthly, quarterly, biannually, or can apply to the end of the year. They are important because they are more current and help project business performance compared to the budget.

Previous Month or Period

These comparisons are important because they identify trends in operations. A goal of any business is to continually improve. Examining month-to-month performance tells us the trend and direction of our operations. They can show improvements that we hope are the results of corrective action implemented by management to keep the company moving in the right direction.

Pro Forma

A new business does not have any historical operating information. Therefore, management, developers, and bankers prepare a pro forma based on market conditions and expected financial returns. The pro formas are estimates or projections of how these financial experts think the business will perform in the first year of operations. The pro forma is used for the first year of business operations and is then replaced by the budget, which is prepared based on the first year's actual performance. Pro formas are used to establish and identify initial business revenues and profits that will generate the cash flow necessary to repay loans and investments.

Other Goals

Occasionally a business will establish other goals or benchmarks to compare actual performance. Examples are improving profit margins to meet an established goal, achieving specific revenue levels, or entering new markets.

1.3.3 Measuring Change to Explain Performance

One of the most important elements of **financial analysis** is to be able to identify where changes occur and what caused the change. In a large business with many products and departments, an effective financial analysis of the financial reports must locate the department that is changing and identify the causes of that change. Is it in revenues—volume or rate? Is it in expenses—cost of sales, wages, benefits, or other operating expenses? Is it a direct or indirect, fixed or variable expense? One department or many departments may be affecting operations with positive or negative changes.

Changes are identified by comparing actual performance to previous performance or a specific goal or measure. These changes can be for a month, a quarter, or a year. The more information that is obtained about the changes, the better chance that good decisions can be made to respond to the changes.

Changes, both positive and negative, are measured in terms of units, dollars, and percentages. These three measurements can tell us a lot about the performance of a business. From our $1,000,000 monthly sales example, we have already looked at the dollar increase (+$50,000 over last year) and the percentage increase (+5.3% over last year). We know that we have $50,000 more sales dollars, a positive change. We know that we increased sales by 5.3%, also a positive change.

Performing that same financial analysis process, our $1,000,000 is $100,000 below the budget of $1,100,000 and 9.1% below the budget. We know that we have $100,000 fewer sales dollars than budgeted, a negative result. Our 9.1% is also a negative result from our budget.

The final measurement is units. If the entire $1,000,000 in monthly sales was from room revenue, our unit will be the number of rooms sold. Our accounting reports would tell us how many rooms were sold and what the average room rate was. Let's assume the average room rate was $80. We can then calculate the number of rooms sold by dividing total room sales of $1,000,000 by the average room rate of $80, which gives us 12,500 rooms sold. That should match the number of rooms sold on our accounting report.

So now we have the units or volume—12,500 rooms sold—but we don't know if this is better or worse than last year's monthly sales of $950,000. The answer will come from last year's accounting reports. If the report tells us that the average rate for last year was $78 and 12,180 rooms were sold, we can multiply these together and get the monthly sales of $950,000. Now we can compare our actual rooms sold this year of 12,500 to last year's rooms sold of 12,180. We can also compare this year's average rate of $80 to last year's average rate of $78.

1.3.4 Using Percentages in Financial Analysis

Percentages are one of the three ways numbers are used to measure financial performance. They provide an additional dimension or perspective in financial analysis. Percentages measure relationships and changes and always involve two numbers.

Calculating Percentages

Percentages are the result of combining two numbers that define a relationship. A change in one number changes the resulting percentage. Both numbers can also change. When a percentage changes, it is important to know which number changed and what caused the change.

What Percentages Measure?

Percentages measure relationships and changes. An example of relationships is the previous wage cost example. A 35% wage cost means that 35 cents out of every revenue dollar is used to pay the wage cost associated with producing that revenue dollar. Another example is food cost percentage. An actual food cost percentage of 40% means that 40 cents out of every food revenue dollar is used to pay for the associated food cost to produce that one food revenue dollar.

The food cost percentage will go up or down based on changes in food costs or food revenues. To become more productive and profitable, the actual food expense that results in a sale would have to decline or stay the same, but the food revenue would increase. To become less productive, our food cost would have to remain the same and our food revenues go down or our food cost would have to increase but our food revenues would remain the same. By looking at each number and identifying any changes, we analyze the numbers and identify what changed and how that affects our operational performance.

Let's look at another example of percentages and change. If our revenues increase from $1,000 to $1,200, the resulting dollar change is an increase of $200. To calculate the associated percentage change, divide the $200 increase by the original $1,000 revenue, and the result is a 20% increase in revenues. The amount of change is always divided by the base, beginning, or original number. Percentage change can be calculated for changes in revenues, expenses, profits, assets, units, liabilities, owner equity, or any other specific account.

Using percentages in the process of financial analysis includes three steps. First is identifying and measuring the change. Second is identifying the cause of the change. Third is developing and implementing corrective action into daily operations.

1.3.5 Four Types of Percentages Used in Financial Analysis

Cost or Expense Percentages

These percentages tell us what dollar amounts of expenses are associated with corresponding revenues or sales. The previous examples of wage cost and food cost demonstrate cost percentages. Cost percentages can be calculated for any expense account or type that has a specific dollar cost associated with it. The formula for cost percentage is expense dollars divided by corresponding revenue dollars.

Profit Percentages

Profit percentages tell how much of the revenue dollar is remaining after all expenses are paid. Profits are measured in dollars and percentages. Dollar profit measures the absolute number of dollars remaining as profit, whereas percentage profit measures how much of the sales dollar is remaining as profit. Profit percentages can be applied to different levels of profit: department profits, house profits, or gross operating profits.

Department profit percentages are important because each department that is a profit center has a different profit percentage resulting in different department profitability.

Mix Percentages

Mix percentages tell you how much of your total comes from different departments, or how much each department adds to the total. Mix percentages can be measured in units or dollars. They are useful because they provide a quantified measure of each part to the whole.

Percentage Change

This percentage is important because it measures progress or lack of progress. Have our restaurant sales increased or decreased compared to last month? Which meal period showed the most improvement, breakfast, lunch, or dinner? Are the sales up because we had an increase in customers served or because our average check increased? The percentage change gives us this information.

Percentage change is calculated by dividing the amount of the change in dollars (increase or decrease) by the base or original amount. In our example, the change or difference would be calculated by subtracting our actual or current month results from the base or previous month. This change amount would then be divided by the base or, in this example, the previous month's results—for example, this month's sales of $4,800 compared to last month's sales of $4,500. Our percentage change is calculated by subtracting this month's sales of $4,800 from the previous month's sales of $4,500 resulting in a difference of $300. This is where it is important to relate the numbers to actual operations. This calculation results in a $300 difference. We then know that this is a positive difference because our current month's sales of $4,800 is larger than the previous month's sales of $4,500.

1.3.6 Trends in Financial Analysis

Trends are important because they show the direction or movement of business operations, industry, and national and international economies. Understanding the different types of trends and how they affect the operations of a business is an important part of financial analysis. We will discuss four types of trends that affect a business.

Short- and Long-Term Trends

It is important to look at both short-term and long-term trends. Short-term trends (less than 90 days) often involve seasonality or the expected cycles of a business or industry. A business that is slowing down because of seasonality or an industry cycle should be evaluated differently from a business that is slowing down because of increased competition, product or service quality, or pricing issues. A long-term tend is a better evaluator of products or services, especially when compared to competitors and industry performance.

When looking at the month-to-month performance of a business, it is important to distinguish between one month of poor financial performance and several months of poor financial performance. It is typical for a business to have a problem or one-time event that results in performance below expectations for a month. One month by itself does not make a trend or signal a major or long-term problem. However, it is important to correct any poor performance to prevent it from becoming an ongoing problem.

If a business has several months of poor performance, this is a trend that could signal continuing major long-term problems. Management might have to make major evaluations and analyses to determine what is causing the ongoing poor performance and how it can be corrected. Correcting the cause of several months or years of poor performance is a much larger task than correcting a problem that has affected only one month.

Revenue, Expense, and Profit Trends

These trends are all shown in the P&L Statement. Each individual trend is compared to the other two to determine if financial performance is improving or declining. For example, if revenue is trending up and expenses are staying flat, the profit trend should also be up. These are good trends and good relationships between revenues, expenses, and profits. However, if revenues are trending up but expenses are trending up at a faster rate, that will result in lower profits. That is not a good trend. Most important, are revenues or expenses trending in the direction to increase or decrease profits? Equally important is which of the three trends are increasing or decreasing faster or slower than the other two. For example, if sales are increasing 5% but expenses are increasing 10%, profits will decrease. The best case for increasing profits is if sales are increasing and expenses are decreasing.

Favorable and unfavorable trends that affect productivity and profits are demonstrated here:

Trends That Increase Profits	Trends That Decrease Profits
Revenues increasing, expenses decreasing	Revenues decreasing, expenses increasing
Revenues increasing, expenses flat	Revenues flat, expenses increasing
Revenues increasing faster than expenses	Expenses increasing faster than revenues

Company and Industry Trends

It is important to compare the trend of a company with the trends of the industry and general economy. Are the company trends the result of the success or failure of your business operations, the result of conditions that are affecting the entire industry, or the result of the general economic environment? Trends can result from any or all of these conditions, and it is important to identify the causes of trends for the business and the industry. Then appropriate action can be implemented.

For example, if your business profits are down 10% from the previous year and the industry average is down 8% to 12%, then you can safely say that your business profits are down as a result of industry conditions and nothing specific to your business. However, if your profits are down 10% from the previous year and the industry average is up 2%, then you can safely say that the reason your business profits are down is because of problems or the inferior performance of your business and not any industry factors. The causes of the 10% decrease in profitability are different from what is occurring in the industry and should be treated in different ways to correct problems and improve efficiencies of the company so that it gets back to desired profit levels.

General Economic Trends—National and International

The world is indeed shrinking, and problems in other countries or other parts of the United States can affect the performance of an individual business operation. Inflation rates, interest rates, unemployment rates, consumer confidence indexes, budget deficits, exchange rates, and social/political environments are all factors that may have major influences on a business. The most dramatic and tragic example of this is the attack that took place on September 11, 2001, which changed the economic, political, military, and social environment for every country in the world. Each industry and business had to develop new policies, procedures, and strategies to survive in such a turbulent and negative environment.

Another element of national economic influences is the understanding of business cycles. Economic growth, bull markets, bear markets, and stable social and political environments do not go on forever. There are business cycles as short as six months and as long as five to eleven years that occur in normal business and economic activities. Financial analysis can assist a business in identifying business cycles and their causes and determining best practices to permit the best possible operations in any economic environment.

1.4 ACCOUNTING DEPARTMENT ORGANIZATION AND OPERATIONS

We discuss accounting structures for large hotels, small hotels, and chain restaurants with a focus on the organization and operation of accounting departments in full-service hotels. Full-service hotels are defined as hotels that have from 250 rooms to more than 2,000 rooms; in addition these establishments provide sleeping rooms, operate food and beverage outlets, provide catering functions and meeting room rentals, and offer gift shops, valet laundry, health workout facilities, bellmen, a concierge, and other services and amenities that are typically included in larger hotels. A wide range of hotels are included in the full-service category, such as corporate hotels, airport hotels, suburban hotels, convention hotels, and resorts. Because of the wide range of activities and the large amounts of revenues and profits generated, full-service hotels have accounting departments in the hotel to take care of all the accounting responsibilities.

Because smaller hotels and select-service hotels do not offer their guests such a wide range of amenities and services, they do not require an onsite accounting department. Their accounting functions are coordinated by a regional or corporate accounting structure, which includes a centralized accounting department that handles the accounting activities of the individual hotels. These hotels provide information daily to the corporate accounting office, which then prepares reports and information and sends them back to the individual hotels for their use and review.

The accounting operations of chain restaurants are similar to the accounting operations of smaller hotels. A regional or corporate accounting office provides the accounting services for each individual restaurant. It is the responsibility of each restaurant to provide the daily operating information to the corporate accounting office, which then prepares the necessary accounting statements and operating information for the restaurant.

Independent operators of small hotels and individually owned restaurants will either do their own accounting or hire an outside accounting company to handle all accounting requirements and to prepare financial reports.

1.4.1 Organization Charts

An organization chart is a diagram of the structure and relationships of a specific business unit. It can include job titles, direct reporting relationships, areas of responsibility, and lines of communication among different job levels. We will discuss several organization charts as we describe the role and relationships of accounting departments.

Full-Service Hotels

Figure 1.4 contains two examples of organization charts for a full-service hotel. It includes four levels of responsibility divided into the two main types of business activities: operating departments and staff departments.

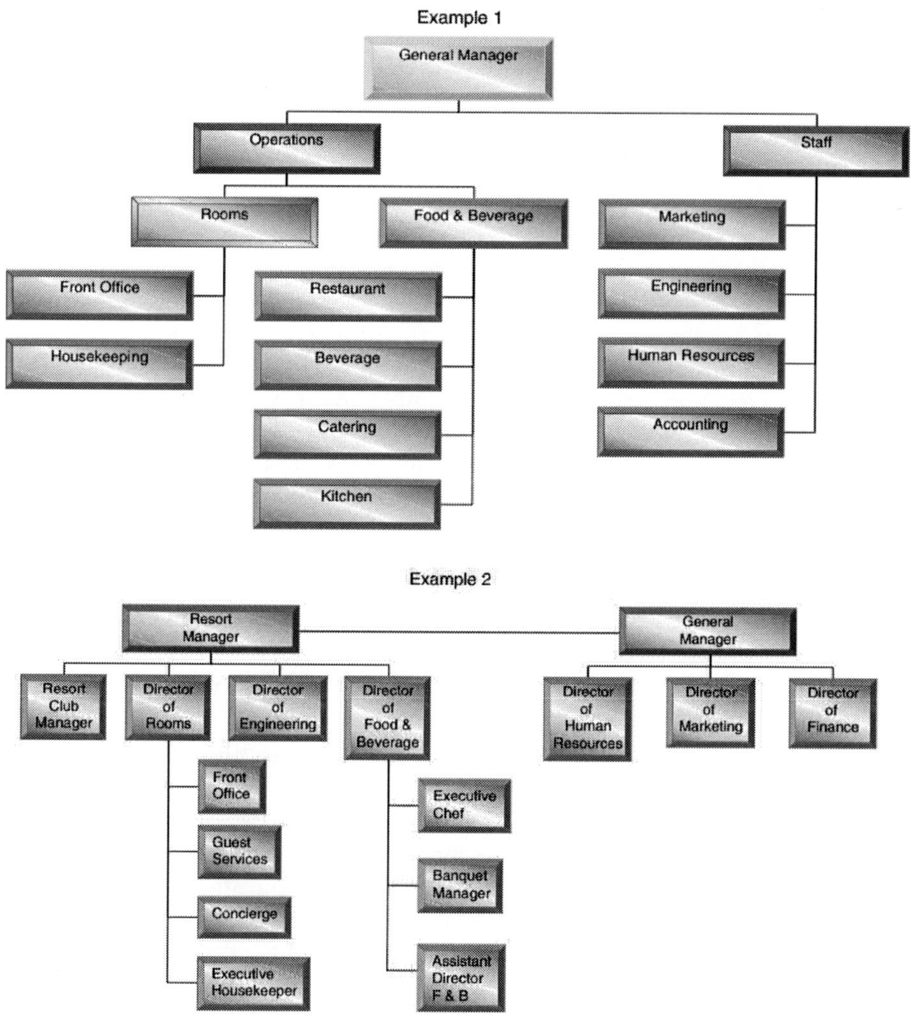

Figure 1.4. Full-service hotel organization charts.

Accounting Departments

We will now discuss in detail the organization and structure of the Accounting Department. As we can see from the hotel organization chart, the Accounting Department is one of the staff departments with the Director of

Finance or Controller responsible for all accounting operations and reporting to the General Manager. The accounting staff includes both managers and hourly employees. Figure 1.5 contains two accounting organization charts for a typical full-service hotel. Following are details about the positions and responsibilities of the accounting department.

Director of Finance/Controller

This Executive Committee member is responsible for all accounting department operations. Although there is a staff that actually perform these responsibilities, the Director of Finance is responsible for ensuring that all accounting information for the hotel is accurate, correct, and conforms to Generally Accepted Accounting Principles. Specifically, the Director of Finance does the following:

1. Prepares the monthly financial statements, primarily the P&L Statement, but also reconciles the Balance Sheet or Asset and Liabilities (A&L) Accounts and the Statement of Cash Flows.
2. Supervises all activities of the different accounting functions.
3. Prepares the annual operating budget and the annual capital expenditure budget.
4. Analyzes and critiques all monthly financial statements and weekly revenue and wage forecasts.
5. Is a financial advisor to all hotel managers and their operations.
6. Coordinates all communication with regional and corporate offices.
7. Prepares all financial statements and presentations for hotel owners.

Assistant Controller of Income Accounting and Operations

The Assistant Controller is often a department head and oversees several of the important aspects of accounting operations and their involvement with hotel department operations. These responsibilities include the following:

1. Assists the Director of Finance in hotel accounting activities including reconciling A&L Accounts, preparing P&L critiques, capital expenditure accounting, weekly revenue and wage forecasts, productivity analysis, and any other activities requested by the Director of Finance.
2. Closes each month and assists in the preparation of monthly P&L Statements, including adjusting A&L Accounts, processing transfers, verifying physical inventories, and coordinating corporate entries.
3. Performs hotel audits.
4. Assists rooms and food and beverage operations managers.

This manager is responsible for the billing and collection of all revenues and accounts receivable due the hotel. He or she oversees several areas of billing and collection and is especially involved in group accounts at larger convention hotels and resorts. These responsibilities include the following:

Example 1

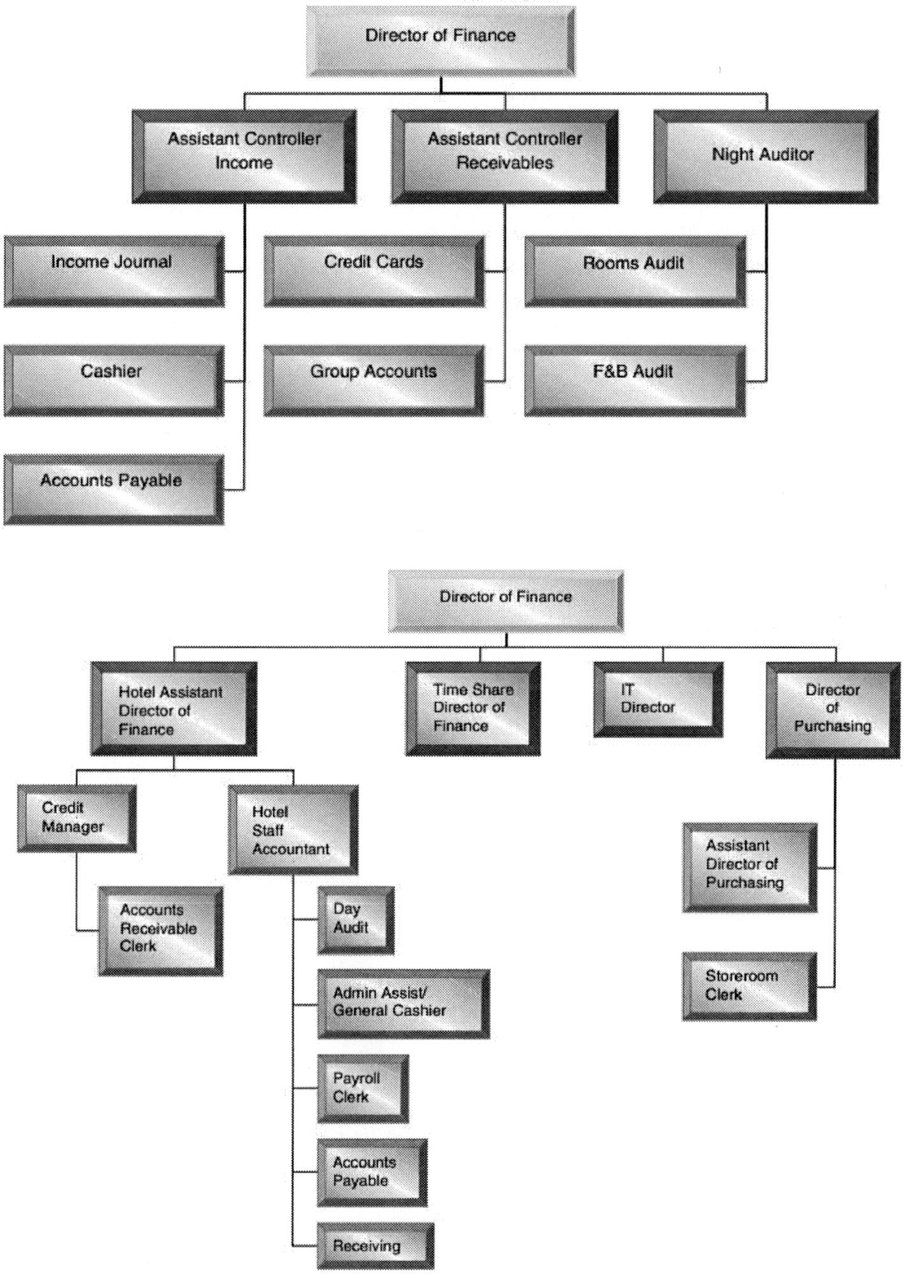

***Figure 1.5**. Accounting department organization charts.*

Assistant Controller Receivables

1. Assists the Director of Finance in hotel accounting activities including reconciling cash accounts (there could be many), reconciling credit card statements, and generating a positive cash flow for the hotel. These are important responsibilities because they have a major impact on maximizing cash flow for the hotel.
2. Assists in closing each month or accounting period and preparing financial statements.
3. Reviews the aging accounts to effectively manage current, 30- to 60-day, 60- to 90- day, and over 90-day accounts. Prepares information for bad debt write-offs and coordinates activities with collection agencies when necessary.
4. Coordinates group billings, including direct billing approvals, account preparation and review, and group account collect.

Night Auditor

This manager is responsible for the processing and auditing of all accounting and operational information for each day. She or he is also responsible for operating the all-night (or 11 p.m. to 7 a.m.) front desk shift.

1. Records and balances the day's transactions for each hotel department. This includes room revenues, food and beverage revenues, catering and meetings revenues, gift shop revenues, and any other revenue-producing departments.
2. Rolls the date after all accounting transactions are audited and in balance. This means closing all the information for the previous day and setting up all the information and systems for the next day.
3. Prepares daily management reports including daily revenue reports, discrepancy reports, and the next-day guest reservations.
4. Ensures that all guests checking in and out of the hotel are taken care of efficiently.

1.4.2 Accounting Operations in Full-Service Hotels

The Accounting department is a staff department that supports all other departments in the hotel with regard to accounting procedures and hotel operations. It works with these departments to provide services and information that will assist them in operating their departments on a daily basis.

Accounting Department Operations

The Accounting Department records and processes the previous day's hotel activities. Refer to the Accounting Department Organization Chart in Figure 1.5. Each day the individual sections within the Accounting Department receive the paperwork and records or processes the information to update accounts and prepare reports.

Hotel Department Operations and Relationships with Accounting

Each department in the hotel is responsible for providing the expected products and services to the customer following established hotel policies and procedures. The accounting department assists the other departments in following appropriate procedures. Following are examples of how an operating department might interact with accounting.

Front Office

Managers in the front office will work with the Income Journal Clerk by reviewing the daily room revenue information that they record. They can look at average room rates by market segment, rooms sold by market segments, and any adjustments to revenues in reviewing the previous day's operations. They can compare actual sales with forecasted, budgeted, and last year's sales. They constantly work with the General Cashier by requesting change for front desk cashiers, helping to research any cash-handling problems such as shortages in banks or deposits, and processing or reimbursing petty cash requests. They work with the Accounts Payable Clerk by forwarding invoices for payments, checking on account numbers, researching invoice problems, and generally ensuring that all invoices approved for payment are correct. They hand the day's work over to the Night Auditor at 11 p.m., who will check in any remaining guests and begin the process of auditing the day's work.

Restaurant and Catering

Managers in the restaurant and catering departments work with the accounting office in much the same manner as do the Front Office managers. Instead of market segments, these managers are interested in meal period information (breakfast, lunch, and dinner) to analyze their sales. The rest of their interactions are the same as those for the Front Office managers.

Staff Departments

The Sales and Marketing, Human Resources, and Engineering departments primarily interact with the Accounts Payable Clerk in processing invoices for payment. Because these departments have no revenues, they do not have any direct interaction with the Income Journal Clerk or General Cashier.

1.4.3 Accounting Operations in Restaurants and Smaller Hotels

The accounting operations of restaurants and smaller, select service hotels are handled in a similar manner.

The accounting process in these operations is based on daily communication with the corporate accounting office. The operating results at the end of the day are transmitted to the corporate accounting office where they are processed and returned to the hotel or restaurant. It is the General Manager's responsibility to ensure that required operating information is submitted in a timely and accurate manner. While the General Manager can delegate this responsibility to his or her managers, it is ultimately the General Manager's responsibility to make sure that all procedures are followed correctly.

Financial Statement Preparation

At the end of each day, the restaurant or hotel will close out the day's operating information accumulated in its POS system. This will include meal period revenues, customer counts, wage costs, and any other expenses for the day. The p.m., or closing manager, is responsible for ensuring that all the day's operating information is sent at the end of each day. The corporate accounting office collects, summarizes, and reports the information and returns it to the restaurant or hotel the next morning. The next day, the a.m., or opening manager, will review the information for accuracy and completeness and make any necessary corrections. This daily information also includes month-to-date information and is used by the restaurant managers in operating their restaurants.

A similar process is followed at the end of the month for the monthly closing. This process is more involved and includes taking physical inventories, verifying revenue and wage information, and ensuring the accuracy of the month-end cutoff date. The corporate accounting office prepares the monthly P&L and any other trend or summary reports and returns it to the restaurant in three to five days.

Customer counts and revenues are forecasted each week for the next two weeks. These forecasts update the budget for the upcoming weeks and are based on the current business conditions that the restaurant is experiencing. These forecasts are used to schedule wages and determine purchase quantities.

Purchasing and Inventories

Food, beverage, and operating supplies are purchased weekly through a centralized purchasing system. This computer program contains inventory level status, daily and weekly consumption amounts, prices, order quantities, and other pertinent purchasing information. The restaurant manager responsible for this function ensures that all the pricing and paperwork are complete and accurate; verifies delivery quantities, prices, and invoices; conducts month-end physical inventories; and processes invoices for payment. Although it is an advantage to have a sophisticated purchasing system to use, it is the manager's responsibility to ensure that all information submitted is accurate. This requires a knowledge of restaurant standards and operations, of the accounting process, and of the importance of current and ongoing communication with the corporate accounting office to ensure that the system is working as intended.

Wage and Cost Controls

Along with food costs, wage and benefit costs are the largest and most important expenses to be controlled in operating a restaurant. Wage costs are reviewed daily to ensure productivity standards are met and waste minimized. This process starts with the preparation of the next week's wage schedule based on the average volumes and employee labor hours for the previous several weeks. Relationships between guest counts and labor hours are established and used to schedule and control wage costs.

The wage departments in a restaurant can be divided into service, bar and hostess, and kitchen or heart of the house. Wage standards are established for each of these departments, and then the wage schedules are prepared for the upcoming week based on forecasted customer counts. An additional part of managing wage costs is controlling overtime. Each overtime labor hour includes a 50% premium—in other words, an overtime labor hour costs 50% more than a regular labor hour.

Another reason controlling wage costs is so important is that for every wage dollar there is an associated benefit cost. Most companies provide benefits to their hourly and management employees. This cost is split between the company and the employees. Typically, a company can pay from 20% to 40% in benefit cost for every wage dollar. This means that for every wage dollar paid, the restaurant will pay an additional 20 to 40 cents for benefits. If a restaurant is effectively controlling wage costs, they will be effectively controlling benefit costs. If they are not effectively controlling wage costs, they will also not be controlling benefit costs.

1.5 FINANCIAL MANAGEMENT CHALLENGES IN HOSPITALITY INDUSTRY

Most hospitality companies are fraught with the challenges of effective financial management in a world where disruption is the new normal. Smooth accounting operations are essential for sustainable growth and scalability in this industry. Those that fail to adopt best practices and tackle the issues with lean, agile solutions are likely to be buried by tedious manual processes and an inability to make strategic moves in a fast-paced, constantly changing world.

Making decisions based on gut feelings is no longer viable. With data becoming increasingly crucial for stakeholders and investors, investments now depend on access to accurate forecasting and reports. Risk management is another motivator for those revamping financial systems. No accounting team wants to stifle the growth of their company, yet, modern compliance standards are increasingly demanding, and there's a degree of transparency required by regulators that is impossible to maintain with outdated solutions.

Many finance teams are weighed down by manual processes, struggling to consolidate multiple entities, keep up to date with leasing requirements, and spend most administrative time on balance sheets and reporting. Often this work involves a degree of correction that should not be necessary when technology can automate many of the workflows that lead to the most common errors on financial statements and reports. Keeping up administrative workloads often leaves little time for teams to adapt to the subscription economy or implement innovative, competitive strategies.

1. Maintaining secure, reliable financial data management across all entities

The Challenge

Given the sheer amount of financial data flowing through the average hospitality company, it's no surprise that one of the biggest concerns accounting team's faces is keeping data clean and free of error while maintaining the security of sensitive information. The bigger a franchise or organization, the more complex things can get, with companies needing to adopt systems that can handle the workload of increased intercompany transactions without causing severe bottlenecks.

With data now at the heart of strategic decision-making, the need for effective data management is a critical component of healthy growth. It's not uncommon for audits or data breaches to slow down productivity for weeks, if not months, a risk most cannot afford to take. Hospitality companies can overcome this financial challenge by introducing several measures to maintain secure, reliable data across all entities and departments.

Suggested Solutions

- Automate time-consuming processes wherever possible and reduce manual data entry
- Introduce standards and processes that ensure accuracy from data input to normalization
- Perform regular audits and data checks to maintain data quality at the highest level
- Centralize data management to avoid introducing errors during data transfers
- Develop consisting accounting rules and naming conventions across all entities
- Invest in solutions with high levels of security and control to maintain data integrity
- Pay particular attention to data management and security during mergers and acquisitions

2. Consolidating financial statements accurately across multiple companies

The Challenge

Effective financial management in the hospitality industry often requires accounting teams to produce consolidated financial statements that allow leadership to get an overview of overall performance across the entire enterprise. Of course, this ties into the challenge of maintaining reliable and secure data, but it's a separate concern with its nuances.

Parent company accounting teams often face significant roadblocks when it comes to consolidating financial information. They may not have access to data from all entities, and other groups may forward reports in inappropriate ways (email, excel files, etc.). Not only does this make it challenging to obtain the necessary data, but it can introduce issues of fraud and data manipulation when the parent companies do not have a clear view of financial processes across all entities.

It's possible to solve this issue by investing in a centralized accounting system specializing in consolidated financial statements. Building a robust financial backbone is essential to sustainable progress when it comes to solving the financial management challenges hospitality faces.

Suggested Solutions

- Ensure the parent company has centralized access to finances from all entities
- Invest in a centralized ERP that specialized in consolidating financial statements
- Implement appropriate access controls given the sensitive nature of finances
- Outline consolidation requirements and implement practical tools across all companies
- Automate workflows for all entities to reduce the possibility of data manipulation

3. Proving compliance with changing global accounting standards

The Challenge

Expectations around data governance and global compliance have never been higher. Most hospitality franchises will be subject to different rules and regulations that govern their accounting practices. Staying on top of fluctuating regulations can strain even the highest performing teams, especially when accounting teams need to maintain compliance for everything from recurring revenue and financial consolidation of multiple entities to lease accounting standards.

It can be a headache, so it's often best to nominate team members to stay on top of requirements, brief the team on any changes and rewrite data management policies to reflect these when necessary. It's also wise to invest in a solution built to handle the complexities of modern compliance, so your team can avoid the risk of hefty fines.

4. Replacing obsolete, on-premise financial management systems

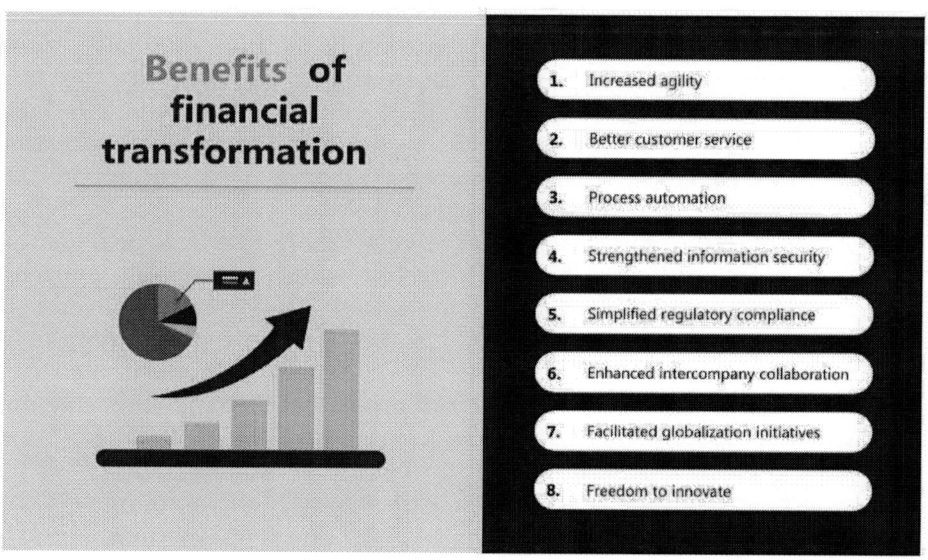

The challenge

The struggle to achieve financial transformation is not unique to the hospitality industry. Across the world, companies face the challenge of introducing agile workflows and replacing legacy, on-premise systems with more comprehensive financial management systems. Add to this the rate of failure of the average transformation, and it's no wonder that accounting teams can be reluctant to undergo the upheaval.

Many issues arise because finance manages the entire transformation in a silo, without any effort made to spread the workload across the whole organization. It's a process that touches on and involves every corner of operations and will require a company-wide effort. The solutions below include a collection of resources to help you navigate the major shifts and challenges of financial transformation.

1.6 POSITIONS WITH ACCOUNTING RESPONSIBILITIES

Someone must be responsible for developing accounting information for line managers. (According to personnel management principles, line positions are held by employees such as managers, department heads, supervisors, and others who are in the chain of command. By contrast, staff positions, held by accounting, personnel, and purchasing department employees, provide specialized and advisory assistance to line officials.)

In a small restaurant, the manager (who is likely to be the owner) develops some of the financial information needed for decision-making. However, because of the increasingly complex process needed to generate financial data, especially for tax accounting purposes, the manager/owner of the small restaurant will likely need the services of an external accountant. As restaurants increase in size, some or all of the accounting responsibilities assumed by the manager of the small operation fall to other employees. Here are some examples:

- **Bookkeeper.** As noted above, bookkeepers are involved in some of the processes by which financial transactions of the restaurant are recorded and summarized. Frequently, bookkeeping services are used by restaurant managers who supply source documents (schedule of hours employees worked, delivery invoices, sales data from electronic registers, etc.) to external bookkeepers who develop records, reports, and financial statements for the manager.
- **Accountant.** Accountants in large restaurants often work under the controller (see below) and perform duties that include designing and monitoring the data collection system and source documents, summarizing information in financial statements, developing management reports, coordinating budget development, collecting information required by tax authorities, and completing required external reports.
- **Controller.** This official is generally the chief accounting officer (CAO) in a large restaurant organization and oversees the development and implementation of the accounting system. The controller may supervise

many employees in large firms (if so, accounting-related activities are generally only part of the responsibilities of the position)

- **Food and beverage controller.** Moderate- and large-sized restaurants may employ a food and beverage controller who is responsible for developing a wide variety of routine operating and control reports. Likewise, for control purposes, product receiving, storing, and/or issuing activities and responsibilities are frequently assumed by this official. (A basic principle [standard] of control involves the need to separate tasks to make it difficult [at least without collusion] for employees to commit fraudulent acts. If products are purchased by a staff purchasing agent and come under the control of production personnel [chef and bartender] after issuing, the control process is tightened when these intermediate tasks [receiving, storing, and issuing] are the responsibility of the controller.)
- **Internal auditor.** Very large restaurants and foodservice chains may employ internal auditors to evaluate the operating effectiveness of the accounting information system. As companies grow into multiunit organizations, corporate-level personnel are often asked to audit records and systems of specific properties.
- **External accounting positions.** There are at least two types of external accounting personnel used by restaurants. An accountant (frequently a Certified Public Accountant—CPA) performs services for a fee as an independent agent rather than as an employee. In this role, he/she may develop and monitor accounting systems and procedures used by the restaurant. External auditors can be used to render an opinion as to whether financial statements reflect fairly the financial position of the restaurant and whether the statements are prepared in accordance with generally accepted accounting principles (GAAPs) and on a consistent basis with the prior year.

1.7 ACCOUNTING AND CONTROL ARE INTERRELATED

The relationship between the management task of control and accounting activities is important. To control any resource (food and beverage products, labor, revenue, energy, etc.), the restaurant manager must use a five-step process:

1. Performance standards (expectations) must be established. (This is done as the operating budget is developed.)
2. Actual financial information must be collected to measure the results of operation.
3. Comparisons must be made between expected performance (Step 1) and actual performance (Step 2).
4. Corrective action must be taken when necessary to bring actual results (Step 2) in line with expected performance (Step 1). Generally, an investigation of alternative causes of problems (negative variances) and their assumed impact on standards is required.
5. Evaluation of the results of the corrective action procedures is necessary.

Collecting actual information (Step 2 above) is done through the formal process of accounting. This provides a clear example of the relationship between financial accounting (with its emphasis on external communication) and managerial accounting (which focuses upon internal management communication).

Generally, the restaurant's accounting system yields information useful for both external and internal purposes. As data is collected for one purpose (financial statements) it can also be used for another (for example, operating reports used by managers). Suppose the manager establishes a budgeted food cost percentage. (If all goes well, a specified percentage of revenue generated from food sales will be used to purchase the food required to generate more food revenue.) Actual operating results (the assessment of dollars actually spent to purchase food) will be measured through the use of an accrual accounting system. (This will require calculating cost of goods sold: Changes between beginning and ending inventory values along with the cost of purchases during the fiscal period and various adjustments that consider employee and promotional meals and transfers between the food and beverage departments will likely be made.) The difference between the budgeted food cost and actual food cost suggests the extent to which operating procedures may need to be revised. Note that actual food costs developed through the formal accounting system could be used both for information on the financial statement and for routine operating control.

1.8 RELATIONSHIP BETWEEN MANAGER AND ACCOUNTANT

The most effective relationship between the manager and the accountant has already been noted; the accountant serves in a staff (advisory) relationship to the manager and provides specialized help to the manager as needed. Sometimes, however, managers are much more passive, because they are unfamiliar with either accounting principles and/or the development/use of accounting systems. These passive managers believe their role in the financial management of the restaurant is to:

- "Do what the accountant says" and provide and accept information using systems and procedures suggested by the accountant.
- Believe that accounting information, regardless of how it is collected, analyzed, or reported, is correct. (In fact, the failure to consider the accuracy of accounting information can be a significant impediment to problem-solving.)
- Use accounting information regardless of how it is presented in formal financial statements. Many managers make decisions with information from various reports and statements that they neither helped to design nor understand. When this occurs, managers often make misinformed decisions.
- Defer to the accountant all or much of the responsibility for making decisions about financial matters. This practice violates the basic distinction between line and staff relationships.

- View the accountant as a "necessary evil" rather than as a partner and helpful provider of useful information.

Each of the above perceptions frequently arises when the role of the accountant in the restaurant operation is not properly understood. In practice, remember that the manager should be the expert who makes decisions. While managers need financial information provided by the accountant, they must determine the meaning of the data themselves. Therefore, a more proper relationship between the manager and the accountant should include the following essentials:

- The manager must know, at minimum, the information required for short- and long-term control of the restaurant's operation. Once the manager has identified what information he or she needs, the accountant can offer advice about the best ways to gather that information.
- Information needed for internal control purposes should be combined with that used to assemble required financial statements. In this way, there is a "dovetailing" effect; the need to keep two sets of books is minimized.
- After receiving input from the manager, the accountant should design an information collection system that assembles information required for both management and accounting purposes.
- After information is developed into financial statements, the accountant can assist the manager in analysis and make corrective action recommendations, if necessary.
- Wise restaurant managers carefully consider the advice of the accountant. They recognize, however, that it is their responsibility, not the accountant's, to make operating decisions.
- The manager should ask questions when fiscal information supplied by the accountant is analyzed. For example, he or she might ask: "How were values of revenues and expenses derived?" "What do the figures mean?" "What are the consistencies and inconsistencies in the way information was collected between fiscal periods?"

The overriding point here is that the manager should be in charge of the restaurant. This means assembling all available talent including that of the accountant to make the best management decisions. Ultimately, the manager—not the accountant—must make decisions. The relationship between the manager and accountant is, then, a team effort. The manager makes use of accounting-related resources to maximize attainment of the restaurant's goals.

1.9 SUMMARY

Hospitality financial management is crucial for ensuring the orderly oversight and organization of the financial aspects of entities like hotels and restaurants, aiming primarily at the judicious handling of a business's monetary resources. This discipline shares commonalities with financial management across various industries, focusing on balancing revenue against expenses such as labor, inventory, and maintenance to secure efficient and profitable operations. It involves the formulation of budgets and financial strategies, facilitating goal setting, resource allocation, and planning for future growth or expansion.

The analysis of financial reports and statements is fundamental, providing insights into performance metrics, productivity improvements, and operational efficiency. Through budget comparisons, businesses can gauge their performance against their financial objectives, identifying areas of success or needed adjustment. The profitability of different departments within a hospitality business is also critically evaluated, considering each department's unique contribution to the overall financial health of the entity.

External economic factors, including inflation, interest rates, and social-political dynamics, significantly influence hospitality businesses, necessitating adaptive financial strategies. The accounting department plays a pivotal role, supporting various operational aspects with accounting procedures and facilitating smooth financial operations.

In an era characterized by constant disruption, effective financial management becomes a cornerstone for sustainable growth and scalability within the hospitality industry. Accounting teams are often tasked with producing consolidated financial statements to provide a comprehensive view of performance across the enterprise, although consolidating financial information presents notable challenges, especially for parent company accounting teams. The continuous evolution of financial management practices is essential for navigating the complexities of the hospitality industry, ensuring its resilience and ongoing success.

1.10 REFERENCES

- Ahmad, S.Z. (2014). Entrepreneurship in the small and medium-sized hotel sector, Current Issues in Tourism, 18 (4), pp. 328-349.
- Ajeyalemi, O. F., & Olarewaju, A. D. (2021). Destination Personality Perception as predictor of Symbolic Consumption in Africa's Tourism Industry.
- Al Najdawi, B.M. Performance measurement system approaches in hotel industry: A comparative study. Int. J. Sci. Technol. Res. 2020, 9, 3504–3507.
- Alexander, D., Britton, A., Jorissen, A., "International Financial Reporting and Analysis", Second Edition, 2005, ISBN 978-1-84480-201-2
- Almansoori, Alia and Nobanee, Haitham. (2019). How Sustainability Contributes to Shared Value Creation and Firms' Value.
- Alvarez, T., Sensini, L., Bello, C., & Vazquez, M. (2021). Management Accounting Practices and Performance of SMEs in the Hotel Industry: Evidence from an emerging economy. International Journal of Business and Social Science, 12(2), 24-35.
- Anthony, R.; Govindarajan, V. Management Control Systems, 10th ed.; McGraw-Hill: Boston, MA, USA, 2000.
- Asche, F., Garlock, T. M., Anderson, J. L., Bush, S. R., Smith, M. D., Anderson, C. M., ... & Vannuccini, S. (2018). Three pillars of sustaina-

bility in fisheries. Proceedings of the National Academy of Sciences, 115(44), 11221-11225.

- Assaf, A. & Cvelbar, L.K. (2010). The performance of the Slovenian hotel industry: Evaluation post privatization, International Journal of Tourism Research, 12 (5), pp. 462-471.
- Barros, C.P. (2005). Evaluating the efficiency of a small hotel chain with a Malmquist productivity index, International Journal of Tourism Research, 7 (3), pp. 173-184.
- Benavides-Velasco, C.A., Quintana-García, C. & Marchante-Lara, M. (2014). Total quality management, corporate social responsibility and performance in the hotel industry, International Journal of Hospitality Management, 41, pp. 77-87.
- Brida, J.G., Esteban, L.P. Risso, W.A. & Such Devesa, M.J. (2010). The international hotel industry in Spain: Its hierarchical structure, Tourism Management, 31 (1), pp. 57-73.
- Brierley, J.A.; Cowton, C.J.; Drury, C. Research into product costing practice: A European perspective. Eur. Account. Rev. 2001, 10, 215–256.
- Briggs, S., Sutherland, J. & Drummond, S. (2007). Are hotels serving quality? An exploratory study of service quality in the Scottish hotel sector, Tourism Management, 28 (4), pp. 1006-1019.
- Burns, J.; Quinn, M.; Warren, L.; Oliveira, J. Management Accounting, 1st ed.; McGraw-Hill Higher Education: New York, NY, USA, 2013.
- Carvalho, F. O 'Uniform System of Accounts for the Lodging Industries': Case Study Hotel Baía. Master's Thesis, ISCTE Business School, Repositório ISCTE-IUL, Lisbon, Portugal, 2009.
- Chan, W.W. & Ho, K. (2006). Hotels' environmental management systems (ISO 14001): creative financing strategy, International Journal of Contemporary Hospitality Management, 18 (4), pp. 302-316.
- Chen, C.F. & Soo, K.T. (2007). Cost structure and productivity growth of the Taiwanese international tourist hotels, Tourism Management, 28 (6), pp. 1400-1407.
- Chen, C.F. (2007). Applying the stochastic frontier approach to measure hotel managerial efficiency in Taiwan, Tourism Management, 28 (3), pp. 696-702.
- Chiang, W. (2006). A hotel performance evaluation of Taipei international tourist hotels – using data envelopment analysis, Asia Pacific Journal of Tourism Research, 11 (1), pp. 29-42.
- Clive Marsh (2009). Mastering Financial Management, Financial Times Prentice Hall ISBN 978-0-273-72454-4
- Cruz, I. How might hospitality organizations optimize their performance measurement systems? Int. J. Contemp. Hosp. Manag. 2007, 19, 574–588.
- Cvelbar, L.K. & Dwyer, L. (2012). An importance-performance analysis of sustainability factors for long-term strategy planning in Slovenian hotels, Journal of Sustainable Tourism, March 2015, pp. 1-18.
- David Annand, Introduction to Financial Accounting, Athabasca University, ISBN 978-0-9953266-4-4

- Della Corte, V., Del Gaudio, G., Sepe, F., & Sciarelli, F. (2019). Sustainable tourism in the open innovation realm: A bibliometric analysis. Sustainability, 11(21), 6114.
- Falk, M., & Vieru, M. (2019). International tourism demand to Finnish Lapland in the early winter season. Current Issues in Tourism, 22(11), 1312-1326.
- Faria, A.; Ferreira, L.; Trigueiros, D. Orçamentação nos hotéis do Algarve: Alinhamento com a prática internacional. Dos Algarves Multidiscip. e-J. 2019, 34, 3–25.
- Fred., Phillips (2011). Fundamentals of financial accounting. Libby, Robert., Libby, Patricia A. (3rd ed.). Boston: McGraw-Hill Irwin. ISBN 9780073527109. OCLC 457010553.
- Gomes, C.; Arroteia, N.; Lima Santos, L. Management accounting in Portuguese hotel enterprises: The influence of organizational and cultural factors. In Fulfilling the Worldwide Sustainability Challenge: Strategies, Innovations, and Perspectives for Forward Momentum in Turbulent Times, Proceedings of the 13th Annual International Conference of the Global Business and Technology Association, Istanbul, Turkey, 12–16 July 2011; Global Businness and Technology Association: New York, NY, USA, 2011.
- Gomes, C.; Lima Santos, L.; Arroteia, N. The influence of the environmental and organizational factors in the management accounting of the Portuguese hotels. In Proceedings of the VII Congreso Iberoamericano de Contabilidad de Gestión y IX Congreso Iberoamericano de Administración Empresarial y Contabilidad, Valencia, Spain, 3–5 July 2013.
- James Van Horne and John Wachowicz (2009). Fundamentals of Financial Management, 13th ed., Pearson Education Limited. ISBN 9705614229
- Johnny Jackson, Introduction to Financial Accounting, Thomas Edison State University.
- Kyrylov, Y., Hranovska, V., Boiko, V., Kwilinski, A., & Boiko, L. (2020). International Tourism Development in the Context of Increasing Globalization Risks: On the Example of Ukraine's Integration into the Global Tourism Industry. Journal of Risk and Financial Management, 13(12), 303.
- Lawrence Gitman and Chad J. Zutter (2019). Principles of Managerial Finance, 14th edition, Addison-Wesley Publishing, ISBN 978-0133507690.
- Li, X., Shi, P., Han, Y., Deng, A., & Liu, D. (2020). Measurement and spatial variation of green total factor productivity of the tourism industry in China. International journal of environmental research and public health, 17(4), 1159.
- Libby, T.; Lindsay, R.M. Beyond budgeting or budgeting reconsidered? A survey of North-American budgeting practice. Manag. Account. Res. 2010, 21, 56–75.

- Lima Santos, L.; Gomes, C.; Arroteia, N.; Almeida, P. The perception of management accounting in the Portuguese lodging industry. In Managing in an Interconnected World: Pioneering Business and Technology Excellence, Proceedings of the 16th Annual International Conference of the Global Business and Technology Association, Baku, Zaerbaijan, 8–12 July 2014; Global Business and Technology Association: New York, NY, USA, 2014; pp. 565–572.
- Lunkes, R.; Bortoluzzi, D.; Anzilago, M.; Rosa, F. Influence of online hotel reviews on the fit between strategy and use of management control systems: A study among small- and medium-sized hotels in Brazil. J. Appl. Account. Res. 2020, 21, 615–634.
- Lunkes, R.J. Manual de Contabilidade Hoteleira, 1st ed.; Editora Atlas, S.A.: São Paulo, Brazil, 2004.
- Makrigiannakis, G.; Soteriades, M. Management accounting in the hotel business: The case of the Greek hotel industry. Int. J. Hosp. Tour. Adm. 2007, 8, 47–76.
- Pezet, A. The history of the French tableau de bord (1885–1975): Evidence from the archives. Account. Bus. Financ. Hist. Taylor Fr. 2009, 19, 103–125.
- Phillips, P.; Moutinho, L. Critical review of strategic planning research in hospitality and tourism. Ann. Tour. Res. 2014, 48, 96–120.
- Zounta, S.; Bekiaris, M.J. Cost-based management and decision-making in Greek luxury hotels. Tourismos 2009, 4, 205–225.

CHAPTER 2

Understanding Financial Statements

INTRODUCTION

The hospitality industry represents a significant and expansive segment of the service sector, encompassing a variety of smaller sectors such as hotels and accommodations, event planning, theme parks, transportation, cruise lines, and various aspects of the broader tourism industry. This industry is characterized by its broad spectrum, catering to the diverse needs of travelers and customers by offering a wide range of services designed to enhance the travel and leisure experience. The complexity and diversity of the hospitality industry necessitate a comprehensive understanding and analysis of its financial health and operational performance.

Given the general and all-encompassing nature of the hospitality industry, it is critically important to establish and utilize a specific set of financial ratios tailored to effectively evaluate companies within this industry, regardless of their specific area of operation. The hospitality sector is notably capital-intensive, heavily relying on fixed and tangible assets such as property, buildings, and equipment, which are fundamental to providing lodging, entertainment, transportation, and other hospitality services. Consequently, this reliance on substantial physical assets demands a unique set of financial metrics and ratios that are capable of providing a detailed and accurate analysis of the industry's financial standing and the performance of individual businesses within it.

Financial ratios play a pivotal role in this context, offering insights into various aspects of a company's financial health, including its profitability, liquidity, efficiency, and solvency. These ratios are essential for comparing the financial performance of companies within the hospitality industry, identifying trends over time, and benchmarking against industry standards and competitors. They help stakeholders to gauge the financial stability and growth potential of businesses, making them invaluable tools for investors, managers, and other interested parties.

The practice of financial accounting in the hospitality industry is foundational to its operational and strategic decision-making processes. Through meticulous tracking and analysis of income, expenses, assets, liabilities, and other financial transactions, hospitality businesses are able to identify their strengths and weaknesses, monitor performance trends, and pinpoint potential areas for improvement. Financial accounting enables these companies to evaluate the cost-effectiveness of their operations, facilitating informed decisions regarding potential investments, resource allocation, and other critical business activities. By leveraging financial data and ratios, the hospitality industry can enhance its financial transparency, operational efficiency, and overall competitiveness in the market.

2.1 FINANCIAL STATEMENTS

Hotel financial statements are designed to provide insights into a specific aspect of your business. As a hotel operator, staying on top of your finances is essential to the long-term profitability of your business. With the right financial information at your fingertips, you can make sound decisions for your hotel, fine-tune your business strategies, deal with any red flags before they become bigger problems and drive sustainable growth.

Financial statements include information about the financial activities of your hotel. The exact information included differs depending on the statement, as we'll cover in more detail below.

Generally speaking, though, financial statements cover information about the incomings and outgoings of your business. This can give you a clear picture of your past, current and predicted future performance.

2.1.1 Importance of Financial Statements

Financial statements are a critical component of running a profitable and sustainable hotel. They can tell you things like:

- Whether you're making enough hotel revenue
- Whether that revenue is translating into hotel profits
- How much you're spending on operational expenses and overheads
- Whether you have enough cash on hand to pay the bills

Financial statements can help with:

- Operations: Financial statements can be used to review the efficiency of your hotel operations and make necessary adjustments to processes, staffing, etc.
- Investments: You use financial statements to figure out if you have the appropriate funds and financial standing to invest in new areas for your hotel.
- Credit and loans: Lenders will ask for financial statements to determine if your hotel is financially stable enough to receive a loan.

- Marketing & pricing: Analysing financial statements can indicate whether your hotel's marketing and pricing strategies are bringing in enough revenue, and whether you need to adjust your approach.

2.1.2 Types of Hotel Financial Statements

There are several different hotel financial statements you can use to look at different aspects of your business. Here are some of the most common types to be aware of.

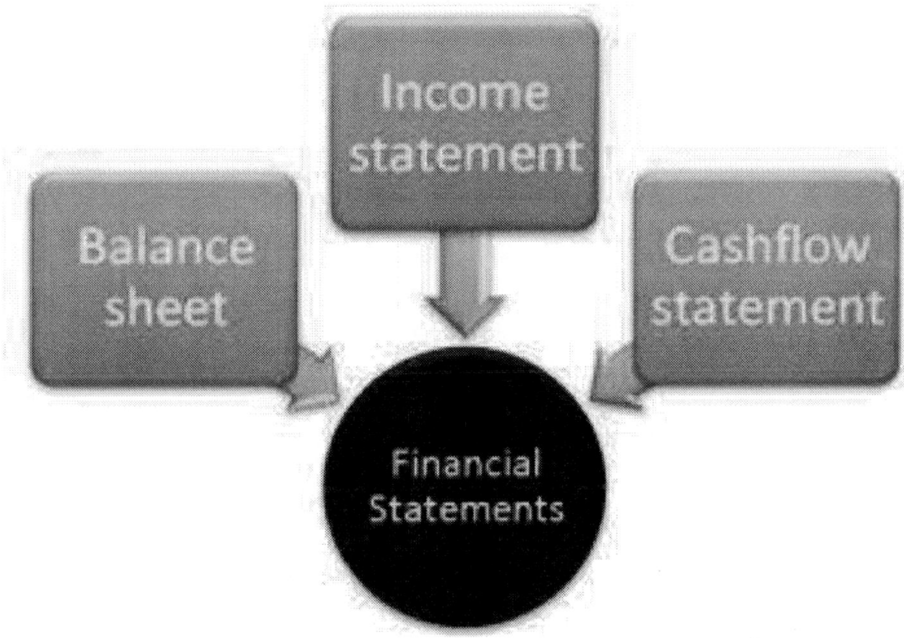

***Figure 2.1:** An illustration of Financial Statements*

Hotel Income Statement

A hotel income statement, also known as a profit and loss statement, P&L statement, statement of operations or statement of earnings, tells you how much money (revenue) your business brought in and how much of a profit you earned from that revenue over a particular period.

Simply put, a hotel income statement shows you how much money your hotel is making, and how much you're losing. You can use an income statement to analyse your profits and losses over any time period you like, but they're most commonly created for a month, quarter or year. You can also use an income statement to compare your profitability against the industry average (as of June 2020, the average hotel profit margin was around 18%).

A hotel income statement gives you a general overview of how your business is performing financially over a specific period. This can be helpful for:

- Setting prices for your rooms or services (to maintain a healthy profit margin)

- Looking at how your expenses are affecting your net profitability
- Understanding whether you're bringing in enough of a profit
- Fine-tuning your sales and marketing strategy

You'll also need a current income statement if you want to apply for a hotel business loan. Banks and lenders will check your net income compared with your expenses to make sure your hotel is financially stable enough to lend money to. The main goal of financial analysis is to measure a company's financial performance over time and against its peers.

Elements of a Hotel Income Statement

There are three main elements of a hotel income statement:

1. Revenue

Revenue, also called sales or income, covers any money received from operating your hotel. This includes income from:

- Rooms
- Food & beverage
- Entertainment
- Guests services such as massages and spa treatments

2. Expenses

Expenses include all your outgoings, such as:

- Cost of goods sold (COGS)
- Rent or mortgage
- Staff wages
- Utilities
- Franchise fees, if applicable
- Property taxes and insurance
- Debts
- Marketing and advertising expenses

3. Net profit

This is calculated by subtracting all your expenses from your revenue.

Hotel Income Statement Example

Here's an example of a simple, hypothetical hotel income statement:

PROFIT & LOSS STATEMENT					
HOTEL NAME				START DATE	END DATE
ABC Hotel				01/07/2022	31/07/2022
INCOME					
REFERENCE ID.	DESCRIPTION				AMOUNT
A1	Guest Reservations				$65,000

A2	Food Purchases	$9,000
A3	Events	$17,000
A4	Other	$7,300
INCOME TOTAL		$98,300
LESS SALES RETURNS / ALLOWANCES (enter "-" negative amount)		$(7,562)
TOTAL REVENUE		$90,738
EXPENSES		
REFERENCE ID.	DESCRIPTION	AMOUNT
R1	Utilities	$2,100
R2	Maintenance	$1,760
R3	Depreciation	$2,950
R4	Staff Wages	$25,400
R4444-5349	Insurance	$1,650
R4444-5350	Legal Fees	$780
R4444-5351	Advertising	$1,850
R4444-5352	Supplies	$475
R4444-5353	Other	$850
EXPENSE TOTAL		$37,815
NET INCOME BEFORE TAXES		$60,485
TAX RATE (enter %)		10.00%
INCOME TAX EXPENSE		$6,049
NET INCOME		$54,437

Balance Sheet for Hotels

A balance sheet, also called a statement of financial position, summarises all of your hotel's business assets (what you own) and liabilities (what you owe).

In a nutshell, a balance sheet shows you how much money you would have left over if you sold all your assets and paid off all your debts at a particular point in time. This is known as your equity.

The formula for calculating your equity is as follows:

Equity = Assets – Liabilities

What is a hotel balance sheet used for?

Like an income statement, a balance sheet provides a picture of the financial health of your hotel.

By analysing a balance sheet, you can assess whether you have borrowed too much money, whether your assets can be converted into cash quickly if needed (i.e. if they're liquid) and whether you have enough cash on hand to cover expenses.

Balance sheets are also used to secure business loans and funding from private investors.

Elements of a Hotel Balance Sheet

The three main elements of a hotel balance sheet are as follows:

1. Assets

Assets cover everything you wholly own, which includes tangible and intangible items such as:

- Property
- Equipment
- Furniture
- Food & beverage inventory
- Other inventory
- Cash
- Vehicles
- Intellectual property
- Trademarks and patents

2. Liabilities

Liabilities cover everything you owe, which includes items such as:

- Short-term and long-term loans
- Accrued bills such as mortgage/rent and utilities
- Staff wages owed
- Taxes owed

3. Equity

Equity is the combined value of all your hotel's assets after deducting your liabilities.

Hotel Balance Sheet Example

Here is an example of a hypothetical hotel balance sheet:

Balance sheet for ABC Hotel		
	2021	2020
Current assets		
Cash	$21,506	$20,000
Petty cash	$200	$200
Accounts receivable	$5,013	$5,000
Inventory	$20,887	$21,000
Prepaid expenses	$1,098	$1,100
Total	$48,704	$47,300
Fixed assets		
Property and land	$150,000	$150,000

Renovations/improvements	$20,000	$12,000
Furniture and fitout	$28,777	$30,777
Vehicles	$32,513	$32,513
Equipment/tools	$21,000	$18,000
Total	$252,290	$243,290
TOTAL ASSETS	$300,994	$290,590
Current/short-term liabilities		
Credit cards payable	$7,523	$6,000
Accounts payable	$18,237	$18,000
Interest payable	$450	$380
Accrued wages		
Income tax	$10,087	$9,870
Total	$36,297	$34,250
Long-term liabilities		
Loans	$148,222	$146,231
Equipment finance	$48,000	$46,500
Total	$196,222	$192,731
TOTAL LIABILITIES	$232,519	$226,981
NET ASSETS (NET EQUITY)	$68,475	$63,609
WORKING CAPITAL	$12,407	$13,050

Cash Flow Statement for Hotels

A cash flow statement shows how much cash is going in and out of your hotel over a specific period. This is known as your cash flow.

Having enough cash on hand to pay the bills and buy goods and assets is an essential part of hotel management. A cash flow statement can tell you whether you're likely to run into any issues in this area.

You might be earning steady hotel revenue but if you're overspending or your expenses are too high, you can quickly end up with negative cash flow. And even if you're profitable, if there's not enough cash landing in your bank at any time, paying the bills such as rent/mortgage, wages and inventory can be a challenge. That's why it's important to keep an eye on your cash flow throughout the year.

What is a hotel cash flow statement used for?

A cash flow forecast tells you how much cash you have coming into and going out of your business. With this information, you can make necessary

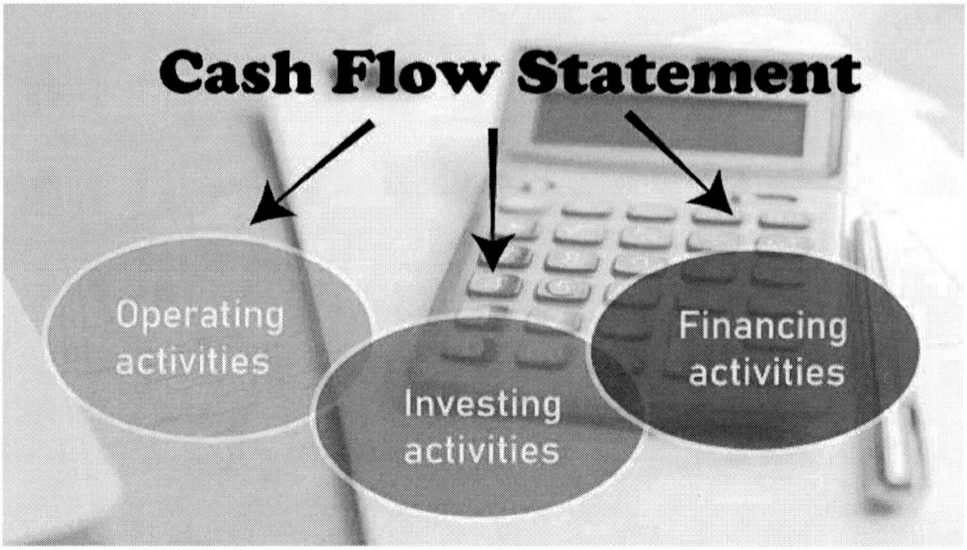

Figure 2.2: Schematic of cash flow statement.

adjustments to improve your cash position, such as cutting expenses, finding new hotel revenue streams or changing your pricing and marketing strategies.

At the other end of the spectrum, if you have a cash surplus, you can consider investing back into your hotel through upgrades and renovations, hiring staff or expanding your operations.

A cash flow statement can be used to see if you:

- Have enough cash to cover expenses
- Need to make adjustments to your pricing or marketing strategies
- Can afford to upgrade or renovate
- Can hire new staff (or need to reduce headcount)
- Should consider borrowing some money

Elements of a Hotel Cash Flow Statement

The two core elements of a hotel cash flow statement are as follows:

1. Cash incoming

This covers all the main cash-generating activities of a business, such as room bookings, food and beverage sales and other sales.

2. Cash outgoing

This includes all the expenses related to running your hotel, including loans, wages, fees, interest and other costs.

The cash balance is calculated by subtracting the total of your cash outgoing from your cash incoming.

Hotel Cash Flow Statement Example

Here's an example of a simple quarterly cash flow statement for a hotel:

Cash flow for ABC Hotel			
	July	August	September
OPENING BALANCE	$85,000	$88,450	$105,099
Cash incoming			
Sales	67000	64399	66500
Asset sales	1200	0	0
Debtor receipts	2500	2800	1300
Loans	1400	1500	1300
Total incoming	$72,100	$68,699	$69,100
Cash outgoing			
Purchases (stock etc)	10000	5700	8500
Accountant fees	800	0	500
Advertising and marketing	2000	0	2000
Bank fees and charges	100	150	120
Interest paid	100	150	120
Utilities (electricity, gas, water)	6700	3000	2500
Telephone	500	600	500
Rent & rates	10000	10000	10000
Motor vehicle expenses	2000	2000	2000
Repairs and maintenance	6000	0	0
Licensing	250	250	300
Insurance	1200	1200	1200
Income tax	5000	5000	5000
Wages (including PAYG)	24000	24000	24000
Total outgoing	$68,650	$52,050	$56,740
Monthly cash balance	$3,450	$16,649	$12,360
CLOSING BALANCE	$88,450	$105,099	$117,459

Financial statements are a key part of running a successful and profitable hotel. Although different types of financial statements show different information, they all provide insights into your hotel's financial standing. The three most common types of financial statements for hotels are:

- Income statement (also known as a profit & loss statement)
- Balance sheet
- Cash flow statement

Together, these three financial statements can tell you:

- Whether you're earning enough revenue

- Whether your hotel is profitable
- How much you're spending
- Whether you have enough cash on hand to pay the bills
- Whether you can afford to invest in growth, such as through renovations and upgrades
- Whether you should adjust your pricing or marketing strategies
- Whether you might need to consider borrowing some money

With these insights, you can make smarter and more impactful decisions about your hote

2.2 RATIO ANALYSIS FOR EVALUATING A HOSPITALITY BUSINESS'S FINANCIAL PERFORMANCE

Ratio analysis is an essential tool for analyzing the financial performance of businesses in the hospitality industry. By comparing different financial ratios, such as profitability ratios, turnover ratios, and financial ratios, one can gain insights into a company's financial health.

Financial ratios are important for hospitality management because they can help you measure your business's strengths and weaknesses, identify areas for improvement, and benchmark your performance against industry standards or competitors. Financial ratios can also help you communicate your results to stakeholders, such as investors, lenders, suppliers, or customers. By using financial ratios, you can make informed decisions and plan ahead for your hospitality business.

***Figure 2.3:** An illustration of financial report.*

2.2.1 Definition of Ratio Analysis

Ratio analysis is the process of analyzing and interpreting the financial statements of a business to assess its financial performance. Financial ratios are used to compare different aspects of a company's performance, such as profitability, liquidity, and efficiency, over time and across different businesses in the same industry.

2.2.2 Classification

The hospitality industry includes hotels, events, tourist destinations, and cruise lines, among others. Because this sector encompasses so many different sub-sectors, it is difficult to compare companies within the hospitality sector. Some helpful financial ratios can be put to use to achieve apples-to-apples comparisons.

Liquidity Ratios

Liquidity ratios provide stakeholders with information regarding a company's ability to meet its short-term financial obligations. The hospitality industry needs a high amount of working capital and has a lot of short-term financial obligations to cover, making liquidity ratios an integral part of the industry's analysis.

Current ratio = (current assets / current liabilities)

The current ratio is a liquidity measure that shows how a company is able to meet all its short-term liabilities with the short-term assets on hand. Assets considered short-term are anything such as inventory and do not include long-term assets such as property, plant, and equipment.

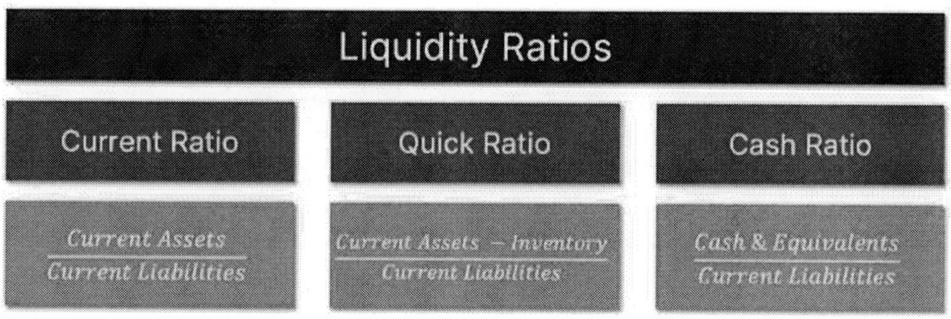

Figure 2.4: *Types of liquidity ratios.*

For the hospitality industry, companies have a lot of current liabilities in the form of salaries and wages, short-term equipment leasing, and other short-term liabilities. Additionally, it is a cyclical industry, making it imperative that companies have enough current assets to cover current liabilities, even in an economic downturn. Stakeholders want to see a high current ratio above one to determine a company within the hospitality industry is strong.

Financial Leverage Ratios

Financial leverage ratios give stakeholders an understanding of the long-term solvency of a firm in the hospitality industry. These ratios measure a company's ability to meet its long-term debt obligations.

Debt ratio = (total debt / total assets)

Companies within the hospitality industry have a lot of long-term liabilities in the form of debt, along with current liabilities. This debt is used to finance large properties such as hotels or large bus fleets for transportation companies. A lot of long-term assets are needed to successfully run a hospitality company, and therefore long-term debt financing is also normally needed.

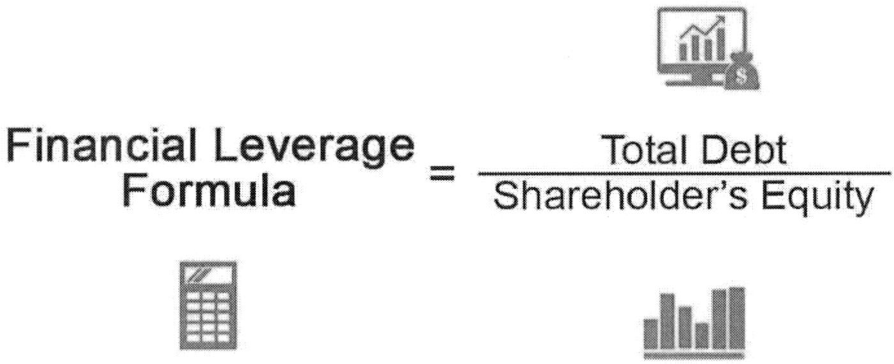

The debt ratio measures a company's ability to meet its long-term debt obligations. For companies within the hospitality industry, it is important to have low debt ratios, meaning long-term assets greatly outweigh the debt used to purchase them.

Profitability Ratios

Profitability ratios measure a company's level of profitability, at the gross profit, operating profit, and net profit levels. For companies in the hospitality industry, billions of dollars are generated, and many companies are long-established, meaning high profit margins should be generated at all levels.

Gross profit margin = ((sales - cost of goods sold) / sales)

Gross profit margin measures a company's gross profit earned on the revenue it generates. For companies in the hospitality industry, most of the costs come from operations and not the cost of goods sold, and the gross profit margin should be high for those businesses that operate within the hospitality industry.

Net profit margin = (net profit) / (total sales)

The net profit margin is similar to the gross profit margin except that it measures the amount of net profit earned on the revenue a company generates. For the companies in the hospitality industry, profits are actually not very high, as there are high associated operating costs to run a company in this industry. However, a stakeholder should always look at a company's net profit margin and compare it to industry averages to ensure it meets or exceeds the benchmark.

***Figure 2.5:** Profitability ratios.*

2.2.3 Practical Applications of Ratio Analysis in Hospitality Industry

Ratio analysis is an essential tool for evaluating the financial performance of businesses in the hospitality industry. The following are some of its practical applications:

- It helps businesses to identify areas where they can improve their profitability, liquidity, and efficiency.
- It enables businesses to compare their performance with that of their competitors and to identify their strengths and weaknesses.
- It helps businesses to make informed financial decisions, such as whether to invest in new equipment or to reduce their debt.
- It helps businesses to communicate their financial performance to their stakeholders, such as investors, lenders, and suppliers.

2.2.4 Limitations of Ratio Analysis

Although ratio analysis is a valuable tool for assessing a company's financial performance, it has its limitations. Some of the limitations are:

- Different businesses may use different accounting methods, which can make comparisons difficult.
- Financial ratios do not always tell the whole story about a company's financial health. For example, a company may have a high debt-to-equity ratio, but if it is using the borrowed funds to finance growth, it may still be financially healthy.
- Financial ratios only provide a snapshot of a company's financial performance at a specific point in time.

Ratio analysis is an essential tool for evaluating the financial performance of businesses in the hospitality industry. By comparing different financial ratios, businesses can gain insights into their financial health and make informed financial decisions. However, it is important to keep in mind the limitations of ratio analysis and to use it in conjunction with other financial analysis tools.

2.3 FINANCIAL ANALYSIS

This section presents some of the fundamental accounting concepts and methods of financial analysis that will be used throughout the book and also throughout the career of any hospitality manager. These are not only fundamental accounting concepts but important management tools used to operate a business on a daily basis

The concepts and terms are explained in a direct and fundamental way. The typical detailed and complicated accounting explanations are missing because they will do no good if they are not understood. The information in this section will form a solid financial foundation, one that will enable students to expand in terms of knowledge and application as they work through problems and deal with business situations. It will focus on hospitality industry operations, but the methods of financial analysis presented are useful and applicable to any business operation.

2.3.1 Methods of Financial Analysis

Analyzing financial reports and statements requires a fundamental understanding of where numbers come from, how they are organized and presented, what they mean, what they measure, and how they are used. This section discusses two concepts of working with numbers to analyze financial statements

Two Important Tools

First, we will talk about two important ways numbers are used in business. They are used to measure financial performance and to provide a management tool to use in operating the business.

To Measure Financial Performance

Numbers provide a way to determine how a business is performing. Measuring financial performance is historical in nature and uses the actual numbers or results from business operations. It tells us what the business has produced, and it compares and evaluates that performance to specific measures. It is looking back through the rearview mirror at operations. The three main financial statements are all used in measuring financial performance. The Profit and Loss (P&L) Statement shows the revenues, expenses, and profits for a specified time period. Each month, accounting period, quarter, or year, the numbers produced by an operation are recorded in the P&L statement and tell whether the business revenue and profits are improving, declining, or staying the same.

The Balance Sheet shows the assets, liabilities, and owner equity of a business at a specific time. These numbers tell us whether the business is getting financially stronger by increasing assets or owner equity or if it is struggling and increasing liabilities. The numbers also tell us how the business is capitalized or started—with more debt than owner equity or with more owner equity than debt. The Statement of Cash Flows shows how much cash is generated by a business and how effectively it is used in operating the business over a specified time period. Cash and liquidity are critical to the success of a business, and the numbers included in the Statement of Cash Flows tells us how cash is being acquired and used.

To Provide a Management Tool

Numbers provide a way for managers to plan for varying levels of business volume. This can take the form of forecasting revenues, scheduling wages, implementing cost controls, expanding business operations, or preparing the annual budget. Numbers give managers feedback on their operations and then assist them in making appropriate changes. This aspect of using numbers is very valuable to a business because it is the process of taking the information numbers provided and applying them back to operating the business.

The Financial Management Cycle

Second is the Financial Management Cycle. It is important to understand this process and how numbers are generated and used in business operations. This cycle deals with the flow and use of numbers in business operations.

1. Operations produce the numbers. All the activities involved in the daily operations produce the numbers that measure performance. In a hotel, the daily operations provide products and services to guests, including the rooms department, food and beverage outlets, gift shop, and any other department that produces a sales transaction with a guest. Numbers used in financial analysis have to come from somewhere, and that is the daily operation of the business.
2. Accounting prepares the numbers and provides financial reports and statements. At the end of the day, week, or month, the numbers resulting from all operations and activities are collected, summarized, and

reported by the accounting department. These reports describe the operations and activities and are distributed to the appropriate managers for their review and use.

3. Accounting and operations analyze the numbers. Operations management and accounting management work together to review and analyze the reports. They look for changes, the cause of the change, and the result of the change to understand operations and determine ways to change and improve. Together they have operational experience and financial analysis experience and can identify any changes or improvements that need to be made to ensure that productive operations continue.
4. Operations applies the numbers back to the business. After reviews and discussions, the operations managers make any necessary changes to operations to correct or improve them. The ability to analyze quickly and accurately and then make any necessary changes is an important part of any business operation. It enables the business to constantly improve by being more productive or creating more value in the products and services that it provides.

2.3.2 Comparing Numbers to Give Them Meaning

Numbers need to be compared to something to have any meaning. A hotel has monthly sales of $1 million. All this tells us is the sales level. How do we know if this is good or bad, up or down, acceptable or not acceptable? A fundamental concept of financial analysis is to compare a number produced by operations to an established number that will tell us if there was an increase or a decrease. The most common comparisons are to (1) last year, (2) budget, (3) forecast, (4) previous month or period, (5) pro forma, or (6) any other established goal.

Last Year

Comparing actual financial results to last year's actual results is a useful comparison. The first evaluation of financial operations is to show if operations are better than the previous year. The best results are if actual operations for the current year are better than last year and the budget. The worst results are if the current year is worse than last year and the budget.

Budget

Actual financial results for a month, quarter, or year are compared to the established budget. The budget is the formal one-year financial operating plan for a company. Budgets include planned increases in revenues and profits, and productivity improvements in costs and expenses. Comparing actual results to the budget shows whether the business is moving in the direction planned and budgeted and how close it is in meeting, exceeding, or missing the budgeted numbers.

Forecast

Forecasts update the budget. Whereas the budget is done once for the entire year, forecasts are done continually to adjust or relate to current business conditions. Forecasts can be weekly, monthly, quarterly, biannually, or can apply to the end of the year. They are important because they are more current and help project business performance compared to the budget.

Previous Month or Period

These comparisons are important because they identify trends in operations. A goal of any business is to continually improve. Examining month-to-month performance tells us the trend and direction of our operations. They can show improvements that we hope are the results of corrective action implemented by management to keep the company moving in the right direction.

Pro Forma

A new business does not have any historical operating information. Therefore, management, developers, and bankers prepare a pro forma based on market conditions and expected financial returns. The pro formas are estimates or projections of how these financial experts think the business will perform in the first year of operations. The pro forma is used for the first year of business operations and is then replaced by the budget, which is prepared based on the first year's actual performance. Pro formas are used to establish and identify initial business revenues and profits that will generate the cash flow necessary to repay loans and investments.

Other Goals

Occasionally a business will establish other goals or benchmarks to compare actual performance. Examples are improving profit margins to meet an established goal, achieving specific revenue levels, or entering new markets. Let's use our example to give meaning to the $1,000,000 in monthly sales. Suppose that last year we did monthly sales of $950,000; this year we increased that by $50,000 to $1,000,000, which is good—sales are increasing. However, if the budget was $1,100,000, we missed the budget by $100,000, which is not good—our sales did not increase as much as we had budgeted.

Now let's analyze our $1,000,000 monthly sales performance. Was it good or bad? We know we increased sales $50,000 over last year, but we missed budget by $100,000. The answer, then, is that our performance was both good and bad. It was good because we improved $50,000 over last year. It was bad because we missed the budget by $100,000. The next question we have to ask is, "Was the budget set too high?" Comparing the budget of $1,100,000 to last year's actual sales of $950,000 tells us that we expected (or budgeted) sales to increase $150,000. We can also measure this increase in percentages by dividing the $150,000 increase by last year's sales of $950,000 to get a budget percentage increase of 15.8%. That is an aggressive budget increase. If I were the manager of this business, I would be very happy to have the $50,000 increase over last year (a 5.3% increase). I would also review the reasons we thought we could increase by 15.8% and analyze why that didn't happen.

Comparing numbers to something concrete is essential to give any meaning to the numbers. This is particularly important for the P&L Statements. The Balance Sheet and the Statement of Cash Flow are analyzed more to look for changes from previous statements or to goals or benchmarks than to budgets. Typically there is no budget for these two financial statements. That is why they are compared to the previous month or period or to a goal. Remember to compare any financial report to last year, last month, the budget, the forecast, the pro forma, or the goal to give it meaning. Then we can tell whether operations are improving or not.

2.3.3 Measuring Change to Explain Performance

One of the most important elements of financial analysis is to be able to identify where changes occur and what caused the change. In a large business with many products and departments, an effective financial analysis of the financial reports must locate the department that is changing and identify the causes of that change. Is it in revenues—volume or rate? Is it in expenses—cost of sales, wages, benefits, or other operating expenses? Is it a direct or indirect, fixed or variable expense? One department or many departments may be affecting operations with positive or negative changes.

Changes are identified by comparing actual performance to previous performance or a specific goal or measure. These changes can be for a month, a quarter, or a year. The more information that is obtained about the changes, the better chance that good decisions can be made to respond to the changes. Changes, both positive and negative, are measured in terms of units, dollars, and percentages. These three measurements can tell us a lot about the performance of a business. From our $1,000,000 monthly sales example, we have already looked at the dollar increase (+$50,000 over last year) and the percentage increase (+5.3% over last year). We know that we have $50,000 more sales dollars, a positive change. We know that we increased sales by 5.3%, also a positive change. Performing that same financial analysis process, our $1,000,000 is $100,000 below the budget of $1,100,000 and 9.1% below the budget. We know that we have $100,000 fewer sales dollars than budgeted, a negative result. Our 9.1% is also a negative result from our budget.

The final measurement is units. If the entire $1,000,000 in monthly sales was from room revenue, our unit will be the number of rooms sold. Our accounting reports would tell us how many rooms were sold and what the average room rate was. Let's assume the average room rate was $80. We can then calculate the number of rooms sold by dividing total room sales of $1,000,000 by the average room rate of $80, which gives us 12,500 rooms sold. That should match the number of rooms sold on our accounting report. So now we have the units or volume—12,500 rooms sold—but we don't know if this is better or worse than last year's monthly sales of $950,000. The answer will come from last year's accounting reports. If the report tells us that the average rate for last year was $78 and 12,180 rooms were sold, we can multiply these together and get the monthly sales of $950,000. Now we can compare our actual rooms sold this year of 12,500 to last year's rooms sold of 12,180. We can also compare this year's average rate of $80 to last year's average rate of $78. Take a minute to calculate the increases from last year in dollars, units, and percentages for this year's monthly sales of $1,000,000 (Table 1).

Table 1: *Comparison Actual to Last Year*

	Sales	Rooms Sold	Average Rate
This year	$1,000,000	12,500	$80
Last year	$950,000	12,180	$78
Dollar difference			
Percentage difference			

The Answers to Table 1 Comparison Actual to Last Year

	Sales	Rooms Sold	Average Rate
This year	$1,000,000	12,500	$80
Last year	$950,000	12,180	$78
Dollar difference	$50,000	320	$2
Percentage difference	+5.3%	+2.6%	+2.6%

2.3.4 Using Percentages in Financial Analysis

Percentages are one of the three ways numbers are used to measure financial performance. They provide an additional dimension or perspective in financial analysis. Percentages measure relationships and changes and always involve two numbers.

Calculating Percentages

Percentages are the result of combining two numbers that define a relationship. A change in one number changes the resulting percentage. Both numbers can also change. When a percentage changes, it is important to know which number changed and what caused the change. For example:

Wage cost percentage equals wage expense dollars divided by the associated revenue dollars

If our department wage expense is $350 and our department revenue is $1,000, our wage cost percentage is 35% ($350 / $1,000). Wage cost percentage can go up or down in two ways. An increased wage cost would result from our actual wage expense increasing or our revenues decreasing. Continuing our example:

1. $400 Wage Expense / $1,000 Department Revenue = 40% Wage Cost Percentage
2. $350 Wage Expense / $875 Department Revenue = 40% Wage Cost Percentage

If our wage cost expense went up, we would analyze the labor numbers to see where the increase was and what caused the increase. In our first example, our wage expense went up $50 to $400, but our department revenue remained the same at $1,000. This is not good because we spent $50 more on wages but did not increase our output or revenues. The business operation was less productive. In our second example, our wage cost remained constant at $350, but our department revenue went down $125 to $875. This is also not good because we spent the same amount on wages, $350, but it resulted in less sales, $875. Again, our business operation was less productive.

When you identify where the changes occurred, then you can look for the causes of the changes and make any necessary adjustments to improve operations. Our corrective action will be different in each example. In the first example, we would look at our work schedule to make scheduling changes to get back to 35% wage cost. In our second example, we would look to the sales department to see what caused the drop in sales to $875 and to determine how we can correct it. In either case, it is an important part of financial analysis to make any necessary changes in our work schedule to adjust to the forecasted production volumes and their corresponding sales.

What Percentages Measure

Percentages measure relationships and changes. An example of relationships is the previous wage cost example. A 35% wage cost means that 35 cents out of every revenue dollar is used to pay the wage cost associated with producing that revenue dollar. Another example is food cost percentage. An actual food cost percentage of 40% means that 40 cents out of every food revenue dollar is used to pay for the associated food cost to produce that one food revenue dollar.

The food cost percentage will go up or down based on changes in food costs or food revenues. To become more productive and profitable, the actual food expense that results in a sale would have to decline or stay the same, but the food revenue would increase. To become less productive, our food cost would have to remain the same and our food revenues go down or our food cost would have to increase but our food revenues would remain the same. By looking at each number and identifying any changes, we analyze the numbers and identify what changed and how that affects our operational performance.

Let's look at another example of percentages and change. If our revenues increase from $1,000 to $1,200, the resulting dollar change is an increase of $200. To calculate the associated percentage change, divide the $200 increase by the original $1,000 revenue, and the result is a 20% increase in revenues. The amount of change is always divided by the base, beginning, or original number. Percentage change can be calculated for changes in revenues, expenses, profits, assets, units, liabilities, owner equity, or any other specific account.

Using percentages in the process of financial analysis includes three steps. First is identifying and measuring the change. Second is identifying the cause of the change. Third is developing and implementing corrective action into daily operations.

2.3.5 Four Types of Percentages Used in Financial Analysis

Cost or Expense Percentages

These percentages tell us what dollar amounts of expenses are associated with corresponding revenues or sales. The previous examples of wage cost and food cost demonstrate cost percentages. Cost percentages can be calculated for any expense account or type that has a specific dollar cost associated with it. The formula for cost percentage is expense dollars divided by corresponding revenue dollars. For example, suppose that the room revenues for January are $40,000, wage costs are $5,000, benefit costs are $2,000, reservation costs are $4,000, and linen costs are $1,500. Our expense formula is dollar cost / department revenue. Our cost percentages for January are as follows:

Wage Cost = 12.5% ($5,000 / $40,000)
Benefit Cost = 5.0% ($2,000 / $40,000)
Reservation Cost = 10.0% ($4,000 / $40,000)
Linen Cost = 3.8% ($1,500 / $40,000)

Profit Percentages

Profit percentages tell how much of the revenue dollar is remaining after all expenses are paid. Profits are measured in dollars and percentages. Dollar profit measures the absolute number of dollars remaining as profit, whereas percentage profit measures how much of the sales dollar is remaining as profit. Profit percentages can be applied to different levels of profit: department profits, house profits, or gross operating profits.

Department profit percentages are important because each department that is a profit center has a different profit percentage resulting in different department profitability. For example, the rooms department typically has a department profit range of 65% to 75%, the banquet or catering department profit typically ranges from 30% to 40%, lounge and retail shop profits range from 25% to 35%, and restaurant profits range from 0% to 10%. It is also possible for some restaurants to operate at a loss, therefore having a negative percentage referred to as department loss percentage rather than department profit percentage.

Mix Percentages

Mix percentages tell you how much of your total comes from different departments, or how much each department adds to the total. Mix percentages can be measured in units or dollars. They are useful because they provide a quantified measure of each part to the whole. The sales mix percentage identifies the portion or amount each department's sales adds to total sales. Following is an example of a hotel sales mix:

Department	Sales Dollars	Sales Mix Percentage
Rooms sales	$1,000	50%
Restaurant sales	300	15%
Beverage sales	200	10%
Banquet sales	500	25%
Total sales	$2,000	100%

If each department has the same profit percentage, the sales mix percentage is not very helpful. In this case, the same amount of profit will result from each revenue dollar regardless of the department. However, the actual department profit percentages are very different as demonstrated in the previous section. Let's add department profit percentages to our example:

Department	Profit Percentage	Sales Dollars	Sales Mix Percentage	Profit Dollars	Profit Mix Percentage
Rooms sales	70%	$1,000	50%	$700	70.7%
Restaurant sales	10%	300	15%	30	3.0%
Beverage sales	30%	200	10%	60	6.1%
Banquet sales	40%	500	25%	200	20.2%
Total sales/profit		$2,000	100%	$990	100.0%

Now we can draw some additional conclusions about the monthly sales and profits:

The Rooms Department generated 50% of sales but 70.7% of total profit dollars.

The Restaurant Department generated 15% of sales but only 3.0% of total profit dollars.

The Beverage Department generated 10% of sales but only 6.1% of total profit dollars.

The Banquet Department generated 25% of sales and 20.2% of total profit dollars.

This information tells us that the Rooms Department is the main contributor of both sales and profits. This department should be our main priority. The Banquet Department is the next highest profit contributor in dollars and percentages. It is still important to focus on Restaurant and Beverage operations, but they do not account for a significant portion of profits—9.1% combined, even though they have a combined 25% of sales.

These mix percentages have given us examples of sales and profit dollar mix percentages. We can also calculate a mix percentage for units sold, market segment, meal periods, or any other unit that we measure and record. Following are examples of the rooms sold market segment mix and the restaurant meal period mix. These are in units, rooms sold, or customer counts.

Rooms Sold Market Segments	Rooms Sold	Mix Percentage	Restaurant Meal Periods Meal Period	Customers	Mix Percentage
Transient	1,500	60.0%	Breakfast	325	41.7%
Group	700	28.0%	Lunch	190	24.3%
Contract	300	12.0%	Dinner	265	34.0%
Total	2,500	100.0%	Total	780	100.0%

Percentage Change

This percentage is important because it measures progress or lack of progress. Have our restaurant sales increased or decreased compared to last month? Which meal period showed the most improvement, breakfast, lunch, or dinner?

Are the sales up because we had an increase in customers served or because our average check increased? The percentage change gives us this information.

Percentage change is calculated by dividing the amount of the change in dollars (increase or decrease) by the base or original amount. In our example, the change or difference would be calculated by subtracting our actual or current month results from the base or previous month. This change amount would then be divided by the base or, in this example, the previous month's results—for example, this month's sales of $4,800 compared to last month's sales of $4,500. Our percentage change is calculated by subtracting this month's sales of $4,800 from the previous month's sales of $4,500 resulting in a difference of $300. This is where it is important to relate the numbers to actual operations. This calculation results in a $300 difference. We then know that this is a positive difference because our current month's sales of $4,800 is larger than the previous month's sales of $4,500.

***Figure 2.6**: The Grand Hyatt Atlanta.*

This 439-room Hyatt hotel is located in the heart of Buckhead, Atlanta's most prestigious and fashionable area. It has over 18,000 square feet of meeting space including a 9,700-square-foot ballroom, 5,500 square feet of pre-function space, and 10 meeting rooms. Food and beverage facilities include a restaurant, 24-hour room service, pool snack bar, and a lounge. From an accounting perspective, consider the banquet and catering operations of this hotel. It is located in a very upscale area of Atlanta that provides many opportunities for profitable social banquets in addition to regular group business. It is also able to command high room rates. Do you think that the rooms sales mix will be higher or lower than a typical business hotel? Do you think the banquets and catering sales mix will be higher or lower than a typical business hotel? Do you think the banquet department will be able to generate a higher profit percent than the banquet department in a typical business hotel?

2.3.6 Trends in Financial Analysis

Trends are important because they show the direction or movement of business operations, industry, and national and international economies. Understanding the different types of trends and how they affect the operations of a business is an important part of financial analysis. We will discuss four types of trends that affect a business.

Short- and Long-Term Trends

It is important to look at both short-term and long-term trends. Short-term trends (less than 90 days) often involve seasonality or the expected cycles of a business or industry. A business that is slowing down because of seasonality or an industry cycle should be evaluated differently from a business that is slowing down because of increased competition, product or service quality, or pricing issues. A long-term tend is a better evaluator of products or services, especially when compared to competitors and industry performance.

When looking at the month-to-month performance of a business, it is important to distinguish between one month of poor financial performance and several months of poor financial performance. It is typical for a business to have a problem or one-time event that results in performance below expectations for a month. One month by itself does not make a trend or signal a major or long-term problem. However, it is important to correct any poor performance to prevent it from becoming an ongoing problem.

If a business has several months of poor performance, this is a trend that could signal continuing major long-term problems. Management might have to make major evaluations and analyses to determine what is causing the ongoing poor performance and how it can be corrected. Correcting the cause of several months or years of poor performance is a much larger task than correcting a problem that has affected only one month.

Revenue, Expense, and Profit Trends

These trends are all shown in the P&L Statement. Each individual trend is compared to the other two to determine if financial performance is improving or declining. For example, if revenue is trending up and expenses are staying flat, the profit trend should also be up. These are good trends and good relationships between revenues, expenses, and profits. However, if revenues are trending up but expenses are trending up at a faster rate, that will result in lower profits. That is not a good trend. Most important, are revenues or expenses trending in the direction to increase or decrease profits? Equally important is which of the three trends are increasing or decreasing faster or slower than the other two. For example, if sales are increasing 5% but expenses are increasing 10%, profits will decrease. The best case for increasing profits is if sales are increasing and expenses are decreasing.

Favorable and unfavorable trends that affect productivity and profits are demonstrated here:

Trends That Increase Profits	Trends That Decrease Profits
Revenues increasing, expenses decreasing	Revenues decreasing, expenses increasing
Revenues increasing, expenses flat	Revenues flat, expenses increasing
Revenues increasing faster than expenses	Expenses increasing faster than revenues

Company and Industry Trends

It is important to compare the trend of a company with the trends of the industry and general economy. Are the company trends the result of the success or failure of your business operations, the result of conditions that are affecting the entire industry, or the result of the general economic environment? Trends can result from any or all of these conditions, and it is important to identify the causes of trends for the business and the industry. Then appropriate action can be implemented.

For example, if your business profits are down 10% from the previous year and the industry average is down 8% to 12%, then you can safely say that your business profits are down as a result of industry conditions and nothing specific to your business. However, if your profits are down 10% from the previous year and the industry average is up 2%, then you can safely say that the reason your business profits are down is because of problems or the inferior performance of your business and not any industry factors. The causes of the 10% decrease in profitability are different from what is occurring in the industry and should be treated in different ways to correct problems and improve efficiencies of the company so that it gets back to desired profit levels.

General Economic Trends—National and International

The world is indeed shrinking, and problems in other countries or other parts of the United States can affect the performance of an individual business operation. Inflation rates, interest rates, unemployment rates, consumer confidence indexes, budget deficits, exchange rates, and social/political environments are all factors that may have major influences on a business. The most dramatic and tragic example of this is the attack that took place on September 11, 2001, which changed the economic, political, military, and social environment for every country in the world. Each industry and business had to develop new policies, procedures, and strategies to survive in such a turbulent and negative environment.

Another element of national economic influences is the understanding of business cycles. Economic growth, bull markets, bear markets, and stable social and political environments do not go on forever. There are business cycles as short as six months and as long as five to eleven years that occur in normal business and economic activities. Financial analysis can assist a business in identifying business cycles and their causes and determining best practices to permit the best possible operations in any economic environment.

Today's major impact player is China. It is such a large and undeveloped market that major companies throughout the world are planning ways to tap into this new and emerging business environment. Yesterday's major impact player was technology. How it will affect business in the next few years is also a major factor for a company or industry to consider in its plans and strategies for the future.

2.4 SUMMARY

Hotel financial statements are vital tools for operators aiming to ensure the profitability and sustainability of their establishments. These statements provide a detailed view of a hotel's financial activities and health, comprising the income statement, balance sheet, and cash flow statement. The income statement, or profit and loss statement, reveals the revenue generated and the profit earned over a specific period, offering insight into the operational success of the hotel. The balance sheet gives a snapshot of the hotel's assets and liabilities, indicating its financial position at a given time. Meanwhile, the cash flow statement tracks the inflow and outflow of cash, highlighting the hotel's liquidity over a particular period.

Financial ratio analysis emerges as a critical tool for dissecting a hotel's financial performance. By evaluating a variety of ratios, such as profitability, turnover, liquidity, and financial leverage ratios, stakeholders can assess the company's financial health, its ability to meet short-term obligations, and its long-term solvency. Profitability ratios, in particular, are crucial for gauging a hotel's capacity to generate income at different levels, which is significant given the billions generated within the hospitality industry and the expectation of high profit margins from established companies.

Understanding and analyzing these financial documents requires a foundational knowledge of their composition, interpretation, and the implications of the figures they present. Identifying changes within these statements and discerning their causes are key components of effective financial analysis. Moreover, the use of percentages and trend analysis offers additional insights, enabling the understanding of financial relationships, changes, and the broader operational, industry, or economic movements they may signify. This comprehensive analysis is instrumental in navigating the complexities of the hospitality industry's financial landscape.

2.5 REFERENCES

- Balteş, N.; Pavel, R.-M. Study on the correlation between working capital and economic value added for the companies relating to the hotel and restaurant industry listed on the bucharest stock exchange. Ovidius Univ. Ann. Econ. Sci. Ser. 2020, 20, 838–844.
- Kratz, N.; Kroflin, P. The relevance of net working capital for value-based management and its consideration within an economic value-added (EVA) framework. J. Econ. Manag. 2016, 23, 21–32.
- Caiado, A.C.P. Contabilidade Analítica e de Gestão, 5th ed.; Áreas Editora: Lisbon, Portugal, 2009.
- Mohan, A. Life Cycle Costing: Meaning, Characteristics and Everything Else. Accounting Notes. 2019. Available online: https://www.accountingnotes.net/cost-accounting/life-cycle-costing/life-cycle-costing-meaning-characteristics-and-everything-else/5783 (accessed on 19 October 2021).
- Aladwan, M.; Alsinglawi, O.; Alhawatmeh, O. The applicability of target costing in jordanian hotels industry. Acad. Account. Financ. Stud. J. 2018, 22, 1–13.
- Freire, L.P.M.M. Rentabilidade Expectável de um Boutique Hotel em Lisboa; Estoril Higher Institute of Hotel Management and Tourism: Estoril, Portugal, 2017.
- Urquidi-Martin, A.; Ripoll Feliu, V. The choice of management accounting techniques in the hotel sector: The role of contextual factors. J. Manag. Res. 2013, 5, 65–82.
- Slattery, P. Reported RevPAR: Unreliable measures, flawed interpretations and the remedy. Int. J. Hosp. Manag. 2002, 21, 145–149.
- Casqueira, N.; Gomes, C.; Lima Santos, L.; Malheiros, C.; Ferreira, R.R. Performance evaluation of small independent hotels through management accounting indicators and ratios. In Proceedings of the EATSA Conference, Lisbon, Portugal, 26–30 June 2016.
- Gomes, C.; Lima Santos, L.; Malheiros, C.; Cardoso, P. Setting up operating indicators and ratios for independent hotels. In Proceedings of the IX International Tourism Congress (ITC'17), Peniche, Portugal, 29–30 November 2017; pp. 241–255.
- Lima Santos, L.; Malheiros, C.; Gomes, C.; Guerra, T. TRevPAR as hotels performance evaluation indicator and influencing factors in Portugal. EATSJ Euro-Asia Tour. Stud. J. 2020, 1, 93–105.
- Mašić, S.I. The performance of Serbian hotel industry. Singidunum J. Appl. Sci. 2013, 10, 24–31.
- Lima Santos, L.; Cardoso, L.; Araújo-Vila, N.; Fraiz-Brea, J.A. Sustainability perceptions in tourism and hospitality: A mixed-method bibliometric approach. Sustainability 2020, 12, 8852.
- American Hotel & Lodging Association. Uniform System of Accounts for the Lodging Industry, 11th ed.; American Hotel & Lodging Association: Lansing, MI, USA, 2014.

- Gómez, A.C. The uniform system of accounts for the lodging industry and XBRL: Development and exchange of homogeneous information. In Research Studies on Tourism and Environment; Jimenez, M., Ferrari, G., Vargas, M., Eds.; Nova Science Publishers: New York, NY, USA, 2013; pp. 269–280.
- Schmidgall, R.S.; Defranco, A. Uniform system of accounts for the lodging industry, 11th revised edition: The new guidelines for the lodging insdustry. J. Hosp. Financ. Manag. 2015, 23, 6–11.
- Yalcin, S. Adoption and benefits of management accounting practices: An inter-country comparison. Account. Eur. 2012, 9, 95–110.
- Zupic, I.; Čater, T. Bibliometric methods in management and organization. Organ. Res. Methods 2014, 18, 429–472.
- Paul, J.; Criado, A.R. The art of writing a literature review: What do we know and what do we need to know? Int. Bus. Rev. 2020, 29, 101717.
- Mudarra-Fernández, A.; Carrillo-Hidalgo, J.; Fernández, I. Factors influencing tourist expenditure by tourism typologies: A systematic review. Anatolia 2018, 30, 18–34.
- Snyder, H. Literature review as a research methodology: An overview and guidelines. J. Bus. Res. 2019, 104, 333–339.
- Wohlin, C. Guidelines for snowballing in systematic literature studies and a replication in software engineering. In EASE '14, Proceedings of the 18th International Conference on Evaluation and Assessment in Software Engineering, London, UK, 13–14 May 2014; Association for Computing Machinery: New York, NY, USA, 2014; pp. 1–10.
- Page, M.J.; McKenzie, J.; Bossuyt, P.M.; Boutron, I.; Hoffmann, T.C.; Mulrow, C.D.; Shamseer, L.; Tetzlaff, J.M.; Akl, E.A.; Brennan, S.E.; et al. The PRISMA 2020 statement: An updated guideline for reporting systematic reviews. BMJ 2021, 372, n71. [PubMed]
- Yang, E.C.L.; Khoo-Lattimore, C.; Arcodia, C. A systematic literature review of risk and gender research in tourism. Tour. Manag. 2017, 58, 89–100.
- Górska-Warsewicz, H.; Kulykovets, O. Hotel brand loyalty—A systematic literature review. Sustainability 2020, 12, 4810.
- Kroon, N.; Do Céu Alves, M.; Martins, I. The impacts of emerging technologies on accountants' role and skills. Connecting to open innovation: A systematic literature review. J. Open Innov. Technol. Mark. Complex. 2021, 7, 163.
- Ouzzani, M.; Hammady, H.; Fedorowicz, Z.; Elmagarmid, A. Rayyan: A web and mobile app for systematic reviews. Syst. Rev. 2016, 5, 210.
- Cardoso, L.; Araújo-Vila, N.; Soliman, M.; Araújo, A.F.; Almeida, G.G.F. How to employ Zipf's laws for content analysis in tourism studies. Int. J. Hosp. Tour. Syst. 2022, 15, 1–16.
- Molinos, D.; Hoff, M.D.D. ZipfTool: Uma ferramenta bibliométrica para auxílio na pesquisa teórica. Rev. Inf. Teór. Apl. 2016, 23, 293–317.

- Cardoso, L.; Dias, F.; Araújo, A.; Marques, M. A destination imagery processing model: Structural differences between dream and favourite destinations. Ann. Tour. Res. 2019, 74, 81–94.
- Cardoso, L.; Araújo, A.F.; Lima Santos, L.; Schegg, R.; Breda, Z.; Costa, C. Country performance analysis of swiss tourism, leisure and hospitality management research. Sustainability 2021, 13, 2378.
- Pavlatos, O.; Paggios, I. Management accounting practices in the Greek hospitality industry. Manag. Audit. J. 2009, 24, 81–98.
- Jones, T. Improving hotel budgetary practice—A positive theory model. Int. J. Hosp. Manag. 2008, 27, 529–540.
- Mia, L.; Patiar, A. The interactive effect of superior-subordinate relationship and budget participation on managerial performance in the hotel industry: An exploratory study. J. Hosp. Tour. Res. 2002, 26, 235–257.
- Sharma, D.S. The differential effect of environmental dimensionality, size, and structure on budget system characteristics in hotels. Manag. Account. Res. 2002, 13, 101–130.
- Pavlatos, O.; Paggios, I. A survey of factors influencing the cost system design in hotels. Int. J. Hosp. Manag. 2009, 28, 263–271.
- Mia, L.; Patiar, A. The use of management accounting systems in hotels: An exploratory study. Int. J. Hosp. Manag. 2001, 20, 111–128.
- Sharma, A.; Upneja, A. Factors influencing financial performance of small hotels in Tanzania. Int. J. Contemp. Hosp. Manag. 2005, 17, 504–515.
- Patiar, A.; Mia, L. The interactive effect of market competition and use of MAS information on performance: Evidence from the upscale hotels. J. Hosp. Tour. Res. 2008, 32, 209–234.
- Devesa, M.J.S.; Esteban, L.P.; Martínez, A.G. The financial structure of the Spanish hotel industry: Evidence from cluster analysis. Tour. Econ. 2009, 15, 121–138.
- Chen, J.; Koh, Y.; Lee, S. Does the market care about RevPAR? A case study of five large U.S. lodging chains. J. Hosp. Tour. Res. 2011, 35, 258–273.
- Amado, C.A.F.; Santos, S.P.; Serra, J.M.M. Does partial privatisation improve performance? Evidence from a chain of hotels in Portugal. J. Bus. Res. 2017, 73, 9–19.
- Lado-Sestayo, R.; Vivel-Búa, M.; Otero-González, L. Determinants of TRevPAR: Hotel, management and tourist destination. Int. J. Contemp. Hosp. Manag. 2017, 29, 3138–3156.
- Kim, S.Y. Predicting hospitality financial distress with ensemble models: The case of US hotels, restaurants, and amusement and recreation. Serv. Bus. 2018, 12, 483–503.

- Campa-Planas, F.; Banchieri, L.-C.; Kalemba, N. A study of the uniformity of the USALI methodology in Spain and Catalonia. Tourism 2017, 65, 204–217.
- Pavlatos, O. The impact of strategic management accounting and cost structure on ABC systems in hotels. J. Hosp. Financ. Manag. 2011, 19, 37–55.
- Rushmore, R.; O'Neill, J.W. Updated benchmarks for projecting fixed and variable components of hotel financial performance. Cornell Hosp. Q. 2015, 56, 17–28.
- Raab, C.; Mayer, K.J. Exploring the use of activity-based costing in the restaurant industry. Int. J. Hosp. Tour. Adm. 2004, 4, 79–96.
- Raab, C.; Mayer, K.; Ramdeen, C.; Ng, S. The application of activity-based costing in a Hong Kong buffet restaurant. Int. J. Hosp. Tour. Adm. 2005, 6, 11–26.
- Raab, C.; Shoemaker, S.; Mayer, K. Activity-based costing: A more accurate way to estimate the costs for a restaurant menu. Int. J. Hosp. Tour. Adm. 2007, 8, 1–15.
- Annaraud, K.; Raab, C.; Schrock, J.R. The application of activity-based costing in a quick service restaurant. J. Foodserv. Bus. Res. 2008, 11, 23–44.
- Pavlatos, O.; Paggios, I. Activity-based costing in the hospitality industry: Evidence from Greece. J. Hosp. Tour. Res. 2009, 33, 511–527.
- Dalci, I.; Tanis, V.; Kosan, L. Customer profitability analysis with time-driven activity-based costing: A case study in a hotel. Int. J. Contemp. Hosp. Manag. 2010, 22, 609–637.
- Bangchokdee, S.; Mia, L. The role of senior managers' use of performance measures in the relationship between decentralization and organizational performance Evidence from hotels in Thailand. J. Account. Organ. Chang. 2016, 12, 129–151.
- Gomez-Conde, J.; Lunkes, R.J.; Rosa, F.S. Environmental innovation practices and operational performance: The joint effects of management accounting and control systems and environmental training. Account. Audit. Account. J. 2019, 32, 1325–1357.
- McManus, L. Customer accounting and marketing performance measures in the hotel industry: Evidence from Australia. Int. J. Hosp. Manag. 2013, 33, 140–152.
- Karanović, G.; Štambuk, A.; Jagodić, D. Profitability performance under capital structure and other company characteristics. Zb. Veleuč. u Rijeci 2020, 8, 227–242.
- Pavlatos, O.; Paggios, I. Cost accounting in Greek hotel enterprises: An empirical approach. Tourismos 2007, 2, 39–59.
- Evans, N. Assessing the balanced scorecard as a management tool for hotels. Int. J. Contemp. Hosp. Manag. 2005, 17, 376–390.

- Phillips, P.; Louvieris, P. Performance measurement systems in tourism, hospitality, and leisure small medium-sized enterprises: A balanced scorecard perspective. J. Travel Res. 2005, 44, 201–211.
- Faria, A.R.; Trigueiros, D.; Ferreira, L. Práticas de custeio e controlo de gestão no sector hoteleiro do Algarve. Tour. Manag. Stud. 2012, 8, 100–107.
- Ni, S.; Chan, W.; Wong, K. Enhancing the Applicability of Hotel Uniform Accounting in Hong Kong. Asia Pac. J. Tour. Res. 2012, 17, 177–192.
- Campa-Planas, F.; Banchieri, L.C. Study about homogeneity implementing USALI in the hospitality business. Cuad. Tur. 2016, 37, 17–35.
- Patiar, A. Costs allocation practices: Evidence of hotels in Australia. J. Hosp. Tour. Manag. 2016, 26, 1–8.
- Capiez, A.; Kaya, A. Yield management and performance in the hotel industry. J. Travel Tour. Mark. 2004, 16, 21–31.
- Tariq, M.; Yasir, M.; Majid, A. Promoting employees' environmental performance in hospitality industry through environmental attitude and ecological behavior: Moderating role of managers' environmental commitment. Corp. Soc. Responsib. Environ. Manag. 2020, 27, 3006–3017.
- Nyide, C.J. Better resource management: A qualitative investigation of Environmental Management Accounting practices used by the South African hotel sector. Afr. J. Hosp. Tour. Leis. 2019, 8, 1–10.
- Molina-Azorín, J.F.; Tarí, J.J.; Pereira-Moliner, J.; López-Gamero, M.D.; Pertusa-Ortega, E.M. The effects of quality and environmental management on competitive advantage: A mixed methods study in the hotel industry. Tour. Manag. 2015, 50, 41–54.

CHAPTER 3

Understanding Pricing Strategies

INTRODUCTION

Pricing is arguably the most potent tool at a company's disposal when it comes to enhancing profitability. When deployed strategically, pricing not only becomes a direct contributor to increased profits but also aligns closely with the broader objectives and strategies of the business. Strategic pricing, therefore, is not a static concept; it is a dynamic and proactive approach aimed at creating conditions that naturally lead to more favorable and profitable pricing outcomes. This concept might seem straightforward, but it encompasses a variety of interpretations and practices that, while distinct, share a common goal of optimizing pricing to the benefit of the business.

At its core, strategic pricing can be viewed through several lenses. Some experts see it as a process of value creation, where the price of a product or service is determined by its perceived value to the customer rather than its cost of production. This perspective underscores the psychological aspects of consumer behavior, acknowledging that purchase decisions are often driven more by perceived value than by rational cost-benefit analyses. Others interpret strategic pricing as maintaining a competitive awareness, ensuring that pricing strategies are responsive to market conditions, competitors' actions, and customers' evolving needs. Another angle is the technical aspect of establishing price levels and bands, which involves setting and adjusting prices within a strategic framework to meet business objectives.

What binds these various definitions together is the recognition that strategic pricing is an integral part of a company's overall strategy. It incorporates best practices in pricing, leveraging analytics and structured pricing processes to align with and support the business strategy. By focusing on strategic pricing, companies can ensure that their pricing strategies are not just reactions to market forces but are proactive measures that create and capture customer value. This approach enables businesses to transform customer value into shareholder value, evidencing the profound impact that thoughtful and strategic pricing can have on a company's financial performance.

In practice, strategic pricing involves a careful analysis of market trends, competitor prices, customer demand, and perceived value. It requires a deep understanding of the customer base, including their preferences, sensitivities, and behaviors. This knowledge allows businesses to tailor their pricing strategies in ways that resonate with customers while also ensuring profitability and competitiveness. Ultimately, strategic pricing is about making informed, deliberate decisions regarding how products or services are priced, with the aim of maximizing both customer satisfaction and business profitability. It represents a sophisticated blending of market insight, competitive intelligence, and financial acumen, all aimed at achieving the best possible pricing outcomes for the company.

3.1 BASE PRICING STRATEGIES

Pricing strategy refers to method companies use to price their products or services. Almost all companies, large or small, base the price of their products and services on production, labor and advertising expenses and then add on a certain percentage so they can make a profit. There are several different pricing strategies, such as penetration pricing, price skimming, discount pricing, product life cycle pricing and even competitive pricing.

What Is A Price?

The ability to price products and services effectively is one of an revenue management (RM) most important skills. You learned that an RM is the individual or team responsible for ensuring that a company's prices match its informed customers' willingness to pay. When this is done, customers perceive value and fairness in the prices they pay. As a result, the business's revenue and profitability are maximized.

First, you should know that in the hospitality industry, there are some very specialized terms that are used when referring to prices. The various terms commonly used to indicate selling price are based primarily on what is being sold. Common examples illustrating this variance in pricing terminology are shown in Table 1.

The generic term *price* when referring to the amount a buyer pays for a hospitality industry seller's product or service because this term is universally understood even by those who work outside a specific hospitality industry segment. When pricing within a specific industry segment is addressed, however, the term most commonly used in that segment will be utilized. Thus, *for example*, the term *room rate* will be used when referring to guest room pricing in the lodging industry and *menu price* will be used when referring to pricing in the foodservice industry.

Unfortunately, RMs who wishes to better understand what the term *price* means based on a dictionary definition will face a dilemma. This is so because the meaning of the word *price* varies based on one's perspective. An economist views price as "the cost at which something is obtained." The accountant prefers to define price as "the amount of money something would bring if or when it is sold.

Table 1: *Common pricing terms used in hospitality and hospitality-related industries*

Industry Segment	Product Sold	Price Referred To As
Lodging	Guest rooms	Rate or room rate
Lodging	Meeting rooms	Room rental
Lodging	Telephone services	Toll charge
Foodservice	Food and beverages	Menu price
Foodservice	Special guest services	Service charge
Special events/theaters	Admission	Ticket price
Golf resorts/courses	Rounds of golf	Greens fee
Amusement parks	Park admission	Pass price or admission fee
Ski resort	Ski area access	Lift ticket price
Parking areas/lots	Parking space	Hourly rate or overnight charge
Taxi	Transportation	Fare
Airlines	Transportation	Airfare
Car rental	Use of vehicle	Daily or weekly rental rate
Casino	Games of chance	Minimum bet

Hospitality professionals with a marketing background will no doubt have encountered a definition of price similar to one of the following:

- *Price*: The value placed by a firm on its products and services.
- *Price*: The amount of money charged for a good or a service.

Each definition has merit. But for RMs, each also has shortcomings. When faced with seeming contradictions about business, or any other ideas, it is always good to remember the quote from Buddha: "Believe nothing, no matter where you read it, or who said it, no matter if you have said it, unless it agrees with the own reason and own common sense."

RMs should understand the meaning of price at a much deeper level. In fact, because effective pricing is the foundation of successful revenue management, it can be reasonably said that RMs should understand price and pricing theory better than any other individuals in the hospitality organization better than the controller; better than the DOSM; better than the general manager; better than the owner.

The hotel chef should understand the art and science required to make a crème Brule better than the hotel's front office manager. In a similar manner, a hotel's chief engineer should be able to diagnose the cause of an electrical malfunction in the boiler system better than the food and beverage director.

Just as understanding the purpose of business first required an appreciation of the buyer and seller in a business transaction, mastery of the term price requires specialized knowledge and understanding of a seller's perspective and a buyer's perspective. Effective RMs must possess that knowledge and understanding.

To begin, it is important to understand that, for an RM, the term price is both a noun and a verb.

A very careful examination of price as defined in this text will reveal two important details are:

- Both the seller and buyer are part of the definition.
- The concept of value "given up" is present whether price is used as a noun or a verb.

Notably missing from this definition of price is any mention of cost recovery, profit, return on investment (ROI), or supply and demand. This is by design. Too many RMs believe that a price, whether noun or verb, is synonymous with a numerical calculation. It is not.

To illustrate the importance of proper price determination in a hospitality setting, consider the hotel RM who is asked to establish a room rate to be quoted for 100 group hotel rooms to be sold on a specific Friday night. If that RM believes that arriving at a suitable price is a matter of applying the appropriate mathematical formula or calculation, they likely have missed the basic fact that an effective and strategic price is a *concept,* not merely a number. Consider the following questions that would be fair to ask such an RM after he or she had determined the rate (price) to be charged to this group:

- How will the price we offer to this group buyer today affect his or her decision to buy from us in the future?
- If this price is accepted by the group, what impacts will that have on the number of room reservation requests for that same night that we will likely be required to refuse to individual buyers because all of our rooms have been sold?
- Does the price take into account the specific type of room desired by the group?
- Does the price consider the probability that this group will:
    - Cancel at the last minute?
    - No-show?
    - Arrive early?
    - Stay more than one night?
- How has this price been influenced by the prices our competitors are likely to quote to the same group?
- What are the likely secondary sources of revenue (i.e., food and beverage sales, meeting room rentals, and the like) that this group could provide if they accept our price?
- What, if any, is the hotel's historical relationship with:
    - This group?

  - o Other groups of this same type?
- Has the quoted price been influenced by the payment form to be utilized by the guest? By the estimated timeliness of the group's payment?
- How has the recommended price been influenced by the source or channel from which this business originated?

Note that most of the questions cannot be adequately addressed by mathematics alone. Despite that, the RM in this example must be able to answer all of these type questions, and more, if they are to establish an appropriate price. To do so, they must completely understand the concept of price.

Seventeenth-century writer Jonathan Swift is best known for penning *Gulliver's Travels*. RMs seeking to fully understand pricing should consider his perceptive statement: "The art of vision is to see what others do not." What too many pricing managers do not see is that price can be truly understood only by exploring the two very different, but complementary, price-related perspectives of the seller and the buyer.

Interestingly, some pricing managers believe they have already mastered pricing from their own (the seller's) perspective, despite the fact that many have not.

Thus, while the buyer's perspective will be presented second in the following examination, that is not a reflection on its relative significance. Rather, it recognizes that it is imperative for RMs to understand them before they seek to understand their customers.

3.1.1 The Seller's Perspective of Price

All sellers must set their prices. To begin the examination of price from the perspective of a sophisticated seller in the hospitality industry, however, consider the following question:

Why do restaurants charge their customers so much for wine at dinner when by lowering the price they could sell more of it?

Put another way, why do not see aggressive price competition among restaurants that sell bottled wine? The same wines are commonly available to consumers in retail stores at one fourth to one third of the price usually found on a restaurant's menu. Industry observers are likely to offer one of six answers:

- There is no competition. The restaurant has a captive audience that cannot bring its own wines in with them.
- It costs the restaurant a lot in licensing, inventory, storage space, equipment, and staff training to make the wines available.
- Wine sales are a significant profit center for the restaurant.
- Only high-quality wines have been selected by management, thus the chances of a guest making a mistake when purchasing a wine is greatly reduced and customers will pay a significant amount to avoid choosing a poor wine.
- Drinking wine with dinner adds to the overall dining experience.
- Many guests will pay the prices charged.

All of these answers appear to make sense, but let's examine each more closely. The first and most common response—that customers are a captive audience with no available alternatives would seem to imply that restaurants should also install pay toilets. Surely their guests are a captive audience in that regard, as well. They do not install them, of course, because they, like you, probably recognize that any extra income derived from pay toilets would be insignificant compared to the number of guests they would lose if they did install them.

Second, it does cost a restaurant a significant amount to offer wine. Licensing, storage, and wine inventory costs are real. But that does not fully explain the higher prices charged, because the operator must also buy, store, and even cook the food. Yet food items are typically sold at a price much closer to the price the restaurateur paid for them.

Third, wine sales may well be a profit center, but so are food sales. Surely restaurants make a profit on meals sold to non-wine drinkers. So, it would seem to make just as much sense to charge a bit more for the food, reduce the markup on wine, and, most likely, sell more of it.

Fourth, if ensuring that a quality product is selected and served makes customers happy, why not charge less for it and make these customers even happier?

If the fifth rationale is correct, and wine does in fact add significantly to the dining experience, why not include wine in the price of all the dinners served, thus maximizing the number of guests with an enhanced dining experience? And if the sixth option is true, why not charge even more?

The fact is that restaurateurs who successfully sell wine to maximize their revenue and profits know something important and deceptively elegant in its simplicity. What they know is that some of their diners like wine more than others do. This is a fact understood by sophisticated price setters in all industries. The fact is that lower wine prices would undoubtedly encourage more diners to buy wine, even if these diners had to pay a bit more for the food they order. But to encourage these diners, the restaurateur would have to increase food prices, and doing so might discourage those diners who prefer to come only to eat food. If there were enough non-wine drinkers, that pricing strategy might backfire.

Sophisticated restaurateurs understand how revenue is generated. The real purpose of high wine prices is *not* to increase the average amount of money spent by each customer.

That goal would be better achieved simply by selling wine for a bit less and raising menu prices to cover the reduction. The reason wine can be sold in restaurants for prices far beyond what the wines could be purchased for and drunk at home is that wine drinkers are not just buying wine. Read that again. They are not just buying wine. What they *are* buying is a valuable enhancement to an elegant dining experience. Some guests desire that enhancement and are willing to pay for it. They are certainly not forced to pay for it. In fact, those wine drinkers who truly seek and then value the experience of having wine with their dinners are pleased to pay more to get that experience. Satisfying these customers' desire to experience elegance is the job of the restaurateur. If the elegant experience is provided, the guests will return. But they will not be returning merely to purchase wine. That product could, in most cases, be purchased and consumed more inexpensively at home. These guests are looking for, and will willingly pay for, the experience of fine dining.

The end goal of a sophisticated restaurateur's wine-pricing strategy is to recognize that different amounts should be charged to different customers because differing customers have different dining goals. Subsequently, there is an increase in the amount of money spent by some, but not all, of the restaurant's customers.

There is no way a restaurateur can easily determine, upon their arrival, which customers are willing to spend more. Many diners for example, large families, students, and those with lower incomes—may not be likely candidates for spending large amounts on wine.

The restaurant needs these customers, and increasing the menu prices charged to them might drive these guests away. Thus, in an effective pricing system, all arriving diners get two choices: enjoy the meal alone, or enjoy the meal with wine. Those who manage revenue will recognize this as a two-tiered price.

Two-tiered pricing is effective and very common; you have no doubt experienced it. Country clubs routinely charge a one-time initiation fee, as well as regular monthly dues. In many amusement parks where country fairs are held there is a fee for entrance to the fair and additional fees for the purchase of rides, games, food, beverages, or souvenirs. Airlines charge one price for a traveler's ticket and add baggage charges for those travelers who check their luggage.

Broadway theater owners charge one price for admission and another for drinks served during intermission. Condominium hotels charge one price for the individual unit its owner buys, as well as an additional monthly maintenance fee. Transient hotels charge a fixed price for a guest room, but add charges for any items purchased from the in-room mini bar and for movies watched on the pay-per-view system.

Business is not financial science; it's about trading: buying and selling. It's about creating a product or service so good that people will pay for it. In a two-tiered pricing system, customers are free to choose whether an additional product or service is so good they will pay for it.

Two-tiered pricing serves both the business and its customers. Consider the situation that would exist if two-tiered pricing were prohibited by law. To maintain their current revenue and profit levels, businesses would have to increase the prices paid by all of their customers—those who value the additional products and services offered, as well as those who do not. The result would not really affect the wealthiest customers. In fact, those who would be hurt the most are those least able to pay higher prices. Lower-income families, senior citizens, and children are some of the groups that would be hurt by a system that prevents businesses from employing a pricing strategy that provides multiple purchasing options to all of their customers.

If you think that the answer to the question of why restaurateurs charge their customers so much for the wines they sell them at dinner has more to do with customers and their buying behavior than the cost of the wines offered, you are correct. And you will likely have an interest in learning more about the strategic pricing and customer-centric revenue management concepts found in the rest. Before you can fully understand strategic pricing from the sellers' perspective, however, it is imperative that you first consider price from a buyer's perspective.

3.1.2 The Buyer's Perspective of Price

If sophisticated sellers can use price to, among other things, determine the willingness of a buyer to buy, how do buyers perceive price? To gain an understanding of the buyer's perspective of price, it is important to first understand the concept of consumer rationality.

Consumer rationality assumes that buyers consistently exhibit reasonable and purposeful behavior. That is, in the overwhelming majority of cases, buyers make purchase decisions based on the sincere belief that it benefits them to do so. For RMs, the implications of accepting as true the concept of consumer rationality are huge. By adopting the rationality assumption, RMs is pledging to treat each customer's behavior as worthy of respectful consideration.

By doing so, RMs will discover possibilities and develop insights that would never arise if they dismissed as "irrational" any customer behavior they did not immediately understand. By rejecting the easy way out, effective RMs can move directly to a careful and creative consideration of why their customers behave the way they do. That is a trait consistently exhibited by effective RMs.

The acceptance of the concept of consumer rationality involves no less than a willingness to look beyond the obvious and seek to understand, in an open-minded manner, exactly how buyers believe they will benefit from a business transaction. In some cases, this is not so easy.

The RMs must resist the temptation to declare that buyers are most often quite irrational. Despite its potential limitations, those who refuse to accept the validity of consumer rationality must be prepared to offer an alternative and equally useful explanation of buyer behavior.

The assumption of rationality is a seller's trait as well. When we earlier addressed the question of why restaurateurs charge so much for wine, the immediate response might be that they are behaving irrationally, because they could sell more wine if it were offered at a lower price. The actual rationale behind this approach to wine pricing, however, is that it serves, in a very rational manner, as a means of separating different types of customers. Effective RMs understands that all rationale buyers do seek to gain an increase in value when they are assessing a potential purchase.

From a buyer's perspective, price is an important part of the seller's value proposition. When a seller states, "I will give you this, if you will give me that," a buyer will make an assessment that will lead to one of three purchase decisions. These three possible reactions to a seller's value proposition are shown in Table 2.

In most cases, it is the seller, not the buyer, who initiates the value proposition. It is also important to recognize that rational buyers do not automatically equate a seller's price with the amount of value they will receive in an exchange. In fact, conventional wisdom advises them not to do so. From a common sense and even from a legal perspective, buyers assessing a value proposition are cautioned not to trust sellers. As a result, "Caveat Emptor," the Latin phrase for "Let the buyer beware," is known and understood by most consumers.

Because most buyers are naturally leery of a seller's value proposition, an important part of an RM's job is ensuring that buyers understand the answers to their very rationale: "What do I get?" and "Why is it of value?" questions just as much as they understand the price they will be charged.

Table 2: *Buyer assessment of a seller's value proposition*

Buyer Assessment	Purchase Decision
1. Perceived Benefit – Price = A value less than "0"	Do Not Buy
2. Perceived Benefit – Price = A value equal to "0"	Do not buy in most cases*
3. Perceived Benefit – Price = A value greater than "0"	Buy

Only then can buyers, who are today very sophisticated and Web-savvy consumers, be convinced they will consistently receive *more* than the worth of the money they must part with when making the purchase.

We conclude this important portion of the by reemphasizing that it is only when both parties to a transaction feel they have received value in excess of what they have given up that a mutually beneficial exchange can occur. Value must always exceed price paid if rational buyers are to become repeat buyers. It is important to recognize that from a buyer's perspective, the prices do not automatically represent the buyer's personal opinion of the product's true value. The prices do, however, provide a quick and convenient way for the customers to rationally evaluate and assess the value proposition.

3.1.3 Different Types of Pricing Strategy

Pricing is one of the four elements of the marketing mix, along with product, place and promotion. Pricing strategy is important for companies who wish to achieve success by finding the price point where they can maximize sales and profits. Companies may use a variety of pricing strategies, depending on their own unique marketing goals and objectives.

Companies will lean on discount pricing as part of product promotions, which are generally used for increasing traffic and attracting new customers. This discounted pricing draws attention to the product and can be used as a hook to bring in customers who will potentially purchase other items. Seasonal changes are good examples of times when companies utilize this strategy, when they discount the prices of the items that are going out of season.

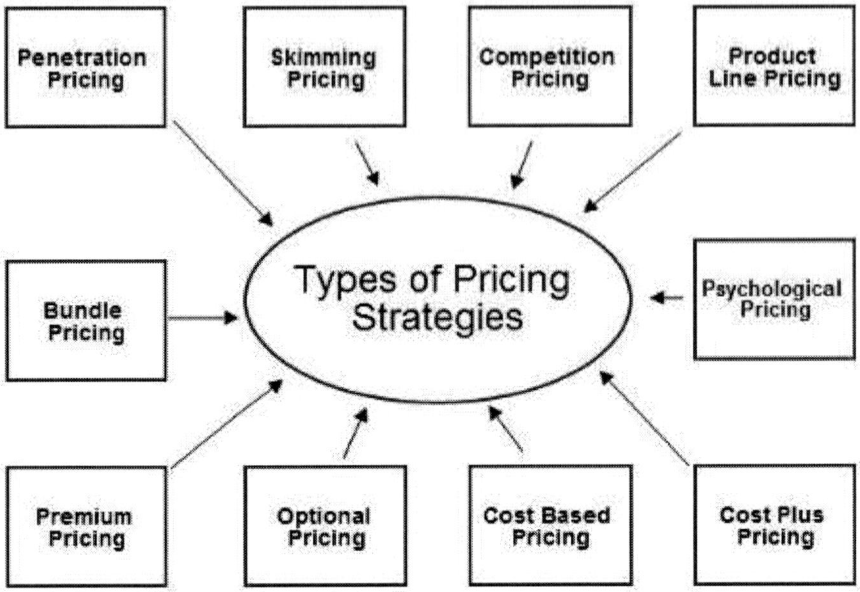

Figure 3.1: *Types of pricing strategy.*

Skim pricing is a technique that companies use to find the optimum price point for a product, usually a unique item with unknown consumer demand. The price skimming strategy consists of the company setting the initial product price high to quickly cover embedded costs, such as production or advertising, and then begins to slowly reduce the price to bring the product to a wider market. The goal with this strategy is to maximize the potential profits layer by layer until the optimum price is reached. Electronic devices are great examples of this strategy, where we see higher prices at market introduction that slowly decrease over time once the initial product buzz weakens.

Every organization needs to adjust the marketing mix for a product as it moves from one stage of the life cycle to the other stage. In course of the marketing mix adjustment, an organization needs to adopt different pricing strategies in the four stages of the product's life cycle.

Premium Pricing

Premium pricing strategy establishes a price higher than the competitors. It's a strategy that can be effectively used when there is something unique about the product or when the product is first to market and the business has a distinct competitive advantage. Premium pricing can be a good strategy for companies entering the market with a new market and hoping to maximize revenue during the early stages of the product life cycle.

Penetration Pricing

A penetration pricing strategy is designed to capture market share by entering the market with a low price relative to the competition to attract buyers.

The idea is that the business will be able to raise awareness and get people to try the product. Even though penetration pricing may initially create a loss for the company, the hope is that it will help to generate word-of-mouth and create awareness amid a crowded market category.

Economy Pricing

Economy pricing is a familiar pricing strategy for organizations that include Wal-Mart, whose brand is based on this strategy. Aldi, a food store, is another example of economy pricing strategy. Companies take a very basic, low-cost approach to marketing--nothing fancy, just the bare minimum to keep prices low and attract a specific segment of the market that is very price sensitive.

Price Skimming

Businesses that have a significant competitive advantage can enter the market with a price skimming strategy designed to gain maximum revenue advantage before other competitors begin offering similar products or product alternatives.

Psychological Pricing

Psychological pricing strategy is commonly used by marketers in the prices they establish for their products. For instance, $99 is psychologically "less" in the minds of consumers than $100. It's a minor distinction that can make a big difference.

Bundle Pricing

A group of products may be bundled together and sold at a reduced price. Supermarkets often use this method through their 'buy one get one free' offers.

Optional Pricing

A company may add optional extra items within the price to increase a product's attractiveness. Car sellers may offer car insurance for the first year for example.

Cost Based Pricing

Simply, a company may determine the exact cost of producing and selling an objective, add a markup that may be desirable for profits and price accordingly. This method may be used in a changing industry where even costs of production are unpredictable.

Cost plus Pricing

A percentage is added to the costs as a profit margin to determine final price.

3.1.4 Advantages of the Pricing Strategies

- *Increases Profits*: High/low pricing allows retailers to charge higher prices to customers who are not price-sensitive and will pay the "high" price and to charge lower prices to price-sensitive customers who will wait for the "low" sale price.

- ***Creates Excitement***: A "gets them while they last" atmosphere often occurs during a sale. Sales draw a lot of customers, and a lot of customers create excitement. Some retailers augment low prices and advertising with special in store activities, such as product demonstrations, giveaways, and celebrity appearances.
- ***Sells Merchandise***: Sales allow retailers to get rid of slow-selling merchandise. The EDLP approach has its own advantages, as follows:
- ***Assures Customers of Low Prices***: Many customers are sceptical about initial retail prices. They have become conditioned to buying only on sale-the main characteristic of a high/low pricing strategy. The Every Day Low Pricing (EDLP) strategy lets customers know that they will get the same low prices every time they patronize the EDLP retailer. Customers do not have to read the ads and wait for items they want to go on sale.
- ***Reduces Advertising and Operating Expenses***: The stable prices caused by EDLP limit the need for the weekly-sale advertising used in the high/low strategy. In addition, EDLP retailers do not have to incur the labor costs of changing price tags and signs and putting up sale signs.
- ***Reduces Stock outs and Improves Inventory Management***: The EDLP approach reduces the large variations in demand caused by frequent sales with large markdowns. As a result, retailers can manage their inventories with more certainty. Fewer stock outs mean more satisfied customers, resulting in higher sales. In addition, a more predictable customer demand pattern enables the retailer to improve inventory turnover by reducing the average inventory needed for special promotions and backup stock.

3.2 MARKET PRICING

Pricing strategies are formulated under the parameters of the pricing objectives and policies. Pricing strategies help the marketer to deal with situations arising in the market as a result of competitors actions or due to change in marketing and environmental variables.

Firms often use different pricing strategies when their products are first launched into the market. The two most common introduction approaches are called price skimming and penetration pricing. The idea behind price skimming is to intentionally set a high price relative to the competition, thereby skimming the profits off the top of the market. Price skimming is designed to recover the high R&D and marketing expenses associated with developing a new product. It may also be used to initially segment the market based on price, or to control the initial demand for the product. Virtually all new high-tech products, new computer technology, and new prescription drugs use a price-skimming approach.

For example, the $80 per month price for Pfizer's cholesterol-lowering drug Lipitor is worth it to patients who suffer from high cholesterol. The high prices associated with prescription medications like Lipitor are designed to recoup the expenses associated with developing and marketing new drugs. However, in the case of pharmaceuticals, price skimming only works as long as the drug is protected by patent in Pfizer's case, the patent on Lipitor expires in 2011. However, the patent on Merck's Zocor, a major competitor, expired in 2006, opening the way for generic pricing. Despite its patent protection, Lipitor sales have declined as managed care companies have forced patients to switch to lower-priced Zocor clones. Eventually, the price support for Lipitor will collapse once its patent expires and generic competition enters the market.

The goal of penetration pricing is to maximize sales, gain widespread market acceptance, and capture a large market share quickly by setting a relatively low initial price. This approach works best when customers are price sensitive for the product or product category; when research and development and marketing expenses are relatively low; or when new competitors will quickly enter the market. Because of its flexibility, penetration pricing can be used to launch a new product or to introduce new product lines to an established product portfolio.

The benefits of penetration pricing rapid market acceptance and maximum sales also have the benefit of discouraging competition from entering the market. This is a powerful advantage that makes a penetration approach quite appealing. However, the strategy is not for all firms. To use penetration pricing successfully, the firm must have a cost structure and scale economies that can withstand narrow profit margins.

Some firms adopt a penetration pricing strategy by selling their products at a loss, hoping to make up the lost revenue via the sale of accessories, add-ons, or subscription services. Although price penetration does not necessarily mean low profit per unit sold, it does require a higher volume of sales to achieve the same total profit that would be achieved using a price-skimming approach. For these reasons, price penetration occurs primarily in situations where the firm has a reasonable expectation of achieving the necessary sales volume to make the product financially viable.

3.2.1 Prestige Pricing

Firms using prestige pricing set their prices at the top end of all competing products in a category. This is done to promote an image of exclusivity and superior quality. Ritz-Carlton Hotels, for example, never wants to compete with other hotels on price. Instead, the company competes only on service and the value of the unique, high-quality experience that they deliver to hotel guests. Prestige pricing is a viable approach in situations where it is hard to objectively judge the true value of a product. In these instances, a higher price may indicate a higher-quality product. Inexperienced wine consumers, for example, might assume that a $40 bottle of wine is better than a $15 bottle. Only a true connoisseur would actually know, but the average wine-buying public would see the $40 bottle as more appropriate for a special occasion or celebration. Consulting and research services are often sold in this fashion as well. Former U.S. presidents and corporate CEOs can command up to $100,000 for a one-hour speech to a company's employees. The presumption held by the firm is that a notable speaker's message will have a stronger impact than a local professional speaker who earns $5,000 for the same amount of time.

3.2.2 Value-Based Pricing

Firms that use a value-based pricing approach set reasonably low prices but still offer high-quality products and adequate customer services. Many different types of firms use value-based pricing; however, retailing has widely embraced this approach, where it is known as everyday low pricing or EDLP. The goal of value-based pricing is to set a reasonable price for the level of quality offered. Prices are not the highest in the market, nor are they the lowest. Instead, value-based pricing sets prices so they are consistent with the benefits and costs associated with acquiring the product.

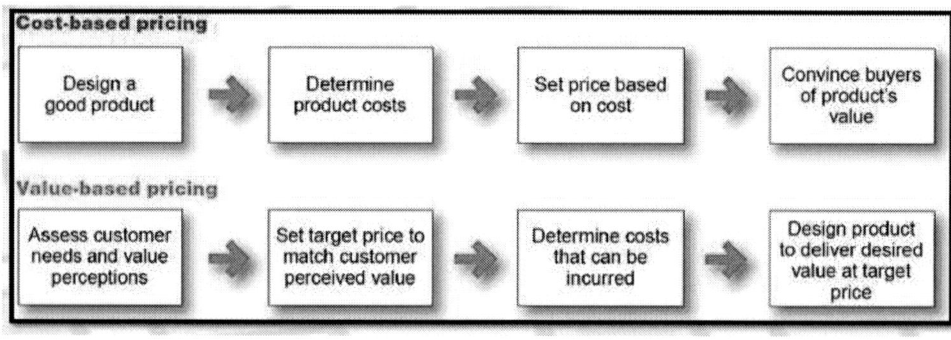

***Figure 3.2**: Value-Based Pricing vs. Cost-Based Pricing*

Market Growth Pricing

Market growth stage of the product life cycle is characterized by a rapid growth in sale. During this stage, marketers need to modify their introductory pricing strategies. Normally, organizations that adopted pricing skimming during introduction stage gradually lower their price in order to expand the product's market size.

Many innovators also face competition in this stage when their entry barriers are low, and hence, are focused to reduce their price. Organizations that started with penetration pricing strategy gradually increase their price level in order to raise profit from the product. Organization that introduced their products under good value price and premium product value price generally may not change their introductory prices during the growth stage.

Market maturity pricing

Products face excessive competition during the maturity stage of the life cycle. In this stage, most products face gradual but slow decline in the sales as there are fewer buyers interested in the product.

During the maturity stage, the product is bought by consumer groups for logical reasons, such as good value reflected in the lower price or premium values reflected in extra benefits attached with the offer. In order to maintain sales levels, some organizations reduce their prices to create good value for consumers, while many others go for non-price competition to crate premium values on the product.

3.2.3 Adjusting Prices in Business Markets

Many of the techniques just discussed are also used in business markets to adjust or fine-tune base prices. However, there are a number of pricing techniques unique to business markets, including these:

- Trade Discounts Manufacturers will reduce prices for certain intermediaries in the supply chain based on the functions that the intermediary performs. In general, discounts are greater for wholesalers than for retailers because the manufacturer wants to compensate wholesalers for the extra functions they perform, such as selling, storage, transportation, and risk taking. Trade discounts vary widely and have become more complicated due to the growth of large retailers who now perform their own wholesaling functions.
- Discounts and Allowances Business buyers can take advantage of sales just like consumers. However, business buyers also receive other price breaks, including discounts for cash, quantity or bulk discounts, seasonal discounts, or trade allowances for participation in advertising or sales support programs.
- Geographic Pricing Selling firms often quote prices in terms of reductions or increases based on transportation costs or the actual physical distance between the seller and the buyer. The most common examples of geographic pricing are uniform delivered pricing (same price for all buyers regardless of transportation expenses) and zone pricing (different prices based on transportation to predefined geographic zones).
- Transfer Pricing Transfer pricing occurs when one unit in an organization sells products to another unit.
- Barter and Countertrade In business exchanges across national boundaries, companies sometimes use products, rather than cash, for payments. Barter involves the direct exchange of goods or services between two firms or nations. Counter-trade refers to agreements based on partial payments in both cash and products, or to agreements between firms or nations to buy goods and services from each other.

Another important pricing technique used in business markets is price discrimination, which occurs when firms charge different customers different prices. When this situation occurs, firms set different prices based on actual cost differences in selling products to one customer relative to the costs involved in selling to other customers. Price discrimination is a viable technique because the costs of selling to one firm are often much higher than selling to others. However, price discrimination also has major legal implications.

3.3 THE IMPORTANCE OF PRICE IN THE 4-P'S OF THE MARKETING MIX

After product, pricing plays a key role in the marketing mix. The reason for this importance is that where the rest of the elements of the marketing mix are cost generators, price is a source of income and profits. Through pricing, the organization manages to support the cost of production, the cost of distribution, and the cost of promotion.

Simplistically, price is the value measured in money term in the part of the transaction between two parties where the buyer has to give something up (the price) to gain something offered by the other party or the seller. Pricing is a complicated element, which needs to reflect supply and demand, the actual value of the object, and the perceived value of it in the mind of the consumer. A price that does not reflect these factors and is either too high or too low will lead to unsuccessful sales. This is why an organization's pricing will change according to circumstances and time.

Figure 3.3: *Importance of price in the 4-P's of the marketing mix*

Thus far, you have learned that price plays a large role in the interactions between buyer and seller. As a result, price is considered to be an important part of an organization's overall marketing effort. The American Marketing Association, the professional association for marketers, defines marketing as "the activity, set of institutions, and processes for creating, communicating, delivering, and exchanging offerings that have value for customers, clients, partners, and society at large.

How important is marketing to the success of a business? Consider management consultant Peter Drucker's perspective on marketing: "Marketing and innovation are the two chief functions of business. You get paid for creating a customer, which is marketing. And you get paid for creating a new dimension of performance, which is innovation.

Everything else is a cost center.

Marketing, as used in this text, will be defined simply as the entire set of activities required to communicate a business's value proposition to a specific market. Although price is one important part of every business's effort to convey the value of what it offers for sale, there are other critical components of that effort. Collectively, these components are known as the "4 P's" of the marketing mix:

1. *Product*: The product or service delivered to the buyer
2. *Promotion*: The means of communication between buyer and seller
3. *Place*: The location or means of delivering the product or service to be sold
4. *Price:* What is given up in exchange for the product or service

Despite some criticism that the 4 P's are overly simplistic and those they may apply better to the exchange of products than to services, the 4 P's do address buyer-related questions of great importance:

- Product: What is the product or service offered?
- Promotion: How will the seller's value proposition be communicated?
- Place: If accepted, where will the value exchange take place?
- Price: What will be the financial terms of the exchange?

In the hospitality industry, product is important. Hoteliers rightly pay a good deal of attention to the color, shapes, sizes, and even textures of the products that make up their guest rooms and public spaces. They know that in the lodging industry, the physical characteristics of the "Product" they sell are vitally important to their guests. The importance of product in the lodging industry was illustrated well when, in 1999, Westin hotels introduced its "Heavenly Bed." Guests loved the significantly improved quality of this product offering. Competitors at all price pointswere forced to copy it, and it forever changed guests' perceptions of what constituted a quality sleep experience.

Key Fact

In the 1990s, the model of 4 Cs was introduced as a more customer-driven replacement of the 4 Ps. There are two theories based on 4 Cs: Lauterborn's 4 Cs (consumer, cost, convenience, and communication), and Shimizu's 4 Cs (commodity, cost, channel, and communication).

3.3.1 The Variables of marketing mix are as follows

Figure 3.4: Elements of marketing mix.

1. Production the Marketing mix

The first thing you need, if you want to start a business, is a product. Therefore Product is also the first variable in the marketing mix. Product decisions are the first decisions you need to take before making any marketing plan. A product can be divided into three parts. The core product, the augmented product and the tertiary product. Before deciding on the product component there are some questions which you need to ask yourself.

- o What product are you selling?
- o What would be the quality of your product?
- o Which features are different from the market?
- o What is the USP of the product?
- o Whether the product will be branded as sub brand or completely new?
- o What are the secondary products which can be sold along with primary (Warranty, services)

Based on these questions, several product decisions have to be made. These product decisions will in turn affect the other variables of the mix. *For example* – You launch a car with is to have the highest quality. Thus the pricing, promotions and placing would have to be altered accordingly. Thus as long as you do not know the product, you cannot decide any other variable of the marketing mix. However, if the product features are not fitting in the mix, you can alter the product such that it finds a place for itself in the marketing mix.

2. Pricing in the Marketing mix

Pricing of a product depends on a lot of different variables and hence it is constantly updated. Major consideration in pricing is the costing of the product, the advertising and marketing expenses, any price fluctuations in the market, distribution costs etc. Many of these factors can change separately. Thus the pricing has to be such that it can bear the brunt of changes for a certain period of time. However, if all these variables change, then the pricing of a product has to be increased and decreased accordingly.

Along with the above factors, there are also other things which have to be taken in consideration when deciding on a pricing strategy. Competition can be the best example. Similarly, pricing also affects the targeting and positioning of a product. Pricing is used for sales promotions in the form of trade discounts. Thus based on these factors there are several pricing strategies, one of which is implemented for the **marketing mix**.

3. Place in the Marketing mix

Place refers to the distribution channel of a product. If a product is a consumer product, it needs to be available as far and wide as possible. On the other hand, if the product is a *Premium consumer product*, it will be available only in select stores. Similarly, if the product is a business product, you need a team which interacts with businesses and makes the product available to them. Thus the place where the product is distributed depends on the product and pricing decisions, as well as any STP decisions taken by a firm.

Distribution has a huge effect on the profitability of a product. Consider a FMCG company which has national distribution for its product. An increase in petrol rates by 10rs will in fact bring about drastic changes in the profitability of the company. Thus supply chain and logistics decisions are considered as very important costing decisions of the firm. The firm needs to have a full proof logistics and supply chain plan for its distribution.

4. Promotionsin the Marketing mix

Promotions in the marketing mix include the complete integrated marketing communications which in turn includes ATL and BTL advertising as well as sales promotions. Promotions are dependent a lot on the product and pricing decision. What is the budget for marketing and advertising? What stage is the product in? If the product is completely new in the market, it needs brand / product awareness promotions, whereas if the product is already existing then it will need brand recall promotions.

Promotions also decide the segmentation targeting and positioning of the product. The right kind of promotions affect all the other three variables the product, price and place. If the promotions are effective, you might have to increase distribution points, you might get to increase the price because of the rising brand equity of the product, and the profitability might support you in launching even more products. However, the budget required for extensive promotions is also high. A promotion is considered as marketing expenses and the same needs to be taken in consideration while deciding the costing of the product.

Figure 3.5: *In diagram, all the four variables of marketing mix are inter related and affect each other.*

By increasing the pricing of the product, demand of the product might lessen, and lesser distribution points might be needed. On the other hand, the product USP can be such that maximum concentration is on creating brand awareness, thereby increasing need of better pricing and more promotions. Finally, the overall marketing mix can result in the customer base asking for some improvement in the product, and the same can be launched as the upgraded product.

The role of Four P's of marketing in Strategy

Marketing mix plays a crucial role while deciding the strategy of an organization. It is the first step even when a marketing plan or a business plan is being made. This is because, you are marketing mix decision will also affect segmentation, targeting and positioning decisions. Based on products, segmentation and targeting will be done. Based on the price, positioning can be decided. And these decisions will likely affect the place and promotion decisions. Thus, the marketing mix strategy goes hand in hand with segmentation targeting and positioning.

3.4 THE ROLE OF SUPPLY AND DEMAND IN PRICING

Economists and others who study how people spend their money have consistently observed several interesting phenomena related to the value buyers place on a seller's goods, as well as the prices they are willing to pay for them. Those who have studied introductory economics are likely familiar with two of these time-tested buyer/ seller realities that have come to be known as the laws of supply and demand.

These two age-old truths or laws were first combined graphically in the late 1800s by Alfred Marshall, a Cambridge University economics professor. His visual depiction of supply (how much of a product is available) and the level of buyer interest in purchasing it looked somewhat like a pair of scissors, with one blade (S) representing the available supply of a product and the other blade (D) representing buyer demand for it. Marshall was most interested in the point at which the two scissor blades would naturally intersect. It was at this natural intersection that Marshall felt the optimum price of a product (P_o) on the price (P) line would match the optimum quantity supplied of it (Q_o) on the quantity (Q) line. To better understand the significance of Marshall's natural price (which has now come to be better known as the equilibrium price), consider that if the price of a product is lower than the equilibrium price (represented by shaded area A), demand for the product, at that price, would exceed its supply, and a shortage would soon exist.

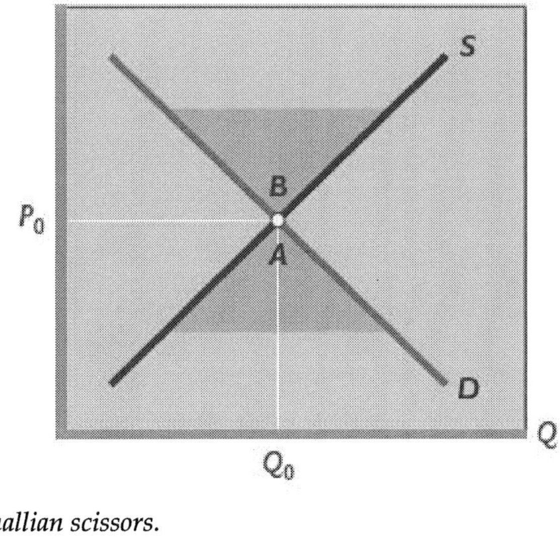

Figure 3.6: *Marshallian scissors.*

Conversely, if the price of a product is higher than the equilibrium price (represented by area B in Figure 3.6), demand for the product, at that price, would be less than the supply of it and a surplus would soon exist.

Unlike Marshall, these later economists were most interested in what would happen to the price of an item (P_1) at a specified demand level (D_1), if demand for that item increased (D_2), or decreased. As seen in Figure 3.7, in a situation where demand increases, the law of supply and demand predicts the new price (P_2) would be higher than the previous price (P_1).

Airfares in the airline industry provide an excellent illustration of how the law of supply and demand following in Figure 3.7 actually works in the real world. If, for example, the consumers demand for airline seats arriving at a specific destination increases, two things will likely happen:

1. The new and higher demand level (D_2) will result in higher ticket prices.
2. At the higher price (P_2) it is likely that the supplier of airline seats (the airlines) will increase the number of seats available for sale, either by adding additional flights or by increasing the size of the plane used on its current number of flights.

In either case, it would be the natural inclination of the seller to produce, and sell, more.

Although supply and demand curves are a very useful way of observing the manner in which changes in demand affect prices, they are much less useful in initially determining prices that should be charged.

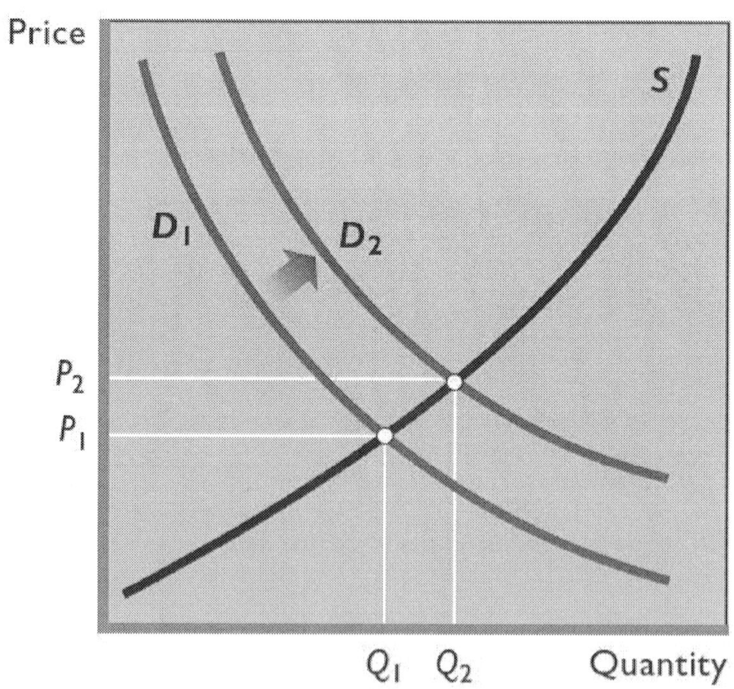

Figure 3.7: Supply and demand curves

may, in fact, serve to raise the selling prices of all rooms in that market because it may actually result in an increase in the number of visitors to an area. For example, few hoteliers would argue that the addition of the several thousand rooms of the Gaylord Opryland Resort and Conference Center located in Nashville, Tennessee, served to reduce the selling prices of rooms in the Nashville area. The resort served as a significant draw to many conventions, and as a result increased the value (and selling prices) of all hotel rooms in the Nashville area.

Finally, when assessing the supply of, and demand for, hospitality products RMs should be careful not to assume that "greater scarcity equals greater value" and thus increased selling prices. That may be true for ancient sculptures and many fine wines, but if it were universally true, the pictures you drew in third grade would now be worth tremendous sums. They were, after all, certainly one-of-a kind and are now scarce.

The more common situation is that the scarcity of a product, in the long run, may actually reflect a lack of interest in it, thus indicating consumers value it less, not more, and its price will be low. If, over the long run, product scarcity actually does yield increased value, the laws of supply and demand would indicate that producers will make more of that product. That may not be possible with diamonds and Picasso paintings, but it certainly is the case with hospitality products. Scarcity of hospitality products does not last long in a free-market economy.

How does the law of supply and demand affect prices?

The law of supply and demand is an economic theory that explains how supply and demand are related to each other and how the relationship affects the price of goods and services. It's a basic economic principle that states that when there is an oversupply of a good or service, prices fall. When there is high demand, prices tend to rise.

There is an inverse relationship between the supply and prices of goods and services when demand is unchanged. If there is an increase in supply for goods and services while demand remains the same, prices tend to fall to a lower equilibrium price and a higher quantity of goods and services. If there is a decrease in supply for goods and services while demand remains the same, prices tend to rise to a higher equilibrium price and a lower quantity of goods and services.

The same inverse relationship holds for the demand of goods and services. However, when demand increases and supply remains the same, the higher demand leads to a higher equilibrium price and vice versa. Suppose a luxury car company sets the price of its new car model at $200,000. While the demand of the luxury car may be high due to the company creating hype for the car, most consumers are not willing to spend $200,000 for a car. As a result, the sales of the new model then quickly falls, are creating an oversupply and lack of demand for the car. In response, the company reduces the price of the car to $150,000 to balance the supply and the demand for the car to reach an equilibrium price.

3.5 THE ROLE OF COSTS IN PRICING

Although it should now be apparent to you that, in the hospitality industry, the "laws of supply and demand" do not dictate specific prices that should be charged, experienced hospitality professionals would correctly point out that, regardless of the supply of a product, the demand for it, or the price consumers are willing to pay for it, unless a seller receives more money when selling a product than was required to produce it, that seller will ultimately go out of business and stop producing. As a result, they would insist that a firm's costs must dictate its prices. Such individuals are certainly correct about cost sustainability, but they misunderstand pricing.

All businesses seek to benefit in the seller/ buyer transactions they initiate. Businesses desire profits. Those businesses that cannot sell their products for more than it costs to produce them will ultimately cease operations regardless of their production efficiency. It is their legitimate concern that income (revenue) must ultimately exceed costs that cause some to overstate the role of **costs** in price determination.

For purposes of this text, a business cost will be defined simply as a business expense. Although it does complicate matters to some degree, it is important to understand that there are actually many types of cost. As a result, cost accountants have identified several useful ways to classify business costs. Among the most important of these are:

- Fixed and variable costs
- Mixed costs
- Step costs
- Direct and indirect (overhead) costs
- Controllable and non-controllable costs
- Other costs including:
- Joint costs
- Incremental costs
- Standard costs
- Sunk costs
- Opportunity costs

These various types of cost are listed simply to demonstrate that the term cost, especially as used by those working in the area of cost accounting, must be well understood before the effect on pricing decisions can be examined. Before examining those costs that most affect pricing, it is important for RMs to understand that not all business costs can be objectively determined in an easy manner. In fact, in some cases, cost can be very subjective. *For example,* the food and beverage director at a Country Club who orders and takes delivery on $1,000 worth of USDA Choice strip steak to be served at a golf outing knows exactly what those steaks cost.

The invoice states the amount

In other cases, however, cost is more subjective. Assume in this example that the golf outing is held as planned. After the event, a final invoice is prepared and sent to the entity sponsoring the outing. Upon receiving the invoice, this buyer has a question about the invoice. Consider now, the salary of the person at the Country Club who originally prepared and sent the bill for the golf outing to the buyer paying it. The cost of "talking with customers regarding invoice questions" is an example of an activity performed inside many hospitality companies and one for which a clear-cut cost cannot be so easily assigned. Some customers will have invoice questions.

Others will not. How then can the true cost of "talking with customers regarding invoice questions" be assigned? A related question would be, "knows the exact cost of such an activity, on an invoice-by-invoice basis, even worth the time it might require to calculate such a cost?" The calculation of costs such as those in the golf outing example can, of course be undertaken. Cost accountants facing such issues could, for example, assign each hospitality employee's time to different activities they perform. They could use surveys to have the workers themselves assign their time to the different activities they perform (such as food preparation, guest service, invoicing, and the like). A cost accountant could then determine the total time and cost spent on each activity by summing up the percentage of each worker's time and pay that is spent on that activity. This process is called activity-based costing, and it seeks to assign objective costs even to the somewhat subjective items such as the payment for various types of labor, as well as the even more subjective management tasks involved with planning, organizing, directing, and controlling a hospitality business. Using activity-based costing when examining expenses is an example of the actions undertaken by accountants to help managers make better decisions and to operate more successful businesses. This is especially true as managers seek to identify their break-even points.

Identification of the break-even point in a sales transaction is critical because, as we have seen, businesses that do not consistently generate revenue in excess of expenses will cease to exist. It is important to note, however, that each of a business's individual sales transactions need not result in more revenue than expense. The sum of all a firm's transactions over the long run, however, certainly must do so.

3.5.1 The Break-Even Point

That a common profit formula used by accountants is:

Profit = Revenue - Expense

Upon initial examination, this seems like a straightforward formula. Experienced RMs, however, know that the profitability of a sale is changeable because, for many hospitality businesses, some sales are simply more profitable than others. One reason for this is the fact that many businesses experience busy periods and slow periods. For example, a Colorado ski resort may experience tremendous sales volume during the ski season, but have a greatly reduced volume, or may even close, during the summer. Similarly, a country club manager working in the Midwestern part of the U.S. may find that revenue from green fees, golf outings, and food and beverage sales are very high in the summer months, but the golf course will likely be closed for several months in the winter.

Hoteliers in many cities also frequently experience varying levels of sales volume. For those hotels that cater to business travelers, the periods around the major holidays result in reduced business travel and as a result, reduced hotel room revenue. Those hotels that cater to family oriented leisure travelers often find their busiest months to be in the summer when school has traditionally been out of session and families take their vacations. Even year-round travel destinations such as Cancun and Florida's coast experience spikes in volume during special events such as college spring break or the Christmas holidays.

It is also important to recognize that many cost percentages change as volume changes. Costs, when expressed as a percentage of revenues (calculated as: Expense/ Revenue-Expense %) are typically reduced when sales are high, and increase when sales volume is lower. This is so because while some costs are variable—*for example,* food and beverage costs—other costs—for example, rent, insurance, and some labor—are fixed, and thus are the same when revenues are high as they are when revenues are low.

The result, in these cases, is greater profits from each dollar's sale during high volume periods, (when a firm's total expense percentages are lower) and lesser profits in lower volume periods (when the total expense percentages are higher). This relationship between sales volume or revenue, costs, and profits is easier to understand when you examine it, as shown in Figure 3.8.

The x-axis (horizontal axis) represents sales volume. In a restaurant, this is the number of covers (guests) served, or dollar volume of sales. In a hotel, it is the number of rooms sold.

The y-axis (vertical axis) represents the costs associated with generating the sales. The Total Revenues line starts at 0 because if no guests are served or no rooms are sold, no revenue dollars are generated. The Total Costs line starts farther up the y axis because fixed costs are incurred even if no guests are served or rooms are sold. The point at which the two lines cross is the break-even point; the point at which operating expenses are exactly equal to sales revenue. Stated in another way, when sales volume in a business equals the sum of the total fixed and variable costs required producing those sales, its break-even point has been reached. Below the break-even point, costs are higher than revenues, so losses occur. Above the break-even point, revenues exceed the sum of the fixed and variable costs required to make the sales, so profits are generated.

While most managers do not calculate the breakeven point on each individual sale, those managers would certainly like to know the break-even point of their businesses on a daily, weekly, or monthly basis. In effect, by determining the break-even point, those managers are answering the question, "How much sales volume must you generate before you begin to make a profit?" Beyond the break-even point, the manager will want to answer another question, "How much sales dollars and volume must you generate to make my target profit level?" To answer these questions, they must conduct a cost/volume/profit

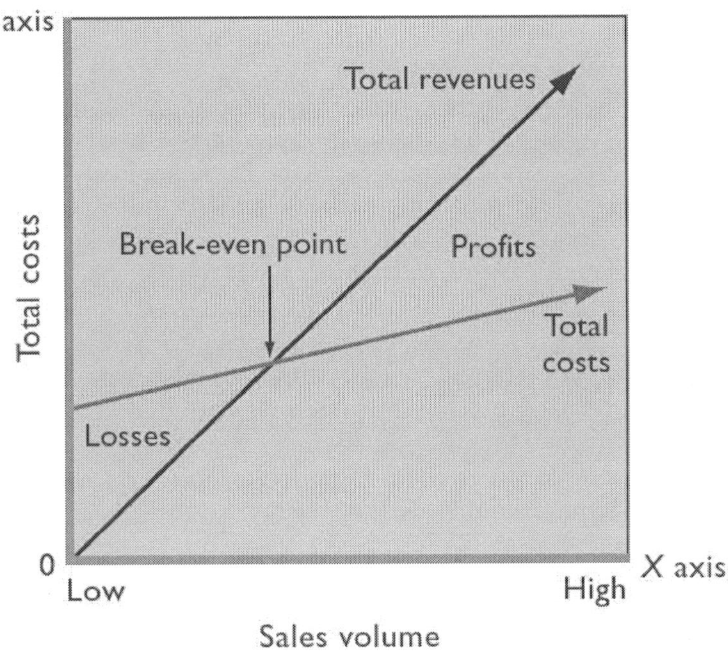

Figure 3.8: *Cost/Volume/Profit relationships*

analysis to predict the sales dollars (volume) required to achieve a break-even point; which is their desired profit based on known costs.

RMs should know how to compute or analyze their break-even points. If they prefer, RMs working in foodservice could compute or analyze their minimum sales point (MSP).

A minimum sales point (MSP) is simply defined as the dollar sales volume required to break even or justify staying open for a given period of time.

When the costs incurred in a sale are known and break-even points are determined, RMs can certainly utilize that information when establishing their prices. The best RMs, however, understand that the identification of costs and the control of costs, as important as they may be, cannot be allowed to unduly influence pricing decisions.

3.5.2 The Confusion over Cost

Perhaps because they have been taught how to compute costs and calculate break-even points, hospitality managers have traditionally utilized cost-based pricing when establishing their prices. The rationale seems straightforward. If a firm knows its costs and has established its break-even point, it can use an established formula, or rule-of thumb, to price its products and services in such a way as to consistently exceed their cost of production and to ensure a profit. It seems like a good way to determine prices. It is not. Sir Rocco Forte, chairman of Rocco Forte (hotel) collection, put it nicely; "A lot of hotels companies tend to be run by accountants these days, which spend their time looking at costs. You need to make a profit these days. If you do not have a top line, you can control costs all you want, but you would not make a profit.

Before examining why Forte's reasoning is sound, it will be helpful to examine why cost based pricing has in the past dominated the price setting philosophy of so many hospitality professionals. There are likely several reasons for the popularity of cost-based pricing in the hospitality industry. They include:

- The relative accuracy with which skilled accountants can calculate costs, thus the relative ease of calculating what are deemed to be accurate prices
- The belief that it is a just system since reasonable profits determined by the firms' owners are legitimized by the business's real costs
- The fact that, thus far, using the system has resulted in little government interference related to unfair pricing
- The belief that, if prices were higher than those calculated using this system, customers would buy less product and revenues would decline, thus reducing profitability
- The belief that, if prices were lower than those calculated using this system, an industry wide price war could result and profits would decline
- The fact that the system is very easy to use and teach to others

Experienced RMs recognizes that a cost-based approach to pricing is simply ineffective. The reasons why are fundamental. First, it is virtually impossible to determine a product's cost before determining its price. Read that line again. Experienced RMs (and honest accountants) knows that unit costs change with volume. This is so because a significant portion of any hospitality business's costs are fixed. As a result, a portion of those fixed costs must be allocated to the total cost of each unit sold. That allocated amount depends on the number of units sold. As Marshall pointed out so well, with changes in price, the concept of a true unit cost inevitably varies based on the unit's selling price.

RMs recognizes that prices dictate revenues and revenues affect costs. In markets where consumer demand is weak, cost-based pricing leads to higher prices than most customers are willing pay. In markets where demand is high, cost-based pricing leads to lower prices than most customers are willing to pay. If you immediately recognize that this is exactly the opposite of the pricing logic that should be used by effective RMs, you are absolutely correct.

The second fundamental flaw in cost-based pricing is the assumption that businesses can charge more for their goods and services simply because the business has added costs to them. Thus, for example, a hotel might assume that because a room has two beds instead of one, it can legitimately charge more to recover the cost of the second bed. In a similar manner, a restaurateur might assume that because cheese has been added to a hamburger, it is reasonable to recover that cost by charging more for cheeseburgers.

Unfortunately, for business owners, however, increased costs do not automatically equate to increases in consumer perceptions of value; a fact recognized by any business owner whose operating costs continually exceed his or her revenues. An increase in costs cannot be automatically allowed to decree an increase in selling price. In fact, the opposite should be true. An appropriate selling price for a product or service must dictate its allowable cost.

It is only when selling prices accurately reflect consumer perceptions of value that a business can ascertain the costs it can incur while still generating the profit levels it requires for long-term sustainability. If you recognize that diamonds of the same size and quality will have equal value even if one was discovered accidentally on the ground and the other took the expense of a year's labor and equipment to uncover, you understand that costs cannot be allowed to dictate price; rather, it is value, as measured by price, which must dictate a firm's costs.

The third and perhaps most fatal flaw of an over dependency on cost-based pricing is the tendency of its proponents to focus on themselves (internally) rather than their customers (externally). This is so because many hospitality managers confuse cost efficiency with business effectiveness. Big mistake. The difference is clear and can be readily illustrated by an example outside of, but related to, the hospitality industry. Consider the rental of audiovisual (AV) equipment, an activity undertaken by many hoteliers whose properties contain meeting space and thus whose meetings clients have need for various pieces of audiovisual equipment. Assume that, five years ago, through hard work, conscientious cost control, and superior managerial skill, an audiovisual rental company became the most efficient source of rental and repair services for the DVD players and recorders used by many of the AV departments of hotels at that time. The result of their efforts was that the company did its work better, faster, and cheaper than anyone else. It owned the market. Today, it still excels at providing DVD-related services. But its customers are few. The problem, of course, is that the company is now very good at doing the wrong thing. In today's competitive meetings market, DVD players are out; and have been for some time. Today, digital video projection units.

The best of AV service companies will survive only if they keep an eye out for what their customers, in this case the hotels, will seek to buy in the future. If they do not, they will go the way of the DVD, VHS, slide projectors, and buggy whip manufacturers. It is a simple truth that cost-effectively doing what the customers do not care about is a sure sign of a business that will not long be in business. Time after time, experience shows that a company's undue focus on the internal cost of operations ultimately leads to a focus on cost containment; more often than not then followed by cost cutting, and all typically enacted at the expense of the customer. Despite the pressure to do so, a reality you must face as an RM is that it is simply not possible to shrink a business to greatness.

Notwithstanding a great deal of lip service to the contrary, there is only so much that can be cut and controlled before a hospitality business begins to compromise product or service quality and as a result causes a perceptible decrease in their customers' assessment of value received. To believe a business can significantly reduce services or quality with no customer impact is simply naïve. As an effective RM, it is important to the success that you focus more on increases in customer value, and thus the long-term profitability accruing to you and the customers, than on reductions in the costs.

3.5.3 Implementing Strategic Pricing

A price must be viewed from the perspective of the seller and the buyer. Sophisticated RMs does just that. Regarding price, this RMs understands that:

- Prices act as signals to buyers and sellers. When prices are low enough, they send a "buy" signal to buyers (customers), who can now afford the things they want and are able and willing to pay for. When prices are high enough, they send a "sell" signal to producers who seek to optimize their profit by offering more products and services for sale.
- Prices encourage efficient production. Prices encourage businesspeople to produce their goods at the lowest possible cost. Despite the illogic of using costs to dictate prices, it is true that the less it costs to produce an item, the more likely it is that its producers will earn a profit. Firms that are cost efficient can produce more goods with fewer materials and lower labor costs than can firms that are inefficient. While these efforts are clearly in the best interests of sellers, buyers also benefit directly because they are provided with the things they want at the lowest sustainable prices.
- Prices help ration scarce resources. Prices help determine who will receive the entire economy's, or a single business's, output of goods and services. The prices charged for some goods are greater than some buyers are willing or able to pay. As a result, prices ensure that goods and services go primarily to those buyers who value them most.

Savvy RMs also appreciate that buyers' perceptions about price are more important than those of sellers. Above all, buyers seek value in what they buy. They are absolutely disinterested in the profits achieved by a business (unless those profits are perceived as too high), and are completely indifferent to a firm's costs or cost structure. Buyers attach importance only to their personal perception of the value they receive for the prices they pay.

Price is an important part of a company's marketing mix. As a result, those responsible for establishing the prices of a firm's products and services are critical to the company's success. But who in the firm should be responsible, and accountable, for its strategic pricing efforts?

Because "Price" is a crucial "P" in the 4 P's of marketing mix, some hospitality marketing professionals feel that pricing is a task best assigned to those in charge of the firm's marketing effort. Some marketing professionals even go so far as to maintain that it is a significant mistake when "Prices are a decision of management, not marketing."

Not surprisingly, hospitality cost accountants generally disagree. Citing the tendency for those in marketing and sales to view pricing as affected chiefly by what the competition charges, many of these financial professionals view pricing as a cost-based activity best left to those who can effectively "crunch the numbers."

Both groups often ignore the fact that while pricing is indeed one of the 4 P's of the marketing mix and that costs should be considered when determining prices, pricing is far too important to be left solely to either a firm's marketing or accounting experts. This is so because, when it is properly performed, pricing actually drives the company's entire business strategy and communicates to consumers its overall business philosophy.

Today's professional hospitality industry RMs must understand well the products their companies create and the customers they serve. As a result, effective RMs can come from a number of diverse areas within the industry. No operational area within hospitality has a monopoly on sensitivity to customer needs. In fact, the closer a hospitality professional is to the actual customer, the better RM he or she will likely become. For example, in 2007, the individual holding the title of Corporate Director of Revenue Management for Hyatt Hotel's 122 properties began his career 27 years earlier as a floor supervisor in the Housekeeping department of the New York Hyatt.

Clearly, effective RMs may have a background in sales, marketing, finance, or operations. In a properly structured revenue management system, the RM provides valuable insight and data that assists in determining whether a specific price will optimize revenues and/or profitability. Typically, he or she is not the sole decision maker. Every significant pricing decision should be reviewed by a team (or individual) capable of representing sales and marketing, finance, operations, strategic planning and the owners of the business. The key to pricing strategically is not the background of RMs but an understanding of a firm's customers and what they value most.

3.6 SUMMARY

Strategic pricing is a nuanced approach that goes beyond traditional cost-plus pricing models, focusing instead on setting prices based on the perceived value of a product to the customer or on a competitive strategy. This method appreciates the psychological factors influencing consumer purchasing decisions, acknowledging that value perception often trumps logical evaluation of cost. This strategy diverges from the common practice where companies calculate their product prices by adding a profit margin to the sum of production, labor, and advertising costs.

In the hospitality sector, for example, sophisticated pricing strategies are evident in how some restaurants manage their revenue through wine pricing, not with the direct intention of increasing the average spend but rather to offer customers a choice that maximizes overall revenue without alienating any customer segment. This reflects a deeper understanding of pricing as part of the marketing mix, which also includes product, place, and promotion. Effective pricing strategies are crucial for companies aiming to maximize sales and profits by finding the optimal price point that attracts and retains customers.

Different pricing strategies, such as penetration pricing, are employed depending on the company's goals, the product lifecycle stage, and market dynamics. Penetration pricing, for instance, involves setting a low entry price to quickly capture market share, with the expectation of raising prices later as brand awareness and customer base grow. As products move through the lifecycle, particularly during the rapid growth stage, it becomes necessary to adjust pricing strategies to maintain momentum and capitalize on market opportunities.

Thus, strategic pricing is a critical component for businesses seeking success in competitive markets. By understanding and applying the principles of strategic pricing, companies can effectively align their pricing with customer value perception and market conditions, thereby optimizing their revenue and profit potential.

3.7 REFERENCES

- Absorption VS Variable costing advantages and disadvantages . (2016, 03 27). Retrieved from The Strategic CF: http://strategiccfo.com/wikicfo/absorption-vs-variable-costing-advantages-and-disadvantages/
- Cohen, Eli; Ghiselli, Richard; Schwartz, Zvi (2007). "The Effect of Loss Leader Pricing on Restaurant Menus' Product Portfolio Analysis". Journal of Foodservice Business Research.
- For a detailed description of the required methodology, see Lea R. Dopson and David K. Hayes, Food and Beverage Cost Control, 5th ed., pp. 419–420(Hoboken, NJ: John Wiley and Sons, 2011).
- Hess J.D., Gerstner E. . (2001). Loss Leader Pricing and Rain Check Policy . Marketing Science (Volume 6), 1-18.
- James Kotler, Philip Bowen and John Makens. Marketing for Hospitality and Tourism, 4th ed. (Upper Saddle River, NJ: Prentice Hall, 2005), 447.
- Marketing Consumer Products: Key Influences on Buying, Selling & Market Growth, ISR/Google Books, 2021. E-book ISBN 9780906321751. Chapter 2, "Consumer Product Affordability", page 4.
- Nagle, Thomas and Holden, Reed. The Strategy and Tactics of Pricing. Prentice Hall, 2002. Pages 84-104.
- Raju, Jagmohan; Zhang, John (2010). *Smart pricing: How Google, Priceline, and leading businesses use pricing innovation for profitability*. Wharton School Publishing. pp. 187–193.
- Robert Reid and David Bojanic, Hospitality Marketing Management, 4th ed. (Hoboken, NJ: John Wiley and Sons, 2006), 17.
- Schindler, Robert (Robert M.) (2012). *Pricing strategies : a marketing approach*. Thousand Oaks, Calif.: Sage Publications, Inc.
- White, J. (2014). "Price Discrimination: A Classroom Exercise". *Business Education Innovation Journal*. **6**: 100–105.

CHAPTER 4

Cost Control Strategies in Hospitality

INTRODUCTION

Cost control within the hospitality industry is a critical management function that directly impacts the financial health and operational success of businesses in this competitive field. With typically narrow profit margins, the ability to effectively manage and reduce costs without sacrificing service quality is fundamental to achieving long-term sustainability and profitability. This involves a multi-faceted approach that includes rigorous budgeting and financial planning, strategic inventory management, labor cost optimization, energy conservation measures, and judicious negotiation with suppliers.

Meticulous budgeting and financial planning form the cornerstone of effective cost control. By setting precise budgets for various operational departments—such as food and beverage, housekeeping, and maintenance—management can monitor expenditures closely, enforce spending caps, and pinpoint opportunities to curtail costs thoughtfully. This proactive financial oversight ensures that resources are allocated efficiently, supporting the dual goals of cost containment and maintenance of service excellence.

Inventory management plays a pivotal role in cost control, requiring businesses to meticulously oversee stock levels to avert waste, spoilage, and pilferage. Adopting advanced inventory tracking solutions can mitigate excessive purchasing and maintain inventory at levels commensurate with actual demand, thereby avoiding unnecessary expenses.

Labor costs, often one of the largest operational expenses in the hospitality industry, demand strategic management. Through careful scheduling, comprehensive staff training, and ongoing performance evaluation, businesses can optimize workforce productivity. Leveraging technology and automation further aids in streamlining operations, potentially reducing the need for extensive manual labor, thus controlling labor costs.

Energy efficiency initiatives are indispensable in reducing operational costs. Investments in energy-saving technologies, like LED lighting and energy-efficient heating, ventilation, and air conditioning (HVAC) systems, not only lower energy consumption but also contribute to significant savings over time. Routine maintenance ensures that equipment operates at peak efficiency, further enhancing cost-effectiveness.

Negotiating advantageous agreements with suppliers, conducting regular cost-benefit analyses, and seizing bulk purchasing opportunities are additional strategies that contribute to cost management. Engaging in strategic partnerships and seeking favorable terms can lead to considerable reductions in the cost of goods and services.

Therefore, achieving effective cost control in the hospitality industry necessitates a comprehensive and strategic approach that encompasses careful budgeting, efficient inventory and labor management, energy conservation, and savvy supplier negotiations. By embracing these strategies, hospitality businesses can bolster their financial performance, ensuring resilience and competitiveness in the dynamic and challenging hospitality market.

4.1 COST MANAGEMENT PRACTICES IN THE HOSPITALITY INDUSTRY

Tourism industry is one of the rapid growing industries around the globe. The boom of mass tourism at the twentieth century becomes widespread with the alternative tourism attendance. According to the WTO (World Tourism Organization) numbers 1.085.000.000 people attended international tourism activities at 2013. In this context, one can see the importance of tourism industry. At the last decades tourism is also one of the rapid growing industries

The conditions today forcing touristic destinations and tourism enterprises for challenging. This competition pressure affecting the choices and activities of the enterprises. Thus, the importance of utilizing the resources more efficient and effective becomes increased. Therefore enterprises should more emphasis on cost management systems.

However cost management concept being started using from the beginning of the 90's, scarcely there is no common and clear definition. There are ongoing differences about the definition of cost management. In the light of these concepts, cost management systems are being used for cost indicators and performance evaluation. Cost management could be defined as; 'improving and using cost management information within a value chain'. From a different point of view cost management could be defined as; 'determining the goods cost accurately, improving the processes, preventing wastages, identifying cost factors, planning and controlling the activities and developing strategies'.

The main goal of any cost management system is to offer timely, accurate, reliable and convenient information for the management. By using this cost information resources could be used efficient and productive in order to produce goods or services. Furthermore, competitive side of the enterprise could be improved by cost and profitability.

In other words, the main goal of cost management information system is 'to supply information to the managers in order to compete at the world market within cost, time and performance dimensions'. Within this context, not only the financial issues but also the non-financial subjects are included in cost management information system. Some aims of cost management could be listed as follows:

- Costing the goods as far as possible by the cost factors.
- Evaluating the life cycle performance of goods or services.
- Realizing and evaluating the process and activities accurately.
- Determining the efficiency and productivity of the activities.
- Controlling and managing costs.
- Facilitating performance evaluation.
- Supporting for performing organizational strategies.

4.1.1 Purpose of Cost Management

Cost management is the process by which companies control and plan the costs of doing business. Individual projects should have customized plans for this process, and companies as a whole also integrate cost management into their overall business model. There is no single accepted definition for this term, because it has such broad applications and possible strategies. When properly implemented, this process will translate into reduced costs of production for products and services, as well as increased value being delivered to the customer.

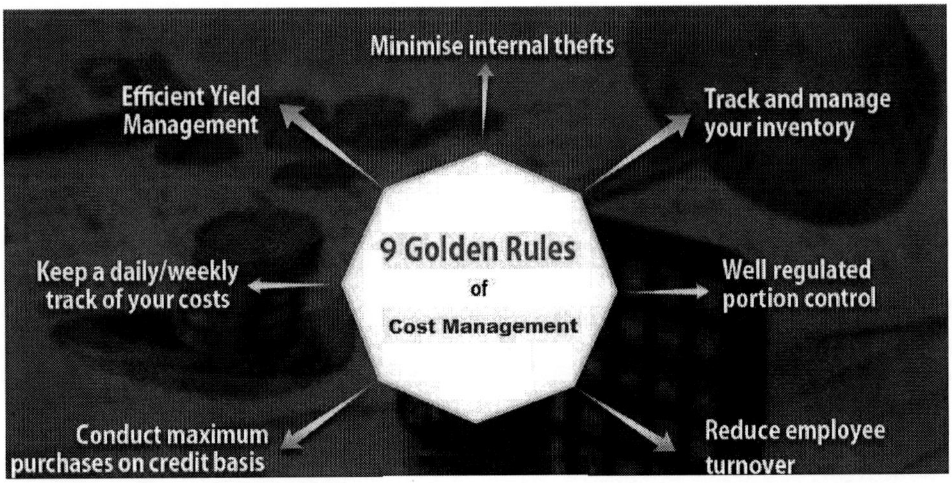

Most of the sales revenue in a hotel or food service enterprise is consumed by costs: as much as 90 cents or more of each revenue dollar may be used to pay for costs. Therefore, cost management is important. Budgeting costs and cost analysis is one way to control and manage costs to improve net income. Another way to improve net income is to cut costs, without regard to the consequences. Perhaps a better way is to look at each cost (expense) and see how it contributes toward net income. If advertising cost leads to higher net income than would be the case if we did not advertise, then it would not pay to cut the advertising expense.

4.1.2 Cost Classifications and Cost Behavior in Hospitality Operations

Cost classifications and cost behavior play a crucial role in the financial management of hospitality operations. The understanding and effectively managing costs are essential for maintaining profitability and providing guests with quality experiences. Cost classifications and cost behavior analysis are fundamental concepts in the financial management of hospitality operations. By categorizing costs correctly and understanding how they behave under different conditions, hospitality businesses can make informed decisions, optimize their cost structure, and ensure long-term profitability while providing high-quality services to their guests. Effective cost control and revenue management strategies are essential in this dynamic and competitive industry.

One of the ways to better manage costs is to understand that there are many types of costs. If one can recognize the type of cost that is being considered, then better decisions can be made.

Direct Cost

A direct cost is one that is traceable to and the responsibility of a particular operating department or division. Most direct costs are variable by nature and will increase or decrease in relation to increases and decreases in **sales revenue**. For this reason, direct costs are considered to be controllable by, and the responsibility of the department or division manager to which they are charged. Examples of these types of costs are cost of sales–food and –beverages, wages and salaries, operating supplies and services, and linen and laundry.

Keyword

Sales revenue is the income a business generates from the sale of goods or services.

Indirect Cost

An indirect cost is one that cannot be identified with and traceable to a particular operating department or division, and thus, cannot be charged to any specific department or division. General building maintenance could only be charged to various departments or divisions (such as rooms, food, or beverage) with difficulty.

REMEMBER

Even if this difficulty could be overcome, it must still be recognized that indirect costs cannot normally be considered the responsibility of operating departments' or divisions' managers. Indirect costs are frequently referred to as undistributed costs.

Controllable and Non-controllable Costs

If a cost is controllable, the manager can influence the amount spent. For example, the kitchen manager can influence the amount spent on food. However, it is unlikely the kitchen manager can influence the amount spent on rent, especially in the short term. The mistake is often made of calling direct costs controllable costs and indirect costs non-controllable costs. It is true that direct costs are generally more easily controlled than indirect costs, but in the long run all costs are controllable by someone at some time.

Joint Cost

A joint cost is one that is shared by, and thus is the responsibility of, two or more departments or areas. A dining room server who serves both food and beverage is an example. The server's wages are a joint cost and should be charged (in proportion to revenue, or by some other appropriate method) partly to the food department and the remainder to the beverage department. Most indirect costs are also joint costs. The problem is to find a rational basis for separating the cost and charging part of it to each department.

Discretionary Cost

This is a cost that may or may not be incurred based on the decision of a particular person, usually the general manager. Nonemergency maintenance is an example of a discretionary cost. The building exterior could be painted this year, or the painting could be postponed until next year. Either way sales revenue should not be affected. The general manager has the choice, thus it is a discretionary cost. Note that a discretionary cost is only discretionary in the short run. For example, the building will have to be painted at some time in order to maintain its appearance.

Relevant and Non-relevant Costs

A relevant cost is one that affects a decision. To be relevant, a cost must be in the future and different between alternatives. For example, a restaurant is considering replacing its mechanical sales register with an electronic one. The relevant costs would be the cost of the new register (less any trade-in of the old one), the cost of training employees on the new equipment, and any change in maintenance and material supply costs on the new machine. As long as no change is necessary in the number of servers required, the restaurant's labor cost would not be a relevant cost. It would make no difference to the decision.

Sunk Cost

A sunk cost is a cost already incurred and about which nothing can be done. It cannot affect any future decisions. If the same restaurant had spent $250 for an employee to study the relative merits of using mechanical or electronic registers, the $250 is a sunk cost. It cannot make any difference to the decision.

Opportunity Cost

An opportunity cost is the cost of not doing something. An organization can invest its surplus cash in marketable securities at 10%, or leave the money in the bank at 6%. If it buys marketable securities, its opportunity cost is 6%. Another way to look at it is to say that it is making 10 percent on the investment, less the opportunity cost of 6%; therefore, the net gain is a 4 percent interest rate.

Fixed Cost

Fixed costs are not expected to change in the short run of an operating period of a year or less, and will not vary with increases or decreases in sales revenue. Examples are management salaries, fire insurance expense, rent paid on a square foot basis, or the committed cost of an advertising campaign. Over the long run fixed costs can, of course, change, but in the short run they are not expected to change.

Variable Cost

A variable cost is one that changes in direct proportion to a change in sales revenue. Very few costs are strictly linear, but two that are (with only a slight possibility that they will not always fit this strict definition) are the cost of sales of food and beverages. The more food and beverages sold, the more costs will be incurred. If sales are zero, no food or beverage costs are incurred.

Semi fixed or Semi variable Costs

Most costs do not fit neatly into the fixed or the variable category. Most have an element of fixed cost and an element of variable cost. As well, they are not always variable directly to sales on a straight-line basis. Such costs would include payroll, maintenance, utilities, and most of the direct operating costs. In order to make some useful decisions, it is advantageous to break down these semi fixed or semi variable costs into their two elements: fixed or variable.

4.1.3 Cost Management Systems

The accounting information system within an organization has two major subsystems: a financial accounting system and a cost management accounting system. One of the major differences between the two systems is the targeted user. Financial accounting is devoted to providing information for external users, including investors, creditors (e.g., banks and suppliers), and government agencies. These external users find the information helpful in making decisions to buy or sell shares of stock, buy bonds, issue loans and regulatory acts, and in making other financial decisions. Because the information needs of this group of external users are so diverse and the information must be so highly reliable, the financial accounting system is designed in accordance with clearly defined accounting rules and formats, or generally accepted accounting principles (GAAP). Cost management produces information for internal users. Specifically, cost management identifies, collects, measures, classifies, and reports information that is useful to managers for determining the cost of products, customers, and suppliers, and other relevant objects and for planning, controlling, making continuous improvements, and decision making.

Cost management has a much broader focus than that found in traditional costing systems. It is not only concerned with how much something costs but also with the factors that drive costs, such as cycle time, quality, and process productivity. Thus, cost management requires a deep understanding of a firm's cost structure. Managers must be able to determine the long- and short-run costs of activities and processes as well as the costs of goods, services, customers, suppliers, and other objects of interest.

Hotel enterprises that are part of a service industry could utilize cost management systems in order to reach their goals. Some of the cost management systems that hotels could utilize are listed as follows:

Activity-Based Costing: Activity-Based Costing (ABC) is a cost accounting system that focuses on an organization's activities and collects costs on the basis of the underlying nature and extent of those activities. ABC focuses on attaching costs to products and services based on the activities conducted to produce, perform, distribute, and support those products and services. ABC system first traces overhead costs to and then to products and other cost objects. The underlying assumption is that activities consume resources, and products and other cost objects consume activities. An ABC system boasts the potential of generating more accurate product costs than functional-based costing system.

Activity-Based Budgeting: Activity-based budgeting is an outgrowth of activity-based costing (ABC), which is similar to zero-based budgeting. This budget type accounts for how staff members allocate their effort among activities. Once the full cost of each activity has been calculated, drivers can be established that link support activities to the primary activities of the organization. By developing a comprehensive activity-based budget executives are able to create a clear nexus between workload and costs. Once developed, executives and managers can exercise control in several ways: 1) assign personnel based upon a demonstrated need, 2) expand or contract personnel proportionately as the need changes, 3) uncover waste and hidden costs, 4) view which activities are most and least expensive, thus subjecting them review, 5) assess the full efficiency of the organization, 6) identify places to cut spending, 7) establish a cost baseline that may be influenced through process or technology changes that reduce effort requirements for the activity and perhaps most importantly 8) argue from an informed, objective position in favor of the organization's budget.

Life Cycle Costing: Life Cycle Costing (LCC) is a technique to get the whole cost of production. It is a special approach that examines all the parts of the cost. It is used to produce a spend profile of the goods or service over its all life-span. The results of an LCC analysis is used to help managers in the decision-making process. The LCC analysis see projects further into the future. It is very valuable as a comparative tool when long term investment in some goods is considered.

Target Costing: Target costing has been introduced as a strategic management accounting system for the management of product costs. It is a costing system to manage a firm's future profits by explicitly including target costs in the product development process. Central to the target costing is 'reverse costing', in which an estimation of the attainable selling price and the required profit margin are used to determine the allowable cost for a new product.

Benchmarking: Competitive-cost benchmarking is an action-oriented tool that enables companies to quantify how their performance and costs compared against competitors, understand why their performance and costs are different, and apply that insight to strengthen competitive responses and implement proactive plans. Benchmarking, by definition, goes beyond competitive-cost analysis, which is often a staff exercise without a structured follow-up implementation program; its goal reaches beyond simple competitor emulation.

Balanced Scorecard: The balanced scorecard is a strategic-based performance management system that typically identifies objectives and measures for four different perspectives; the financial perspective, the customer perspective, the process perspective, and the learning and growth perspective. The objectives and measures of the four perspectives are linked by a series of cause-and effect hypotheses. This produces a testable strategy that provides strategic feedback to managers. Alignment with the strategy expressed by the balanced scorecard is achieved by communication, incentives, and allocation of resources to support the strategic initiatives.

Value Chain Analysis: Value chain analysis (VCA) is described as a technique that can play an important role in the management of supply chain relationships. VCA is used to analyze, coordinate and optimize linkages between activities in the value chain, by focusing on the interdependence between these activities. A value chain is defined as; the linked set of value-creating activities all the way from basic raw material sources for component suppliers through the ultimate end-use product delivered into the final customer's hands.

Transfer Pricing: The transfer pricing issue is typically portrayed as a problem of finding the price or pricing schedule that comes closest to inducing an efficient level of trade between two divisions of a firm The optimal design of a transfer pricing policy is a solution to a mechanism design program, which seeks to induce information revelation at the lowest possible cost-that is, with minimal allocation distortions.

Kaizen Costing: Kaizen costing is a new costing system that utilizing by Japanese companies. Target costing is an effective system at the design of the product. On the hand kaizen costing is specifically utilized by high technological companies in order to cut costs. Kaizen costing is a process that firstly a target cost is determined and then production methods improved in order to achieve that costing goal.

4.1.4 Analysis of Cost Management Practices at the Hotel Industry

When evaluating the institutionalism of the hotel companies, one can say that using accounting information systems and cost management systems are more widespread at chain hotels than the independent ones. Nevertheless, at the last decade both chain and independent hotels are more familiar with cost management systems in order to support strategic goals. By better understanding of the contemporary cost management philosophy hotel companies –like the other companies- change their paradigm and traditional systems are becoming lesser while contemporary systems becomes more popular. Contemporary cost management systems have more contribution for cost information and decision support in order to achieve companies' goals.

Before the changing period of the companies it was feasible to focus on standardized and detailed methods. Nowadays within the rapid changing environment companies should be more dynamic, customer and market oriented. Therefore, hotel companies should improve their cost management systems in order to facilitate strategic management. Nowadays only financial information are inadequate for decision making. Within this context, non-financial critical success factors gain importance. Managing costs at the hotel companies are highly important like the other companies. Cutting costs, planning and control is critical for hotel companies. For achieving competence, profitability, raising service quality, focusing at market and continuous improvement strategic cost management is becoming crucial for the enterprises. Strategic cost management is focusing on these success factors. Likewise the other part of the world hotel companies in need strategic cost management in order to survive, efficient and productive. One can say the hotel companies in hospitality have to utilize contemporary cost management systems in order to reach their goals.

4.2 STRATEGY OF COST CONTROL IN HOSPITALITY

Cost control is the practice of identifying and reducing business expenses to increase profits, and it starts with the budgeting process. A business owner compares the company's actual financial results with the budgeted expectations, and if actual costs are higher than planned, management has the information it needs to take action.

As an example, a company can obtain bids from different vendors that provide the same product or service, which can lower costs. Cost control is an important factor in maintaining and growing profitability.

Corporate payroll, for example, is often outsourced, because payroll tax laws change constantly, and employee turnover requires frequent changes to payroll records. A payroll company can calculate the net pay and tax withholdings for each worker, which saves the employer time and expense.

4.2.1 Cost Control and Analysis

In business, cost control is defined as "the practice of identifying and reducing business expenses to increase profits." To find all your costs, run through your credit card statements and other places where your spend will documented. If you're using software with accounting or reporting functions, this should be easily accessible.

Next you want to run a quick analysis to see where you're spending money and where you may need to cut back you're spending.

With your list of expenses in front of you:

- **Compare** your expenses to your budgeted expenses: are you going over budget and, if so, which areas seem to be the problem areas?
- **Categories** your expenses (labor, food and beverage, utilities, marketing, subscriptions, accounting, legal, insurance, maintenance and repairs, office expenses and other relevant areas) to get an understanding of where your money is going
- **Classify** costs as fixed or variable: fixed costs are those that remain the same regardless of business activity while variable costs go up and down with changes in business activity levels
- Find **controllable** costs: the expenses that can be adjusted or influenced by a person are the ones you really want to focus on – for example, switching off lights can bring down electricity bills but your monthly accounting software fees are generally fixed
- **Calculate** return on investment to work out which expenses are justified by the amount of money they bring back into the business.

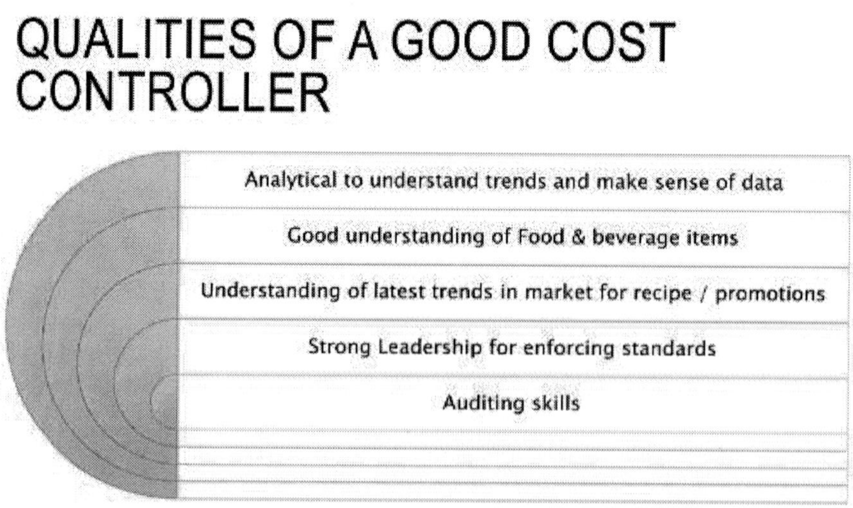

4.2.2 Methods and Techniques for Cost Control

If it looks like things have gone from bad to worse after your analysis, don't panic! There are plenty of ways you can start cutting costs, including:

- **Outsourcing**: moving tasks that are currently handled in-house to an external provider often cuts costs through economies of scale (and by lowering your labor costs)
- Focusing on efficiency: money could be seeping from your business simply because your processes are letting you down (or you're not allocating and using resources to maximize profits)
- **Bulk buying** and other ways to reduce supply costs: negotiating a better deal across all your suppliers can add up to significant cost savings
- Finding errors and unused services: running an eye over your bills to find costly errors or services you simply don't use or need anymore can deliver quick money-saving wins
- Focusing on small savings: remember that making small changes consistently can add up to big costs savings in the long run.

4.2.3 Hotel Cost Control Procedures

Ready to take action and start saving money now? Here are some practical ideas to get you started:

- **Reach out and make some calls**

Call around and get a few quotes for major expenses such as insurance. At the same time, check in with your vendors and ask if they offer loyalty incentives or have any better deals for bulk purchases.

- **Review how you manage staff**

If you employ staff at your property, could you train them to complete tasks outside their role when they have downtime? Could you better forecast when you'll need additional staff and when you won't? Could additional staff training allow more flexibility in roistering? Cut down labor and other costs by tweaking the way you manage staff.

- **Keep staff happy**

Lose a staff member and you lose their experience along with the time and energy you've put into welcoming and training them. There are plenty of ways to keep your people happy (and avoid the costs of having to train someone else) from setting clear goals to recognizing achievements, providing a few perks and adding flexibility and work-life balance to the mix.

- **Optimize your front desk operations**

Your front desk is the heart of your hotel, and focusing on improving your front desk operations can lead to a better guest experience and a more efficient hotel – adding up to significant cost savings.

- **Fix it before you have to replace it**

It can be more cost effective to fix something rather than letting it go and eventually having to replace it. Boost your maintenance schedule and work out if this helps cut down on replacement costs.

- **Go green**

Going green in even small ways will help save the environment and also save you dollars. Educate staff on turning off lights. Install efficient lighting. Encourage guests to reuse towels. When replacing appliances, buy with the best energy rating high on your priority list.

- **Re-allocate your marketing spend**

Effective marketing is critical in the small hotel industry, but traditional marketing can take out a big chunk of your budget. Consider reducing your spend and channeling the money into digital marketing, which is often more affordable and has the potential for massive reach and results.

4.2.3 Food and Beverage Cost Control

A small restaurant or other food and drink offering can be a draw card for guests, however the costs can quickly escalate.

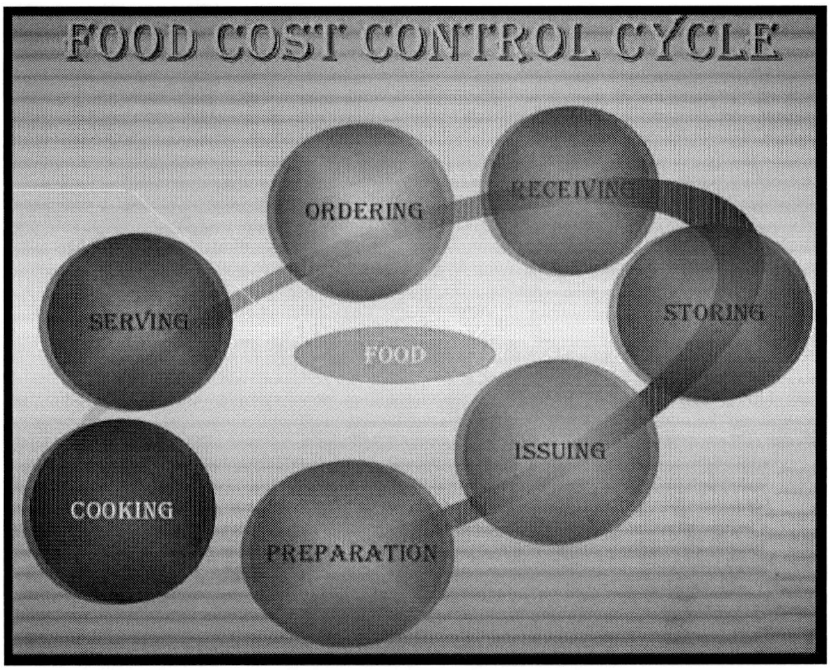

Food and beverage cost control is one area that deserves special scrutiny. While some of the general areas can help you cut costs, including looking at suppliers and labor costs, there are some additional ways to improve your food and beverage profits:

- Get the pour size precise for alcohol by training staff or using jiggers
- Reconsider portion sizes if meals are often praised but often left partly uneaten
- Design menus so some ingredients and prep work are shared among dishes

- Shrink the menu and go for quality over quantity
- Make sure the kitchen isn't over-prepping or failing to efficiently store ingredients, leading to waste
- Consider whether a breakfast buffet would work more efficiently as a "grab and go" style breakfast menu
- Cut down the hours or room service if it's becoming a drain on resources.

4.2.4 Tools to Help Control Hotel Operations Costs

If you are examining and managing your costs manually, using pen and paper or Excel spreadsheets, this time drain can also become expensive for your business – undoing your efforts to save costs.

Investing in hotel technology and software can not only help you manage costs, it can improve efficiency and decision-making across your entire business and boost your guests' experience.

Imagine being able to:

- Connect your channel manager and booking engine
- Take direct bookings on your website
- Track and measure which online sales channels are generating the most bookings
- Manage reservations with a simple drag and drop calendar
- Organize and streamline housekeeping
- Use a mobile app to manage your property from anywhere
- Get more time back to spend in the business or simply doing what makes you happy.

4.2.5 Ways to Reduce Hotel Operating Costs While Sustaining Customer Service

In the hospitality industry, customer service is the name of the game. This fact represents both a challenge for hotels to meet and an opportunity that hotels can maximize.

The challenge, of course, is in controlling costs while keeping customer service high. It's as true in hospitality as it is in any industry: bad service will lose you customers. The opportunity, however, is somewhat unique to hospitality.

The savvy hotelier will be on the lookout for ways to reduce costs while continuing to delight customers. Here are useful ways to start:

1. Optimize labor scheduling and staff training. Labor cost is a significant proportion of a hotel's operating expenses: roughly 50 percent, on average. Labor is an obvious place to begin looking for savings, but solutions require creative thought and careful balancing. Of course, you don't want your staff overscheduled and underutilized, but at the same time, you don't want to be caught short-staffed with disgruntled guests and stressed employees.

The first step in optimizing labor scheduling is to forecast staffing needs and plan accordingly"ideally on a timeline that makes sense with staff scheduling. Be sure to segment your forecasts: luxury suites and check-outs take longer to clean than smaller rooms and stay overs.

Then, consider cross-training employees so staff members can lend a hand in another role when needed. Cross-trained staff can provide coverage during another staff member's vacation or a staffing emergency (such as a sudden sick day), and they can pitch in during a rush in their secondary function or a lull in their primary function.

Research suggests training staff members in just one additional responsibility is best, as is cross training staff members in skills they like. A waiter who enjoys his work, for example, may prefer cross training in another customer-facing position, such as host, more than he would enjoy a grounds keeping role.

2. Attend to utilities. Labor may be the highest operating cost for hotels, but according to the EPA's Energy Star information for hotels, utilities are the fastest-growing. There is a well-established case for energy efficiency as a sound business practice, they write, and expectations for hoteliers to demonstrate their climate stewardship are growing. In other words, done right, this makes good business sense AND builds customer goodwill.

You can't measure what you don't track: Energy Star's first low-cost recommendation is to track energy performance with their free and easy benchmarking tool. Or, if you'd like to outsource the whole process, look into energy audits in your state or region. Certain programs provide energy audits for free, with no obligation. Audits may examine lighting, HVAC, insulation and refrigeration systems, and make recommendations for reducing energy use. Other programs that vary by region provide rebates for purchasing energy-efficient equipment: look into these when it's time to replace laundry, restaurant, or HVAC equipment.

Low-cost options that Energy Star recommends include:

- Switching to energy efficient light bulbs like compact fluorescent or LED
- Training staff to turn off lights, TVs, and heating or cooling in empty rooms
- Installing timers on bathroom heat lamps
- Installing occupancy sensors for lighting (Turning off fluorescent lights for 12 hours per day extends their calendar life "the time between replacements "by 75 percent, to nearly seven years! According to Energy Star, compact fluorescent bulbs tend to start paying for themselves after nine months.)

Let guests know about your energy-saving measures. Signs about the environmental friendliness of reusing towels, for example, can produce both cost savings and customer goodwill.

3. Stay on top of maintenance. Don't defer it! According to the US Department of Energy, clogged HVAC filters can increase energy consumption by 15 percent. Maintaining systems will minimize energy consumption, extend equipment life, and reduce the likelihood of a catastrophic breakdown. System breakdowns or other maintenance issues are costly to the hotel, inconvenient to guests, and give the hotel the aura of an undesirable, hassle-filled experience.

Develop and implement a schedule for maintaining your building's equipment. For the HVAC system, this might mean scheduling the replacement of filters every one to six months, inspecting fans, bearings, belts, and the area around the air intake every six months, and inspecting for leaks, and cleaning and testing dampers yearly.

4. Improve the employee onboarding experience. Employee turnover is famously high in the hospitality industry. That's a costly problem: It costs an employer an estimated 33 percent of a worker's salary to find, hire, and train a replacement. Start your valuable employees off on the right foot by making your hotel employee onboarding as positive as possible. Standardize your onboarding with a process that helps employees feel welcome, understand expectations, and get up to speed successfully.

Consider using checklists to keep onboarding on track "before, during, and after an employee's first day. Before their first day, for example, send an email outlining essential information like how to dress (including uniform requirements and costs, if applicable), where to park, who to report to, and when to arrive. Standardize the email with a template, but don't forget to personalize it with the new hire's name.

On the first day, move through a checklist of orientation items, paperwork requirements, and essential training. Provide the employee with information to keep about policies, procedures, and acronyms or hotel lingo. Assign a mentor who can answer questions, help them get their bearings, explain work tasks, and introduce them to the team.

5. Take advantage of technology to automate processes. The thoughtful and directed use of technology can increase efficiency, save time, reduce labor costs, and provide a positive experience for your customers.

Consider the many steps involved in event booking and F&B coordination. A sales & catering CRM can set automatic reminders for the sales team to follow up with leads, schedule onsite visits, send contracts, and get signed contracts returned. Streamlining this process saves staff time, keeps details organized and attended to, and makes planners' lives easier.

Or consider offering a check-in and check-out app, eliminating the need for customers to wait in line. Beacon technology can even automatically push a mobile check-in option when guests walk in the door, and deliver a mobile check-out option the morning of departure. (Be aware that although the cost per beacon is low, the cost of developing an app and maintaining the beacon system can be several times greater. Look into pricing and pre-developed apps to determine whether this is a cost-effective measure.)

According to IBM, 85 percent of customer interactions will be handled with artificial intelligence by 2020. In the hotel industry, this percentage is likely to be lower, since customer service is a significant component of our product. But still, as consumers become used to AI instantly answering routine questions, there will be room for individual hotels and chains to test this type of technology, saving staff time or cutting down on call center needs.

For human-mediated customer service and remember, hotels might always need more of that than other industries direct human-to-human contact is a mainstay.

Telephone calls to the front desk or a centralized call center are familiar and appreciated by many groups. The ability to text the front desk for requests or directions is increasingly popular as well. Some systems let hotels preload answers to common questions, or even use AI to generate an answer that the front desk staff can confirm or correct, and send on with a click.

Hotel managers can automate many processes with technology, freeing up employees to deliver services tech can't manage. But it only happens that way when employees can use the systems, and the systems work well together. As you choose systems for your CRM, PMS, customer service, online booking, accounting, labor scheduling, housekeeping, EAM/CMMS or other needs, prioritize ease of use and integration with other systems. Then devote the necessary time to staff training.

6. Streamline F&B to reduce waste. Especially if you provide banquet F&B, streamline collaboration and execution with a computerized F&B system. Such a system can make measurable impacts on your profits: According to research from STR, hotels that use Social Tables Event Services Platform have higher F&B profits than those that don't have the software.

Make F&B more efficient with restaurant and banquet menu options that use similar ingredients and prep. That way, although two groups in two different event spaces might have settled on two different menus, some ingredients and prep work can be shared. Use your event management system to examine the menu requirements for each day and make prep sheets for cooks so that they don't over-prepare.

Watch your waste: Pay attention to what your end-of-meal plates say about portion size. You don't want to send people away dissatisfied, but consider scaling back if food is often left uneaten. For beverages, decide whether you want bartenders to use jiggers or free-pour. Either way, train your staff to the standard and review every so often to ensure they are pouring accurately.

4.3 COSTING METHOD APPLIED IN HOTEL INDUSTRY

For this purpose expenses are classified according to their relation to the production variations into two categories: variable expenses (that depends on the production variations) and fixed expenses (that are independent to the production variations).

Fixed expenses, according to the simplified direct-costing method, are treated like a unitary mass that affects the period costs and are not allocated on the cost bearers. Therefore, fixed expenses are not considered when the product cost of goods, works or services is calculated, but they are transferred directly upon the income statement of the period referred to. In the simplified direct-costing method only variable costs are taken in account and subjected to distribution upon the cost bearers.

In order to calculate the variable costs accordingly to the simplified direct-costing method, the following steps must be complied:

- In the first step the effective expenses of a certain period must be structured accordingly to their relation with the production volume, and then divided on the economic function (production, sales, and administration). Expenses incurred in the reporting period consist of:
    - Variable expenses (production and sales);
    - Fixed expenses (production, sales and administration).
- In the second step the cost of the cost bearers (goods, works or services) are calculated taking in account only those expenses that vary accordingly to the production volume. This step is divided into two phases:
    - First, the direct variable costs are collected on the costs centers;
    - Second, the variable costs identified on the costs centers are attributed to the cost bearers.

In the hotel industry expenses are collected on the costs centers based on the supporting documentation of the different activities undertaken. On each supporting document registered by the primary accounting, the character of the expenses must be stated (variable or fixed), according to classification scheme of the production, sales and administration expenses. Thereby, the variable expenses recorded in the primary documents are easily tracked on the cost centers, and then they are centralized and transmitted to the central accounting department. In other words, each cost center officer is interested only in the variable expenses (because they are cost elements), the **fixed expenses** registered in different documents are transmitted directly to the central accounting department.

The statements regarding the variable expenses identified by their nature are transferred to the general accounting compartment that centralizes all these expenses on the economic entity. The centralized statements regarding the variable and fixed expenses are the basis of the simplified direct – costing calculation.

The informational cycle, on which the centralized statements of the variable and fixed expenses are based, is presented in figure 4.1.

Simplified direct costing calculation retrieves the effective variable cost value from the statements of variable expenses presented for each cost center. Although the usage of standards is possible, the simplified direct costing calculation dose not appeal to them because its purpose is not the forecast of expenses and results, this being proper to the evolved direct costing method. If the hotel management consider the information revealed by the simplified direct costing calculation to be sufficient, standards and budgets can be used because they are very useful tools for an efficient management.

4.3.1 Applying the Simplified Direct Costing Method

In order to apply the simplified direct costing method, as for any other direct costing method, information regarding the activity volume is necessary. This statistical information is identified for every operational cost center. The sales

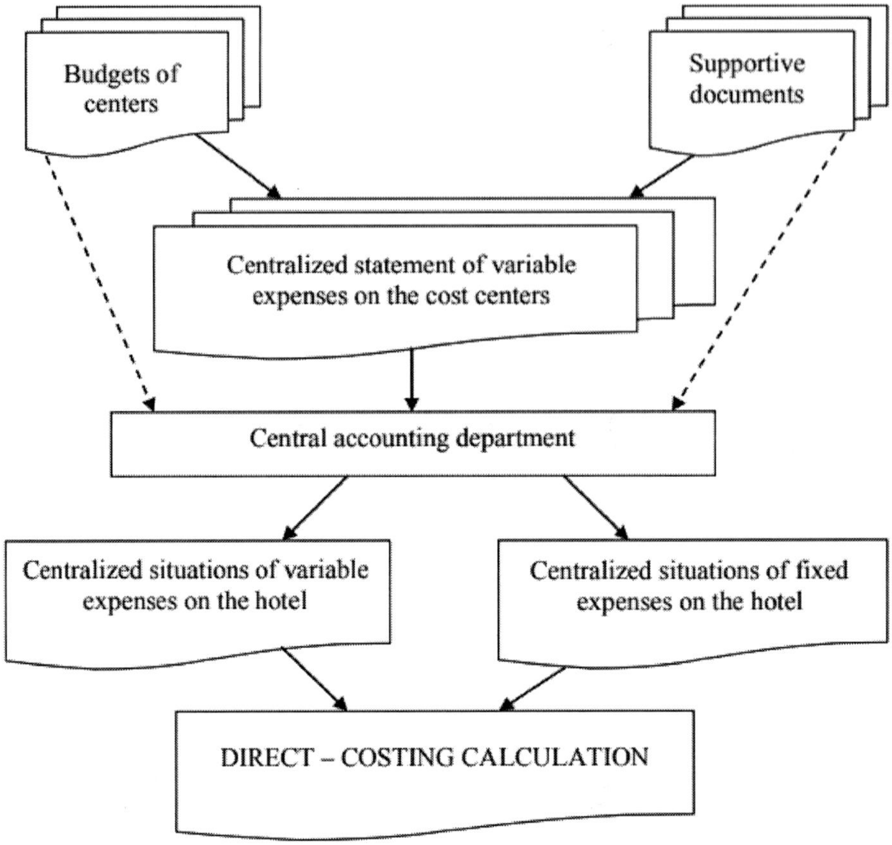

***Figure 4.1**: Direct – costing calculation informational cycle.*

center is responsible for research regarding the number of rooms occupied in the calculation period, real average rate, number of places occupied in the restaurant, restaurant's turnover, the number of clients that asked for other services (besides accommodation and restaurant) and the turnover of the "other services" cost center. These are the information from which the simplified direct costing method is starting. The hotel activity, in its nature, doesn't allow a single cost bearer for its entire activity, specific cost bearers for every cost centers being necessary.

The simplified direct costing calculation model for the hotel activity is presented in Table 1. The necessary data, the effective variable expenses for each cost center, have been taken from the statements of variable expenses. The variable expenses have been separated on the cost bearers identified for the hotel activity ("accommodation", "restaurant" and "other services"). Once this information is obtained, the next stage is the calculation of the contribution margin (total turnover minus total variable expenses) in two steps: contribution margin of production and contribution margin after sales. This way the contribution of each step to covering the fixed expenses and the positive or negative effect on profit can be established. Next, the contribution margin of each cost bearer and of the total hotel activity for the two steps identified is presented:

***Table 1**: Contribution margin calculation according to the simplified direct – costing method*

Indicators	**Accommodation**	**Costs bearers Restaurant**	**Other services**	**Total**
Turnover	3,389,998	1,749,996	433,125	5,573,119
Variable production costs	717,423	778,803	144,139	1,640,365
Contribution margin of production (1-2)	2,672,575	971,193	288,986	3,932,754
Variable sales costs	100,144	51,697	12,795	164,636
Contribution margin after sales (3-4)	2,572,431	919,496	276,191	3,768,118
Total fixed expenses	-	-	-	2,300,389
Profit				**1,467,729**

The contribution margin of production, for the analyzed hotel, is very generous being able to cover all the fixed expenses, therefore placing the hotel in the profitability area. Contribution margin of production represents 70.57% of total turnover and the fixed expenses represent only 41.28% of total turnover. If the variable expenses of distribution are taken in account, then the contribution margin after sales represents 67.61% of total turnover. Therefore, the contribution margin after sales assures the full coverage of the fixed expenses a surplus of 1,467,729 lei remaining in the form of profit. The difference between the contribution margin after sales share (67.61%) and the fixed expenses share (41.28%) of total turnover represents the profit rate of 26.34%. Simplified direct-costing calculation increases the information value of the contribution margin because it is highlighted in steps and on cost bearers.

The fixed expenses, in the concept of the simplified direct-costing method, are not directly connected to the main production activity; therefore, they offer the possibility of consumption evaluation. In figure 4.2, the relative sizes of fixed expenses of production, administration and sales, are presented.

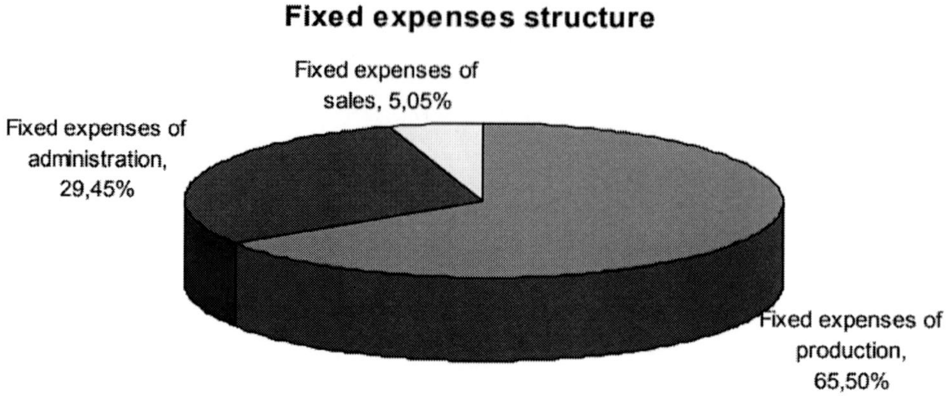

Figure 4.2: *Fixed expenses structure.*

The above presented figure shows that the fixed expenses of production have a share of 65.50%, the fixed expenses of administration have a share of 29.45% and the fixed expenses of sales have a share of 5.05% of the total fixed expenses. Form the calculation obtained with the simplified direct-costing method, presented in table 2, it is easily observed that all the fixed expenses have been covered by the contribution margin, placing the hotel in the profitability area. In other words, the break-even point has been exceeded in the analyzed period. When it comes to fixed expenses, it is needed to refer to the degree of stiffness (Gr) of the organization, which is nothing else than the share of fixed expenses in total expenses. The formula is shown:

$$G_r = \frac{Chf}{CT} x100 \text{ , where:}$$

Chf – fixed expenses of the organization;
CT – total expenses of the organization.

For the analyzed hotel, the degree of stiffness is:

$$G_r = \frac{2,300,389}{4,105,390} x100 = 56.03\%$$

The degree of stiffness of 56.03% is absolutely normal, given the field of activity of the organization. It also shows the extent of the organization's technical and material support.

If the degree of stiffness registers higher values, it highlights the need of stimulating more efficient usage of the organization's technical and material support for an optimal exploitation of its capacity. The maximum usage of the technical and material support happens rarely for reasons not entirely related to the organization's management.

With the simplified direct-costing method, the global analysis is left behind and the passing to a more detailed analysis is made, an analysis on cost bearers, as far as the method allows. In the effective calculation it can be observed that the largest share of the total turnover is obtained by the "accommodation" center, followed by the "restaurant" center. Regarding the variable expenses, things are the same, if we consider the cost bearer share in the total amount of variable expenses. Also, the analysis shows that the "accommodation" center is the most profitable, because the variable expenses that actually form the production cost represent only 21.16% of the center's turnover, and the contribution margin represents 78.84% of the center's total sales. This is perfectly normal given that the accommodation activity is the most important activity of any hotel, providing part of the dissolution of the other two operational centers.

However, besides the analysis of variable costs and contribution margin, the relative levels of fixed costs identified for each cost bearers should be taken into account. So, in table 2, we shall submit the attention to a number of rates, which reveal, from different angles, the production expenses that do not depend on the volume of activity. We are referring to the fixed expenses identified directly on the cost bearers.

The degree of stiffness for the "other services" cost bearer is the highest (55.52%), followed by the "accommodation" cost bearer (53.09%) and finally by the "restaurant" cost bearer with a degree of stiffness of only 39.80%. The same rate calculated for the production fixed expenses of the entire hotel has a result of 47.88%, which means that the hotel is well equipped and the facilities are relatively new.

From the analysis of the fixed expenses rate relative to the contribution margin, this expresses the relative size of the amount of fixed expenses covered by the contribution margin, and results that the "accommodation" cost bearer needs only 30.38% of the contribution margin to cover all of its fixed expenses. The "restaurant" cost bearer needs 53.01% of the contribution margin to cover the fixed expenses and the "other services" cost bearer needs 62.25% of the contribution margin.

***Table 2:** Fixed expenses rates*

Indicators	**Accommodation**	**Activity Restaurant**	**Other services**	**Total**
Turnover	3,389,998	1,749,996	433,125	5,573,119
Contribution margin of production	2,672,575	971,193	288,986	3,932,754
Fixed expenses	811,956	514,836	179,904	1,506,696
Total production expenses	1,529,379	1,293,639	324,043	3,147,061
Degree of stiffness of production (%)	53.09%	39.80%	55.52%	47.88%
Fixed expenses rate on the contribution margin (%)	30.38%	53.01%	62.25%	38.31%
Fixed expenses rate on turnover (%)	23.95%	29.42%	41.54%	27.04%

The third rate is also favorable to the hotel, in total and on cost bearers. It receives an increase of relevance if analyzed in conjunction with the first two rates calculated and presented in table 2. The rate of fixed costs relative to turnover provides information on how many percent of total turnover are needed to cover fixed expenses. The percentage is pretty good, considering that the amount of fixed costs is approximately equal to the volume of variable costs.

4.3.2 Types of Costing

In case of ascertaining cost, following types of costing are used:

Uniform Costing

It is seen that if a number of firms in an industry agree among themselves to follow the same pattern or system of costing in details by adopting common terminology for various items and processes, in such cases they are said to follow a system of **uniform costing**. Under such circumstances, a comparison of the performance of each of the firms can be made with that of another, or with the average performance in the industry. With the effect of particular system it is also promising to find the cost of production of goods which is best and true for the industry in total. It is found useful when tax-relief or protection is sought from the Government.

Marginal Costing

Marginal Costing is such type of costing where the ascertainment of marginal cost is differentiated in the midst of the fixed cost and in variable costs. It is used to ascertain effect of changes in volume or type of output on profit. It is believed that the marginal cost at each level of production includes an additional costs required to produce the unit. If in era of producing extra vehicles requires, for example, in lien of building a new factory, the marginal cost of those extra vehicles are covered whose cost is required for the new factory. In practice, it is analyzed that the cost is segregated into small and long-run cases, and over the long run, all costs are marginal. At every stage of production and time period being taken into consideration, marginal costs should cover all costs that vary with the level of production, and other costs are considered fixed costs. Basically if the cost function which is differentiable by joining and the cost of the next unit produced which is called as the basic volume, the formula used can be:

$$\frac{dC}{dQ}$$

If on the other hand, the cost function is not differentiable, then the marginal cost can be written and explain as follows:

$$\frac{\Delta C}{\Delta Q}$$

In this, various factors that affect marginal cost and its applicability to real world problems covers market failures. These include information related to:

- Asymmetries
- Presence of negative or positive externalities
- Transaction costs
- Price discrimination

Standard Costing and Variance Analysis

Standard Costing and variance analysis is the method or the tool where the standard costs are pre-determined and afterward compared with the recorded actual costs. Under such technique of cost ascertainment and cost control, can be used in conjunction with any method of costing if it is required. On the other hand, it is especially fitted where the manufacturing method uses production of standardized and quality goods of repetitive nature. It may also be defined as a technique of cost accounting which compares the standard cost of each product or service with the real cost in order to determine the efficiency of the operation, so that any remedial action may be taken immediately. It is a programmed cost which determines and calculates what each product or service should cost under given circumstances.

It should therefore be seen that the standard costing involves:

- Setting of standards
- Ascertaining actual results
- Comparing standards and actual costs to determine the variances
- Investigating the variances and taking appropriate action where necessary.

4.3.3 Uses of Costing

It is seen that the direct costing is of great use which involves the use of direct costs as an inputs to the decision models. They contain no allocations of overhead, which are not only irrelevant for many short-term decisions, but which can be difficult to explain to someone not trained in accounting

Automation Investments

In case of company investment, automated production equipment lowers the amount it pays to its direct labor staff. Under direct costing, the main information is to gather and collect the incremental labor cost of any employees which will be terminated, along with the new period costs to be received as part of the equipment purchase that led to occurrence of depreciation on the equipment and maintenance costs.

Cost Reporting

It was observed that direct costing is useful for controlling variable costs as it can create a variance analysis report which can be compared with the actual variable cost to what the variable cost per unit should have been. Under this, fixed costs are not included in this analysis, as they are associated with the period in which they are received, and so therefore are not covered under the direct costs.

Customer Profitability

It is seen that some customers require a great deal of support, but also place such large orders that a company still earns a considerable profit from the relationship. If there are such resource-intensive situations, it gives the meaning to calculate how much money the company actually gains or earned from each customer. This analysis may revealed that the company would be at better side in order to eliminate certain customers, even if this results in a way of noticeable revenue declination.

Internal Inventory Reporting

Usually accepted accounting principles and international financial reporting standards require that a company allocate indirect costs to its inventory asset for external reporting purposes. In this the overhead allocation requires a long-drawn-out amount of time to complete, so that it should be relatively common for company controllers to avoid updating the overhead by sharing during reporting periods when there will be no external reporting. Instead, they believe mostly on direct cost updates, and either avoid all changes to the overhead allocation, or make an estimated guess at the correct overhead allocation based on a proportion of direct costs, and make a more accurate adjustment when a reporting period arrives for which the company must report monetary statements to outside parties.

Profit-volume Relationship

It is seen that direct costing is of much use in plotting changes in profit levels as sales volumes change. It is easy and simple to create a direct costing table that points out the volume levels at which additional direct costs will be received, so that management can find or estimate the amount of profit at various levels of corporate activity.

Outsourcing

Direct costing is useful for deciding the manufacturing of items, whether the item can be manufactured in-house or to maintain a capability in-house, or whether to outsource the production. If the decision involves manufacturing in-house or elsewhere, it is crucial to determine how many staff and inventory which includes machineries will actually be required in certain cases, these resources are simply shifted elsewhere within the company, so there is no net profit improvement by shifting production to a supplier.

4.3.3 Cost-Volume-Profit (CVP) Analysis

Cost-Volume-Profit (CVP) analysis is a valuable tool for businesses, including those in the hospitality industry, to make informed decisions about pricing, production levels, and profitability. This analysis examines the relationship between costs, sales volume, and profit to help managers plan and strategize effectively.

At its core, CVP analysis revolves around three key components: costs, volume (or quantity of units sold or services provided), and profit. Let's delve deeper into each of these components and how they interplay within the context of hospitality operations.

Costs

Costs in CVP analysis are typically categorized into two main types: variable costs and fixed costs.

- **Variable Costs**: These are expenses that vary in direct proportion to changes in sales volume. In the hospitality industry, common examples of variable costs include the cost of food and beverages, housekeeping supplies, and hourly wages for front-line staff. As sales increase, variable costs increase as well, and they decrease when sales decline.
- **Fixed Costs**: Fixed costs are expenses that remain constant regardless of changes in sales volume. In hospitality, fixed costs may include rent or lease payments for the property, insurance premiums, management salaries, and depreciation on fixed assets. These costs are incurred even if the hotel or restaurant is not operating at full capacity.

Volume (Sales/Service Quantity)

Volume represents the number of units sold or services provided. In the hospitality industry, this could refer to the number of room nights booked, the number of meals served, or the quantity of drinks and beverages sold. Understanding how changes in volume affect costs and profits is a central aspect of CVP analysis.

Profit

Profit is the ultimate goal of any business, and CVP analysis helps assess how different levels of volume and associated costs impact profitability. Profit in CVP analysis is often referred to as contribution margin, which is the difference between total revenue and total variable costs.

Now, let's explore the key insights and uses of CVP analysis in the hospitality industry:

- **Break-Even Analysis**: One of the primary applications of CVP analysis is determining the break-even point. This is the level of sales volume at which total revenue equals total costs, resulting in zero profit. Knowing the break-even point helps hospitality businesses set pricing strategies and sales targets necessary to cover fixed costs and start generating a profit.
- **Pricing Strategies**: CVP analysis allows hotels and restaurants to evaluate how changes in pricing affect their bottom line. By analyzing the impact of price adjustments on contribution margins, businesses can make informed decisions about setting prices that maximize profitability.
- **Profit Planning**: Hospitality businesses can use CVP analysis for profit planning and forecasting. By projecting sales volume and estimating costs, they can develop budgets and financial plans that guide their operations.
- **Cost Control**: Understanding cost behavior through CVP analysis helps identify areas where cost control efforts are most needed. Businesses can

focus on managing and reducing variable costs while also optimizing fixed costs to improve overall profitability.

- **Expansion and Investment Decisions**: When considering expanding operations or making significant investments in new facilities or services, CVP analysis can assess the potential impact on profitability. It helps in evaluating whether the expected increase in sales volume justifies the associated costs.
- **Scenario Analysis**: Hospitality businesses can conduct scenario analysis using CVP analysis to explore different what-if scenarios. For instance, they can assess the impact of a new marketing campaign, changes in menu offerings, or renovations on their financial performance.
- **Risk Management**: CVP analysis can highlight the sensitivity of profit to changes in volume and costs. This insight allows businesses to identify potential risks and develop strategies to mitigate them, ensuring financial stability.

Cost-Volume-Profit (CVP) analysis is a powerful tool for hospitality businesses to assess the relationship between costs, sales volume, and profit. By using CVP analysis, hotels, restaurants, and other hospitality establishments can make data-driven decisions regarding pricing, break-even points, profit planning, and cost control, ultimately leading to improved financial performance and sustainability in a competitive industry.

4.4 CONTROLLING FOOD, BEVERAGE, AND LABOR COSTS

Controlling food costs is an important component of ensuring the profitability of your food service operation. However, food costs are only part of the picture. It is also necessary to control labor costs and forecast labor demands accurately if your business is to succeed. If you have more staff than is required, your labor costs will be too high and the company will lose money. If you have insufficient staff for a particular time period, customer service will suffer. Your goal in planning staffing and scheduling needs is to match labor supply with customer volume so that you can provide quality service without excessive cost.

The food service industry is labor intensive. Technology has not replaced people with equipment, though some foodservice operations are experimenting with robots which cook and assist in service. Unlike an automobile manufacturing plant, a restaurant cannot store its product until tomorrow or the next day if customers are not buying today. The same seat in the restaurant can only be sold a fixed number of times, based on the operating hours and number of turns (rate of turnover of customers). Therefore, it is critical to be able to forecast the number of customers you will have, the peak customer periods, and the staffing needed to provide service to those customers.

4.4.1 Food and Beverage Control in Restaurants

There are primarily four Food Service categories that need to be controlled in a restaurant.

1. **Food Cost-** Food cost is the cost incurred in preparing a dish. The food cost includes the plate as well as the period cost. It includes the cost of the raw materials utilized, such as meat, dairy, vegetables, grain, spices, etc. Non-alcoholic beverages are also included in the Food Cost.
2. **Beverage Cost-** Beverage cost is the cost related to alcoholic beverages served in restaurants and bars.
3. **Labor Cost-** Labour Cost includes the expenses incurred in maintaining the restaurant staff. It also consists of the taxes incurred on the payrolls of the employees.
4. **Other Expenses–** Other expenses include all the other costs that are incurred while running a restaurant. These can be utilities, rent, kitchen equipment, etc.

1. Food Cost Control in Restaurants

The first step of food and beverage control is Food Cost Control. But before you go ahead and take steps to control your Food Costs, you must analyze your actual food expenses and your Food Cost Percentage. This can be deduced by using predefined food and beverage cost control formulas. Food Cost Percentage is the portion of sales that was spent on food expenses. The cost of food sold divided by total sales gives you the Food Cost Percentage.

Once you know your exact food cost percentage, you can control your restaurant's Food Cost by following certain practices. These are:-

(i) Menu Item Forecasting

Menu item forecasting is an integral part of the Food and Beverage Control. Food Cost Control begins with forecasting the menu. Forecasting the menu is ascertaining the demand for different menu items. It is required to make decisions regarding raw materials to be ordered, the workforce to be supplied, time to be given, etc. Menu item forecasting will decrease your food waste and save you the cost of labor and raw materials. Depending on your customer psychology you must forecast your menu to ensure that your menu bolsters your sales.

Only after understanding the requirements of a particular item should you decide how much of a specific item should be prepared in your restaurant. You can forecast the sales of a dish by calculating its Popularity Index.

Popularity Index= Total number of a specific menu item sold/ Total number of all items sold

Predicted Number of Item Sold= Number of guests to visit your restaurant X Popularity Index

Save some unexpected surprises, it is usually quite easy to predict the number of guests to visit your restaurant. The footfall depends on several factors that must be taken into consideration, such as quality of your service, competition in your area, season, etc.

Over a period, you can predict the trend of footfall. Refer to the reports generated by your POS software that would give you a detailed insight into the amount of footfall in your restaurant, the busiest time of the day, the most popular dish, etc.

(ii) Standardized Recipes

Simply put, a standardized recipe consists of the detailed procedures to be used in preparing and serving each of your menu items and is integral to Food and Beverage Control. They give a set measure of the exact amount of ingredients to be used, declare the number of servings, set portions for each meal, and of course the preparation method. They are critical for controlling food and beverage costs as even a slight imbalance in the servings, cascaded over a period could lead to a severe dip in your margins.

(iii) Inventory Management

Stocking up the inventory is the first thing that restaurant owners do to get the operations going. However, managing the inventory is arguably the most important part of Food and Beverage Control. Before you go and start stocking up your inventory, you first need to define what inventory levels are needed in your restaurant. That is, you need to have a clear understanding of how much stock of which items would be needed in your restaurant kitchen, and for how long would those items last.

This comes from menu forecasting and yield management. When you forecast your menu, you determine how much of a dish will be required. When you manage yield per dish, you estimate how much raw material will be necessary to avoid wastage. Both of them together will work towards your food and beverage cost control by determining exactly how much inventory would be needed.

You need to consider the storage capacity of your inventory and shelf life and perishability of each item in mind before purchasing.

(iv) Purchasing

Much care needs to be given while purchasing inventory items or your food costs might escalate. You need to have a list of all the items that need to be purchased and how many to be purchased. You should also order enough to maintain a steady supply so that you don't run out of an item.

Inventory Management Software comes extremely handy in such cases. You can mark levels for each item in the inventory, and set reminders in the POS software that would alert you when the items run low, thus giving you ample time to order more. It is also advised to order items in a 'Purchase Group.' Purchase Groups because of the increased number of buyers gives you an edge over the supplier and so you can bargain for the price better.

Another factor that is crucial to Purchasing while keeping food and beverage cost control in mind is the Product Yield. Product yield essentially gives the amount of the item ordered that can be used for preparing the dish, that is, the Edible Portion. You must also consider the Waste Percentage of the item. Few items can be utilized whole while cooking; a significant portion is often lost while chopping, trimming, and cooking. Fortunately, you can calculate this loss, and thus order accordingly.

Waste Percentage is given by,

Waste Percentage= Product Loss/ Total Weight of the item when purchased.

(v) Vendor Management

Before you choose a vendor to supply the raw ingredients to your kitchen, you need to have the Purchase Order. It is essential to have a Purchase Order (PO) for all orders, no matter how trivial they are, and their records should be maintained.

Once you have the Purchase Order prepared, you need to decide on a vendor for supplying the stock to your restaurant kitchen. It is better to purchase from the same vendor to maintain the quality and taste of your food. Buying from the same vendor at the same price also helps in keeping the Fixed Cost of your menu. Also, to lower your purchasing costs order on credit instead of cash. That way you can order more for a considerably lower price. You can easily manage all your vendors through your restaurant POS.

(vi) Receiving

Receiving is one aspect of Food and Beverage control that is often overlooked, but it is just as important. The maximum discrepancy in stock happens while receiving the order. A not so honest employee may be tempted to steal from the inventory while receiving the order. Dishonest employees are also known to often strike an agreement with the Vendor and receive only half the amount of the ordered items while pocketing the money of the entire order.

To reduce the possibility of thefts, you should ensure that the purchasing agent and receiving clerk are two different individuals and that the entire purchasing and receiving procedure is carefully monitored.

Receiving clerks should be adequately trained to verify the weight, quantity, quality, and price of the products while collecting the stock items. They should be adequately equipped with the necessary tools for weighing and measurement of the stock.

(vii) Storage

All Food Costing and Control methods can go in vain if the stock items purchased are not stored properly, as food items are highly perishable. You must follow proper stocking practices to ensure longevity of the stocked goods. There should be separate areas for storing dry, refrigerated, and frozen products. Storage can be done in the following ways-

- **First In First Out:** In this method, the items are purchased first and consumed first. The items that are purchased first are more likely to spoil than the items purchased later. This method is preferred in cases of grocery, dairy, etc., and is the most popular method of storage utilization.
- **Last In First Out:** In this method, the items that are purchased last are consumed first. The idea behind this storage is that certain items such as

baked goods are best consumed when fresh. Last in First Out method helps to maintain quality and deliver high customer service.

The best way to store your inventory items is to ensure that the items are kept in a cool, dry, and sterile place. The items should also be appropriately rotated.

2. Beverage Cost Control in Restaurants

The second part of the Food and Beverage Control is Beverage Cost Control. The process of controlling Beverage costs is pretty much similar to Food Cost control. Keeping a check on the Beverage Costs can be more tedious as over pouring, and spilling is quite common and leads to inflated costs. You can track and control your beverage cost using this formula:-

Cost of beverage sold/ Beverage sold= Beverage Cost percentage

(i) Forecasting Beverage Sales

When you predict the number of guests you will serve and the revenues they will generate in a given future period, you have created a Beverage Sales forecast. Doing so will provide you a clear picture of the costs that you are looking at so that you can take definite steps to ensure there is no wastage or theft, and the beverage cost is controlled.

(ii) Standardized Drinks and Recipe Portions

The most important aspect of controlling Beverage Costs is setting up a Standardized drink recipe. You should also have a pouring policy through which you can regulate the drink size. Standardized portions are essential, and tools must be ensured to maintain the quality and quantity of the drink. Train your staff to use measuring cups or jiggers to avoid over pouring.

Also, decide how you wish to serve different types of liquor. For example, do you want to sell wine by the glass or by the bottle?

3. Labor Cost Control in Restaurants

The Restaurant Industry witnesses one of the highest attrition rates among all sectors, especially at the junior level, leading to high overall restaurant costs. You must be able to control your overall restaurant costs, to sustain your restaurant. Several factors contribute to a high Labor Cost, making it a significant part of the entire Restaurant Cost. Labor expense includes salaries and wages, but it consists of other labor-related costs as well such as employee meals, training, uniform, etc.

Calculate the Labor Cost Percentage of your restaurant using this formula-

Labor Cost Percentage: Cost of labor/ *total sales*

(i) Assessing and Managing Labor Productivity

While hiring employees for your restaurant, it is important first to determine the number of staff you'll be needing. However, it is not just sufficient to employ the staff and expect everything to fall miraculously into place. You need to assess the Productivity Ratio of each staff member to maintain a Productive Workforce.

Productivity standards represent what you should reasonably expect in the way of output per unit of labor input. A productivity standard merely is management's expectation of the productivity ratio of each employee. Establishing productivity standards for every employee is an essential management task and the first step in controlling payroll costs.

Schedule employees using productivity standards and forecasted sales volume.

Output/Input= Productivity Ratio

Eg: 60 guests/4 servers= 15 guests per server

(ii) Ensuring Employee Productivity

Follow these tips to enhance employee productivity in your restaurant.

1. **Employee selection-** Selecting the right employees plays a vital part in controlling costs. Create a clear Job Description and hiring criteria for each role and sort the applications on their basis. Conduct detailed interviews and background checks before getting anyone on board.
2. **Training and Supervision-** A trained employee is a productive employee. Before a new employee joins the team, ensure that he/she has been thoroughly trained. Do not hesitate from on-the-job training and even re-training if the need arises. Supervise the tasks wherever possible, or assign your manager to oversee the process.
3. **Scheduling-** Proper scheduling ensures that the correct number of employees is available to do the necessary amount of work. If too many employees are scheduled for a particular time, the productivity ratios will decline. If too few employees are scheduled, customer service levels may suffer or necessary tasks may not be completed on time or as well as they should be.

Scheduling efficiency can often be improved through the use of the split-shift, a technique used to match individual employee work shifts with peaks and valleys of customer demand.

4. Other Expenses Control

Apart from the Food, Beverage, and Labor, certain other expenses add up to the overall Restaurant Costs. A lot of you may ask the question of how to control restaurant costs with the least possible resources. These may seem trivial, but you need to give just as much attention to these for Food and Beverage Control. These can be categorized as Controllable and Non-Controllable, and Fixed and Variable Costs.

For example, rent is a Non-Controllable, fixed cost, while repairs and maintenance are variable costs.

Food and Beverage Control is an integral part of restaurant operations, and the points mentioned above of Food and Beverage Cost Control, Labor Cost Control, and Other Costs.

You need to consistently track and analyze the performance of your restaurant to identify the areas where you're bleeding money. Smart restaurant management software gives you the details of all the operations and helps you reduce your restaurant costs.

4.4.2 Food Cost Control

Cost control has been defined as the guidance and regulation of the costs of operating an undertaking. To guide and regulate costs means to ensure that they are in accordance with the pre-determined objectives of the business. Hence the notion of the guidance and regulation of costs pre supposes the existence of stated objectives as expressed in the policy statements and the budgets of the undertaking. Food cost control is simply cost control as applied to an undertaking operating food facilities. Food cost control is therefore cost control as applied in hotels, restaurants, canteens and similar establishments.

It is quite common in certain catering circles to regard food cost control as something wholly negative designed to cut costs in all directions. This is quite wrong. The object of food cost control is to ensure that costs are neither more or less than they ought to be that they are in line with the financial and catering policies of the establishment. An important feature, which distinguishes food cost control from systems of cost control in other industries, is its materials costs orientation. In most aspects of food cost control, attention is directed to primarily to the cost of materials (cost of sales) leaving the cost of labor and other operating costs very much in the background. This is mainly due to the fact that in the short run, labor and other operating costs tend to remain fixed and are thus largely uncontrollable

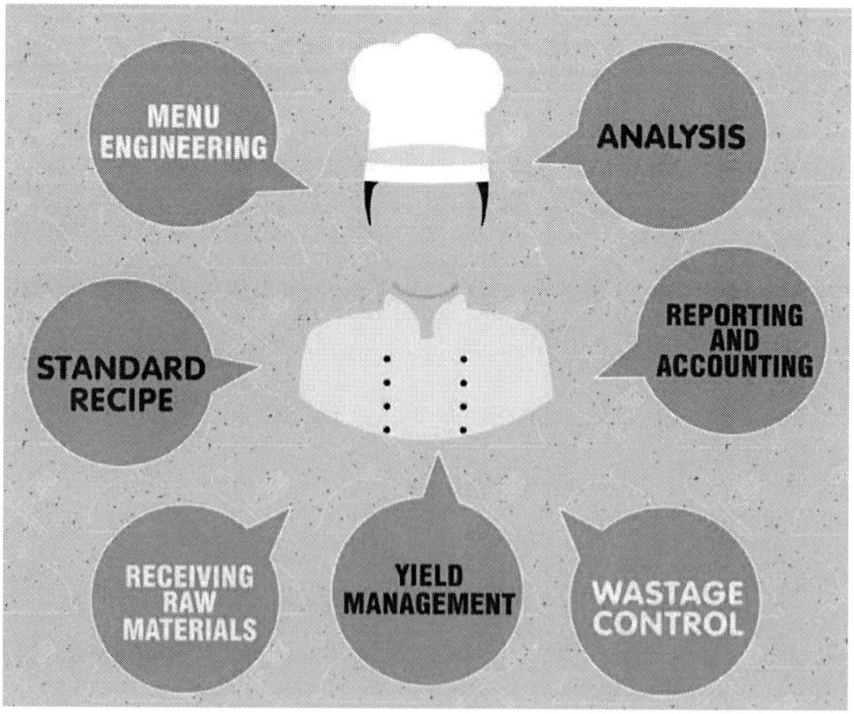

Restaurant margins are notoriously slim, so figuring out how to control costs, more often than not, boils down to a do or die scenario. Food cost plays a major role in any restaurant's success or failure—that French foie gras may be awesome, but not if it kills profit. Controlling food costs is the most important tasks for a restaurant owner. With proper menu planning, sales forecasting and employee training, a restaurant can prevent overspending on staff and supplies and still provide excellent quality dishes and service. Using a variety of planning, monitoring and evaluation techniques, you can continually manage these expenses to ensure you remain profitable without sacrificing quality.

The first step in controlling foods costs is to determine what they are, per diner. You can do this by calculating the expense of each ingredient that goes into each dish, or divide the total number of diners you serve per month by your monthly food costs. Food costs include the cost of the food, delivery, interest on those purchases, spoilage, theft and make-good meals returned for lack of quality.

Knowing the food costs of individual dishes lets you determine whether they belong on your menu. For example, if you're overhead cost per customer is $7 and your food cost for a specific lunch dish is $4, your cost to serve that customer is $12. Customers must pay $11, as well as for a drink, tip and tax, and your desired profit margin, which brings the bill to more than $15. If your target customer wants to spend $12 or less on lunch, this item doesn't belong on your menu. Some menu items can be loss leaders, used to attract customers who spend more on appetizers, drinks or desserts. Eliminate items that don't sell well, reducing your food costs.

Food cost may be defined as the cost of material used in producing the food sold. In other words, it is the cost of food consumed less the cost of staff meals. The main objects of food cost or material costing are:

- To ascertain the food cost of particular item on the menu
- To ascertain the total expenditure on food over a period of time.
- To control cost, price, profit margins and provide information for formulating an effective pricing policy.
- To disclose faulty purchasing and inefficient storing.
- To prevent pilferage and wastage.
- To ensure customer satisfactions.
- To bring cost- consciousness among the employees.
- To reduce cost and improve quality.
- To provide cost estimates to manager for developing budgets.
- To assist manager in making control decision.
- To evaluate pricing and establish future pricing.

4.4.3 Objectives of Food Cost Control

In many hotel and catering establishments, the expenditure on food is the largest single element of cost. The maintenance of Food cost at pre-determined levels are therefore of the greatest importance in ensuring the satisfactory profitability of each establishment. Even where catering is undertaken as a welfare facility food cost targets and costs ceilings are invariably imposed from above either in total or on a per unit basis. The main objectives of food cost control may be summarized as follows:

- Analysis of Income and Expenditure: In financial accounts, stress is usually placed on an ascertainment of total quantities e.g. sales, cost of sales, gross profit and net profit. In Food cost control on the other hand, much stress is placed on the analysis of such total quantities as between the various departments of the business. We are thus not satisfied with the ascertainment of the total gross profits of the business as a whole, but attempt to ascertain the cost of the profit on each department and each unit produced.
- Pricing of Food and Quotations: Another major objective of food cost control is to provide a sound basis for menu pricing and quotations in respect of banquets and special parties. Whilst often, menu prices are fixed by caterers by reference to prices charged by competitors, the correct approach to the problem is to determine menu and other prices in the light of the main costs and market considerations. Thus in addition to a knowledge of prices charged by competitors, the customers spending power etc., it is necessary to take into account the costs of the establishment. This can only be done by installing a sound system of Food Cost Control.
- Prevention of Waste and Inefficiencies: The purpose of control is to ensure that current results are in accordance with the pre-determined objectives of the business. Invariably, such objectives are expanded in terms of targets for turnover, cost ceilings and profit margins. Clearly, if such targets are to be reached, all possible forms of waste and inefficiencies must be prevented. In order to be effective in preventing waste and inefficiencies, a system of food cost control must cover the whole field of catering operations – from the purchase of the foodstuffs to the sale of the meals. It will be appreciated that as the catering process proceeds along the line along the line, linking the purchase of foodstuffs to the sale of the meals, there are numerous critical areas (e.g.: receipt of the incoming goods, preparation of meals and cash control) at which considerable losses may be incurred. An effective system of food cost control will therefore place particular stress on such critical areas of control and in this way help the establishment to reach its pre-determined targets.
- Data for Management Reports: An important function to be fulfilled by the food cost control system is the provision of data for periodical reports on food operations. It is said that the manager is like a judge. His judgment is only as good as the information supplied to him. Effective catering management pre supposes adequate food cost reporting which can only be based on a sound system of control.

4.4.4 Obstacles to Food Cost Control

In many respects food cost control is more difficult than systems of control in operation in other industries. The specific factors which make food cost control relatively more difficult are discussed here:

- Unpredictability of the Volume of Business: Sales instability is inherent in almost all catering operations. The changes, which occur in the volume of catering, are of several kinds. Firstly, the intensity of demand for food and drink will in most cases vary during the day. As a result, in the majority of establishments, it is possible to observe more or less, peaks of activity during the workday. Secondly, there are changes in the volume of business occurring from one day to the next. (Weekends). Finally, in catering establishments which are to some degree seasonal (resorts), turnover in season will be considerably greater than in the off season.
- Perishability of Food: Food is perishable both as a raw material and in the form of prepared meals. This presents the catering businesses with two major problems. Firstly, when buying perishable foodstuffs it is necessary to ensure that while current supplies are adequate there is no over buying. This applies particularly to highly perishable items such as soft fruits, salads and certain vegetables. Secondly, the quantity of food prepared for each service should be in line with the anticipated demand (forecast). Extra food necessitates re heating and re processing before sale thereby incurring further operating costs. Over production also leads to wastage because most of the times, this excess is not suitable for resale thereby leading to spoilage and wastage.
- Daily Variations in Food Production: In addition to changes in volume of sales there is continual change in the assortment of meals produced by catering units. The assortment of meals will change from one meal to another during the working day. Also, there are considerable changes of emphasis from one item on the menu to another. All shifts of emphasis entail considerable problems relating to all phases of the catering cycle and present many control problems relating to the purchase of the food stuff, preparations of the meals, pricing, cash collection etc. The nature of the products require considerably more control than is the case in many other industries.
- Short Cycle of Operations: Another characteristic feature of catering establishments, which presents an acute control problem, is the short cycle of operations. Whilst in many other manufacturing units the time taken by the production process sometimes lasts weeks (from the time of purchase of raw materials to the sale of the finished product), in a catering operation the cycle is fairly short and lasts at the most a couple of days. Therefore there is little time to exercise control and remedial action if and when required. As a result, checks are done retrospectively. Hence a daily and at times weekly control check needs to be applied.
- Multiplicity of Low Value Transactions: The spending power of customers will vary from one type of organization to another. Even when the customer spending power is high, the total amount spent by the customer consists of a number of small payments for the individual items comprising his meal. The turnover of the catering establishments is therefore the result of a number of low value transactions. This presents

several control problems. Control tasks such as forecast of sales, stores, pricing and cash collection are therefore made more difficult.

- High Degree of Departmentalization: Whereas some catering units have one selling outlet, there are many, which have several revenue producing units (e.g. Birdy's, Croissant Etc.). This also applies to the large hotels, which have several F&B outlets including Banquet facilities and Bars. The larger the number of outlets, the greater the difficulties and the more arduous the problems of control. Whilst the analysis of total revenue presents some difficulties, these are magnified when the number of outlets increases. One of the problems of food cost control is to determine the results of each department (outlet), even though the production unit is the same.

4.4.5 Methodology of Food Cost Control

We have defined Food Cost Control, described its objectives and dealt with the difficulties which its application presents. Now, we must deal with the method which should be applied in the development of a system of Food Cost Control.

The development of an effective system of Food Cost Control resolves itself into three distinct phases:

- Phase I consists of basic policy decisions in relation to the financial and catering policies of the establishment.
- Phase II consists of the necessary routine operation controls revolving around the catering cycle.
- Phase III consists of what may be described as control after the event or post operational control.

Phase I Basic Policy Decisions: Food cost control is a byproduct of the interplay of two basic and sometimes conflicting considerations. When one reflects on what most forms of catering are about, the inevitable conclusion is that in the final analysis, only two things finally matter profitability and the customer. The profitability of the establishment is the ultimate objective whereas the provision of a satisfactory standard of food and service is the means by which the ultimate objective is reached. Hence, before a system of cost control is developed, it is important to evolve the following:

- *A Financial Policy* – setting out the intentions of the management with regard to the forecasted profitability. This involves setting up a profit target, the determination of departmental profit target and the planning of a whole pattern of differential profit margins in respect of each menu.

The financial policy of a catering establishment should be determined as in the five steps listed are:

- o Determine the overall profit target. (return on capital employed)
- o Determine what percentage of net profit on sales must be aimed at.
- o By reference to the budgeted volume of sales, the type of service and the degree of comfort to be provided to the customer. Determine what percentage of revenue will be required to cover labor costs and

overheads, and what percentage of revenue can therefore be available to cover costs of sales.

- o By reference to the projected sales mix, determine the cost of sales for each department of the business: food, beverages, alcoholic drinks and tobacco.
- o Having determined the overall cost of sales for each department, plan the differential profit margin for each group of items offered on the menu, wine list etc.

- **A Catering Policy** - defining the market to be aimed at and describing how it is to be catered for

Phase II Operational Control: We have now outlined the first stage in Food Cost Control. The second stage consists of a sum total of built in checks (inspection of incoming goods for quality and quantity), technological procedures (yield testing) and clerical procedures (writing out requisitions). These should be planned so as to cover the whole cycle of catering operations. We must therefore deal with operational control in relation to:

a) Buying/Purchasing
b) Receiving
c) Storing and Issuing
d) Preparation
e) Sales

Each of the above stages constitutes a highly critical stage of Food Cost Control. Any system installed must therefore cover all the five stages.

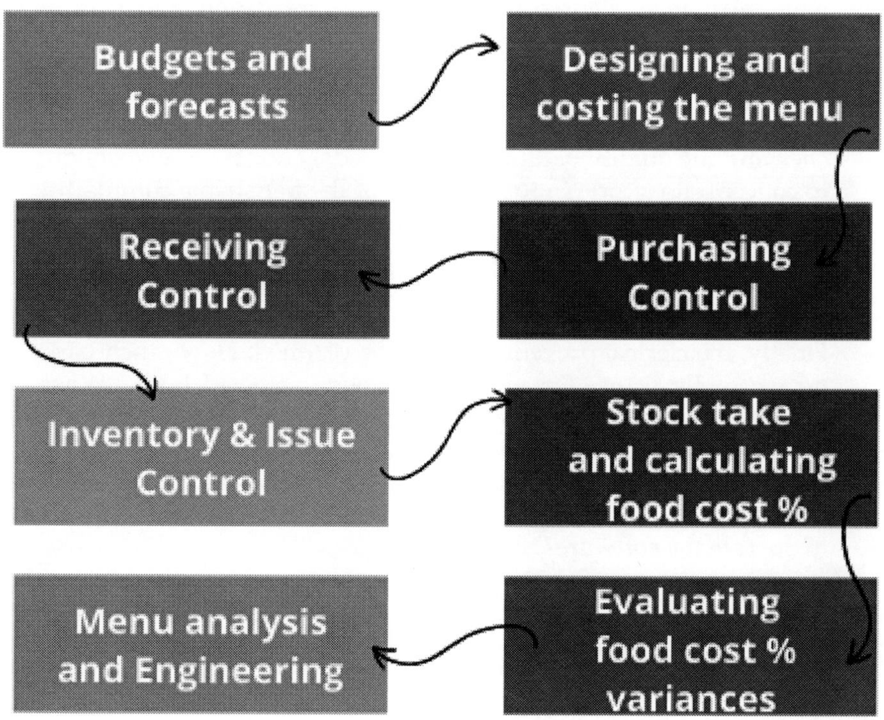

a). Buying – There are four main points to be considered at this stage.

- Firstly, there is yield testing. We have already evolved a catering policy, identified the type of customer, decided on the type of the menu and established a set of costs and gross profit targets. The object of yield testing is simply to discover the respective of yields of a whole range of commodities available for any one purpose and so determine the costs concerned. It is only on the basis of yield testing that we can compile the necessary purchase specifications. By the way, understand that there is a difference between yield testing and product testing. In product testing, we are mainly concerned with the physical properties of the food – texture, composition, keeping quality, flavor etc. In reality, tests are carried out which would combine the two objectives.
- Secondly, we have Purchase Specifications, which are concise descriptions of an item of food. This helps the caterer to communicate with the supplier. Varieties of tomatoes are available, some suitable for salads and some that may be used for soups and gravies.
- Thirdly, the methods of buying must be considered. It is clear that no single method of buying is suitable for all types of food. Hence, in relation to each type of commodity, we must decide whether it should be bought open market, via a tender or local purchase/imported.
- Finally, we must determine clerical procedures. It is necessary to decide who originates, sanctions and places purchase orders and what sort of documentary evidence is to be used. The use of the computer and material management packages is widespread and will help generate reports, which helps immensely with food cost control procedures.

b) Receiving – There seem to be three main points here.

- The first is quality control. Some person must be made responsible for checking the quality of all incoming goods, and it is obviously important to concentrate efforts in the direction of the perishable commodities. The quality of nonperishables tends to be constant over a period of time.
- Secondly, we must assign responsibility for the quantity inspection. The goods receiving clerk normally perform this task. Blind receiving is now quite a popular receiving technique especially in large-scale operations.
- Finally, the clerical procedures must be planned. How much paper work do we really want? Do we keep a goods received book? What action should be taken in the event of non-delivery or short delivery? These questions need to be answered and the policies framed. Today, the computer helps to eliminate a lot of paper work. But, is the organization financially equipped to install computers? Do they possess the personnel to operate the software??

c) Storing and Issuing – Several important matters must be planned for the third stage of the cycle.

- First, there is the problem of stock records. It is necessary to decide whether or not these will be kept at all and also for how long!

- Secondly, the matter of pricing of issues must be decided upon. In other words, we must choose one or more of the following for computing the cost of food consumed:
    - o Actual purchase price
    - o Simple average price
    - o Weighted average price
    - o Inflated price
    - o Standard price
- Thirdly, stocktaking must be considered. Decisions must be made with regard to its frequency, the pricing of stocks, methods with dealing with discrepancies etc. Finally, the necessary clerical procedures must be established and introduced. Who writes the requisitions? How many copies? Who will sanction? These are some of the questions that must be answered.

d) Preparing – This is possibly the most critical stage of the cycle. The cost of food consumed depends on two factors: the number of meals produced and the food cost per meal. In order therefore to control food costs we must be able to control the numbers being catered for (we must have some method of volume forecasting) and control the food cost per meal in advance (standard recipes and portion control). Volume forecasting is a method of predicting the sales volume for a future period. In order to be of practical value, the forecast must predict the total number of covers as well as the choice of menu items. The process of volume forecasting consists of two stages:

- First, we have what we know as the initial forecast. This is done once a week in respect of each day of the following week. The initial forecast is based on sales histories, data relating to advance bookings as well as current trends. When the initial forecast has been completed, the predicted sales are converted into quantities of raw material. Purchase orders can then be prepared and sent out to the suppliers.
- The second stage is known as the final forecast. And this usually takes place a day before. The final forecast takes into account the latest developments including weather etc. If required, supplier's orders can be amended. It must be understood that volume forecasting is not a perfect method of prediction. We cannot really tell the future. It does however help to minimize over and under production of food.

e) Selling – At this last stage of the catering cycle, we are concerned with three main problems. The financial and catering policies will have defined the price policy of the business. In operational food cost control, we are therefore only concerned with the routine pricing of food. Where differential profit margins have been evolved, this is a relatively simple matter. A more important tactical task that has to be faced is to ensure that any increase in the quantity of food prepared is matched by a corresponding increase in cash received from the customer. This will require a restaurant checking system. The final problem is of cash control. We must ensure that all amounts received by the waiting staff are paid to the cashier. He in turn has to deposit each day's takings.

Phase III – Control after the Event: The last phase of cost control is concerned with three important matters:

- Food Cost reporting
- Assessment of Results
- Corrective Action where appropriate and necessary

The *first* point is obviously a matter of some importance mainly for reasons of the specific character of catering operations. Food is a highly perishable commodity and whether in the form of cooked meals or raw materials, it cannot be stored indefinitely. Moreover, the demand for catering facilities shows unpredictable trends and unexpected changes. The cycle of production is extremely short, unlike other manufacturing operations such as automobiles for example. All this means that current operations must be reviewed frequently and that there is a need for a short review period.

The *second* important aspect of food cost reporting is concerned with analysis. A catering business, unlike most other businesses performs a dual function: production and selling. Furthermore, many catering establishments are highly departmentalized, especially large hotels and industrial canteens. The assortment of production (large menus) changes from day to day. All these factors mean that from the point of view of control; analytical reports showing separate results for each branch of the catering operation are necessary. The assessment of results is concerned with an appreciation of how far the actual results of food operations correspond with the actual results. This means that assessment is not possible without a yardstick for measurement. We could assess current results in relation to those of food cost review periods or we could assess current actual results in relation to budgeted results. Obviously, the second is the preferred one.

This brings us to the ***last*** stage: corrective action. Surely, any action that is taken following receipt of a food cost report depends on circumstances and reasons of each case. Therefore, it is difficult to lay down specific guidelines for corrective action and it here that the manager's tact and experiences as well as his feel for the job come into play. Questions of praise, reprimand, authority and responsibility are very largely a matter of human relations.

4.4.6 Labor Cost Control

Labor cost control is a process used by managers to direct, regulate, and restrain employees' actions in order to obtain desired levels of performance at appropriate levels of cost. To the inexperienced, labor cost control is sometimes mistakenly taken to suggest the mere reduction of payroll costs to their irreducible minimum. This can be achieved by employing a bare minimum number of people paid the minimum legal wage. But there is much more to labor cost control than just minimizing dollar wages, a fact sometimes ignored by owners and managers who take the short-term view of operations, thinking only of immediate profits and not taking into account the long-term effects of their policies and actions

Short-term policies geared strictly to minimizing immediate costs may have undesirable long-term effects, including decreased dollar sales, increased operating costs, and even business failure. For example, hiring a full staff of employees at minimum wage may minimize immediate labor costs but lead to poor-quality products, high labor turnover, customer dissatisfaction, decreasing sales volume, and a host of other long-term problems. Obviously, management should pay the wage rates necessary to attract and retain qualified personnel, but not more. To overpay may make for an operation that cannot be profitable.

Appropriate performance levels differ from establishment to establishment. For some (fast-food restaurants serving frozen, portioned products that need only be heated and served by comparatively unskilled labor), desired levels of performance may be such that minimum-wage employees are appropriate; for others (fine restaurants attempting to offer the finest food, wines, and service in their areas), appropriate levels of performance may be such that wages considerably above those prevailing in the area may be required.

But level of performance is not simply a function of wage rates. Unskilled employees in fast-food establishments cannot perform at appropriate levels unless they are provided with appropriate equipment, given suitable training, placed in a working environment conducive to getting work done, and supervised in a manner that will inspire them to work and remain on the staff. This is also true for highly skilled employees in the finest restaurants. Suitable wage levels do not guarantee appropriate performance. Many other factors are involved in ensuring suitable levels of performance.

The Purpose of Labor Cost Control

The primary purpose of labor cost control is to maximize the efficiency of the labor force in a manner consistent with the established standards of quality and service. Ideally, each employee's services will be utilized as effectively as possible. There should be a sufficient number of dishwashers working to ensure that dishes are washed as efficiently as possible, but there should be no time when dishwashers stand around with no work to do. Similarly, a sufficient number of servers should ensure that all customers are served as quickly as possible while standards of service are maintained, but at no time should there be more than a sufficient number to serve the customers then in the restaurant.

4.4.7 Identifying Labor Costs

Labor costs in the foodservice industry continue to increase from year to year. This can be due to an increasing minimum wage and pressure to pay all employees a "living wage" rather than relying on tipping to make up the difference. In addition, costs have increased because of the stiff competition for skilled service employees, which has not only increased wages but also fringe benefits covered by the employer.

Most students understand that wages and salaries are labor costs, but there are many other labor-related costs in addition to the wages/salaries paid. Employee benefits or "fringe benefits" include various types of non-wage compensation provided to employees in addition to their normal wages or salaries.

This list includes such costs as:

- Social security taxes (employer share)
- Medicare taxes (required employer tax)
- Unemployment taxes
- Worker's compensation
- Group Insurance, such as health, dental, vision, life, etc.
- Vacation, personal and sick leave
- Disability income protection
- Retirement benefits
- Uniforms and laundry
- Employee meals (free or discounted)
- Employee training
- Tuition reimbursement or employer student loan contributions
- Use of a company car, or even company housing or a housing allowance
- Mileage for using a personal car for business
- Daycare (free or subsidized)
- Moving expenses
- Profit sharing

Some operations may even have other labor-related costs not included in the above list. The real cost of an hour of work is not simple to compute because of the fringe benefits and hidden costs. The first step to identifying labor costs is to categorize costs so they can be picked up as labor costs. For example, employee meals and laundering of employee uniforms are fringe benefits that may be hidden in other cost categories.

Labor costs may be divided into the following categories:

- Management (fixed labor/payroll cost)
- Full-time employees (fixed labor/payroll cost)
- Overtime/substitute employees (variable labor/payroll cost)
- Part-time employees (variable labor/payroll cost)
- Fringe benefits

Overtime should be nonexistent or nearly nonexistent. Management needs to keep an eye on those employees whose time is nearing 40 hours. Money spent on overtime usually indicates poor management and inefficiency.

There is much to learn from calculating the real cost of a labor hour. For instance, it is shocking when you consider that in some cases only about 50% of the labor hour is spent productively. It helps when evaluating labor costs to break down the costs by 15-minute intervals and relate the cost to the amount of work that can be produced. When management looks at the cost of a break, idle time, and "leaning" time, it is easy to see the value of training in efficiency, good scheduling of employees, and planning work carefully.

4.5 SUMMARY

Cost management is a fundamental process for companies aiming to regulate and plan the expenses associated with conducting business. This entails customizing cost control strategies for individual projects as well as integrating such practices into the broader business model. In the hospitality industry, understanding and managing costs—ranging from fixed and variable costs to labor and food costs—are crucial for maintaining profitability while still delivering quality experiences to guests. The structure of an organization's accounting information system, which includes both financial accounting and cost management accounting systems, plays a significant role in facilitating effective cost management.

The approach to cost management in modern business practices has evolved to encompass a wider perspective than traditional costing systems. It focuses not only on the expenses incurred but also on the factors that influence these costs, such as cycle times, quality, and process efficiency. This broader focus is more commonly observed in chain hotels, where the implementation of sophisticated accounting and cost management systems is more prevalent compared to independent hotels.

Cost control strategies start with the budgeting process and extend to the meticulous management of business expenses to enhance profitability. The application of different costing methods, such as Marginal Costing and Standard Costing, helps in understanding the impact of production volume and efficiency on profits. Variance analysis, comparing predetermined standard costs with actual incurred costs, serves as a crucial tool for cost management.

Moreover, Cost-Volume-Profit (CVP) analysis is highlighted as a valuable tool for making informed decisions about pricing, production levels, and profitability, crucial for hospitality businesses. Beyond food costs, controlling labor costs and accurately forecasting labor demands are pivotal for the financial success of food service operations. Labor cost control is thus emphasized as a key managerial activity aimed at achieving desired performance levels without incurring excessive costs. Together, these components form the bedrock of effective cost management, enabling businesses in the hospitality industry and beyond to optimize their operations and achieve financial sustainability.

4.6 REFERENCES

- Abdel-Kader, M. & Luther R. (2006). Management Accounting Practices in the British Food and Drinks Industry. British Food Journal 108(5): 336-357.
- Cadez, S. & Guilding C. (2008). An Exploratory Investigation of an Integrated Contingency Model of Strategic Management Accounting. Accounting, Organizations and Society. 33(7-8): 836-863.
- Guan, L., Hansen D. R. & Mowen M. M. (2009). Cost Management. Mason, Ohio: South-Western Cengage Learning.
- Hansen, D. R. & Mowen M. M. (2006). Cost Management: Accounting and Control. Mason, Ohio: Thomson South-Western.
- Joe A, 2009. Control your food cost, genuine Hospitality consulting. Available on www.genuinehc.com/articles/restaurant-startup-andgrowth/27-control-your-food-cost. January, 2009.
- Joe D, 2008. Essential food cost control. Available on www.hotelfandb.com/biol/march-april2008-food-cost-control.asp

- Makrigiannakis, G & Soteriades M. (2007). Management Accounting in the Hotel Business: The Case of the Greek Hotel Industry. International Journal of Hospitality and Tourism Administration 8(4): 47-76.
- Mishra HA (2012) How to manage food cost in hotels. Available on http://articles.economictimes.indiatimes.com/2012-10- 25/news/3472 990 7_1_cost-hotel-industry-food-service.(accessed 25 October, 2012)
- Mongiello, M. & Harris P. (2006). Management Accounting and Corporate Management: Insights into Multinational Hotel Companies. International Journal of Contemporary Hospitality Management 18(5): 364-379.

CHAPTER 5

Revenue Manager's Role in Hospitality Industry

INTRODUCTION

Revenue management is an extremely important concept within the hospitality industry, because it allows hotel owners to anticipate demand and optimize availability and pricing, in order to achieve the best possible financial results.

Revenue manager is responsible for management of the revenues coming into the hotel through various channels. In simple words: Sales is responsible to generate demand and revenue manager is responsible to manage the demand.

Revenue managers are generally given the responsibility to generate business through electronic channels and in-house reservation department. Yes, pricing and managing online channels is responsibility of a revenue manager.

Revenue manager predicts the market and hotel demand through forecasting. There are many actions we can take to change the demand level for a hotel. Some of the actions are: Pricing, yield management – LOS (length of stay restrictions), CTA (closed to arrival), channel management – opening and closing certain channels. Revenue managers must have a concrete understanding and familiarity with perishable inventory and the pricing strategies and demand management required for this unique set.

While non-perishable inventory examples include cars, consumer electronics and many other items without a specific shelf life, perishable inventory creates other challenges. A deep understanding of the perishable set is highly important for the hotel revenue manager as once a hotel room night passes, it's gone.

Incentivizing revenue manager may be more important than incentivizing sales teams. Both functions need to be highly motivated and passionate about moving the hotel's business forward. Making reward commensurate with performance means the revenue manager must be measured over time from a start point. Logically that's when they took responsibility for your hotel's revenue and profitability. After that it's between periodic performance reviews.

Revenue managers can be evaluated against a select number of KPI metrics. Which metrics to use depends on the objectives and strategies senior management set for the hotel or the enterprise? Some organizations are primarily revenue driven.

Successful revenue managers all need to work in close collaboration with GMs, heads of finance, directors of operations, marketing and food and beverage. It follows that the revenue manager must have a solid working knowledge of each of these functional areas. A full working knowledge of the challenges and business drivers for each business function head is ideal. Seek candidates with broad hotel operations experience (in addition to education) who can interact with leaders of other hotel departments.

5.1 REVENUE MANAGEMENT IN THE HOSPITALITY INDUSTRY

Revenue management in the hospitality industry has taken great strides since its early and simplistic days of applying yield management as one seeking to maximize revenues by varying prices in response to buyer demand. A truly effective hospitality revenue manager must do much more than merely react to guests. Today, revenue management in the lodging industry is an overarching approach that considers total dollars spent on rooms as well as across all other areas of a property. In foodservice, revenue management means optimizing revenues through strategic pricing and the effective management of production and service capacity.

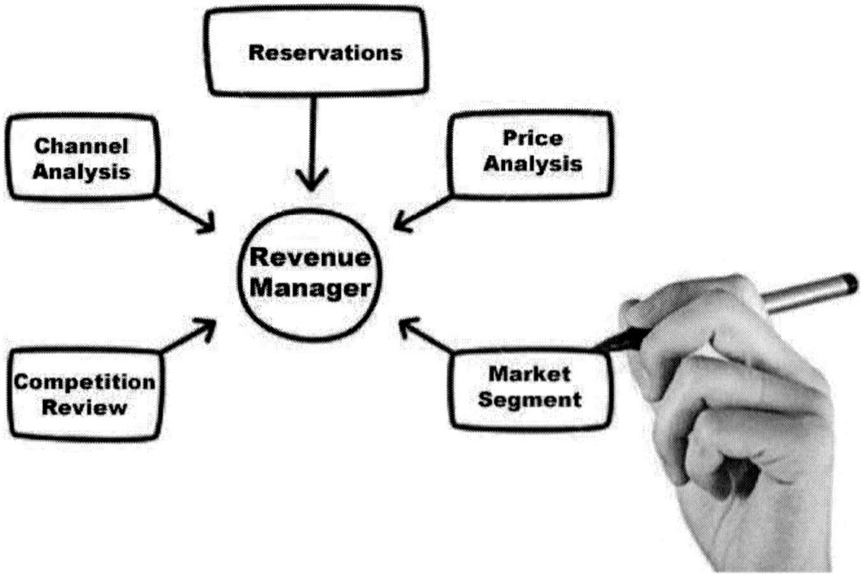

Figure 5.1: Revenue management elements.

Revenue management has advanced from a focus on variable demand for those products offered for sale to a focus on how customers and channels respond to pricing and how to use that information to direct and shape consumer behavior. This means RMs must increasingly focus on forecasting demand, distribution channel management, internal communications, and training staff in modern revenue management concepts and strategies. Doing so makes good sense for many businesses; thus, a reasonable question to be asked is, "Why is revenue management in the hospitality industry any different from revenue management in other fields?"

The rationale for revenue management as a distinct field of study within the hospitality industry stems from the fact that, unlike revenue managers in many other industries, RMs in hospitality must manage both hard and soft supply constraints.

A hard supply constraint is a restriction on product availability that, in the short run, cannot be remedied at any price; while a soft supply constraint can at some cost allow for additional product availability. Understanding the implications inherent in managing hard and soft constraints makes the hospitality RM's job quite unique.

5.1.1 Hard Constraint Management

In some cases, sellers can produce as much of a product as they can possibly sell. In such a situation, producers calculate their production costs, forecast buyer demand, and seek to charge a price that exceeds their costs, maximizes their income, and ensures a profit. To illustrate, consider the maker of a breakfast cereal. To optimize revenues the selling price chosen by the manufacturer is of critical importance. In all likelihood, as the price of the cereal is reduced, sales will increase but profits per box sold would decline. As the cereal's selling price increases, sales will likely be reduced—however, profits per box sold would increase.

The challenge for the cereal seller is to determine the optimal price at which to sell the product, producing more if more cereal were sold and making less if fewer boxes were sold. Consider further that such a producer could, at the end of each day, assess the amount of cereal produced and sold and then use that information to adjust the next day's cereal production. In such a business, the job of the revenue manager would not be extremely complex. It would essentially consist of establishing the optimum price, monitoring cereal sales, and then adjusting the amount produced (inventory) each day to equal buyers' demand.

Assume, however, that our cereal producer encountered the following set of interesting circumstances:

- Once the cereal factory was built, the amount of cereal produced each day could not be increased or decreased each day regardless of how much was or was not sold on previous days.
- Demand for the cereal produced will vary widely, based on the time of year or even the day of the week.

- Any cereal not sold on the day it was made could not be sold the next day; rather it would disappear from inventory forever at the end of that day.

To summarize, consider that production levels cannot change, demand for the product will vary greatly and no unsold product from today can be sold tomorrow. Clearly, this cereal producer now faces a world filled with significant challenges. That world is the daily world of RMs in the lodging industry. This is true because, for hoteliers:

- The number of rooms offered for sale each day cannot vary.
- Demand for rooms varies widely, based on the time of year or even the day of the week.
- Any room night not sold on a given day disappears forever at the end of that day.

RMs in the lodging industry face hard supplies constraints because the number of rooms they have available for sale cannot be increased, at any price, in response to increased short-term demand. Nor can the number of rooms offered for sale is reduced in periods of slackened demand. In addition, while the cereal producer in our hypothetical example can keep enough unsold stock on hand to supply buyers in short-term periods of heightened or unanticipated demand, while reducing production during periods of weak demand, the hotelier cannot.

The lodging industry is not the only one in which hard supply constraints are encountered. A business selling gas through its pipelines is constrained by the capacity (size) of the lines. Hair salons are constrained by the number of chairs and hair stylists available to service their customers. In each of these businesses, as well as in other businesses facing hard supply constraints, RMs are forced to implement one of three income-management alternatives when demand for their products is high:

1. Establish one fixed price, and then sell to customers on a first come-first served basis until they have exhausted their supply of products.
2. Allocate the limited supply to selected customers who meet established criteria (i.e., they are volume buyers, repeat buyers, or they hold other favored buyer status).
3. Raise their prices until demand is reduced sufficiently to equal the available supply.

5.1.2 Soft Constraint Management

Lodging industry RMs face hard supply constraints. Most foodservice operators face soft supply constraints. As a result, the revenue management challenges faced by foodservice operators are different from those encountered by hoteliers. The first of these differences relates to capacity. Consider the fact that limited-service hotels, which make up over 75 percent of the hotels in the United States, essentially sell just one product: guest rooms.

Full-service hotels sell additional products and services, but their guest room night sales are as constrained as are those of their colleagues in the limited-service lodging segment. On any given night, hoteliers simply cannot increase their number of room nights available for sale at any price. Unlike the supply of hotel rooms foodservice supply is based on two factors, rather than one product.

In this context, foodservice supply in a sit-down restaurant can be defined with the following formula:

Number of seats available × Hours of seat availability × Total available seat supply

Thus, for example, a restaurant with 150 seats that is open for 12 hours per day would have a total available seat supply of 1,800 seat hours (150 seats 12 hours 1,800 total available seat hours). With 1,800 seat hours available, longer dining times reduce the number of customers that can be served in that number of seat hours, while shorter dining times increase the number of guests that can be served.

Excluding, for this illustration, the ability of the foodservice operation to increase supply via the use of carry-out or delivery sales, the manager of this business could also increase the available supply of seat hours by increasing the number of seats in the operation or by extending its operating hours. Thus, for example, a restaurant currently closing its doors at 10:00 P.M. could elect to increase available seat supply by extending its closing time until 11:00 P.M. Doing so would increase its operating costs somewhat but it would also increase the seat hours available and thus its supply capacity. In response to reduced demand, the operator could, of course, elect to reduce operating hours. That's the good news. The less good news is that demand for dining between 10:00 P.M. and 11:00 P.M. will likely be quite limited.

Recall that a hard or soft supply constraint affects an RM's decision making primarily when demand exceeds supply. Also, it is important to recognize that despite its importance, restaurateurs do not gain increased revenues merely from increasing seat capacity or supply, but rather from the amount of money spent by those guests occupying each available seat.

Thus, RMs in the foodservice industry should be especially concerned with RevPASH (revenue per available seat hour).

From a revenue management perspective, it is also interesting to note that hotels and restaurants vary greatly in their knowledge about their customer's spending. Hoteliers know that a guest occupying a room will pay the room rate agreed upon in advance and confirmed at check-in. In contrast, restaurateurs do not know the income-producing capacity of an occupied seat until the guest has placed his or her order. This, of course, presents an additional challenge for RMs working in the foodservice industry. Even with this setback, foodservice operators benefit from a positive difference between themselves and those in the lodging industry. Recall that an unsold room night is lost forever. The restaurateur, however, who does not sell an aged Porterhouse steak on a given night, will likely have the opportunity to sell that same item the next day. Again, some additional costs may be incurred due to product shrinkage, spoilage, and the like, but the ability to recover at least some of the business's lost revenue-generating capacity related to products sold is retained.

A final difference between the lodging industry and the foodservice industry is that of daily price variation. RMs working in the lodging industry is accustomed to price changes made on a monthly, weekly, daily, and even hourly basis in response to changes in demand. Their foodservice counterparts have not adopted this custom and thus do not typically adjust their prices in a similar fashion, although some restaurateurs do vary prices between meal periods—for example, a lunch price versus dinner price for the same menu item

Table 1. *Revenue management characteristics in the hospitality industry*

Issue	Cereal Maker	Hotelier	Restaurateur
Supply constraint	None	Hard	Soft
Ability to increase supply	Unlimited	None	Limited
Ability to decrease supply	Unlimited	None	Limited
Ability to carry over excess supply to the next day	Yes	Service capacity: No Product: No	Service capacity: No Product: Yes
Practice price modification in response to variation in short-term demand	Optional	Almost always	Almost never
Can benefit from effective Revenue Management practices	Yes	Yes	Yes

Table 1 summarizes some of the significant differences, similarities, and common practices that distinguish hospitality industry RMs from those in other businesses, such as, in this example, the breakfast cereal industry.

5.2 ROLE AND ACTIVITIES OF REVENUE MANAGER BETWEEN INDIVIDUAL AND TEAM COMPETENCIES

Revenue management (RM) is one of the most significant innovations to have affected the tourism industry in recent years. The meaning of RM has evolved over time, shifting from the initial practice of optimizing the yield of the **average daily rate (ADR)**, which is instrumental for maximizing revenue, to the current philosophy that is aimed at maximizing general profits at the level of property and not just the optimal management of rooms.

For this purpose, the companies that adopt this approach should match customer purchase intention at a specific time with the price of the product at that time. A company optimizes the revenue if it charges for the service the maximum price that it could seek from each segment of demand "in that context and at that moment". The result is an extreme mutability of the price of the

product: here variations no longer defined ex ante according to the time of year (e.g. hotel season, discount periods, promotions days) but instead specified in an extemporaneous manner based on a series of factors. These factors include external variables (e.g. competitors' product demand, combination of events, meteorological situation) and business situations (e.g. request for the asset, availability, monitoring of the costs and revenues of the structure, target objectives).

This dynamic price management is based on an important pillar: information. However, though information is a common assumption, companies carry out RM in the most diverse ways, depending on the variety of the incoming information considered in the pricing definition, the level of complexity, detailed information used to identify company performance, or the type of support used in information management processes. Regarding the support, different RM systems depend on the presence and type of software dedicated to this activity.

Scholars have dwelt extensively on the information and variables to be considered in RM activities, the importance of forecasts, the measurements of chamber performance, and the tools for implementation, and the impact on performance, the main problems and erroneous beliefs, as well as the challenges for the future.

Linked with these aspects, revenue management was examined regarding different levels (the strategic level, the management level, the operational level), with growing attention towards a strategic and holistic vision from an initially more tactical and instrumental approach

There is no doubt that though there are many advantages linked with a decision support system, RM is not a mechanical activity; it is a management approach that depends on the will, sensitivity, and skills of the revenue manager and the team of people who collaborate with him.

On these aspects and on the role and competences required by RM, the literature is less abundant. Therefore, there are many aspects of a more organizational nature on which greater depth is needed. For instance, who plays this role in hotels? Is it a subject inside or outside the structure? Is it a single individual or a team of people? Where does this choice come from and what does it involve? In terms of content, what does a revenue manager really do and what does the extent of the revenue manager's activities depend on?

Numerous contributions focus on operational aspects that include the techniques and tools for dynamic pricing of the products offered and a whole series of connected choices such as decisions relating to the ranges of variation, sales channels, statistical techniques used, etc. Writings on operational aspects can be distinguished between non-pricing RM tools and pricing RM tools.

Beyond the technical and managerial aspects, it was immediately clear to scholars that RM is a strategic approach and that many writings have highlighted its important role in determining the economic and financial success of hotels as well as other hospitality organizations. With time, RM is increasingly orienting itself towards a strategic and holistic vision, abandoning the tactical and instrumental approach.

This view raises the problem of how to measure global performance —i.e. which measurement metrics to consider (average daily occupancy, revenue per available room (RevPAR), **or gross operating profit per available room (GOPPAR), among others.**

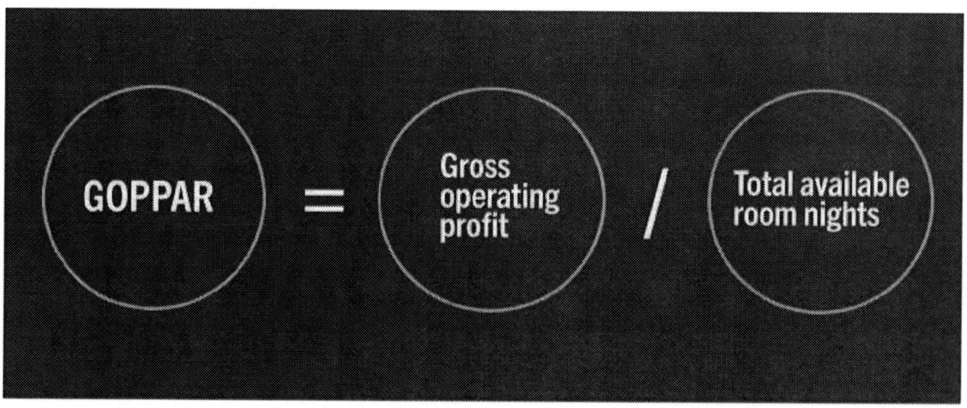

But all, owing to an increasingly strategic approach, a topic assumes particular importance—the complexity of the role played by those involved in revenue management and the consequent extent of the skills that must be possessed.

Compared to many topics of study on RM contained in the literature, the organizational aspects related to those who carry out the RM activities, how they are distributed within various company functions and the competencies of revenue managers are less present in the studies. They have begun to draw more attention in recent years, although the impact of this technique on the skills of hotel management has still not been completely investigated.

There is no single way to understand the role and relative place of the RM function. Ferguson and Smith have examined the revenue manager in an evolutionary key and identified three stages in the role and practices of the revenue manager. In the first phase of RM, which is characterized by seasonal price policies (linked to high-, medium-, and low-demand periods), some basic restrictions on high demand (e.g. minimum night stay), discount contracts for particular categories (e.g. groups, companies), and usually the position of a hotel revenue manager did not exist. The reservation manager implemented the pricing policies, but they did not generally decide about such policies. Where the position of the revenue manger was created as a separate and distinct position from the reservation manager, this role was assigned for providing reports to others, who, in turn, made decisions regarding strategic pricing and allotment. It was a supporting role to the sales and marketing director, for whom they prepared reports and other material for business decisions, focusing on RevPAR as a key metric for measuring the hotel's performance.

The revenue manager is considered an expert who reports directly to the general manager of the hotel and makes instant decisions daily relating to price dynamics in collaboration with the sales and marketing director. This has led to the additional expansion of RM responsibilities to include overseeing of other revenue-producing departments such as restaurants, meeting rooms, and others. In Stage 3, the expansion of the RM technique, even in small hotels that cannot afford a special representative, has led the Alberghire chains to provide this type of service with the centralization of the role even at the level of property and to assign responsibilities to a single subject who is often located remotely, away from the properties. The revenue manager, therefore, becomes a consultant, taking on an increasingly specialized and proactive role that requires special training and skills to manage diverse variables and information.

In some companies, the RM unit reports directly to the senior management and the revenue manager function is central to the big functions of the organizational chart. In other companies, the RM unit reports to an assistant management position and its responsibility is shared Whether it is a centralized or widespread function, RM requires a high level of information- and knowledge-sharing between different areas of hotel management (e.g. marketing, sales, finance, operations) on various elements (e.g. forecasting demand, strategies). The role of the revenue manager has been examined as a node of a network (the RM team) in which they exchange knowledge. Through social network analysis, the authors have highlighted that the revenue manager plays a more active role as an information broker to provide enhanced support to the decision-making group.

The role played by human resources in dealing with RM and the related competences are considered very important. Regarding skills and competences, Cetin, Demirciftci, and Bilgihan, through qualitative research conducted in two steps, propose the nomenclature of knowledge, skills, and abilities (KSAs). The KSAs are connected with the challenges that RM must face and which are internal (relating to the department and organization of the RM), external (relating to the requests and changes in the general context), industrial (relating to industry and the related characteristics of demand and supply), personal (relating to the individual characters of the RM team), and organizational (relating to the organization to which it belongs, to its power relations and rules of operation, etc.).

Depending on the type of challenge, the KSAs are divided into the following categories: analytical (e.g. ability to make quick decisions, ability to prioritize, flexibility, analytical and numerical intelligence); technical (e.g. knowledge of RM software, RM indicators, and forecasting techniques); social (e.g. interpersonal communication, empathy, leadership); generic (e.g. marketing, human resource management, strategy knowledge); ethical (e.g. integrity, fair competition). These skills are always complex even considering that RM activities are increasingly integrated with those of social media and therefore special training is necessary.

5.2.1 RM and ICT Support

As stated by Hendler: "Room, as limited resources, must be allocated to the segment that generates the most profit", considering both direct profit generated by selling the rooms and indirect profit generated by guests that spend money in other services offered by the hotel. This consideration, which is the basis of RM, requires technological support to be operational.

Indeed, in a context where tourism is increasingly linked to the digital world, RM is also lacking in support technology, as well as all the decisions that concern the client and that must descend from his in-depth knowledge, on which the technology gives a high help. Today, customer bookings arrive almost exclusively via online travel agencies (OTAs) or through the hotel website, the use of customer relationship management (CRM) makes it possible to automate most of the processes relating to customer relations before and after their stay, online review sites influence the choices of potential customers, and social networks are a driving force for tourist destinations and drive market trends.

In this panorama of high computerization, RM techniques in the hotel sector have found fertile ground to grow and to integrate this world. RM techniques have therefore evolved, moving from complex systems developed specifically for the first hotel chains that have made use of them to widely used economic systems. Hundreds of software solutions were born to support decisions for revenue managers. Many of these are integrated with CRM platforms and have made the possibility of exploiting RM techniques accessible to the ever-increasing users. The research highlights how often the software used concerns more general property management than RM alone. There is no doubt that the integration of systems allows the creation of wider databases and profiles on users facilitating cross-selling and up-selling; therefore, more and more hotels and chains invest in integrated software solutions, such as between RM and CRM.

Reducing costs and increasing the simplicity of using IT platforms to support RM decisions has allowed small and medium-sized hotels to use these tools. To use them effectively, a deep knowledge of RM techniques is required. This is confirmed by managers' perception of the still fundamental role of the people who deal with them.

The term revenue management and revenue manager—even though they are much present and discussed in the literature—in practice are not associated with a univocal concept and clearly understood by the operators. The research has shown that the terms dynamic pricing and revenue management are often overlapped in the destination considered and that they do not coincide even if they have common elements. In fact, although the number of those who declare that they carry out dynamic pricing corresponds to the number of those who claim to carry out RM activities. The change in tariffs in some cases is linked exclusively with sales policies and not with global revenue and costs of the structure. In other words, dynamic pricing is not derived from the monitoring system of all the external and external variables that must be controlled in a real RM system.

The result is a smaller number of structures where RM techniques and activities are present in the destination considered.

Regarding organizational aspects, there seems to be an RM model where the figure of the revenue manager is not very present—the activities there are carried out by the manager of the structure or by managers of other areas under the supervision of the former.

Regarding the ICT support, the structures that claim to carry out RM policies use software packages—mostly Ericsoft—even if the use of some software packages, especially CRM, is more widespread than the number of companies that claim to implement RM policies. This can be explained by the fact that the software in other companies is used for some specific activities, without any 360-degree view of RM.

Regarding the competencies of the revenue manager, the range of skills involved in the survey and associated with the role of the revenue manager is very broad: they indicate as necessary a structured set of skills.

Considering the technological support, the use of specific software is present, although this is not widespread and there is often no systemic view. The work provides first results on a revenue management model and on a competence profile of the revenue manager that are consistent with the characteristics of the hotel management in the destination considered. This result arouses interest in exploring the role that the local entrepreneurial culture can have on this approach, in particular on the centralized or shared role and on the competences of the revenue manager.

5.3 PROFIT MAXIMIZATION

Revenue management evolved from yield management, expanding beyond the traditional areas of airline seats, car hire and hotel rooms. It is an integral tool for service businesses, used to optimize revenue from both the use of space (occupancy/capacity utilization) and the price per unit sold (hotel room, restaurant seat, cruise-ship cabin, beauty session. The technology revolution will continue to provide firms with access to cheaper but increasingly sophisticated RM tools that already allow real-time decisions to be taken in reaction to market forces. However, the efficacy of the tools is correlated to forecast accuracy and business as usual scenarios. In periods of economic uncertainty or of unpredictable customer behavior, the skills of a revenue manager can effectively optimize profit opportunity. However, detecting the impact of `good' and `bad' RM decisions on customers is complex.

The increasing demands of stakeholders for improved profits have affected all aspects of business and especially in those with very high fixed costs structures, such as hotels, restaurants, cinemas Optimizing revenues is an effective way of achieving high levels of contribution to fixed costs. This places increased pressure on those managers with a RM role especially in complex environments such as resort/city/casino/conference hotels, cruiseships or tourist attractions, with many different departments and often a 24-hour operation. A total asset revenue management approach is complex and hence many skills are required.

There has been increasing awareness of the importance of management development in improving business objectives. The Chartered Institute of Personnel and Development see this as `the entire structured process by which managers learn and improve their skills for the benefit of the employing organization and themselves'. The achievement of professional qualifications shows a person's ability and allows them to better demonstrate their expertise and professional competence. Specialist skills are of major importance, both

Mabey and Doyle, for instance, arguing that management development generally should be contextualized to specific roles, and Gosling and Mintzberg emphasis that this should be `concurrent and integrated' into the workplace, hence leading to increased personal achievement and respect with benefits such as loyalty, long-term tenure and achieving goals as well as financial gains. As a result, organizations are increasingly committed to investing in the development of their managers.

Attitudes towards management development in hotels have improved where a more long-term perspective is seen as an investment rather than a cost. Within the finance area, the professional association, The British Association of Hospitality Accountants (BAHA) has provided professional and management development qualifications for many years (see baha-uk.org). They have now been approached by senior financial personnel in industry to develop a professional qualification for revenue managers, as an extension of their existing programs. In order to do this, the range of skills required of future revenue managers must be identified, so that appropriate learning outcomes can be developed. At the same time, performance benchmarks must be identified to allow the efficient evaluation of the impact of a formal certification program.

In western economies, organizations are under increasing pressures from various stakeholders to optimize profits to provide a required return to investors. The movement away from manufacturing to a more service –based economy has increased the emphasis on service organizations' performance at all levels. However, many service-based businesses operate high fixed costs structures, with limited opportunities to control costs in a volatile market. Tourism businesses have a variety of different operating departments, with a leisure hotel, for instance, having rooms, restaurants, bars, room service, conference, leisure and other facilities in addition to the non-operating departments such as administration, marketing, accounting and maintenance. These all have separate (and different) cost and revenue structures and hence all require different types of financial management. Hotels are particularly vulnerable to fluctuations in demand as they often have high initial capital investment and high fixed payroll, maintenance and administrative requirements, with a consequent lack of opportunity to match costs to peaks and troughs in sales. Only the budget sector operates with a very limited departmental structure.

If an organization has high fixed costs, the opportunities for improving profits are focused on the revenue aspects of the business. Most traditional manufacturing organizations are able to match production to demand but many service organizations operate in a perishable environment where, if the product is not used, it then `expires' and is no longer available for sale. Examples are airline or cinema seats, holiday accommodation, tours, hotel rooms, conference space or car hire, all of which can vary in demand. A sale lost cannot be recouped later, and so management must operate in an environment where all available space is sold at optimum rate through effective pricing decisions. Where a limited product structure exists, the loss of a single sale may have little impact on other aspects of the business. However, if the unit is multi-departmental then other sales may be lost as a result of lack of sale of the product. For a theatre, as an example, the loss of a single seat booking may cause a loss of sales in the bar, for programs and ice creams and perhaps from car parking and retail sales. Hotels are even more liable to loss of peripheral sales, as not only do they have many different departments, as discussed earlier, they also operate multinight stays and hence the loss of a single booking may cause reduced sales for several days.

Further complications can emerge in an environment where revenues are gained from different types of customer with different purchasing behavior and in many service sector environments customers may come from a variety of sources, with different purposes. A bank, for instance, may have both business and personal account customers with vastly different incomes and expenditures. The budget airlines have seen both business and leisure customers use their flights, and the same customer may travel on business on one occasion, and for pleasure on another. Similarly a hotel guest may stay in a single hotel on business or as part of a conference (where their employer is paying) or for pleasure where they are paying their own bill. All of these market segments may have different lengths of stay and different buying behavior for both room type and for peripheral spending.

As a business guest, a customer may stay a single night in a `luxury' single room, eat breakfast and drink in the bar, but not use any other services. When attending a conference the room occupied, perhaps for four or five days, would be lower grade, perhaps shared with another conference guest, and all meals would be taken in a conference suite. Their expenditure in the bar at night, however, could be considerable. When staying with their family for a two-night leisure break in a family room (children may stay free but consume hotel resources), they would eat breakfast and perhaps dinner (with wine but limited other drinks) and utilize the leisure facilities.

All these departments also have different costs, and so predicting the profits of the various market segments is extremely difficult. Although Activity-Based-Costing (ABC) and Customer Profitability Analysis (CPA) techniques have been widely adopted in manufacturing organizations the more complex the operating structures, the less likely they are to be used. Establishing the costs associated with different segments is complex and technical, and only recently, with the development of more sophisticated systems and technology, has ABC/CPA become a remote possibility, with a recommended practice guide recently published. Without this type of technical support, making decisions becomes much more difficult, with further pressures on the person making those decisions - the revenue manager.

How does a manager decide which customer will generate the most contribution to fixed costs, and subsequently most positively impact profits? Strategies need to be multi-faceted as different demand periods have different demand patterns. For example, in major European cities the month of August is quiet, with few trade fairs, and consequently leisure customers have a wide variety of choice of where to stay, making the competitive arena extremely tough. In cases like these price becomes the tool to attract business to generate at least a contribution to fixed costs. The customer that is most valuable in this case would be where the highest net rate is achieved (rate less commission, booking fees etc.), where the least hotel resources are utilized, where the spend on extras is highest and where the bill is settled in cash. Alternatively in trade fair periods, the best customer may be the customer that is paying a high rate, has booked directly, requires few hotel services or amenities, does not have breakfast (although included in the rate) recycles the towels and leaves the room in a tidy state.

Firstly it is important to differentiate between the role of revenue manager and revenue manager role. Revenue management positions reviewed on www.hcareers.com in June 2008 showed that the skill-set required depended on the level of the revenue manager. In addition, when the keywords, "Revenue Management" were utilized, a range of other positions were also shown. In the same way that customer relations can be the job of a customer relations officer, all staff in contact with customers can have an impact, and all staff that is in contact with revenue/profit generating activities (including contact with customers) has a role to play in the firm's revenue management program.

It is apparent that the role of Revenue Manager encompasses a range of skills with a greater strategic emphasis where the position is at a senior corporate level. Abilities required may encompass skills which range across interpersonal, database management, analytical and reporting tools, the ability to ensure maximization of all distribution systems, an understanding of trends in strategic pricing and selling strategies to enhance revenues.

Regional/ cluster director of revenue manager positions required candidates to have both strategic thinking as well as hands on skills that may encompass some or all of the following abilities:

- forecasting,
- revenue budgeting
- daily, weekly, monthly reporting
- competitive analysis
- develop, train and provide guidance to the regions RM teams
- leading/coordination weekly selling and inventory strategy meetings.
- monitor/manage the RM system and ensure the hotels position in distribution channels
- coordinate rate and availability audit.
- conduct research to assess RM strategies and opportunities and develop internet revenue products.
- monitor transient and group guest mix and evaluate group booking requests and set group ceilings and target rates.
- maintain relationships with distribution partners.
- analyze events, market trends for seasonality and critique past pricing.
- prepare demand forecasts and conduct revenue analysis to identify revenue improvement opportunity.
- maximize property revenues through development and implementation of effective inventory and pricing strategies based on future forecasts. Set internet rate structure in brand and third party booking engines.

From the revenue perspective, a new paradigm is emerging. In the past, revenue managers were limited to making decisions based on rate allocation and inventory control, but now need to be aware of the wider CPA aspects so as to optimize profits. Typically hotel revenue managers were also employed first in the operational areas, usually front office or reservations and were then trained on-job in revenue management techniques as systems became more sophisticated. However, formal training – as for other managers in hotels – in other financial aspects was sporadic and often non-existent, and hence the revenue managers frequently has little awareness of the wider financial impacts of their decisions (Upchurch et al, 2002). Now, however, with increasingly sophisticated systems, revenue managers are being required to demonstrate a wider range of skills and attributes which are difficult to develop effectively while on the job, therefore recruitment of the best RM talent has become key to establishing a competitive edge. Although there is a preference for recruiting university graduates as revenue managers, there is a need for ongoing training and development especially as the role is in evolution as technological tools evolve. There has been only limited research into the skills and attributes of revenue managers, with the most useful data being found on careers websites. When scanning positions available it was evident that there are a wide range of RM responsibilities throughout service organizations. In general, a revenue manager's time can be divided into the following main activities: evaluating RM activities and forecasting, setting and maintaining rates, interacting with other managers and developing strategies. Developing credibility with the executive management team together with strong communication skills were areas where training was seen as particularly critical together with the ability to analyze financial data. The ability to analyze and interpret financial statements and market data was seen as important. Development of skills such as writing, conflict resolution, development /implementation of revenue management strategies were also seen as topics for development.

For whatever background a revenue manager comes from, it is unlikely that they will have a complete set of required skills. Therefore the question arises - how will they attain these additional skills? Attitudes towards qualifications and developing managers within hotels have been variable in the past. Traditionally managers were trained on-job and developed their skills through the workplace, with little opportunity for more formalized management development– most taking place within the organization rather than externally. In recent years there has been more encouragement for managers to gain professional qualifications by undergoing formal management development, and Harper have shown how this can benefit general managers, for example. In the broad financial area, Burgess' research into managers' financial skills also showed overall support for more skills training in specific areas, but contradicted this by a lack of opportunities for recruiting more qualified managers. Her 2008 research confirms this, with senior financial executives stating that, although they supported managers' desires to gain more qualifications, they could not then afford to recruit professionally qualified staff. This is indicative of attitudes throughout the industry – there is support for specific training needs but not for more generalized management development. What were supported – sponsored with both time and money - was industry-designed programs for specific purposes, such as the BAHA Education and Training program to develop assistant controllers' financial skills. This existing program was developed in response to demands from the hotel industry for more formal qualifications for hotel financial controllers, and following a review of skill needs of financial controllers.

Revenue management is growing in importance with the need to optimize contribution to satisfy the needs of stakeholders. In a complex operating environment, such as a hotel, there are many variables that can influence the revenue and profit gained from a particular customer, and hence decisions on accepting customers must be made by the revenue managers utilizing all the resources that are available to them. Effective decision making can be greatly enhanced by the manager having appropriate skills and knowledge to optimize these resources, but the limited evidence available suggests a lack of formal development of these skills, particularly within the hotel environment. As RM has developed rapidly in recent years, much of the limited data that is available is accessed via, for instance, careers websites. Accordingly, if a clear view as to the required skills and attributes was to be established, further primary research needed to be performed within the field.

Technical and operational skills and knowledge revenue managers required, experts responded as follows:

- ***Rooms Division/Front Office experience:*** Contemporary approaches to pricing and the ability to integrate marketing efforts into pricing and inventory decisions: Processes are in place, what is going on locally, regionally and globally, the role of RM and linkages to other functions. Rate allocation and Inventory control, reservation process, technology, segmentation and the rate loading process. How to build rate structures/a pre-set level of rate grids, tactical offers and use business intelligence.
- ***Product Management:*** How to achieve optimization of the selling potential all year, independent of occupancy and demand. The importance of coordinated marketing activities to achieve RM objectives.
- ***Distribution and e-channel management:*** How to manage the hotel's online presence and use e-channels as a tool towards (complex) demand generation. Comparative value of transactions from each e-mediary to ensure value added.
- How technology works especially that used towards the production of accurate long-term forecast. Systems are constantly changing and updating, they must be able to adapt and grasp change easily
- Exposure across various brands (economy to luxury), managed and franchised properties and experience in various markets/countries. Sensing the market i.e. the conditions, underlying factors for different market behavior, competitors. Trends and opportunities, hotels/airlines/etc. business pattern. Customer-centric data management: How to track and analyze buying behavior of individual consumers over

time: How distorted recommendations from RM system are caused. How the consumer shops: how and why they make their buying decisions.

- ***Analytics***: Analysis of related RM reports using statistics. Aside from RevPAR, other measures need to be utilized to assess opportunity costs and how revenues interact to maximise the profitability of individual transactions. Total asset revenue management: what is it? How can it be implemented? Total guest value
- ***Communication***: effective people management and efficient relationship building to influence colleagues and executives. How to sell pricing strategies to co-workers e.g. How to influence sales teams to move away from negotiated price to best rate guarantee. Quality Interaction with operational managers to be able to understand all needs expectations and how the product is delivered. Ability to multi task, implement and reinforce processes and procedures, interpret data to the members of the revenue management committee, make recommendations that are clear and well-reasoned.
- ***Creativity***: How to capitalize revenue opportunities using out of the box thinking applying creative approaches. How to develop an innovative RM vision. Entrepreneurial thinking is important as well as training and coaching to enable staff be unconventional way.
- ***Other***: Comfortable with figures and budgets, time management, inquisitive, resourceful and a team player, able to use spreadsheets for reporting and developing demand projections, leadership skills, outgoing, convincing with good presentational skills, decision maker and risk taker.

5.4 ETHICAL ASPECTS OF REVENUE MANAGEMENT

RMs must, of course, obey all of the laws that directly affect their decision making. In the majority of cases, however, decisions made about prices and selling are affected more by ethics than by the law.

Certainly, RMs should ensure the prices they charge, as well as the way those prices are managed is fair. The difficulty, of course, comes in making the determination of exactly what constitutes a fair price. The question is important for a variety of reasons:

- Buyers must be convinced the prices they are paying are fair if they are to become repeat customers.
- Employees of a business must be convinced the prices charged by their employers are fair if they are to be effective salespersons for the business.
- Business owners must be convinced the prices they receive for the products and services they sell are fair or they will not continue their businesses.
- Regulatory agencies must be convinced prices charged are fair or they will be motivated to increase their oversight and control over any industry (including hospitality) that is perceived as pricing its products unfairly. RMs in hospitality need look no further than those lawmakers

vocally supporting legislation that would tax airlines if they charged carry-on luggage fees to see the legal and public relations impact of pricing that appears to be unfair.

The question of what constitutes a fair price is closely related to the question of who should determine the fairness of prices. As you have learned, in the long run it is always the buyer who will ultimately determine the fairness of a price. The decision to buy, or not to buy, not only shapes the answer to what is a fair price but also affects the continued existence of a product or service in the marketplace. Just as buyers will not continually pay more for a product than they believe it is worth, sellers will not continue to sell for a price that does not return a sufficient profit for the risk they undertake in operating their businesses operating their businesses. In most cases, it is not the actual price charged for an item that makes consumers question the fairness of the price. Rather, it is the perception of profit made by the seller that cause the accusations of price gouging or unconscionable selling prices that can result in government regulation.

Note that, while the annual average return for the 20-year period was just over 9 percent, the volatility of returns is significant. Any consumer group or governmental agency protesting the excessive business returns achieved in 1995 would also be required to address the dismal returns of 2002 and 2008. Few critics of business, however, could seriously argue that a 9 percent average return on investment over a 20-year period is excessive. Ultimately, in nearly all cases, the prices charged by businesses simply cannot be excessive or buyers will simply reject the products and services sold by that business. In many cases, they will reject the business as well. From the perspective of an RM, there are four pricing-related ethical issues that must be considered:

1. Are the actions I am taking ethical?
2. Are the profits resulting from my actions ethical?
3. Are my prices presented fairly?
4. Are my prices perceived as fair by customers?

Are the actions I am taking ethical?

The first question; "Are the actions I am taking ethical?" simply addresses the fact that RMs face ethical dilemmas on a regular basis. Consider, for example, the RM whose hotel consists of 300 rooms. On a specific night, the hotel has 200 arriving reservations (reserved rooms) and 100 occupied rooms. As a result, each room has been sold. The RM knows, however, that historically 5 percent of all reservations made for any given night will be no-shows.

At two in the afternoon, the RM is approached by a member of the hotel's sales and marketing department to make a decision regarding a repeat customer's request to reserve 11 rooms, at full rack rate, for that night. Would you advise the RM to approve the sale? When you do the required calculations, you can see why for many RMs the answer to this question may be as much an ethical one as a financial one.

Most questions related to **ethical behavior** are, by their very nature, of two types. The first are those where the decision is easy, and the great majority of

RMs would follow the same course of action. For example; "Should RMs accept money (a kickback) for them in exchange for giving a customer a price-reduction?" Such a course of action would, in the opinion of nearly all RMs, be a clear violation of professional ethics.

The more difficult ethical questions are of the second type. In these cases, there are no clear-cut answers. RMs must examine their own moral conduct codes and then make their own decisions. Answers to what is ethical behavior in such situations may be unclear. Although there often are no easy or universal answers to many ethical dilemmas, RMs questioning the ethics of a decision or course of action can be guided in their decisions by utilizing the following questions:

- Is the intended action legal?
- Would boss be O.K. with the action and advise me to do it?
- Would potential future employers be pleased to learn we had initiated the activity?
- Is the action fair to all parties involved?

If you can answer yes to each of these, the proposed action is likely ethical. If you cannot, it indicates that great care should be taken before you engage in the activity or make the decision because the ethics of it are clearly suspect in your own mind.

Are the Profits Resulting from My Actions Ethical?

The second question posed, "Are the profits resulting from my actions ethical?" is unfortunately one that is not addressed often enough. Its answer is not easy. The notion of what constitutes a "fair" or "just" profit has for centuries vexed philosophers, religious leaders, politicians, and businesspersons. Throughout this book we have taken the position that it is the free market that determines fair prices, with buyer's willingness to pay as the true measure of an item's worth.

As you have learned, price gouging (the charging of unreasonably high prices for goods and services) is sometimes illegal, but it is universally considered unethical. The difficulty, of course, lies in addressing the question of who gets to decide if a price is fair and thus if the profit resulting from it is, in fact, reasonable or unreasonable.

Some in business would argue that it is no more immoral for a producer to charge premium prices than it is for a consumer to pay low prices. Others state that the fairness of a price depends on the alternatives available to the buyer.

To charge $10.00 for a 12-ounce bottle of spring water during a normal time period would simply be bad business because few bottles would be sold. To charge the same $10.00 per bottle in the aftermath of a hurricane when no alternative water sources are available would clearly be unethical (and illegal in some states).

A customer willing to pay a high price simply because they have no reasonable alternative is not truly a willing customer, and RMs must recognize that. It is also true, however, that a legitimate function of a price is to allocate scarce resources. When for example, only one hotel ballroom in a city is available for hosting a June wedding, the value of that space is legitimately higher than during alternative months when fewer weddings take place and thus more alternative rental space is available.

The question of what constitutes ethical pricing is one that RMs will encounter frequently. This is especially true of those working in hard constraint industries such as lodging. It is critical, however, that RMs are able to defend and justify their pricing policies. It has been said that ethics is doing the right thing when no one is watching. For RMs, the fact is that their customers, their supervisors, and their employees are watching, and they are watching closely.

Despite lip service to the contrary, experienced businesspersons recognize the simple truth that "honesty and integrity often do not pay off in the short run." There are frequently real costs involved with maintaining these values. These costs may take the form of lost business or in reduced profits resulting from charging prices lower than those that could feasibly be charged. For ethical reasons alone, however, these costs are worth paying. For business reasons, it is unquestionable that, in the long run, honesty and integrity yield tremendous payoffs. This is so because the value to RMs and their businesses of ethical behavior and impeccable integrity is priceless. Customers expect sellers to act with integrity every time, not just sometimes. This was summed up nicely by Tom Peters, the bestselling author of In Search of Excellence, when he stated, "There is no such thing as a minor lapse of integrity."

Are my prices presented fairly?

The question of "Are my prices presented fairly?" is an important one. Certainly it is fair for RMs to use their knowledge of consumer behavior to take advantage of the known ways consumers react to prices. Thus, for example, it makes sense for all RMs working in the lodging industry to add $0.99 to the end of their advertised room rates because they know that consumers perceive very little difference between a rate of $299.00 per night and $299.99 per night. This phenomenon exists even at lower rates (i.e., a rate of $59.00 per night is perceived about the same as $59.99). In a similar manner, restaurateurs whose menu prices end in $0.95 or $0.99 can do so fairly because they know that buyers tend to overweight the first digits in a price8 and lower numbers are perceived as providing more value. Thus, for example, a $7.99 menu item seems to be a much greater savings from an $8.00 price than $7.92 is from $7.99. In both of these examples, the prices are presented openly with no intent to disguise them. That should always be the case. RMs must be fully aware that, regardless of the justification, their customers will react to hidden charges or charges revealed after the fact in much the same way they themselves would.

Are My Prices Perceived as Fair by Customers?

The final question, "Are my prices perceived as fair by customers?" is the most difficult of all. Because customers naturally seek to pay low prices, they have a tendency to feel nearly any price is "too high." That is, their preference, much like your own, would always be to pay a lower price for all of the things they want or need to buy. Seasoned RMs understands this natural tendency. As stated earlier, however, the simple fact that a potential customer feels a price is too high is not a legitimate reason for granting that customer a price reduction. The issue of too high a price, however, is vastly different from that of an unfair price. Prices can often be beyond a customer's willingness to pay; but prices should never be unfair.

RMs will have little control over the inherent tendency of buyers to seek low prices. They have a great deal of control, however, over buyer perceptions of price fairness. In general, customers evaluate price fairness based on two different perspectives. The first relates to the perceived profit that the seller will earn. The second relates to the price a buyer believes other buyers are being charged.

Most buyers believe that it is simply unfair for sellers to charge excessively high prices, even if the majority of buyers are willing to pay those prices. Dual entitlement theory explains why.

Consumers feel they have a right to a reasonable price just as sellers have a right to a reasonable profit. Prices that appear to customers as having been established for the sole purpose of increasing profits beyond reasonable levels will be viewed as being unfair. Thus, if prices are raised in response to a business's increased costs, the higher prices will likely be perceived as fair. Raising prices simply to increase profits excessively is most often viewed as unfair. Ignoring this customer viewpoint can often be the cause of pricing fiascos.

To illustrate, consider the hardware store normally selling snow shovels for $25.00. The morning after a major snowstorm, the store raises the price on its ten remaining snow shovels to $35.00. Is such an action and the resulting new price "fair"? The overwhelming majority of buyers (over 82 percent of respondents in one study) found such an action to be unfair. Interestingly, in an identical study, 76 percent of University of Chicago economics students found raising the prices of the shovels to be "fair," a strong indicator that pricing debacles and the strong consumer reactions they generate will not disappear in the foreseeable future. Buyers found the hardware stores new prices unconscionable. The economics students saw strong demand as the justification for a significant price increase.

RMs must remember that buyers will sympathize with a seller's cost increases much more than with the seller's supply shortages. Thus a seller who finds that it has only one or two of an extremely popular item in stock (e.g., the season's most popular new video game release, or a single hotel room) must be careful. While the price of the item could, of course, be raised significantly, or even auctioned to the highest bidder, doing so would certainly be perceived as unfair by the majority of consumers. Buyers use a variety of information to establish a reference price or the selling price they believe to be fair. They will then evaluate all other prices for that same item in comparison to that reference price.

It is for this reason that discounts from "normal" prices—even those normal prices that are set very high—are popular with buyers. Experienced sellers know it pays to keep reference prices high, and when it is advantageous to them, to offer discounts from those regular prices.

The second consumer view of price fairness relates to perceptions of the prices that are paid by others. Buyers who are perfectly happy with the price they paid for an item can instantly become irate if they find that another buyer has paid less for the same item. This phenomenon is familiar to many professionals, including those professionals working in human resource management. They know that a specific employee may be quite satisfied to be paid a salary of $50,000 per year, but if that employee discovers another worker is doing exactly the same job for $60,000 per year, he (or she) will likely become angry.

Similarly, the employee who gets a $5,000 raise may be thrilled with it, but not if a co-worker doing similar work was granted a $10,000 raise. Astute readers will recognize that from a purely economic perspective, this price-related reaction is irrational. A buyer's own consumer surplus is dependent only on what that buyer has paid for an item, not what someone else has paid. But RMs must also remember that the axiom "Consumers will always behave rationally, except when they don't" is all too often true.

The implications of the importance of fairness perception to pricing and revenue optimization are several, and they dictate six important pricing concepts that RMs would do well to remember:

1. Prices should be presented fairly. Hidden or after-purchase charges will be perceived as unfair.
2. Buyers prefer rewards to punishments. Rewarding guests for buying more or more frequently, is preferable to penalizing them for buying less or less frequently.
3. Discounts are viewed more favorably then surcharges.
4. Price increases justified only by supply shortages (or even increased consumer demand) are likely to be viewed unfavorably.
5. Lower prices (when offered) should be available to all buyers willing to meet the low price criteria or fences established for them. When lower prices are offered to all, potential buyers can decide for themselves whether they wish to meet the qualifying criteria.
6. If they do vary from traditional pricing approaches, a seller's pricing offer must be easily explained and understood. Deviations from traditional pricing approaches must be presented carefully and fully to consumers who must then perceive them to be fair.

5.5 REVENUE MANAGER JOB DESCRIPTION

Developing pricing strategies and forecasting revenue for hotels and other lodging establishments are the main activities of a revenue manager. Revenue Managers work closely with sales teams, reception desk employees and the hotel general manager in areas of promotion, business planning and reservation costs. They might conduct analyses of prices offered by other hotels to develop competitive prices and discounts.

RMs seeking continuous improvement in their revenue optimization efforts undertake the following steps:

Figure 5.2: Key activities of a revenue manager

Step 1: Establish prices

The importance of price and strategic pricing has been extensively addressed. Because the word price communicates strongly to potential customers the value placed on a product or service by its seller, the ability to properly establish pricing is a critical aspect of every RM's job.

Step 2: Forecast demand

After a price has been established, customer demand for products and services can be estimated or forecasted. Of course, if prices are changed, forecasts of demand may be changed as well. Some RMs specialize in this task and use sophisticated mathematical modeling tools to help them. All RMs seeking to optimize revenue, however, must have the ability to forecast demand for their products and services.

Step 3: Manage inventory

This crucial step requires RMs to understand how to withhold or make available to specific buyers the products and service capacity held in inventory.

This task is made more challenging by the fact that revenue optimization must be viewed from a long-term as well as a short-term perspective.

Step 4: Manage distribution

In nearly all segments of the hospitality industry intermediaries are used to assist in the selling process.

Customers themselves will vary in the amount of revenue they generate. For example, some hotel guests will reserve their rooms and stay longer than do other guests. Similarly, some identifiable types of restaurant customers purchase more food and beverages while dining than do others. When it is known that specific distribution channels deliver guests whose buying patterns are significantly higher or lower than that of guests produced by other channels, RMs must consider and manage these source-related factors.

Step 5: Evaluate results

The thoughtful evaluation of results is one of an RM's best tools for improving performance. Assessing the outcome of revenue management-related decisions that have been made in the past helps improve the quality of future decisions.

Often, a precise evaluation of an RMs' efforts can be challenging. The best metrics for ascertaining success in revenue optimization decision making may be uncertain. As well, success in some measures may mask a lack of success in others; thus providing RMs with conflicting information. The best RMs, however, understand the importance of evaluating their performance—and the very best RMs do it well. As Winston Churchill pointed out "True genius resides in the capacity for evaluation of uncertain, hazardous, and conflicting information." Despite the inherent difficulties of assessing uncertain and conflicting historical information RMs must learn to modify their future actions in direct response to the outcomes they have achieved, the actions of their customers, their competitors and the general business environment.

While it would no doubt be pointless to argue that any one step in the five-step revenue management process is the most important, simply recognizing that revenue management is a process should help you better understand some of the reasons why RMs' jobs vary so much among different companies. Because of the segment in which they work some hospitality professionals may place greater emphasis on any one of the steps than they do on another. In addition, some businesses are large enough to have revenue management specialists who work only in one or two of these processes while other companies employ a single RM to perform all of these tasks

Lastly, as the importance of revenue management has grown, some advisory companies have been formed specifically to assist RMs in one or more of their specialized duties. The decision by a business to utilize these companies' services can also have a significant impact on the daily tasks assigned to their own RMs.

Reviewing a sample position description is a good way for you to become more familiar with the typical duties of an RM.

RMs in full-service hotels manage revenues related to guest rooms, foodservices, meeting space, and other hotel services. RMs in limited-service hotels will focus more of their efforts on guest room sales.

5.5.1 Job Title: Revenue Manager

Job Description

The primary responsibility of the Revenue Manager is to optimize the hotel's revenues by working closely with the GM, DOSM, and FOM and implementing strategies agreed upon by this team.

Job Duties

The following are specific responsibilities and contributions critical to the successful performance of the position:

- Optimize RevPAR by analyzing and forecasting demand and establishing effective selling strategies.
- Work with the director of sales and marketing and hotel team to establish strategies to increase room revenue.
- Manage and update current selling strategies and product information in all available internal and external distribution channels and reservation sources.
- Facilitate weekly revenue strategy meetings.
- Conduct ongoing competitor price analysis to ensure proper rate positioning relative to the competition.
- Generate and distribute daily, weekly, and monthly revenue management reports.
- Maintain historical data from all distribution channels in all market segments.
- Continually monitor all pertinent travel related web sites to ensure competitiveness in both availability and price.

Job Requirements

- Prefer previous revenue management experience
- Strong analytical skills
- Ability to identify relevant data and use it to draw inferences with reference to impact on hotels revenues
- Excellent communication skills and interpersonal skills
- Ability to use PMS/reservation/revenue management systems to forecast, implement, and evaluate optimization strategies

It is important for you to recognize that the same principles and practices applied by RM in lodging and foodservices can be applied to many other of the specialized segments within the hospitality industry. This is so because the hard constraint RM techniques utilized by RMs in lodging and the soft constraint RM techniques applied by foodservice industry RMs can be directly applied to any hospitality product or service in which these same supply constraints are encountered.

5.5.2 Reporting Relationships

Just as there is no single job description that would address the activities of all RMs, there is no single best organizational structure representing an RM's ideal reporting relationship. In fact, even within the same industry segment, the reporting relationships of RMs vary greatly. This can reflect the objective of the business employing the RM, the specific revenue management philosophy of its managers, or both. In most cases, RMs will find that their reporting relationship will be to one of the following individuals:

The director of sales and marketing (DOSM)

Organizations utilizing this structure emphasize the RM's role in demand forecasting and in the selling process. Because the DOSM is typically responsible for group room sales, this scenario is also common in those lodging properties in which group room sales constitute a significant portion of total rooms revenue. The title of the customer may change from guest, to diner, to client, to attendee, but the RM in this scenario plays a supporting role to the DOSM.

The room's manager

Exclusive to the lodging industry, in this scenario, the RM reports to the room's manager, the individual traditionally responsible for the management of a hotel's front office and the housekeeping departments. In other properties, the RM may report directly to the FOM. This scenario is common in those lodging properties in which transient room sales constitute a significant portion of total room's revenue. In this role, the RM supports the efforts of the hotel's front office in establishing room prices, managing reservations, and maintaining relationships with the property's various intermediaries and distribution channels.

The controller

The controller is responsible for a hotel's on-property accounting procedures. Those entities selecting this placement for the RM's position emphasize the pricing and results analysis duties of RMs. Typical in this role are activities related to the forecasting and evaluation of the organization's financial results as well as preparation of financial reports related to the management of revenues.

The property GM

In some properties, the RMs position is valued so highly the reporting relationship is directly to the general manager or even the owner of the business.

A corporate-level executive

In multiunit organizations, it is common for property level RMs to report directly to an area or regional RM. This structure helps ensure revenue management consistency across properties and where more than one property exists in the same geographic market, allows for cooperative revenue management activities.

Those intermediaries and service companies advising or supporting the efforts of property-level RMs are also likely to be structured in this way.

5.6 THE REVENUE MANAGEMENT TEAM

In the hospitality industry it is essential to have revenue a management team in place to capitalize on the market and profits. There is more competition than ever in the industry as well as more channels for travelers to book. Revenue management is the process of using data to predict consumer behavior in order to enhance product availability and increase revenue.

For example, Fred is the general manager of a local hotel. He needs to know the probability of selling out next week. His revenue management team provides him with data including pricing of competitors, the demand in the market, and availability in the market. This helps Fred decide on pricing for his hotel in order to maximize his revenue. The revenue management team can consist of a revenue manager, operational management, the sales team, and the line level employees. We will take a look at how each member of the team plays a role in the revenue management of the business.

Every revenue management team has a revenue manager. This is a role that has developed over the years as the hospitality industry has seen the need to use revenue management. At one point the operational teams were in charge of revenue management before the creation of the revenue manager. Now there is a need for a revenue manager that is only focused on the revenue management of the business.

The primary role of the revenue manager is to maximize the businesses' opportunity for revenue and profits. In order to do that, the revenue manager is in charge of compiling and analyzing data to make decisions regarding pricing.

The revenue manager compiles data on the business as well as the competition. They keep up with market changes and identify trends.

For example, a hotel in a corporate location will see high demand for hotel rooms during the week versus on the weekend. This is a trend that a revenue manager would be aware of and take into consideration when setting pricing. The revenue manager is in charge of setting rate strategies that will help the business capitalize their profits. The revenue manager will know what the competition is selling and how the competition is fairing.

Given the diversity of duties, responsibilities areas, and reporting relationships encountered by RMs an extremely useful way of reviewing the RM's role is that of a vital member of the revenue management team.

Each member of the revenue management team plays an important role:

Revenue manager

As an RM, your own role in the revenue management team will likely be one of planning, organizing, directing, and evaluating your team's revenue manager activities.

Organization administrators

Business owners, corporate or property level managers, and department heads all will have input into your revenue management decision making. They must be kept informed about your actions and their own goals must always be kept foremost in your mind.

Sales and marketing staff

Pricing and revenue management activities are closely related to sales and marketing activities. In nearly all cases, members of the sales and marketing departments will be part of the revenue management team and their specific goals will strongly influence the actions of your team. As well, in many cases an RM may report directly to an individual holding a position within this area of their organization.

Financial administrators

An organization's financial accountants and controllers as well as those department heads responsible for the financial management of their own areas will most often be important members of your revenue management team. Historically many of these individuals have viewed pricing and revenue management from a cost-based, not value-based perspective, yet their insights and points of view should always be among those you understand and fully appreciate.

Line-level employees

Line-level employees as well as those holding mid-supervisory positions interact directly with guests. In many cases, revenue management plans fail because these individuals have not been given the information and training they need to properly communicate those plans to guests. It will be part of your responsibility as an RM to ensure these individuals are prepared to implement the strategies and tactics you devise.

Intermediaries and channels

Although not directly employed by your organization, these professional partners in your RM efforts are crucial to your success. Coordinating information exchange with them, understanding their own needs, and working hard to maintain good relationships with them are all crucial aspects of your own success as a revenue management team member.

Guest and buyers

A recurring theme of this book has been the importance of guests in the revenue management process. It is only by keeping the needs of your guests, clients, customers, and buyers clearly in focus that your revenue management team can achieve its goals. Whether purchasing your products and services for themselves or for others, continuous feedback from these individuals will be essential to the quality of your own future decision making.

An additional and important team member role of many RMs is the coordination of revenue management strategy meetings. Often headed or chaired by the RM, these monthly, weekly, daily, and in some cases even hourly meetings are essential for coordinating the efforts of those team members with direct revenue management related responsibilities.

Which member of the revenue management team is most important? All of them! Few individuals understood this as well, or embodied the concept of teamwork more, than Vince Lombardi, legendary coach of the championship Green Bay Packers football team. Understanding his statement, "Individual commitment to a group effort—that is what makes a team work, a company work, a society work, and a civilization work,"16 is critical to your success as an RM. It is only through the efforts of talented individual RMs, serving at the center of the revenue management team, that organizations will achieve the financial success they desire.

5.7 SUMMARY

Revenue management (RM) in the hospitality industry is a critical function that has significantly evolved over time, transcending its initial focus on maximizing room yields through pricing strategies sensitive to buyer demand. Today, revenue management encompasses a broader goal of maximizing overall profits, not just through room sales but across various revenue streams within a property. This shift represents a departure from the traditional practices of yield management, marking RM as a cornerstone of modern hospitality operations.

The role of a revenue manager is pivotal in managing and optimizing the influx of revenues through multiple channels. While the sales team is tasked with generating demand, the revenue manager's responsibility lies in managing this demand effectively. This involves not only maximizing occupancy through dynamic pricing and inventory management but also developing comprehensive pricing strategies and revenue forecasts for the hotel or lodging establishment.

Given the fixed nature of the supply, particularly in the lodging sector where the number of available rooms cannot be increased overnight to meet short-term demand surges, revenue managers face unique challenges in optimizing revenue.

One of the key innovations in RM is the daily variation in pricing, a strategy that differentiates the lodging industry from other sectors like food service. This dynamic pricing model allows hotels to adjust rates based on fluctuating demand, thereby maximizing revenue potential. Furthermore, the advent of advanced IT platforms has democratized RM, enabling small and medium-sized hotels to leverage these tools for cost reduction and simplified decision-making processes.

Despite its critical importance, the concept of revenue management and the role of revenue managers are not universally understood, with varying interpretations and applications in practice. Nevertheless, RM's impact on the tourism industry is undeniable, extending its influence beyond traditional domains such as airline seats and hotel rooms to encompass a wide range of services within the hospitality sector. This evolution underscores the importance of RM as a strategic tool for achieving profitability and sustainability in the highly competitive hospitality industry.

5.8 REFERENCES

- Abrate, G. and Viglia, G. (2016) Strategic and Tactical Price Decisions in Hotel. Tourism Management, 55, 123-132. https://doi.org/10.1016/j.tourman.2016.02.006.
- Adams, D. and Waddle, C. (2004) `Evaluating the return for management development programs: individual returns versus organizational benefits', International Journal of Contemporary Hospitality Management Vol.14, No.1, pp.14-20
- Altinay, L. and Altinay, M. (2003) `How will growth be financed by the international hotel companies'. International Journal of Contemporary Hospitality Management, Vol.15, No.5, pp.274-282.
- Anderson, C.K. and Xie, X. (2010) Improving Hospitality Industry Sales: Twenty-Five Years of Revenue Management. Cornell Hospitality Quarterly, 51, 53-67. https://doi.org/10.1177/1938965509354697
- Barclays Bank PLC. (2006) Hospitality and Leisure Services Review. August. Portfolio Optimisation, Barclays Bank PLC. Bowie, D. and Buttle, F. (2004) Hospitality Marketing: An Introduction. Oxford: Butterworth-Heinemann.
- Beals, P. (2006) `Hotel asset management – will a North American phenomenon expand internationally?'. In P. Harris and M. Mongiello (Eds). Accounting and financial management: developments in the international hospitality industry. Oxford: Butterworth Heinemann.
- Burgess, C and Varini, K. (2008) ` Optimizing the Future of Hospitality Businesses', EuroChrie conference paper, October

- Burgess, C. (2007)`Do managers have sufficient financial skills to help them manage their areas?' International Journal of Contemporary Hospitality Management. Vol.19, No.3, pp.188-200.
- Cannell. M. and Taylor, J. (2009) Management Development. Factsheet., Chartered Institute of Personnel and Development, September, available from www.cipd.co.uk.
- Cetin, G., Demirciftci, T. and Bilgihan, A. (2016) Meeting Revenue Management Challenges: Knowledge, Skills and Abilities. International Journal of Hospitality Management, 57, 132-142. https://doi.org/10.1016/j.ijhm.2016.06.008
- Chiang, W.-C., Chen, J.C.H. and Xu, X. (2007) An Overview of Research on Revenue Management Current Issues and Future Research. International Journal of Revenue Management, 1, 97-127. https://doi.org/10.1504/IJRM.2007.011196
- Davis, S. and Albright, J. (2000) `The changing organizational structure and individual responsibilities of managerial accountants: a case study'. Journal of Managerial Issues, Vol.12, No.4, pp.446-464.
- De Vita, G. and Tekaya, A. (2015) Hotel Outsourcing under Asset Specificity: The Good, the Bad and the Ugly. Tourism Management, 47, 97-106. https://doi.org/10.1016/j.tourman.2014.09.012
- Di Foggia, G. and Lazzarotti, V. (2014) Assessing the Link between Revenue Management and Performance: Insights from the Italian Tourism Industry. Measuring Business Excellence, 18, 55-65. https://doi.org/10.1108/MBE-11-2013-0059
- Doyle, M. (2000) `Managing development in an era of radical change: evaluating a relational perspective', Journal of Management Development Vol.19, No.7, pp.579-601.
- Emeksiz, M., Gursoy, D. and Icoz, O. (2006) A Yield Management Model for Five-Star Hotels: Computerized and Non-Computerized Implementation. International Journal of Hospitality Management, 25, 536-551. https://doi.org/10.1016/j.ijhm.2005.03.003
- Evans, C. (2005) `Developing effective managers', British Journal of Administrative Management June/July, Vol.47, pp.i-111.
- Field, H. (2006) `Career directions in financial management in the hospitality industry'. In P. Harris and M. Mongiello (Eds). Accounting and financial management: developments in the international hospitality industry. Oxford: Butterworth Heinemann.
- Gosling, J. and Mintzberg, H. (2004) `The education of practicing managers', MIT Sloan Management Review Summer Vol.45, No.4, pp.14-22.
- Gregory, S. and Beck, J. (2006) `The activities, training and reporting relationships of today's revenue managers'. HSMAI Marketing Review, Autumn.
- Hardesty, D. M., Goodstein, R. C., Grewal, D., Miyazaki, A. D., Kopalle, P. (2014). The Accuracy of Scanned Prices. Journal of Retailing, 90(2): 291-300.

- Hastak, M., & Mazis, M. B. (2011). Deception by Implication: A Typology of Truthful but Misleading Advertising and Labeling Claims. Journal of Public Policy & Marketing, 30(2): 157-167.
- Holcomb, T.R. and Hitt, M.A. (2007) Toward a Model of Strategic Outsourcing. Journal of Operation Management, 25, 464-481 https://doi.org/10.1016/j.jom.2006.05.003
- Hubert, M., & Kenning, P. (2008). A current overview of consumer neuroscience. Journal of Consumer Behaviour, 7(4-5): 272-292.
- Ivanov, S. and Zhechev, V. (2012) Hotel Revenue Management: A Critical Literature Review. Tourism: An International Interdisciplinary Journal, 60, 175-197. https://hrcak.srce.hr/84562?lang=en
- Kimes, S.E. (2011) The Future of Hotel Revenue Management. Journal of Revenue and Pricing Management, 10, 62-72. https://doi.org/10.1057/rpm.2010.47
- Knutson, B., Rick, S., Wimmer, G, E,, Prelec, D., & Loewenstein, G. (2007). Neural predictors of purchase. Neuron, 53(1): 147-156.
- Kukar-Kinney, M., Xia, L., & Monroe, K. B. (2007). Consumers' perceptions of the fairness of price-matching refund policies. Journal of Retailing, 83(3): 325-337.
- Lamminmaki, D. (2011) An Examination of Factors Motivating Hotel Outsourcing. International Journal of Hospitality Management, 30, 963-973. https://doi.org/10.1016/j.ijhm.2010.10.010
- Ng, F., Rouse, P. and Harrison, J. (2017) Classifying Revenue Management: A Taxonomy to Assess Business Practice. Decision Sciences, 48, 489-522 https://doi.org/10.1111/deci.12230
- Orkin, E.B. (1988) Boosting Your Bottom Line with Yield Management. Cornell Hotel and Restaurant Administration Quarterly, 28, 52-56. https://doi.org/10.1177/001088048802800416
- Pechmann, C., & Silk, T. (2013). Policy and Research Related to Consumer Rebates: A Comprehensive Review. Journal of Public Policy & Marketing, 32(2): 255-270.
- Plassmann, H., O'Doherty, J., & Rangel, A. (2007). Orbitofrontal cortex encodes willingness to pay in everyday economic transactions. Journal of Neuroscience, 27(37): 9984-9 988.
- Sanfey, A. G., Rilling, J. K., Aronson, J. A., Nystrom, L. E., & Cohen, J. D. (2003). The neural basis of economic decision-making in the ultimatum game. Science, 300(5626): 1755- 1758.
- Upchurch, R.S., Ellis, T. and Seo, J. (2002) Revenue Management Underpinnings: An Exploratory Review. International Journal of Hospitality Management, 21, 67-83. https://doi.org/10.1016/S0278-4319(01)00027-5
- Villas-Boas, J. M. (2004). Price cycles in markets with customer recognition. Rand Journal of Economics, 35(3): 486-501.
- Vinod, B. (2004) Unlocking the Value of Revenue Management in the Hotel Industry. Journal of Revenue and Pricing Management, 3, 178-190. https://doi.org/10.1057/palgrave.rpm.5170105

- Wang, X.L. (2012) The Impact of Revenue Management on Hotel Key Account Relationship Development. International Journal of Contemporary Hospital Management, 24, 358-380. https://doi.org/10.1108/09596111211217860
- Xia, L., Monroe, K. B., & Cox, J. L. (2004). The price is unfair! A conceptual framework of price fairness perceptions. Journal of marketing, 68(October): 1-15.
- Yao, J., & Oppewal, H. (2016). Unit Pricing Increases Price Sensitivity Even When Products are of Identical Size. Journal of Retailing, 92(1): 109-121.

CHAPTER 6

Forecasting Demand for Hotel Revenue and Occupancy

INTRODUCTION

Demand forecasting is a pivotal process for businesses aiming to navigate the complexities of market dynamics effectively. It involves making informed predictions about future customer demand based on a comprehensive analysis of historical data and other market indicators. This forward-looking approach provides enterprises with critical insights into their market potential, enabling managers to devise robust pricing strategies, business expansion plans, and assess new market opportunities. Without the insights gleaned from demand forecasting, companies may find themselves at a significant disadvantage, leading to suboptimal decision-making that adversely affects inventory management, customer satisfaction, supply chain efficiency, and overall profitability.

In the hospitality industry, the concept of demand forecasting might seem daunting or even novel to some professionals. There's a tendency to rely on short-term decision-making at the expense of long-term planning due to apprehensions about the accuracy of predictions. However, leveraging available data for informed decision-making is indispensable for the strategic growth and sustainability of the business. Demand forecasts in hospitality are inherently dynamic, subject to change based on various factors including seasonal trends, economic conditions, and consumer behavior, thereby necessitating a flexible approach to forecasting.

Effective demand forecasting impacts numerous operational aspects such as budgeting, staffing, scheduling, inventory management, setting average room rates, pricing, and formulating marketing strategies. These areas underscore the importance of accurate forecasts in optimizing resource allocation and enhancing operational efficiency.

To refine the accuracy of demand forecasting, businesses should embrace a structured approach encompassing several key steps. Maintaining organized and accurate records forms the foundation for reliable forecasting. Utilizing past performance data, staying attuned to industry trends and competitor activities, continuously reviewing and adjusting forecasts based on actual performance, and collaborating with marketing teams for insights into market trends and consumer behavior are crucial strategies for enhancing forecasting accuracy.

Although forecasting can appear as a challenging task fraught with uncertainties, adopting a systematic approach that leverages data, industry insights, and continuous evaluation can significantly improve its effectiveness. Recognizing the inherent complexities and potential pitfalls of demand forecasting, businesses, especially in the hospitality sector, are encouraged to seek professional advice. This ensures the development of realistic and accurate forecasts, thereby minimizing risks and positioning the business for success in a competitive market environment.

6.1 BASIC CONCEPT OF DEMAND FORECASTING

Demand forecasting is a combination of two words; the first one is Demand and another forecasting. Demand means outside requirements of a product or service. In general, forecasting means making an estimation in the present for a future occurring event. Here we are going to discuss demand forecasting and its usefulness.

It is a technique for estimation of probable demand for a product or services in the future. It is based on the analysis of past demand for that product or service in the present market condition. Demand forecasting should be done on a scientific basis and facts and events related to forecasting should be considered.

Therefore, in simple words, we can say that after gathering information about various aspect of the market and demand based on the past, an attempt may be made to estimate future demand. This concept is called forecasting of demand. Suppose we sold 200, 250, 300 units of product X in the month of January, February, and March respectively. Now we can say that there will be a demand for 250 units approx. of product X in the month of April, if the market condition remains the same.

6.1.1 Usefulness of Demand Forecasting

Demand plays a vital role in the decision making of a business. In competitive market conditions, there is a need to take correct decision and make planning for future events related to business like a sale, production, etc. The effectiveness of a decision taken by business managers depends upon the accuracy of the decision taken by them.

Demand is the most important aspect for business for achieving its objectives. Many decisions of business depend on demand like production, sales, staff requirement, etc. Forecasting is the necessity of business at an international level as well as domestic level.

Demand forecasting reduces risk related to business activities and helps it to take efficient decisions. For firms having production at the mass level, the importance of forecasting had increased more. A good forecasting helps a firm in better planning related to business goals.

There is a huge role of forecasting in functional areas of accounting. Good forecast helps in appropriate production planning, process selection, capacity planning, facility layout planning, and inventory management, etc.

Demand forecasting provides reasonable data for the organization's capital investment and expansion decision. It also provides a way for the formulation of suitable pricing and advertisement strategies.

Following is the significance of Demand Forecasting:

- Fulfilling objectives of the business
- Preparing the budget
- Taking management decision
- Evaluating performance etc.

Moreover, forecasting is not completely full of proof and correct. It thus helps in evaluating various factors which affect demand and enables management staff to know about various forces relevant to the study of demand behavior.

6.1.2 The Scope of Demand Forecasting

The scope of demand forecasting depends upon the operated area of the firm, present as well as what is proposed in the future. Forecasting can be at an international level if the area of operation is international. If the firm supplies its products and services in the local market then forecasting will be at local level.

The scope should be decided considering the time and cost involved in relation to the benefit of the information acquired through the study of demand. Cost of forecasting and benefit flows from such forecasting should be in a balanced manner.

6.1.3 Types of Forecasting

There are two types of forecasting:

- Based on Economy
- Based on the time period

Based on Economy

There are three types of forecasting based on the economy:

i. **Macro-level forecasting:** It deals with the general economic environment relating to the economy as measured by the Index of Industrial Production(IIP), national income and general level of employment, etc.

ii. **Industry level forecasting:** Industry level forecasting deals with the demand for the industry's products as a whole. For example demand for cement in India, demand for clothes in India, etc.

iii. **Firm-level forecasting:** It means forecasting the demand for a particular firm's product. For example, demand for Birla cement, demand for Raymond clothes, etc.

Based on the Time Period

Forecasting based on time may be short-term forecasting and long-term forecasting

i. **Short-term forecasting:** It covers a short period of time, depending upon the nature of the industry. It is done generally for six months or less than one year. Short-term forecasting is generally useful in tactical decisions.

ii. **Long-term forecasting casting:** Long-term forecasts are for a longer period of time say, two to five years or more. It gives information for major strategic decisions of the firm. For example, expansion of plant capacity, opening a new unit of business, etc.

6.1.4 Demand Forecasting Methods

There are many different ways to create forecasts. Here are five of the top demand forecasting methods.

Trend projection

Trend projection uses your past sales data to project your future sales. It is the simplest and most straightforward demand forecasting method.

It's important to adjust future projections to account for historical anomalies. For example, perhaps you had a sudden spike in demand last year. However, it happened after your product was featured on a popular television show, so it is unlikely to repeat. Or your **e-Commerce** site got hacked, causing your sales to plunge. Be sure to note unusual factors in your historical data when you use the trend projection method.

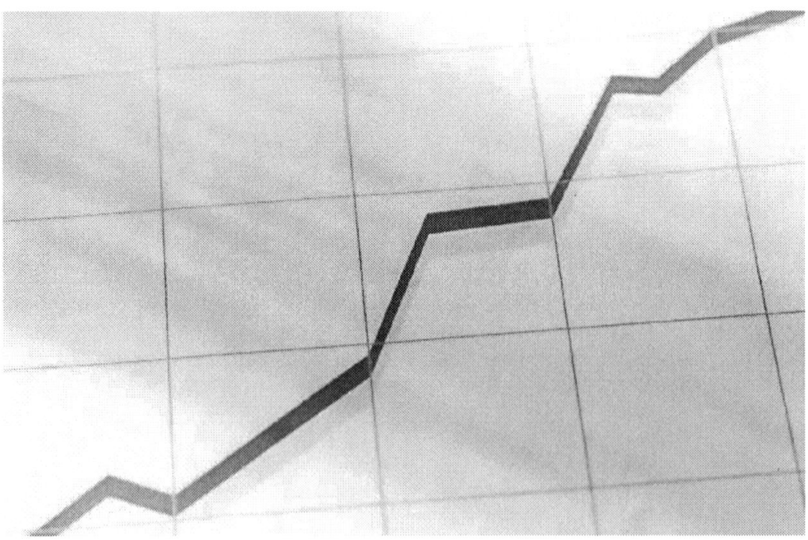

Market research

Market research demand forecasting is based on data from customer surveys. It requires time and effort to send out surveys and tabulate data, but it's worth it. This method can provide valuable insights you can't get from internal sales data.

You can do this research on an ongoing basis or during an intensive research period. Market research can give you a better picture of your typical customer. Your surveys can collect demographic data that will help you target future marketing efforts. Market research is particularly helpful for young companies that are just getting to know their customers.

Sales force composite

The sales force composite demand forecasting method puts your sales team in the driver's seat. It uses feedback from the sales group to forecast customer demand.

Your salespeople have the closest contact with your customers. They hear feedback and take requests. As a result, they are a great source of data on customer desires, product trends, and what your competitors are doing.

This method gathers the sales division with your managers and executives. The group meets to develop the forecast as a team.

Delphi method

The Delphi method, or Delphi technique, leverages expert opinions on your market forecast. This method requires engaging outside experts and a skilled facilitator.

You start by sending a questionnaire to a group of demand forecasting experts. You create a summary of the responses from the first round and share it with your panel. This process is repeated through successive rounds. The answers from each round, shared anonymously, influence the next set of responses. The Delphi method is complete when the group comes to a consensus.

This demand forecasting method allows you to draw on the knowledge of people with different areas of expertise. The fact that the responses are

anonymised allows each person to provide frank answers. Because there is no in-person discussion, you can include experts from anywhere in the world on your panel. The process is designed to allow the group to build on each other's knowledge and opinions. The end result is an informed consensus.

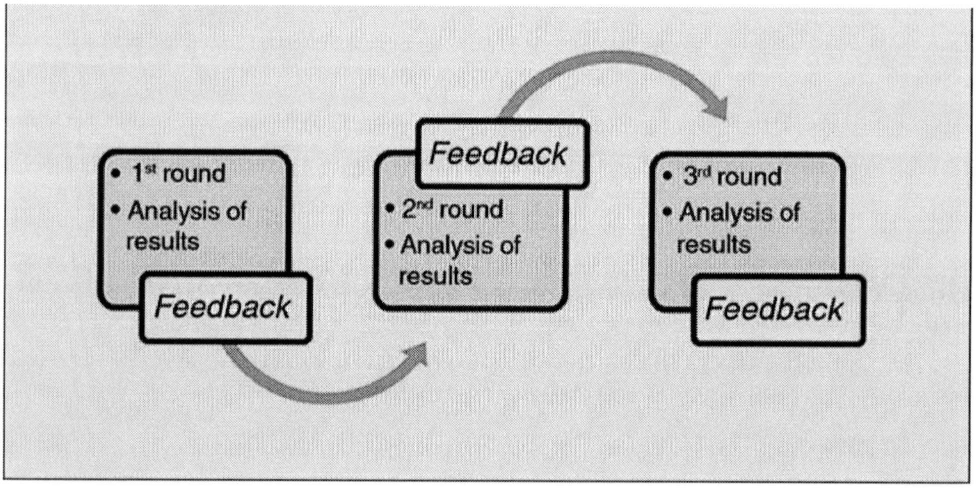

Econometric

The econometric method requires some number crunching. This technique combines sales data with information on outside forces that affect demand. Then you create a mathematical formula to predict future customer demand.

The econometric demand forecasting method accounts for relationships between economic factors. For example, an increase in personal debt levels might coincide with an increased demand for home repair services.

enjoyed the luxury of being able to price items at their discretion as their geographical location is not easily accessible for an eCommerce business to deliver to.

However, a large chain grocery store recently opened in their area that offers lower prices on many items that they carry. The grocery small business owners are unsure about how the competition will affect their customer demand or future sales potential.

Using historical data alone, the business would not likely make any adjustments to their marketing strategy. However, after performing a combination of demand forecasting methods they decide to make some changes.

With a low cash flow due to stocking their inventory levels abundantly in anticipation of the holiday season, the business is unsure how to make their short term demand increase. They research some case studies they find online and meet with a small business owner in their area for advice.

The small business decides on offering extra discounts to customers for a short time period and their Thanksgiving sales exceed their original projections. As a result, they decide to develop a customer loyalty program that even further increases long term customer retention.

6.2 THE KEY TO PROFITABILITY: UNDERSTAND YOUR DEMAND FORECAST

A hotel that is constantly jam-packed with guests is not automatically a profitable one. The goal of a successful hotel is not necessarily to achieve 100 percent occupancy, but rather to optimize revenue. And developing a way to more accurately forecast daily demand is a key operational challenge for hoteliers.

Today's hospitality landscape is characterized by increasing room supply and tight margins. In addition, stiff competition makes it imperative for hotel revenue managers to continuously adjust strategies to remain relevant. Predicting how many customers your hotel will have on any given night, anticipating the sales of products and services, and understanding how those bookings break down into business segment and respective profitability help hoteliers develop effective business growth strategies and make the most of revenue opportunities.

6.2.1 Unconstrained vs. Constrained Demand

Your operations team benefits from the use of a constrained demand forecast for supply purchases and planning purposes. However, to develop an effective revenue management strategy you must understand your forecasted unconstrained demand. Unconstrained demand is an estimate of the total demand for your hotel, ignoring rate and capacity constraints - essentially, how many rooms could be sold on a given day if your hotel had unlimited inventory. It's only through an analysis of total demand that you can optimize your profits, capturing yield opportunities at those points when demand exceeds supply and where it becomes necessary to turn away customers that are less profitable in favor of those who may be more willing to pay higher rates.

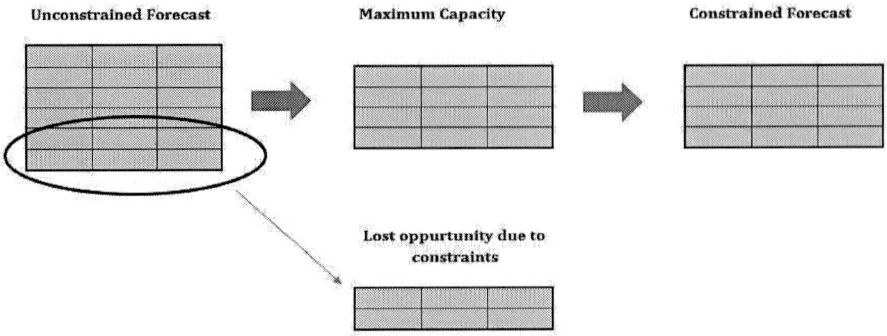

6.2.3 What's Powering Your Forecast?

By relying on science to power your demand forecasting - as opposed to using legacy methods - you leverage sophisticated processes and produce intelligent insights that reduce uncertainties and better equip managers to optimize financial results and business performance.

Better Accuracy

A major pillar supporting a demand forecast is accurate data. A good science-based forecast not only captures valuable historical data, but continuously updates real-time data as well, examining broad factors such as seasonality, market conditions, competitive landscape, length of stay patterns, pricing elasticity, geographical data, booking pace, and lead time. And it should automatically detect outliers and anomalies as well. By incorporating the right data - and avoiding "noisy data" that dilutes the reliability of a demand forecast - revenue managers can refine their approach and adjust pricing with greater precision, transforming data into accurate and actionable revenue-enhancing strategies.

Machine Learning & Artificial Intelligence

Machine learning (ML) is fueling next-generation solutions, allowing revenue managers to improve forecast performance by adapting quickly to changes in the business or marketplace. Scientific models enhanced with ML have the ability to automatically learn and improve from experience without being explicitly programmed, and are especially valuable in forecasting applications. Examples of ML used in forecasting include:

1. Machine learning (ML) is fueling next-generation solutions, allowing revenue managers to improve forecast performance by adapting quickly to changes in the business or marketplace. Scientific models enhanced with ML have the ability to automatically learn and improve from experience without being explicitly programmed, and are especially valuable in forecasting applications Examples of ML used in forecasting include: Anomaly detection mechanisms that identify and remove booking or rate observations that could skew historical statistics and degrade the accuracy of the forecast.

2. Advanced competitor configuration algorithms that automatically choose a best-fit competitive set based on relationships in pricing actions among a subject hotel and its competitors
3. Customer segmentation analysis used to predict customer value

Valuable Segmentation

A good forecast is granular enough to capture the nuances of market segmentation, understanding that each customer segment reflects different preferences, booking trends and patterns, and purchase intentions. A family taking a leisure vacation will have different requirements than a business traveler attending a convention. Predicting demand and requirements for each of these customer segments helps you better target your marketing, budget your operational expenses, and achieve an optimal business mix - knowing at any given time which business to take and which to turn down.

Incorporating Events

Incorporating events and promotions into your demand forecasting process is crucial for accuracy in your revenue management strategy. Beyond considering major holidays, you want to add in significant events that are specific to your city or property. Events typically mean a big influx of traffic and demand to your area, and when they're omitted from your forecast, you not only don't have a full picture of demand, but you'll be unable to develop an accurate pricing strategy. By separately forecasting events and promotions, you'll determine how far in advance guests book rooms around these two things, providing you with a more accurate analysis of future demand. And you'll also avoid letting them affect your day-in/day-out forecast.

Add Science to Group Forecasting

Group business can markedly impact hotel profits. And without forecasting for groups, you can't effectively yield nor truly optimize your business. Group

demand forecasting affects transient business and business from other groups, as well as ancillary revenue generators. It allows revenue managers to accurately assess the financial impacts of accepting a group during periods of high and low transient demand.

Most RMSs don't have the capability to forecast for group business. And many hotels still utilize traditional methods that rely on transient displacement analysis. This type of analysis, however, only projects what is required in group revenue to break even with displaced transient bookings, and it doesn't consider the significance of one group displacing another group. It also doesn't factor in how to optimize a property's meeting space.

Inaccurate group demand forecasting risks significant revenue losses. When group forecasts are too high, a property loses profits on rooms that could have been sold to high-value customers but instead lie empty. And if group business is forecasted too low, a property risks accepting transient business at suboptimal rates, or even booking to overcapacity. When forecasted accurately, hotels get a clear picture of the constraints that groups produce on sleeping rooms, providing opportunities for hotels to capture the appropriate rates from transient customers or other groups.

By choosing an RMS that incorporates science into group demand forecasting, you have the sophistication and flexibility you need to handle the complexities of predicting demand and establishing pricing for group business. Next-generation group forecasting provides a comprehensive daily analysis of allocation and pricing for both sleeping rooms and function space. It also incorporates the differences between transient and groups in terms of booking windows - understanding that groups book earlier in the booking horizon, while transient customers book closer in. A scientific solution can also handle the inherent fluctuations involved in group demand - preventing potential revenue losses by dynamically updating rates across market segments as it evaluates whether anticipated demand from RFPs actually occur.

Demand forecasting is germane for revenue management in the hospitality industry. An RMS with demand forecasting capabilities backed by science significantly improves accuracy - leveraging complex algorithms and extensive data sets that guide hoteliers in making fact-based decisions that lead to substantially higher profits. By integrating pricing with market demand intelligence, you can achieve the best business mix across both transient and group segments. Demand forecasting provides a strong foundation for an effective growth strategy, and it leads to a number of downstream positive effects on metrics and bottom-line income.

6.3 FORECASTING HOTEL REVENUE WITH OPTIMIZED PRECISION

No reasonable forecaster can identify the 'best' method from the various forecasting competitions and adopt that method for his/her specific forecasting problem.

Instead, the accuracy of hotel revenue forecast results benefits from taking multiple outcomes across forecasting methods to reach a more comprehensive, robust analysis. The revenue manager's responsibility is to consider the multiple outcomes produced by a forecast and efficiently deal with the implications and possible deviations from the adopted strategy.

In this way, a critical reflection on the achieved results can take place, and if any potential optimization can be achieved in the future by adjusting strategy.

Demand forecasting is of critical importance when optimizing hotel revenue, as it anticipates future business performance. It does this by identifying outliers in the form of data points that deviate from average performance to maximize results.

Valuable insights that hotel managers glean from forecasting can form the foundation for strategic decision-making to optimize hotel revenue performance. As hotel rooms are a perishable asset, forecasting is an indispensable means to maximize hotel occupancy rates.

6.3.1 Creating a successful forecasting model for your hotel

There are various types of tools available for your hotel to carry out a thorough, accurate forecast, which differ depending on your needs and budget. To complement available information to revenue managers, leading hotels tend to use a hotel Revenue Management System (RMS), as they are affordable, efficient, and high-performing. The main strength of an RMS is that they use advanced algorithms to improve forecasting precision.

6.3.2 Exploring 3 Popular Hotel Revenue Forecasting Models

Forecasting falls into three main categories: 1, operational forecasting; 2, financial forecasting; and 3, revenue management forecasting (unconstrained demand forecasting). Each of the three increases revenue in a different way.

Operational forecasting

i. This method focuses on operations areas across the hotel. Chiefly, these are:
ii. Staff allocation per department and with seasonal peaks and troughs taken into consideration.
iii. Reception, with peak times front of mind.
iv. Restaurants, including the number of covers for breakfast, lunch and dinner, and average spend per cover. It also scrutinizes the purchasing

obligations for both perishable and non-perishable restaurant produce, products, and equipment.

v. Risk management, including contingency plans to offset any type of damage.

Financial forecasting

This forecast type offers a prediction of revenue and **profitability** for owners and investors. It anticipates desired cash flow per month to compensate for periods of low demand – otherwise known as seasonality reserves. An example is a beach resort that closes during winter and so must generate enough revenue during busy season.

Key metrics for financial forecasting include payments for any property mortgages, insurance, licence fees, amortization of loans and assets that are constant, regardless of whether the hotel's doors are open or not.

Additional key metrics include any planned renovations and maintenance operations during the off-season, and the impact of any tax payment or interest rate obligation changes.

Revenue management forecasting (unconstrained demand forecast)

Revenue management gives hotel managers insights over future demand management. At its core, it takes into account room rate decisions and displacement reviews for possible group reservations. It incorporates market data, including competitor pricing and overall market performance, and applies seasonal pricing models to increase occupancy rates at the optimal revenue maximization price. Revenue management also offers hotels a marketing and sales advantage, as it advertises for rooms with lower demand and hyper-targets the buyer persona that is likeliest to visit.

The unique advantages that revenue management forecasting offers.

The main difference is that revenue management forecasting begins by actually taking figures that the hotel already has on their books, using them as a base point to map out possible future revenue scenarios by leveraging intricate analysis processes.

Revenue manager output is used as a foundation to inform hotel departments and set parameters for optimal performance according to expected demand. This includes opportunities and initiatives that various departments within hotel can implement. A revenue manager also increases marketing efforts and determines which customer segments to target and periods in which to use certain tactics and strategy. For instance, in low demand periods, promotions can be used to attract a demographic with lower disposable income.

Other areas that revenue management forecasting target include required staffing adjustments and product purchase, including linen, food and drink, and so forth, to prevent shortages and excess waste. Hotel departments can adjust their strategy and execution accordingly with richer insights that revenue managers provide. After all, a revenue manager's core responsibility is to deliver precise, rich information that generates key business insights, that in turn accelerate revenue across the hotel.

6.3.3 Key Focus Areas for Outstanding Revenue Management Forecasting Success

There are various areas within revenue management forecasting that contribute to your results. Addressing all of these areas with the requisite attention, determination, and diligence will position your hotel for optimized outcomes.

Date :	Days	31	Rooms	120			
Month : December	**Monday 1**	**Tuesday 2**	**Wednesday 3**	**Thursday 4**	**Friday 5**	**Saturday 6**	**Sunday 7**
Rooms on the Books	60	70	55	70	85	87	40
Segmentation							
Direct	8	10	8	8	20	22	8
Website	10	12	10	10	23	24	8
OTAs	20	22	18	20	28	27	16
Corporate	12	11	12	12	2	1	0
Groups	8	14	6	8	11	11	4
Promo´s	2	1	1	2	1	2	4
Others	0	0	0	0	0	0	0
Totals	***60***	***70***	***55***	***60***	***85***	***87***	***40***
% Occupancy on the Books	*50.0%*	*58.3%*	*45.8%*	*58.3%*	*70.8%*	*72.5%*	*33.3%*
Expected pickup	0	4	5	5	3	15	17
Forecast - Room Nights	60	94	60	75	100	110	58
Forecast - ADR	€ 109	€ 108	€ 96	€ 96	€ 124	€ 139	€ 88
Forecast %	50.0%	78.3%	50.0%	62.5%	83.3%	91.7%	48.3%
Room Night Pick Up							
Direct	0	8	2	2	6	8	6
Website	0	5	1	0	2	6	2
OTAs	0	9	2	3	7	8	8
Corporate	0	2	0	0	0	0	0
Groups	0	0	0	0	0	1	0
Promo´s	0	0	0	0	0	0	2
Others	0	0	0	0	0	0	0
Totals	***0***	***24***	***5***	***5***	***15***	***23***	***18***
ADR							
Direct		€ 108	€ 96	€ 96	€ 122	€ 140	€ 88
Website		€ 109	€ 97	€ -	€ 126	€ 136	€ 86
OTAs		€ 110	€ 96	€ 96	€ 124	€ 138	€ 89
Corporate		€ 100	€ -	€ -	€ -	€ -	€ 0
Groups		€ -	€ -	€ -	€ -	€ 137	€ 89
Promo´s		€ -	€ -	€ -	€ -	€ -	€ 88
Others		€ -	€ -	€ -	€ -	€ -	€ 0
Totals	***€ -***	***€ 107***	***€ 96***	***€ 96***	***€ 124***	***€ 138***	***€ 88***

You can use data from previous financial years to build a naive forecast (baseline forecast), before elaborating on it with anticipated data for upcoming periods. This naive forecast starting point can also be used as a reference to compare with your final forecast, with the aim of assessing where potential revenue-building opportunities may arise.

Past performance data

Historical hotel data acts as a strong indicator for future performance. However, while nothing is guaranteed, some trends in hotel revenue can always be identified, such as spikes and lulls in guest demand.

On-the-book (OTB) data

Revenue management should analyze current reservations that have already been made, upcoming promotions and offers that the hotel has in the pipeline, and website traffic, specifically its level of success as a contributor to bookings.

Accurate future data

It is essential to follow a robust process to ensure quality of data, such as distribution channel performance and customer preferences, guest nationalities, and travel type (business or leisure).

Top Accounts Expectations

Top-performing hotels anticipate production for their top accounts, including direct, corporate, consortia, and wholesale. Managers can then compare outcome of anticipated returns with their expectations and whether or not it fits with general OTB trends. This enables you to visualise discrepancies and, therefore, take action to make up any deficit.

Market trends

Market trends are, of course, very broad and general. Nevertheless, they are so important that they must be taken into account. For instance, trends may include increase/decline of hotel visitors in your local area or city; increase/decline in competitor hotels in your area or city; and changes in the local, regional, national, and, if applicable, international economies.

Holidays and events

Certain periods of the year, such as Christmas, summer holidays, New Year's Eve, and national events such as Thanksgiving in the United States, significantly help boost hotel revenues. Revenue managers can anticipate these periods and events for spikes in demand.

Influence of the competitors

Strong revenue management largely incorporates a record of all the available competitor data, kept up to date periodically. This data includes room rates, availability, fully booked dates, low and high demand periods, sales strategy shifts, management changes, and opening and closing of hotels.

Repeats and rebookings

Revenue managers should also be aware of occurrences that can skew forecast accuracy. Examples are repeat customers that are erroneously recorded as new guests and occasions where guests cancel and rebook at a reduced rate.

Additional trends

It is so important to assess trends between similar days from previous weeks to achieve accurate forecasting. It simply isn't enough to compare year-on-year. An efficient revenue management forecasting system compares and finds comparable booking trends on similar days from past weeks and seasons.

The same principle also applies to events and special periods, such as a national holiday or celebration. The greater the comparison data sample, the richer the data that the process has to work with, which can produce more informed, more precise results.

6.3.4 Revenue management precision in forecasting

The overarching objective for hotels is to forecast with as much accuracy as possible. Aiming for a maximum of 5% helps position your hotel to act in such a way to achieve your targets, while also giving you room to prepare for less-than-desired performance. Constant accuracy measurement is also essential, including analyzing differences between your forecast and reality as the days, weeks and months go by. This applies to both negative and positive differences.

It is critical to ascertain the causes of any differences by day of the week and segments in order to improve future forecasting accuracy.

Forecasts can also be inaccurate because of an incorrect OTB. To minimize the chances of such an outcome, you can systematically check for the following, with periodic procedural reviews too:

- Is your segmentation correct?
- Are room blocks up-to-date? Is there an increase or decrease?
- Is the group tentative correct? (apply materialisation factor)
- Are there any duplicate bookings?
- Are they any pending reservations that haven't been entered in your PMS)
- Are any oversold rooms removed, basing your forecast on the number of rooms available to sell?
- Are all room blocks and reservations attached to a correct rate or rate code?

6.3.5 Setting your hotel up for extraordinary revenue management forecasting outcomes

Forecasting process and results can vary across different hotels. Important differences often exist across companies and even within the same hotel group between different properties in their portfolio.

The longer forecasting is performed in a consistent, comprehensive manner, the better the accuracy. And when it comes to establishing your variance, once you achieve 5%, you can make it sharper, such as 3 or 4%. On this note, it is also worth keeping in mind that setting too ambitious target can demotivate personnel. It should be a realistic variance that provides you with a strong target that is good for business and helps motivate your team. By using a proven revenue management system with market-leading technology at its core, you can take advantage of a powerful tool that is also an affordable way to produce strong forecasting results.

6.4 DIFFERENT WAYS HOTELIERS CAN LEVERAGE STRATEGIC MANAGEMENT TOOL

Human minds are inherently prone to biases. Isn't it? In hotel revenue management, biases can be your worst nightmares since these can result in imprecise conclusions. And, inaccurate conclusions often equal to missed revenue opportunities.

Look, either you have a crystal ball that empowers you to know how much will be the average length of stay for varied rate categories in your hotel or what will be the occupancy percentage for "x" number of room nights and many more. Does that imply you've got to sit back and wait for the results to pan out? Of course not!

That's why room demand forecasting is so critical for effective planning and quick decision making. In fact, an improvement of 10% in forecasting accuracy can result in a surge of 1.5% to 3% in revenue generated from a revenue management system.

In this section, let's discover how you can improve your hotel demand forecast approach and maximize your hotel's profitability manifold with better pricing.

You already know it – profit maximization is your key KPI as a revenue manager, while that includes optimum room pricing (that's influenced by demand forecasting) and also cost reduction. The more accurate and clear demand picture you have, the better you can strategize your staffing, front desk, housekeeping, marketing, operations, and pricing. This also helps you resurrect your revenue management strategy based on projected upcoming demand.

Let's face it – demand forecasting is a complex discipline. But you can master it with a smart approach that ultimately helps you understand how to price your hotel rooms optimally to maximize your revenues. Put, this strategic management tool helps you become proactive in managing your inventory and prices smartly to boost your hotel's profitability.

6.4.1 Big Data, Big Revenue Opportunities

Many hotel industry players across the world still rely on their guesswork and instincts for forecasting. However, some smart revenue managers embracing technology strategize using information from tools with scientific algorithms that employ various statistical models like exponential smoothing, moving average, etc.

PMS, home to mountains of historical as well as future data, was traditionally used to understand the scope of upcoming demand across different room categories, length of stays, guest segments, and other data points such as booking pace, weather, etc. Hoteliers used to turn to the historical booking information available, recreate past booking curves, and compare the pace of bookings. However, those pricing decisions were not reliable.

Fortunately, with more and more technology adoption, Big Data has made inroads into the fabric of the hotel industry and emerged as a game-changer for hoteliers. It's here to stay and has brought about a paradigm shift (look ahead, not back!) in the hotel demand forecasting been done so far.

Today a lot has changed or better to say, more evolved– customer segments, customer behavior, etc. We have piles of competitor pricing information available too. *Pro Tip:* Not all data is the right data. So beware!

Then we have other data sets that can be taken into consideration while taking pricing decisions:

- **Macroeconomic Factors:** Some trigger events (either in source market or travel destinations) like conferences, holidays, conventions, events, economic development, citywide transport changes can cause a shift in demand patterns.
- **Reviews and Rating Information:** Good reviews lead to a spike in demand that implies you can increase your prices while maintaining occupancy levels.
- **Weather Impact:** If you run your hotel in a weather-driven market, the impact of weather is an important parameter. Good date can boost demand and vice versa.
- **Web-shopping regrets and denials:** Customer browsing behavior and booking activity/inactivity can reveal good insights for you. By layering in this information into your forecasts, you can get a more accurate picture.

All these factors and wealth of information can help a modern hotelier understand market demand much better and build an accurate demand forecasting picture well in advance to make profitable rate adjustments and sell more inventory at the best possible rates.

6.4.2 Track Web Shopping Behavior

To be able to build optimal price points, a hotel needs to forecast unconstrained demand. And for that, it's imperative to look at the hotel's denials and regrets. And thus, website data is a crucial source for these. If you wish to determine the popularity score for your hotel on a given day, look at your hotel's website traffic. The valuable web insights can help you get a clearer picture of your current and upcoming true unconstrained demand by unraveling details such as your website visits that reflect the frequency of last-minute arrivals. You will also be able to see as to how many website visitors are you attracting to your hotel's website at a certain time on a specific day.

If you can analyze the website visitors' data vs. future date bookings, you can build an accurate future demand picture. You can also determine the price sensitivity of your customers by assessing the prices at which consumers are making bookings and their site abandonment rate (due to rate controls or inventory limitations).

But it's Not as Easy as it looks! You must be able to capture the accurate difference between denials and regrets, which is tough. Some hotels use CRS data to track this. The Internet has also empowered hoteliers like you to collate the bulk of consumer shopping data. You can easily find out now as to how many bookers landed up on your website but did not finish the booking.

This customer lost data reflects on the latent demand but only if you have a clear picture of denials and regrets as mentioned above too. However, you can fall prey to miscalculating the latent demand if you use multiple distribution channels as again for every channel you need to clearly distinguish between denials and regrets. As a revenue manager, you can utilize this data to determine the conversion rates and plan the roadmap to recover from the site abandonment.

6.4.3 Competitive Intelligence and Competitor Pricing

Besides the deep analysis of your hotel's web shopping data, competitive intelligence and competitor pricing can also help you make accurate demand forecasts. You must identify a competitive set (similar to your property size, consumer segment, and comparable pricing model) that you need to set your eyes on. Then, glean their demand by fetching and analyzing their room rates using some price intelligence tools across various distribution channels, GDS and their brand websites. If your competitor makes any change(s) to their price, it can impact your demand since it might be the strategy of your competitor to acquire your customers. Thus, competitor pricing can influence price-sensitive consumers. It can also have an indirect impact on your demand if you (as a revenue manager) make rate adjustments to combat the price challenge thrown by your competitors.

Hotel revenue management has emerged as an important discipline that entails ever-changing consumer behavior, new age channels, varied pricing models, lean booking windows, and many more aspects. Amidst all this, accurate demand forecasting is the jumping pad to maximizing your revenue and hotel profitability.

> **Key Fact**
>
> The forecast error needs to be calculated using actual sales as a base. There are several forms of forecast error calculation methods used, namely Mean Percent Error, Root Mean Squared Error, Tracking Signal and Forecast Bias.

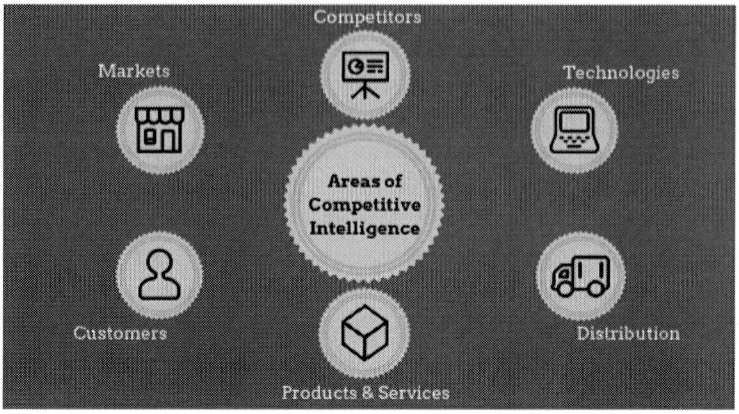

6.5 HOTEL FORECAST MODEL AND TOOL

According to your yield opportunities, you may decide of a more or a less developed forecasting tool. You may also consider Computerized – Revenue Management System. Here some examples of hotel forecasting tools in excel.

Forecasts are not perfect. It is a strategic management tool. A basic Forecast is better than none. It is the path to market and customer knowledge. It reinforces your pro-activeness in terms of inventory and rate management.

Your forecast module can help to forecast the double occupancy, the number of arrivals and departures: useful for the front-desk and housekeeping. On the basis of your forecasted number of nights by segment, you can anticipate the number of guests: it helps housekeeping to forecast their costs, and the restuarant the number of breakfasts. The forecast can help you to prevent and identify challenges in reaching your objectives: it gives time to adapt strategies or work out additional actions.

The forecast can help to identify low demand period: you can develop it as a communication tool taken over by sales department to focus their efforts on sales.

6.5.1 Basic Forecasting Model

Date : 30th November   Days 31   Rooms 120

Month : December	Wednesday	Thursday	Friday	Saturday	Sunday	Monday	Tuesday
	1	2	3	4	5	6	7
Rooms on the books	60	70	55	70	20	40	45
% Occupancy on the books	50%	58%	46%	58%	17%	33%	38%
Expected Pick up	0	4	5	5	3	15	17
Forecast	60	74	60	75	23	55	62
Forecast % Occ	50.0%	61.7%	50.0%	62.5%	19.2%	45.8%	51.7%
Pick Up Room Nights							
Individual	2	5	10	10	3	15	17
Groups	-2	-1	-5	-5	0	0	0
TOTAL	0	4	5	5	3	15	17

6.5.2 Advanced Hotel Forecast

Month : December	Wednesday	Thursday	Friday	Saturday	Sunday
	1	2	3	4	5
Rooms on the books	87	112	88	108	93
Individual Business	10	15	11	16	21
Companies	45	50	15	15	10
Wholesale	15	20	25	30	5
Meeting and Congress	10	15	20	25	30
Groups Leisure	7	12	17	22	27
% Occupancy on the books	73%	93%	73%	90%	78%
Expected Pick up	3	2	11	12	7
Forecast RN	90	114	99	120	100
Forecast ARR	109,2	108,0	96,1	96,4	95,8
Forecast % Occ	75%	95%	83%	100%	83%
Pick Up Room Nights					
Individual Business	5	5	10	10	7
Companies	-1	-2	0	0	0
Wholesale	-1	-1	5	5	2
Meeting and Congress	0	0	-2	-1	0
Groups Leisure	0	0	-2	-2	-2
TOTAL	3	2	11	12	7
ADR					
Individual Business	125	125	110	115	105
Companies	115	115	125	125	120
Wholesale	90	90	80	80	80
Meeting and Congress	100	100	100	100	100
Groups Leisure	90	90	75	75	75
TOTAL ARR	109,17	107,98	96,06	96,38	95,75

6.5.3 Occupancy Forecast

The most important short-term planning is forecasting the number of rooms available for sale on any future date for making pricing decisions.

Obviously, a forecast is only as reliable as the information on which it is based, not just guesswork. Forecasting is a difficult skill to develop. The skill is acquire through experience mainly, effective recordkeeping, and accurate counting methods.

Occupancy Forecast Data:

- **Number of expected room arrivals:** based on existing reservations and historical trends for new reservations and on cancellations prior to arrival date.
- **Number of expected room walk-ins:** (guests how arrive at a hotel without reservation) based on historical records. Percentage of Walk-ins = Number of Room Walk-Ins/Total Number of Room Arrival = (96/ 335)x100

- **Number of expected room stayovers** (rooms occupied on previous nights that will continue to be occupied for the night in question): based on existing reservations.
- **Number of expected room no-shows:** based on historical records. Percentage of No-shows = Number of Room No-Shows/Number of Room Reservations = (49/288)x100
- **Number of expected room understays** (check-outs occurring before expected departure date): based on historical data. Percentage of Understays = Number of Understay Rooms / Number of Expected Check-Outs = [30/(290-30+47)]x100
- **Number of expected room check-outs:** based on existing reservations.
- **Number of expected room overstays** (check-outs occurring after the originally reserved departure date): based on historical records. Percentage of Overstays = Number of Overstay Rooms / Number of Expected Check-outs = [47 /(290-30+47)]x100

Forecast Formula. Once relevant occupancy statistics have been gathered, the number of rooms available for sale on any given date can be determined by the following formula (Hotel example has 130 rooms):

Total Number of Guestrooms: 130
– Number of Out-of-Order Rooms
– Number of Room Stayovers
– Number of Room Reservations
+ Number of Room Reservations x no-Show Percentage
+ Number of Room Understays
– Number of Room Overstays
———————————————-
= Number of Rooms Available for Sale

Once this figure is determined, Hotel can decide whether or not to accept more reservations but planning decisions must remain flexible because they are subject to change a cause for cancellations and modifications. Note that the above formula does *not include walk-ins* because the number of walk-ins a hotel can accept is determined by the number of rooms available for sale; if a hotel is full due to existing reservations, stayovers, and other factors, it cannot accept walk-ins!

6.6 SUMMARY

Demand forecasting is a crucial analytical process in business planning, involving estimations of future customer demand through the analysis of historical data and other market indicators. This practice is fundamental for making informed decisions in a competitive market, guiding strategies related to sales, production, capital investment, expansion, pricing, and advertising. The accuracy of demand forecasting significantly influences the effectiveness of these decisions, underscoring its importance in achieving business objectives and optimizing revenue.

The scope of demand forecasting varies according to the geographical and operational reach of a business, ranging from local to international levels. Various methods are employed to project future demand, including trend projection, market research, sales force composite, the Delphi method, and econometric models. Each of these approaches offers different insights and relies on distinct data sources, from internal sales data to expert opinions and customer surveys, highlighting the multifaceted nature of forecasting.

In the hospitality industry, particularly in hotel revenue management, the goal is not merely to achieve full occupancy but to maximize profitability through optimized pricing and occupancy strategies. This involves understanding both constrained and unconstrained demand forecasts, the former aiding in operational planning and the latter in developing effective revenue management strategies. Advances in machine learning (ML) have further enhanced forecasting accuracy, allowing for rapid adaptation to market changes and more granular analysis of customer segments, booking trends, and purchase intentions.

Incorporating external factors such as events, promotions, and group business into demand forecasting is critical for achieving precision in revenue management strategies. However, no single forecasting method is universally best; the choice depends on the specific needs and context of the business. Employing sophisticated forecasting techniques can significantly reduce uncertainties, enabling businesses, especially hotels, to optimize financial results and improve overall performance by anticipating future trends and adapting strategies accordingly.

6.7 REFERENCES

- "Groups & Total Hotel Revenue Management." HSMAI, 2016, www.hsmai.org/knowledge/summary.cfm?ItemNumber=24710.
- Ampountolas, Apostolos. "Forecasting Hotel Demand Uncertainty Using Time Series Bayesian VAR Models - Apostolos Ampountolas, 2018." SAGE Journals, 4 Oct. 2018, journals.sagepub.com/doi/abs/10.11 77/1354816618801741.
- Boulton, Clint. "Starwood Taps Machine Learning to Dynamically Price Hotel Rooms." CIO, CIO, 13 May 2016, www.cio.com/article/3070384/starwood-taps-machine-learning-to-dynamically-price-hotel-rooms.html.
- Lynn, Michael. "Segmenting and Targeting Your Market: Strategies and Limitations - Lynn - 2012 - Wiley Online Books." Wiley Online Library, The Cornell School of Hotel Administration on Hospitality: Cutting Edge Thinking and Practice, 2 Jan. 2012, onlinelibrary.wiley.com/doi/abs/10.1002/9781119200901.ch23.
- Morse SC, Beckman E (2016) A Decision Model for Hotel Revenue Management Displacement Analysis for Transient Room Demand vs. Group Room Demand. Journal of Hotel & Business Management 5: 141. doi: 10.4172/2169-0286.1000141, https://www.longdom.org/open-access/a-decision -model-for-hotel-revenue-management-displacement-analysisfor-transient-room-demand-vs-group-room-demand-2169-0286-1000141.pdf.
- Thompson, Gary. "Revenue Management Forecasting Aggregation Analysis Tool." Cornell Hotel of School of Administration, Center for Hospitality Research Tools, Sept. 2009, scholarship.sha.c ornell.edu/chrtools/21/.
- White Paper: Innovative Forecasting & Demand Growth Strategies for Fueling Hotel Bookings. Cvent, Social Tables, Rainmaker, cdn2.hubspot.net/hubfs/3226550/eBook%20Fueling%20Hotel%20Bookings%20-%20Rainmaker%20and%20Social%20Tables.pdf.
- Willmore, Simon. "12 Advantages of Revenue Management Technology." Travel Daily, 71 Sept. 2017, www.traveldailymedia.com/12-advantages-revenue-management-technology/.

CHAPTER 7

Inventory Management in Hospitality Industry

INTRODUCTION

Effective inventory management is pivotal for the success of any business or e-commerce platform, ensuring a delicate balance between meeting customer demands and minimizing costs. This equilibrium involves maintaining sufficient stock levels to meet consumer expectations while also controlling inventory expenses. Employing strategies rooted in pricing psychology can play a significant role in managing excess inventory efficiently.

One such strategy is "price anchoring," where a higher-priced item from the same category is positioned alongside the product targeted for clearance. This tactic not only captures customer interest but also enhances the perceived value of the discounted item, thereby increasing its sale probability. Another approach is the "bundle offer," where combining two distinct products at a special price can expediently reduce surplus stock, particularly of those items that yield lower returns. Additionally, offering a free product with a popular item can significantly boost the sales rate of the latter, effectively moving inventory while delighting customers.

In the hospitality sector, inventory management systems are indispensable tools for mitigating losses, preventing theft, and optimizing stock orders from vendors. These systems furnish hotels with critical reports on various aspects such as vendor performance, accountability, and order management. Vendor performance reports provide insights into the timeliness, cost, accuracy, and quality of deliveries, enabling hotels to assess and select reliable suppliers. Accountability reports are crucial for tracking and resolving delivery discrepancies, ensuring order accuracy. Moreover, order management functionalities aid in preventing both surplus stock and shortages, allowing for precise stock ordering.

Comprehensive inventory controls are essential not only for shrinkage prevention but also for regulatory compliance, including adherence to vendor agreements and accounting standards. Hotels, in particular, must implement robust inventory control measures to ensure accurate reporting and optimal stock levels. These measures are fundamental to maintaining vendor relations, financial integrity, and operational efficiency. By integrating strategic pricing techniques with advanced inventory management systems, businesses and hotels can navigate the complexities of inventory control, achieving both customer satisfaction and cost-effectiveness.

7.1 INVENTORY MANAGEMENT IN HOSPITALITY

Inventory management can be difficult for the hospitality industry because of the somewhat intangible nature of their product or difficulty associated with tracking it and stocktaking. However, do not fall into the trap of thinking that it can simply be forgotten about as this will cost you thousands per year in revenue. Here we consider some ways in which better inventory control can be achieved in hospitality environments.

Effective inventory management for hotels involves both revenue management (creating and managing demand) and yield management (maximizing returns). The investment backing a hotel is tied up in its real estate and the returns can only be gained from renting out that real estate optimally.

Pricing. By driving prices up during high peak periods and knowing how much to discount prices by to ensure rooms are rented during low peak periods, hotels can maximize their return. Through dynamic pricing, businesses can provide discounts and incentives in a controlled way during different seasons.

Distribution. Hotels generally advertise their rooms through multiple channels, such as online travel agencies, to optimize reach and promote sales. Distribution management is essential and this involves calculating the minimum numbers of rooms needing to be sold for any given period by each channel. In doing so, you then have the ability to make informed choices regarding reallocation from cancellations or where to list spare rooms to maximize sales.

Market Segmentation. Being aware of your market and the variable preferences, demands and affordability of different demographics are paramount to understanding how to price and distribute your room sales across the various channels. Not only does this help in managing your existing rooms, but it can also allow you to capture more of the market and increase sales and revenue. Flexibility is an important virtue required of hoteliers and being able to understand your clientele and adapt to their needs is vital to building loyalty and guaranteeing profitability.

7.1.1 Effectiveness in Inventory Management

Inventory management is a very critical aspect of revenue management or yield management. To start with first we need to understand what inventory means in the Hospitality industry. As per the hospitality sector, their inventory means hotel rooms to be rented each night. The Hospitality industry is an immensely competitive business and effective inventory control plays a critical role in the hotel's success in term of profitability.

Effective inventory management for hotels involves both revenue management (creating and managing demand) and yield management (maximising returns). The investment which done in the hospitality industry is closely related to its real estate and returns on investments can only be maximized from selling (renting) these real estate (Hotel rooms) wisely.

There are several ways that you can manage your inventory, let's discuss some of those.

- **Integrate your system with your sources of reservation**

In today's era, automation and well-connected systems are utmost necessary for the improvement of the overall performance of your hotel. A hotels channel manager (CRS) solution should interface, seamlessly connect, and share data, in a real-time manner with both the PMS and revenue management systems. With the help of an integrated system as it comes with real-time inventory management it makes easier for hotels to manage reservations, rates and allocation of inventory across several channels and properties in single go. These channels have to be updated in efficient way, otherwise it will face problems like reservation errors, Overbooking and missed booking. Integration helps in making sure that rates and inventory availability updates in real time and accurately across all reservation sources. Thus, gives the flexibility to operators to optimise inventory for maximise occupancy and revenue.

- **Take control of your Inventory**

The OTAs are integral part of any hotel's success strategy. However, it is seen that the channel partners like OTAs making profit at the expense of property owner. This situation is dangerous as well as debilitating. These channels should be used very cleverly as a part of hotels overall mix of business.

Using and promoting direct booking strategy will help hotels to recapture their financial destiny and gaining control over pricing and managing inventory.

- **Find an effective use of Market Segmentation**

You should be very much aware about your market. The variable preferences demand and rate sensibility in different segment of market will give you the basic idea about how to price and distribute your inventory across the various channels. This will not only help you in managing your inventory but it can also help you to capture more of market and increase in revenue and sales. You have to very flexible being an inventory manager of the hotel, you should be able to understand your clientele and adapt to their needs is very important in building loyalty and guaranteeing profitability.

7.1.2 Optimizing Room Inventory

Here's why your hotel needs a comprehensive room inventory strategy:

It allows you to improve your distribution strategy. Your room inventory strategy should identify the various channels that need to be used to maximize bookings during a specific period of time, and also minimize the costs associated with achieving those bookings.

For example, your room inventory strategy should identify the best times of year to employ OTAs to sell a high number of rooms. While these bookings are more expensive than direct bookings, they may be necessary to book the highest number of rooms possible during a specific time of the year. With an effective room inventory strategy in place, you will be able to better identify which distribution partners and channels to include in your overall distribution strategy.

It allows you to accurately forecast. A comprehensive room inventory strategy will allow you to predict when your rooms will be in higher demand and determine how room rates should fluctuate during those peak times.

Beyond simply forecasting when demand will rise and fall throughout the travel season, the best hotel inventory strategies also explain the reasoning behind those trends using accurate, relevant data. You should priorities data collection efforts in order to create a refined room inventory strategy that predicts and forecasts future demands with precision.

Ultimately, forecasting has a direct impact on your ability to balance your room inventory levels with their revenue levels, giving them the opportunity to earn as much revenue as possible with each booking.

It allows you to segment your target markets. Knowing that not every room is right for every traveler, it's important for you to use a room inventory strategy to better develop segmentations. For instance, the luxury suite at the highest level of your hotel property is not going to be within reach for every market segment you sell to.

It's critical your room inventory strategy accommodates the various types of people who book your hotel, including their interests, age groups, demographics and budget levels, and matches them accordingly with the right rooms to meet their needs. By using segmentation strategies, you will be able to sell as many rooms as possible across all of your different price points at any given moment.

Hotel Room Inventory Advice for Hoteliers

Your hotel's inventory is its greatest asset and represents a major part of your investment.

That investment is tied up until rooms are sold, making the effective management of inventory a key task. No longer just an idea, hotels that have mastered the art of inventory management are seeing big benefits to their bottom line. It is estimated that Marriott Hotels increased their annual revenue by as much as $200 million when they first introduced their inventory management strategy.

Creating a balanced strategy. It costs time and money to store, track, and promote inventory across multiple booking channels. Because mismanagement of inventory can cause significant financial problems, hotels must be vigilant in tracking their data and implementing findings on a regular basis with an eye to controlling the costs associated with inventory. Technology will help you make the most of your data and create a balanced inventory management strategy, this includes:

- **Lead Time.** In order to maximize sales, you need to understand how long it takes to sell hotel rooms through each of your key channels. With booking lead times shrinking, creating more forecasting uncertainty, hotels must have a better grasp of what consumer behaviors and trends are driving lead times from the search-to-booking window.
- **Distribution.** What is the minimum number of rooms you have to sell through each type of booking channel in order to maintain effective sales levels? By understanding the minimum number of rooms to be sold (across day, week, and month) and across specific channels (direct and indirect), you can both reallocate any cancellations, and more importantly, decide how and where to utilize spare rooms for promotional offers and seasonally adjusted rates. For maximum efficiency, your inventory management strategy needs to work hand-in-hand with your sales and marketing strategy.
- **Demand Management.** Monitoring demand and sales trends via your channel manager or in-house reporting system allows for real-time, effective inventory management, promotion, and reallocation of rooms so that you are aware of your available inventory at any given time. To this end, centralization of all hotel staff resources is essential so that everyone is on top of your hotel's current inventory, the prices they should be quoting, and any discounts or promotions they can offer. This centralization is particularly important for hotels that receive high volumes of phone reservations and walk-in guests, or have call centers or central reservation systems.

A holistic approach. You need to think of inventory management holistically: it doesn't happen in isolation from your other management, sales, and marketing strategy. With the right technology to help you integrate the different functions, you will be able not only to collect the right data and analyze it in a way that is meaningful, but also use it to drive your marketing campaigns through all your different sales channels and maximize your return on your inventory.

Understanding Distressed Inventory

Distressed inventory refers to hotel rooms that are not expected to be sold at full price. Inventory can become distressed for a number of reasons, but the most common is cancellations in close proximity to the booking date.

For these rooms, hotels often significantly reduce prices to encourage consumers to book last-minute and to avoid their rooms remaining empty. After all, what is the value of a hotel room if it is empty?

Also, a hotel that is full to capacity is good for business in other ways. It conveys the impression that there is always high demand for rooms, enhancing a hotel's reputation.

Additionally, when people stay at a hotel, they don't just pay for the room. Other revenue can be generated from food services, recreational activities and other in-house services. Sometimes, the discounted amount of money on a reduced price room can be made up through the late-coming guests' extra spending.

Why your hotel needs pooled inventory

A pooled inventory model means you can sell all your rooms on all channels at the same time, as opposed to splitting your inventory and allocating a certain number of rooms to each channel you connect to.

Pooled inventory can be achieved by using a channel manager and will ensure your hotel avoids double bookings and overbooking.

If a hotel is not using a channel manager, then they have to fracture their inventory splitting between all the online booking channels they are using.

The hotel then has to constantly monitor and shuffle its inventory, with the real risk of missing bookings, as they run out of inventory on the smaller – but still valuable – OTAs.

By giving all of the OTAs your entire inventory at once – which is what pooled inventory supports – most of the OTAs will reward you with, better visibility in their ranking algorithm.

By using pooled inventory, there is no barrier to the number of online booking channels you can work with; by broadening your distribution, you increase your opportunity and can target individual markets and segments. This will increase your bookings and then by providing loyalty and re-marketing strategies, marketers can turn these booking clients into direct clients.

7.1.3 Hotel Inventory Management Software

Technology is changing the way people plan, book, and enjoys travel – and it can also be used to combat these changes from a hotel's perspective. Just as technology empowers travelers and guests to explore their online options and conveniently book their chosen accommodation, intuitive technology can eliminate the manual processes that dominate your daily routine in your hotel.

One great example of how you can use technology to positively impact your hotel's operations is last-minute bookings.

We know that mobile devices are changing everything. More than half of the world's population now has a mobile device. That in turn means that more guests are booking your hotel on Smartphone and tablets, and crucially, they're doing it increasingly at the last minute.

This trend represents a huge opportunity for hotels to sell their very final rooms, right up to the last minute. But only hotels with the right channel management technology in place will be able to take advantage.

Ultimately your hotel needs one single connection that can shield you from the madness; a seamless two-way connection to your hotel's various booking sites is key to ensuring the constant flow of information is reliable.

This allows you to increase your revenue and reduce waste, by ensuring your entire inventory is available across all channels – and you can keep all available rooms listed right up to the last minute. When a room is booked, a channel manager automatically updates it across all channels. You can change the room rates across all channels without logging into multiple sites to make updates, and maintain or increase your rates.

There are a lot of systems that help support inventory management:

- Property Management System (PMS)
- Point of Sale System (POS)
- Revenue Management System (RMS)
- Channel Management System (CMS)
- Central Reservation System (CRS) and Hotel Reservation System (HRS)
- Global Distribution System (GDS)
- Internet Booking Engine (IBE)

Choosing the right hotel inventory software

Given a channel manager is the most powerful asset, it's important to make the right choice since not all of them include the same features.

Choosing the right channel manager will also enable you to:

- Get your hotel booked faster
- Remove manual entry with complete real-time automation
- Have all your rooms online at once to increase revenue
- Understand deep reporting to help analyze trends such as last-minute bookings

Here are some questions to ask potential channel manager providers no matter what size your property is:

- Do they offer full integration with your property management system?
- Do they support global channel connections, integrated with reliable XML connection?
- Is the user interface user friendly?
- Is adequate support and training offered, especially in your native language?
- Do they use a pooled inventory model?
- Is comprehensive reporting part of the system?
- Will they integrate with your online booking engine?
- Do they automate and update in real-time?
- How long does it take to implement the technology?
- Is the software PCI DSS compliant?
- Are there product feedback avenues?
- Can the product support multiple users
- Is there a free trial period?
- Is the pricing model per channel, per reservation, or flat fee?

7.1.4 Hotel Inventory Management System

A revenue management system is another vital piece of technology that can significantly aid your inventory management strategy.

What an RMS can do. We live in an era of big data. In order to create accurate demand forecasts and update room prices in real-time, you are going to be reliant on technological solutions. At the most basic level, an RMS can mine your reservation, booking and data, producing demand generation forecasts for every type of room for every day of the year. You will be able to see historic booking channels, lengths of stays, prices paid and the yield generated on each room, as well as any patterns in cancellations.

These forecasts work alongside optimization programs in order to set inventory controls, enabling you to automatically set different rates for room types and lengths of stay up to specified overbooking levels. This approach allows you to cherry pick the highest value bookings (which given differences in underlying costs are not necessarily those with the highest room rate), thereby optimizing the yield on your inventory.

Pricing precision and pricing optimization is the two most important parts of your inventory management strategy and is key drivers of your revenue per available room and profitability. Even a $1 reduction in the ADR (average daily rate) for a 500-room hotel with 70% occupancy would cost that hotel over more than $100,000 in lost revenue per year.

In order to take advantage of dynamic pricing, you need a system that can respond to information in real-time, allowing you to stay on top of any emerging trends or shifts in customer behavior.

Integrating your RMS with your channel manager. By integrating your Revenue Management System with your channel manager, you can quickly distribute real-time rate recommendations from your RMS, making sure your rooms are selling for the right price. An important piece of the inventory management puzzle, your channel manager ensures that rates and availability are automatically adjusted in real-time across all booking channels in order to reduce the time it takes to update room prices and increase revenue. By monitoring demand and sales trends via your RMS, channel manager, and in-house reporting you can effectively manage, promote, and reallocate your rooms.

Leverage technology for more powerful inventory management. Technology can not only help inform human decision making, but also show the impact of those decisions in real-time, enabling you to streamline your marketing strategies and capitalize on emerging trends. And by bringing your technological and human resources together, you can help maximize your inventory yield through more targeted marketing opportunities.

The theory behind a good hotel inventory system

Every principle and strategy has best practice, which allows you to achieve the best possible results. Inventory management is no exception.

Here are four ways to streamline inventory management to maximize revenue opportunities:

1. Integrate your channel manager. Integrated systems are now necessary to improve the overall performance of your property. A channel manager solution should interface, seamlessly connect, and share data, in a real-time manner with both the PMS and revenue management systems. With an integrated system comes real-time inventory management, making it easier for hotels to manage room bookings, rates, and distribution of inventory across multiple channels and properties in a single click. Channels that are not updated properly encounter reservation errors, overbooking and missed booking opportunities. Integration ensures that room rates and inventory availability update simultaneously and accurately across all booking channels and provides operators with the flexibility needed to optimize inventory for maximum occupancy and revenue.

2. Make data-based decisions. When it comes to rate setting and inventory allocation decisions, data, not instinct, should drive marketing moves. With seamless integration, hoteliers can monitor performance metrics such as RevPAR, ADR, occupancy, booking source etc. and not only determine their best-performing channels and price points that are best fit for their target market but also gauge the impact of their decisions. Similarly, hoteliers can combine and analyze various data sets simultaneously such as customer segmentation, seasonality, special events, booking trends, competition rate setting etc. allowing hoteliers to forecast demand and create appropriate pricing and promotional strategies aimed at different customer segments. Armed with the relevant data and utilized effectively, owners and managers can then make more timely, informed and sophisticated rate and distribution decisions, maximizing revenue opportunities and hotel performance.

3. Leveraging mobile technology. Real-time visibility is important in making timely informed decisions. With a cloud-based mobile PMS managers' can view live performance, monitor operations, access key reports etc. remotely, on the go, anytime, anywhere, even if they are not physically on site. Likewise, revenue managers can access the PMS and make strategic decisions about rates and inventory and can react to hotel and market conditions in real time and make inventory adjustments. Information that can be accessed instantly from almost anywhere helps to further streamline inventory management; employees are better informed, can make more accurate, faster decisions, deliver the right inventory to the right people at the right time, maximizing revenue opportunities.

4. Push your book direct channels. We all know that it is far cheaper to encourage a repeat visit than it is to find a new customer. And while that is all well and good since we have become tethered to our digital devices in recent years, our booking habits have moved online and as a result, the fight for online bookings between hoteliers and third parties has grown. The issue is also compounded by a number of factors, such as the unwavering contracts that exist between the OTAs and hoteliers, the commission paid by the hoteliers – anywhere from 15-25% of top-line revenue in commissions (painful!), the strong online presence OTAs have (supported by unbelievable marketing budgets) along with the consumers belief, and have been trained to believe, that the best prices can be found on third-party sites.

With the right technology in place, maximizing return on your inventory and increasing the hotel's revenue is much more achievable.

7.1.5 Online Inventory Management for the Hospitality Industry

In the highly competitive hospitality industry, hotel operators and small business owners need access to valuable data to facilitate informed decision-making. This data plays a particularly pivotal role in developing the revenue and inventory management strategies for hotels and resorts to ensure business success and sustainability.

Online inventory management software is a great tool for facilitating and analyzing this information. It provides a variety of inventory control solutions that businesses in the hospitality industry would find life-changing.

Food manufacturing software

Inventory mistakes can be costly, make sure what you ordered is what you receive. Cross-check that units of measure correspond with orders and stock taking measures; counts, for example, may be recorded per unit, by weight or by volume.

Take time to inspect inventory stock as it arrives, particularly any perishable produce to ensure it has been delivered fresh and undamaged. Check the best-before and use-by dates on non-perishable items so that you are aware of the product shelf life of your entire on-hand inventory.

7.2 HOTEL INVENTORY MANAGEMENT AND DISTRIBUTION

We are all aware of the health and economic crisis that we are experiencing around the world, and we have already assimilated that the tourism industry has been forced to stop its activity either by government mandate or by the lack of demand.

However we tend to get bogged down in the immediate future rather than think about what we'll find when recovery begins. What actions can we take now to prepare for when the situation improves? Let's go back to basics and look at different tips and approaches to rethink strategies and processes for the coming months.

First focus on Inventory Management. Here are some activities to review how you classify your rooms and configure your product so when things stabilize, you will be ready with an optimized inventory.

- **Review your room types and attributes**

Since the last time you set up the distribution of room types, some things may have changed in your property. Are they currently defined in the most efficient way? Can you create new room types or join room types that are not so different?

Review the results of past sales and the production provided by each room type, as well as guest reviews, and consider if you could make changes to improve results. For example, if your double rooms have different sizes, perhaps you can differentiate a XL Double room type that will bring you additional income.

In the same way, you should review which attributes you can use that can be added through price supplements. In recent times we have seen how the tendency of the user is to customize their own product, adding certain features that they are willing to pay a little more for: sea view, double bed, bathtub, etc. If you work in a hotel group, do your best to create a basic structure that is homogeneous and applicable to all properties, as this will make operations, team training and distribution easier.

- **Reconfigure your product**

With this new revision of room types and attributes, you can already consider a global reconfiguration of your product before putting it back on sale:

Meal plans – What meal plans do you want to work with? What are the ones that have given you better results in the past? Are there any that you should stop using because it doesn't produce much revenue? Find ways to innovate in this area.

Cancellation policies and restrictions -Think about the booking conditions you have used so far and keep in mind the current market situation: we are facing a time of low demand, where people need to regain confidence and seek flexibility. Temporarily remove strict restrictions and prepayments. You must reassure your customers.

Added value – Find a way to add value for your client, beyond offering a bed and a shower. Think in terms of experience: How does staying at your hotel change the life of a guest? Can you improve their experience in the destination? Can you offer an environment that meets their needs? Can you personalize their stay? This approach will also allow you to keep a certain level of rates and avoid the dreaded price drop.

- **Review your rate structure**

You should consider the role of room type, occupancy, attributes, meal plan, cancellation policy and restrictions when restructuring your rate plans. We advise you to take time to see if your rate plans and rate codes are correctly configured and in the most efficient way.

- Remove or deactivate all those rate codes that have not produced anything or almost nothing in the last year.
- Decide if you need new rate plans, but try to keep a simplified and efficient structure.
- Review the basic plans and indexed rates and make the changes you think are appropriate to optimize results. Try to keep a clear difference of prices and conditions between one rate and another.
- If you work in a hotel group, try to make a standard of the basic structure to simplify operations and facilitate distribution.
- Is your rate structure understandable to the customer or does it hinder the purchase process? Does it build trust?

- **Manage your inventory on the sale channels**

Sometimes we tend to think about closing hotel + flight rates (packages) or opaque rates because they have very strong discounts. However, with demand far below your hotel room supply, it is important to consider activating all rates at least temporarily to reach all segments.

In times of low demand we must use open door strategies, so that we improve occupancy with less restrictive policies. We recommend you read our e-book about Forecasting, where decision-making is explained for periods without excess demand versus periods with over-demand.

- **Boost your direct sales channel**

Currently we have a great opportunity to rethink our distribution, launch actions that generate greater loyalty, and satisfy the needs of our current or future guest.

It is very likely that some of them have had a tedious experience of cancelling or postponing their trip with an OTA, while we have the option of giving direct treatment and immediate solutions. The added value that we can provide from personalized and direct treatment, our knowledge of the product and the greater ability to adapt to customer needs plays in our favor.

Collaboration with the marketing and e-commerce teams in this area is crucial, to optimize SEO and SEM strategies, ensure that the hotel website and booking engine are working properly, keep presence on social media and Meta search engines, and define Ads strategies.

- **Pay attention to dollar exchange rates**

We think it is important to highlight the situation of those properties that are affected by the fluctuation of the exchange rate. This is more uncertain today than ever, especially in countries in Latin America and the Caribbean. For example, data from experts in the field expect the dollar to rise to 30 MXN per USD (in recent years it has fluctuated between 18 and 20). This is why it is very important to ensure that a correct adjustment of individual and group rates is carried out for this kind of hotel. The best way to do this is by shopping your competitive set in the OTA's, but searching in local currency.

- **Revenue management never stops**

It is important to not let your guard down in these moments of low activity, but on the contrary, take advantage of this pause to focus on your strategies. Going back to basics may seem simple, but it can give us the opportunity to discover areas for improvement and better prepare ourselves for what is to come. The objective should be to go on sale with a very well configured and stronger product for a good competitive positioning in the market.

7.2.1 Clarify the Inventory Levels

Better inventory management is possible by setting inventory levels, like maximum level, reorder level and minimum level.

Maximum stock level represents the quantity of inventory beyond which the stock should never move up. Reorder level refers to the level of stock at which an order for replenishing the inventory has to be placed. Minimum level or safety level is the stock level below which the size of inventory should not normally fall. Lead time, lead time consumption and the economic order quantity (EOQ) determine these inventory levels. Lead time refers to the time lapse between order placement and receipt of goods. Lead time consumption refers to the requirement/demand during the lead time. Lead time is not a constant factor, neither lead time consumption is. So, minimum, average and maximum lead times and minimum, average and maximum lead time usage rates (per period) are found from experience. EOQ is a fixed quantity which the square root of twice the period (say a year) requirement of material times ordering cost per order divided by carrying cost of a unit of material per period (a year).

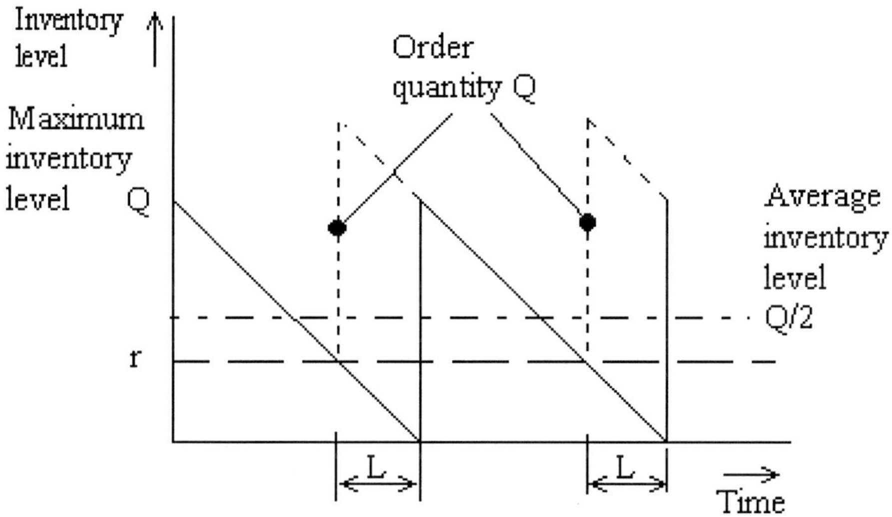

The different inventory levels are given by:

1. Reorder stock level = Maximum lead time x maximum usage rate or Minimum stock + (Average lead time X average usage rate)
2. Maximum stock level = Reorder level + EOQ – (Minimum lead time X Minimum Usage rate)
3. Minimum stock level = Reorder level – (Average lead time X Average Usage rate)
4. Average stock level = Minimum level + ½ of EOQ or (Minimum level + Maximum level)/2
5. Danger stock level = Minimum usage rate X Emergency lead time.

7.2.2 Factors that Affect Inventory Management in Distribution

Inventory management is fundamental for a business and its profitability. Monitoring and maintaining stock levels will enable organizations to optimize the pricing strategy of products and overall revenue.

Well-managed inventory processes will also guarantee that customer expectations are met, inventory-related expenses are minimized, and profits are maximized.

There are multiple variables that can influence inventory management, which in turn impacts expenses, processing time, and pricing decisions. Organizations should be aware of these factors, which include

Inventory models can greatly impact the pricing strategies of products. Having too much or too little of a product can cause its value to change.

For instance, under stocking, which refers to when a company has low levels of inventory than desired? This can lead to product prices increasing. This generally occurs when an item is popular or highly demanded by consumers but the quantity of the product is low in inventory.

Since the item is exceedingly sought after, consumers are generally more willing to pay a higher price to obtain it. Organizations can use this to their advantage and increase their profits and sales.

Despite this competitive edge, businesses should monitor inventory and use digital tools to forecast sales and to prevent under stocking. This will help establishments avoid losing potential sales from customers seeking a certain item.

Overstocking, which is when companies over-order and have too many inventory items, can also impact prices. Excess inventory can enable businesses to be more competitive in their market by selling items for lower prices than their competing establishments. Not only will owners be able to increase sales, but they can relieve their warehouse of excess products.

It is important that business offload overstocked products because it can lead to dead stock or items that do not sell and remain in the warehouse. Obsolete items in storage facilities can also lead to increased carrying costs.

To offset surpluses, companies may have to lower their prices or bundle excess items with other products to increase the sales rate.

Businesses can also offer overstocked items for free when customers purchase merchandise that typically sells well. Although these methods may lower profit margins, businesses will have a better chance of grasping customer interest and removing items from their inventory.

Businesses should implement proper inventory management systems to avoid price sensitive setbacks created from over and under stocking. Managing inventory will ensure that prices are maintained appropriately and that businesses secure their optimal profit margins.

Integrating inventory management software can streamline this process, in which organizations can access real-time data reports related to expenses and track inventory levels and waste.

These digital tools provide user-friendly interfaces and mobile app features that allow businesses to quickly identify popular items and make informed ordering decisions to guarantee advantageous inventory levels.

7.2.3 Optimization of Inventory and Distribution in the Hotel Industry

Inventory management is an umbrella concept that involves understanding, overseeing and controlling your hotel's room inventory.

By analyzing your inventory and rates on a regular basis, you can make adjustments in anticipation of peaks and troughs in demand, allowing you to cherry-pick the highest value bookings during peak times, as well as deploy discounts and other customer incentives to drive up demand and increase occupancy during quieter periods. This strategy is what is referred to as dynamic pricing, and the benefits include simplified revenue processes, increased speed and agility of a hotel's responses to customers, as well as greater rate integrity. Inventory management also enables you to set your prices relative to competitors, which is essential given that OTAs are leveling the playing field for hoteliers through increased pricing transparency.

Hotel operators need to create an efficient and effective distribution strategy to thrive in a competitive global industry.

Here's how to optimize your hotel's distribution strategy:

Collect data and utilize it effectively. No matter how good your distribution strategy is, you need to recognize that there's always room for improvement. The best way to enhance and improve your distribution strategy is to collect data and initiate a better understanding of your guests and distribution partners.

Through data collection, you will be able to understand which channels drive the most revenue, and when. Be sure to run regular reports so that you can make frequent adjustments based on the most relevant, accurate and recent data available.

Consider your target market segment when adding agents to your distribution network. Certain distribution agents will appeal more to different market segments, so it's important to form partnerships with the right agents for your property. For example, if your hotel appeals to international travelers from China who is searching for luxury experiences, you will want to find OTAs that attract those specific individuals.

Increase opportunities for direct bookings. Many travelers use large distribution agents, such as OTAs, as a starting point for their travel-related research. They're likely to discover your hotel on OTA search results pages, but they may also head to your website or begin following your social pages in order to learn more about your brand. At these key moments, make sure your potential guests know they can book directly with you.

Make online booking simple on your website, and prominently display your booking button. Include booking capability on your social pages, such as Facebook or Instagram.

Use OTA marketing strategies to your advantage. The fact of the matter is, OTAs have more money to spend on marketing than you do. Use this to your advantage, and let them promote your property for you. Leverage their marketing spending in order to increase bookings at your brand, without increasing your own marketing budget.

7.2.4 Tips To Do Hotel Inventory

Here are some additional tips for doing hotel inventory.

- Estimate the Cost of Your Inventory: Take into account your ordering, shortage, and carrying costs to optimize your entire merchandising and stocking operation. You will be able to generate more revenue and prevent losing revenue due to running out of items.
- User Relevant Software: Doing everything manually is daunting. After all, why would you do it when software can help you completely automate it? The latest property management system tool can help you track your entire hotel inventory, manage it on the go, and get valuable reports and insights.
- Always Use Data to Support Your Decisions: Don't base your inventory management decisions on your experience or hunch. Use the data from your spreadsheets and software tools to support your decisions, such as item re-stocking and adding/removing a distribution channel.

Hotel inventory management is a complex topic. The ultimate goal is to optimize the inventory with your business goals and guests' needs and wants in mind. Given that hotel inventory management is a very dynamic process, spreadsheets and manual work can only get you so far. Leveraging cutting-edge software tools definitely yields better results, both in the short and long run.

7.2.5 Step by Step Process on How to Do It

Every hotel and inventory is unique. However, the same hotel inventory management method can be applied across all hotels. The scope of work depends on the size of the hotel, the size and how diverse the inventory is, and the occupancy rates.

Collect Data on Your Current Hotel Inventory: The first step is to collect the data on your current hotel inventory. You will need to catalog all rooms and every secondary inventory item available at your hotel. That includes everything ranging from food and drink to linen and cleaning products. The goal is to end up with the ultimate list of your hotel inventory so that you can streamline your next steps.

Cross-reference Your Inventory with Occupancy Rates: Primary hotel inventory management requires you to cross-reference your entire room offer with the room occupancy rates. To manage means to utilize your resources so that they generate more revenue. Look for rooms that are rarely occupied. These are usually deluxe suits that you can offer as affordable upgrades. The information will also help you optimize your distribution network.

Assess the Purchasing Behavior of Your Guests: When it comes to secondary hotel inventory, to efficiently manage it, you need to take a closer look at the purchasing behavior of your guests. Do you have items and services that you rarely manage to sell? Are some of your items constantly below safe stock level? You will find answers to these questions only if you try to learn what your guests want and don't want.

Identify Patterns: When you collect the data, you will be able to identify patterns. Patterns will help you stay on top of your management efforts. For instance, you will know when to expect occupancy rates to drop or spike and which items you need to regularly re-stock.

Use Data to Optimize Hotel Inventory Management: Finally, with all this data at your disposal, you'll be able to make informed decisions. The insights will enable you to optimize hotel inventory, maximize revenue, and make your guests happy.

7.2.6 Hotel Inventory Template

Since you need all the help you can get to take your hotel inventory management game to the next level, we've done some research and found the following hotel inventory templates you can use for free.

- Stock Inventory Template – a comprehensive stock inventory template. Use it to create a complete list of items you keep in stock, reduce excess inventory, locate items in storage, and find out when you need to re-stock.
- Linen Inventory Template – use this template to effectively manage your linen inventory and track the movement of linens between laundry and housekeeping.
- Food Inventory Template – stay on top of your food stock. If you have a restaurant in your hotel, this template will help you organize and optimize your inventory based on categories (meat, vegetables, food, desserts).
- Equipment Inventory Template – this template allows you to track the location, condition, and value of your hotel equipment. You will be able to track various metrics, including depreciation and operating costs.

7.3 COSTS ASSOCIATED WITH INVENTORY MANAGEMENT

Inventory carrying cost is the expense associated with maintaining inventory. Inventory expense is calculated by multiplying annual inventory carrying cost percent by average inventory value. Standard accounting practice is to value inventory at purchase or standard manufacturing cost rather than at selling price.

Inventory procurement, storage and management is associated with huge costs associated with each these functions.

Inventory costs are basically categorized into three headings:

1. Ordering cost
2. Carrying cost
3. Shortage or stock out cost and cost of replenishment
    a) Cost of loss, pilferage, shrinkage and obsolescence etc.
    b) Cost of logistics
    c) Sales discounts, volume discounts and other related costs

Ordering Cost

Cost of procurement and inbound logistics costs form a part of Ordering Cost. Ordering Cost is dependent and varies based on two factors - The cost of ordering excess and the Cost of ordering too less. Both these factors move in opposite directions to each other. Ordering excess quantity will result in carrying cost of inventory. Whereas ordering less will result in increase of replenishment cost and ordering costs.

These two beyond costs together are called total stocking cost. If we plot the order quantity *vs.* the TSC, we will see the graph declining gradually until a certain point after which with every increase in quantity the TSC will proportionately show an increase.

This functional analysis and cost implications form the basis of determining the Inventory Procurement decision by answering the two basic fundamental questions:

- How much to order and when to order?
- How much to order is determined by arriving at the economic order quantity or EOQ?

Carrying Cost

Inventory storage and maintenance involves various types of costs namely:

- Inventory storage cost
- Cost of capital

Inventory carrying involves inventory storage and management either using in house facilities or external warehouses owned and managed by third party vendors. In both cases, inventory management and process involves extensive use of building, material handling equipment, IT software applications and hardware equipment coupled managed by operations and management staff resources.

Inventory Storage Cost

Inventory storage costs typically include cost of building rental and facility maintenance and related costs. Cost of material handling equipment, IT hardware and applications, including cost of purchase, depreciation or rental or lease as the case may be. Further costs include operational costs, consumables, communication costs and utilities, besides the cost of human resources employed in operations as well as management.

Cost of Capital

Includes the costs of investments, interest on working capital, taxes on inventory paid, insurance costs and other costs associate with legal liabilities.

The inventory storage costs as well as cost of capital are dependent upon and vary with the decision of the management to manage inventory in house or through outsourced vendors and third party service providers.

Current times, the trend is increasingly in favor of outsourcing the inventory management to third party service provides. For one thing the organizations find that managing inventory operations requires certain core competencies, which may not be in line with their business competencies. They would rather outsource to a supplier who has the required competency than build them in house.

Secondly in case of large-scale warehouse operations, the scale of investments may be too huge in terms of cost of building and material handling equipment etc. Besides the project may span over a longer period of several years, thus blocking capital of the company, which can be utilized into more important areas such as R & D, expansion etc. than by staying invested into the project.

Ordering and Carrying Costs

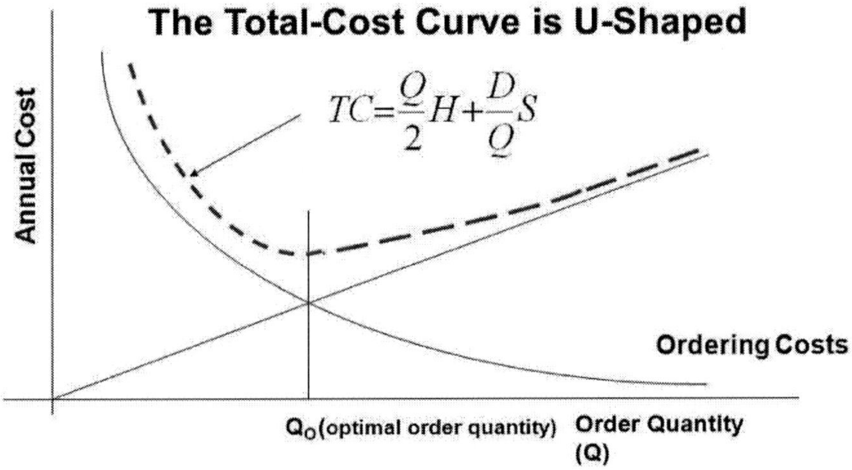

7.3.1 Inventory Planning

Key parameters and procedures, namely, when to order, how much to order, and inventory control, guide inventory planning.

Determining when to Order

The reorder point defines when a replenishment shipment should be initiated. A reorder point can be specified in terms of units or days` supply. This discussion focuses on determining reorder points under conditions of demand and performance cycle certainty.

Determining how much to Order

Relationships involving the inventory performance cycle, inventory cost, and economic order formulations are useful for guiding inventory planning. First, the EOQ is found at the point where annualized order cost and inventory carrying cost are equal. Second, average base inventory equals one-half order quantity. Third, the value of the inventory unit, all other things being equal, will have a direct relationship with replenishment order frequency. In effect, the higher the product value, the more frequently it will be ordered.

Every organization that is engaged in production, sale or trading of products holds inventory in one or the other form. While production and manufacturing organizations hold raw material inventories, finished goods and spare parts inventories, trading companies might hold only finished goods inventories depending upon the business model.

When in case of raw material inventory management function is essentially dealing with two major functions. First function deals with inventory planning and the second being inventory tracking. As inventory planners, their main job consists in analyzing demand and deciding when to order and how much to order new inventories.

Traditional inventory management approach consists of two models namely:

- Economic order quantity (EOQ)
- Continuous ordering
- Periodic ordering

EOQ: Economic Order Quantity method determines the optimal order quantity that will minimize the total inventory cost. EOQ is a basic model and further models developed based on this model include production Quantity Model and Quantity Discount Model.

Continuous Order Model: Works on fixed order quantity basis where a trigger for fixed quantity replenishment is released whenever the inventory level reaches predetermined safety level and triggers re ordering.

Periodic System Model: This model works on the basis of placing order after a fixed period of time.

Economic Order Quantity

Economic Order Quantity (EOQ) is the number of units that a company should add to inventory with each order to minimize the total costs of inventory such as holding costs, order costs, and shortage costs. The EOQ is used as part of a continuous review inventory system, in which the level of inventory is monitored at all times, and a fixed quantity is ordered each time the inventory level reaches a specific reorder point. The EOQ provides a model for calculating the appropriate reorder point and the optimal reorder quantity to ensure the immediate replacement of inventory with no shortages. It can be a valuable tool for small business owners who have to make decisions about how much inventory to keep on hand, how many items to order each time, and how often to reorder to incur the lowest possible costs.

The EOQ model finds the quantity that minimizes the sum of these costs.

The basic EOQ formula is as follows:

$TC = PD + HQ/2 + SD/Q$

Where TC is the total inventory cost per year, PD is the inventory purchase cost per year (price P multiplied by demand D in units per year), H is the holding cost, Q is the order quantity, and S is the order cost (in dollars per order). Breaking down the elements of the formula further, the yearly holding cost of inventory is H multiplied by the average number of units in inventory. Since the model assumes that inventory is depleted at a constant rate, the average number of units is equal to Q/2. The total orders cost per year is S multiplied by the number of orders per year, which is equal to the annual demand divided by the number of orders, or D/Q. Finally, PD is constant, regardless of the order quantity.

Taking these factors into consideration, solving for the optimal order quantity gives a formula of:

HQ/2 = SD/Q, or Q = the square root of 2DS/H.

Managing Uncertainty

Two types of uncertainty have a direct impact upon inventory policy. Demand uncertainty is rate of sales during inventory replenishment. Performance cycle uncertainty concerns inventory replenishment time variations.

Demand Uncertainty

Sales forecasting estimates unit demand during the inventory replenishment cycle. Even with good forecasting, demand during replenishment cycle often exceeds or falls short of what is anticipated. To protect against a stock out when demand exceeds forecast, safety stock is added to base inventory. Under conditions of demand uncertainty, average inventory represents one-half order quantity plus safety stock.

Performance Cycle Uncertainty

Performance cycle uncertainty means that inventory policy cannot assume consistent delivery. The planner should expect that actual performance cycle experience will cluster near the average and be skewed in excess of the planned duration. If performance cycle uncertainty is not evaluated statistically, the most common practice is to base safety stock requirements on the planned replenishment time. However, if there is substantial variation in the performance cycle, a formal evaluation is desirable.

Determining Safety Stock with Uncertainty

Treating both demand and performance cycle uncertainty requires combining two independent variables. The duration of the cycle is, at least in the short run, independent of the daily demand. However, in setting safety stocks, the joint impact of the probability of both demand and performance cycle variation must be determined. Safety stock requirements can be determined by either numerical or simulation procedures.

Dependent Demand Replenishment

Three basic approaches have been used to introduce safety stocks into a system coping with dependent demand. First, a common practice is to put safety time into the requirements plan. A second approach is to increase the requisition by a quantity specified by some estimate of expected forecast error. The third method is to utilize the previously discussed statistical techniques for setting safety stocks directly to the component rather than to the item of top-level demand.

7.3.2 Policy and Practices of Inventory Management

Inventory management is the process companies use to order, receive, account for and manage the various products sold to consumers. Business owners and managers focus on this activity because inventory typically represents the second largest expenditure in a company behind payroll. Policies and procedures help companies actively manage the different products in their facilities. While standard policies and procedures exist for inventory management, owners and managers have some latitude to develop standards for their own companies.

Procurement

Procurement is the purchasing process individuals must use to order and receive inventory. Companies typically require individuals to have a purchase order with a manager's authorization prior to ordering inventory. A procurement manager is responsible for reviewing the purchase order to ensure it includes authorization and other information relating to the cost of items purchased. While larger organizations can hire individuals to work in the procurement department, smaller companies often have the business owner perform this function.

Valuing Inventory

Valuing inventory is the policy in which inventory sells first and is removed from the accounting ledger. Methods include first-in, first-out (FIFO), last-in, first-out (LIFO) and the weighted average method. FIFO requires companies to sell older inventory first, leaving more expensive inventory in the general ledger and increasing the company's gross profit during an accounting period. LIFO is the opposite of FIFO; therefore it has the opposite effects in the accounting ledger. The weighted average method does not require older inventory to be sold first as inventory costs are recalculated each time the company purchases inventory.

Inventory Accounting System

An inventory accounting system is the specific procedures a company uses to update its accounting ledger. The two types of systems are periodic and perpetual. Periodic systems start with an opening balance and only record purchases, sales or adjustments on a monthly, quarterly or annual basis. The perpetual system starts with the opening inventory balance and updates inventory after each purchase, sales or inventory adjustment. Companies create their policies depending on their business models.

Physical Controls

Physical controls relate to how a company stores and counts inventory items. Storage is important because companies must safeguard their inventory against loss, theft and employee abuse. This can include limiting access, locking up valuable products and using tracking devices on products. Business owners and managers must also use periodic counts to verify the number of items on hand.

Cycle counts counting a specific number of items each day or week and annual inventory counts are the most common physical counting methods in the business environment.

7.3.3 Inventory Management Practices

Inventory management practices in the company help by adding value in terms of having control over and maintaining lean inventory. Inventory should not be too much or too less. Both the situations are bad for the company. However often we see that inventory is not focused upon by the management and hence lot of inefficiencies build up over a period of time without the knowledge of the management. It is only when we start a cost reduction drive that the inventory goof ups and skeletons come out of the cupboard and results in revamping the entire operations.

However those companies, which have always focused on inventory as a principle function and recognized that the inventory effects their sales, as well as the books of accounts and profits, have managed to introduce and improve inventory management processes. Many business models work on lean inventory principle or JIT inventory along with other models like VMI etc. Inventory management to a large extent is dependent upon the supply chain efficiency as well as operations.

We have covered below briefly few of the points which when followed, can go a long way in ensuring that the inventory is lean and clean.

Review Inventory Periodically and Revise stocking Patterns and Norms

Inventory is dependent upon the demand as well as the supply chain delivery time. Often companies follow one stocking policy for all items.

For example, all A, B & C categories may be stocking inventory of 15 days, which may not be the right thing that is required. While some items may have a longer lead-time thus affecting the inventory holding, the demand pattern and the hit frequency in terms of past data may show up differently for each of the inventory items. Therefore one standard norm does not suit all and can lead to over stocking of inventory as well as in efficiencies in the system.

Get into detailed inventory planning: One size does not fit all

Understand the inventory types and the specific characteristics of the items we are carrying. Then build the inventory stocking parameters taking into account the unique characteristics of the particular inventory.

From amongst our inventory list, we will find that all types of materials are not of the same value. Some might be very expensive and need to be carried in stock for a longer period, while another item might have a shorter lead-time and may be fast moving. Quite a few items often have shelf life and hence require separate norms and focus to manage such items.

Getting into the detailed understanding will help us identify the inventory-stocking norm required to manage these characteristics to ensure optimum efficiency. The solution quite often may not be to carry stocks; rather it may involve setting up the customer service standard for such items and specifying a delivery time depending upon the frequency of demand. Quite a few items often have shelf life and hence require separate norms and focus to manage such items.

Study demand pattern, movement patterns and cycles to build suitable inventory norms for different categories of inventory

Companies which are into retail segments and dealing with huge inventories in terms of number of parts as well as value will necessarily need to ensure they practice review of inventory list and cleanup operations on ongoing basis.

Popularly known as catalogue management, inventory norms review should be carried out based on detailed study of the sales data, demand pattern, sales cycles etc. Understanding of the business and sales cycles specific to the product category helps one manage inventories better.

For example, in case of retail garments, with every season certain skus become redundant no matter how their demand was in the previous months. This helps identify those stocks which are required to be managed at a micro level and identify the high value and fast moving items that need to be always on the radar to avoid stock outs.

It does not help for example to carry standard stocks of all items including low value items as well as high value items. If the low value items are locally available and the lead-time is less, one can cut down on the inventory and change the buying pattern. Similarly high value items too can be managed by cutting down the delivery lead times and in turn reducing inventory.

It helps to periodically study the past data and extrapolate the same to identify slow moving and obsolete items. The dead stocks should be flushed out and active catalogue items should be made available.

7.4 PRICING MANAGEMENT IN HOSPITALITY

Pricing is an important parameter; organizations need to take care of while launching a new product or service in the market. Before deciding the price of a new product, it is essential for organizations to understand and also calculate total costs involved in the entire process of the product development be it designing, manufacturing or delivering the same. No organization works for charity and thus the price of a new product or service ought to be decided keeping in mind all such factors.

While everything looks smooth front of house, at the back end of the hotel, things are a little more complex. Regardless of the type of the hotel or the number of rooms at your property a good pricing strategy is necessary for success.

Having the right pricing strategy can set you apart from your competitors and prevent new businesses from entering a competitive marketplace. Of course, having the wrong pricing strategy can also ruin your own chances!

Having a pricing strategy that consistently works for your business is essential to increasing your market share.

Forecasting Methodology

You can't just wake up in the morning and decide that today your double room will cost €100. Prior to this decision, you need to do some forecasting, to better understand where your guests are coming from; and also how much they are willing to pay!

Anticipating demand and performance is key to forecasting, giving hotel management the ability to make strategic decisions on pricing. Accurate forecasting should give a business a clear snapshot of how it will perform in the future and allow management to then make any adjustments necessary. Looking at industry trends and past performance can also assist in making decisions about pricing and promotions.

Whilst forecasting isn't full proof, you can make pretty reasonable assumptions based on the time of week, day and economy.

Here are four tips to accurate forecasting;

- **Use Historical Data**

Refer to your PMS system for your historical data; it's a good indicator of what's next.

- **Monitor your Competitors**

Always have an eye on what's happening in your local area. Has a similar hotel recently closed or relocated or has a competitor decided to renovate? These are all factors which could affect your market share. Not sure who the competition is?

- **Consider Special Events and Holidays**

Working special events and holidays into your calendar is essential. Customers expect to see special offers and additional inclusions during seasonal events.

- **Market Trends**

Take a wider view and look at what's happening within both the local and global economy. Pay attention to market trends within the hospitality industry and observe the arrival figures in your part of the world.

Establishing Rate Parity

When making a pricing strategy, the first thing we do is establish Rate Parity across all channels. We do that by maintaining consistent rates for the same product in all online distribution channels, based on the actual revenue you are getting from a booking - that means not counting the commission paid to OTAs.

For instance, an OTA reservation might be €100 but you are only getting €85 (assuming a 15% commission). The same reservation from your website will bring you €100 (but you will have to discount from that the cost of marketing and running your website).

For the consumer point of view, it's beneficial if your room rates match across the web: it shows that you are dependable and helps build a relationship of trust that might eventually motivate him/her to book directly on your website.

Of course, paying OTA commission and charging the lowest rates possible can eat into your profit margins. Never fear the primary focus is to help you to increase direct bookings! Over the years we've practiced multiple techniques and strategies. Here are our top tips:

- Have a responsive and clean website with an Integrated Booking Engine, making the booking process as easy as or even better than booking your room.
- You might not be able to run campaigns and discounted offers, but you can definitely be unique. Agoda.com and HRS cannot offer free tours, a welcoming gift or free breakfast at your property, but you can!
- You can lower your rates for specific audiences on Social Media. Engage directly with your guests with special offers on:
    - Facebook,
    - Twitter,
    - Instagram

Customers Segmentation

Different guests look for different things and are willing to pay different rates to get what they want. Therefore, by properly segmenting potential guests, you can be more efficient with marketing and distribution. You can then take a different approach when defining your pricing strategy!

Having in mind the different customer segments, we can then implement basic rates:

- **Best Available Rate (BAR)**

This is the lowest, non-restricted rate which guests can book. It's available to all and can change from several times per day to per week.

- **Corporate and/ or Partners rates**

This is a restricted rate that has been set through an agreement between the provider and an entity such as a corporation. This rate is normally calculated based on the assumption that bookings will continue to generate repeat business.

- **Group rates**

A group rate is generally given to a large travel party who book a significant number of rooms during a specific period of time. In many cases, groups are given a discounted group rate by hotel operators.

As the channel connectivity grows and guest booking sources expand, we can look into more pricing options too.

Building the Pricing Strategy

While forecasting and segmentation are steps that must be done before you make the actual decision about your prices, there are other elements you should pay attention to:

Use Length of Stay (LOS) restrictions. This strategy revolves around adjusting pricing based on the length of the stay. When demand outweighs supply, it can be beneficial to implement a rule where guests are obligated to stay a minimum number of days.

For example, you already know that booking too many one-night stays on a popular night, such as a Saturday, means you're forced to turn away more customers who want to book multiple night stays. More importantly, you will end up having an empty hotel on Sunday because you are already booked out on Saturday and all potential multi-night bookers cannot stay at your property. In these cases, you should add a longer minimum stay policy, both to increase your occupancy and your revenue.

Alternatively, when demand is lower, you can potentially encourage guests to stay longer by offering them a lower rate if they stay for multiple days, or simply lower the minimum length of stay to one night only.

Improve your Cancellation Policy. Cancellation policies can also factor into a pricing strategy and help to increase revenue. Rates can be lowered on the agreement that there are no refunds in the event of cancellation. Alternatively, higher rates offer guests greater flexibility with cancellations.

Hotels in high demand can really benefit from no refund cancellations. By charging lower rates in exchange for foregoing a refund, busy hotels are able to sell the same room twice in event of cancellation.

Still have rooms to be sold? Here, you can implement some of the following strategies to reach 100% full occupancy:

Setup Discount Codes. One highly effective strategy to encourage future direct bookings is discount codes. Share discount codes with former guests or with guests via a third party booking channel to encourage future **direct bookings.**

Create and Offer Packages. Another great option to maximize revenue is creating packages. The room rate may actually be lower than the equivalent rate for the same room only, but this will be hidden inside of the package. Creating attractive packages can mean including local experiences, special meals and so on.

Plan last-minute offers. Last minute offers are usually given in the days prior to room availability ending. If your strategy is to gain 100% occupancy, last minute offers are a good idea.

7.4.1 Hospitality Industry and Predatory Pricing

Hotels that can afford to take a hit may employ predatory pricing strategies when they want to thwart competition. Predatory pricing is the practice of lowering your prices so much that your competitors cannot match them, thus losing business. While predatory pricing may appear unfair or unethical, in the hospitality industry it is a viable marketing strategy commonly employed by hotels, motels and restaurants.

- **Advantages**

By lowering its prices, a hotel in a certain neighborhood gains an advantage over competitors who offer basically the same services on their properties. According to the CATO Institute, predatory pricing typically does not last long enough to create a monopoly in a certain industry. Instead, competitors often match the lower prices and put the properties back on equal footing. The first property that starts the price lowering strategy has a window of opportunity to lure new guests and introduce its line to visitors who might not have visited initially.

- **Winners**

Consumers are the winners when hotels, restaurants and entertainment establishments start a price war. In a capitalistic society, competition is key and allows businesses to employ a wide range of strategies to lure business. Consumers can retain loyalty to their chosen brands or try a new property that may be offering lower prices in a predatory fashion. While the hospitality businesses may lose money in the process, consumers can take advantage of the practice to save money while trying out a new establishment. Eventually, they may even receive the same lowered prices from their preferred business.

- **Ambiguity**

Sometimes there is a thin line between using predatory pricing as a marketing strategy and trying to obtain a monopoly, according to the American Bar Association. Predatory pricing certainly can lead to a monopoly, which would eventually hurt consumers. If a hotel or restaurant forces competition out of the marketplace, it is then free to raise prices without fear of losing business. On the other hand, hospitality industry businesses are not considered essential for human life and would not warrant monopoly litigation.

- **Warning**

A number of consequences can occur if you decide to use predatory pricing as a marketing strategy or to drive out the competition. Once you're the only property around, you must be ready to accommodate the market with staffing and inventory. You must eventually counter your low-pricing strategy with increases to maintain a profitable margin. This could draw criticism from your customers and lead to a backlash, since your services are considered a luxury for most people. Additionally, your pricing strategy may create an unfriendly business environment in your community that could lead to even greater losses as the entertainment consumers go elsewhere.

7.4.2 Pricing Strategies to Increase the Hotel Revenue

For those operating in the hotel industry, maximizing revenue is a top priority, and achieving this goal often requires the right pricing strategy, at the right time. In fact, making room rate adjustments based on demand, customer segmentation and other factors can be the key to overall business success.

1. Pricing Strategy Based on Forecasting

The single most important pricing strategy for hotels to master is the use of forecasting to set their prices based on anticipated demand. Essentially, this should mean that the hotel room rate being charged will depend on how high demand is. For instance, times of high demand may lead to higher room rates, in order to maximize revenue.

A robust forecasting strategy relies upon accurate records being kept, with historical data – such as occupancy, revenue; room rates and average spend per room – proving particularly useful. In addition, it is important to make use of data that is already in the books, such as reservations, as well as any wider market trends.

This data can then be used to make pricing decisions. So, if your hotel has historically experienced low demand in January, there are strategic considerations associated with that. As an example, you could consider lowering prices in January to try to build demand, or you could raise prices, to get more out of the smaller customer base.

2. Rate Parity Strategy

In simple terms, a rate parity strategy involves maintaining consistent rates for the same product, across all online distribution channels. The key benefit of this is that it provides transparency for consumers, while it is also often a prerequisite of advertising rooms through online travel agents, such as Expedia and Booking.com.

The primary challenge of this is the fact that OTAs charge commission, and paying this while charging a low rate can eat into the revenue you would have earned through direct bookings. However, direct bookings can be stimulated in ways aside from simple room rate adjustments.

3. Price per Segment

One of the most commonly used pricing strategies for those in the hotel industry is price per segment, and this is where you offer the same product at different prices to different types of customers.

While "open market" prices should be subject to a rate parity strategy, prices for corporate segments could be lower, especially if they commit to a certain number of rooms, or a certain number of meals. Another option would be to sell multiple rooms to travel agents for a lower rate, so the travel agent can include the rooms in packages.

4. Discount Codes to Stimulate Direct Bookings

Although a price parity strategy may prohibit some of the pricing incentives that can stimulate direct bookings, one highly effective strategy involves the use of discount codes to encourage future direct bookings.

So, when a guest visits your hotel or property after booking through a third party, you could offer them a discount code for any future direct bookings they make with you. This has the dual benefit of encouraging repeat business and encouraging them to book directly if they opt to stay in your hotel again in the future.

5. Offer a Package

Another solid option for those in hotel management attempting to maximise revenue is to create packages, allowing customers to pay for more than just a room. Additional items, services or products that may feature in a package deal include meals, bicycles, access to golf courses and equipment, and so on.

With packages, the actual room rate may be lower than the equivalent rate for an identical room on its own. However, your hotel will be able to sell more products at the same time.

6. Length of Stay Strategy (LOS)

As the name implies, a length of stay strategy is based around adjusting pricing based on the length of the stay. In some instances, such as when demand outweighs supply, it can be beneficial to implement a rule where guests are 'obligated' to stay a minimum number of days. In such cases, lower rates may not always be necessary.

On the other hand, when demand is lower, you can potentially encourage guests to stay longer by offering them a lower rate if they stay for multiple days, resulting in fewer unused rooms overall.

7. Cancellation Policy

The cancellation policy of a hotel can also factor into a pricing strategy and help to increase revenue. For instance, one option is to charge a lower rate on the condition that a guest cannot receive a refund in the event that they cancel the room, while higher rates are charged when guests have greater flexibility with cancellations.

This can be of particular value in hotels with high demand. By charging lower rates, in exchange for no refunds, busy hotels can benefit from effectively being able to sell the same room twice in the event of a cancellation.

8. Upselling

The basic principle of upselling involves encouraging customers to spend more on their existing purchase or booking, and it is a vital component of any effective hotel revenue management strategy within the hotel industry.

It may mean encouraging a guest to upgrade to a better room, or pay a higher room rate for a more desirable view. It could also mean persuading them to pay more for a king size bed. Upselling is often most successful during the booking process, so it can be beneficial to promote upgrade options while guests are making their choices.

9. Cross Selling

Cross selling is a similar concept to upselling, but rather than encouraging customers to spend more on an existing purchase, it involves encouraging customers to make additional purchases on top of the one(s) already made.

Within the hotel industry, this will typically refer to additional services, such as local tours, massages, or gym services. Generally, cross selling is most effective after the initial booking has been made, but before the guest actually arrives. For this reason, it is often best achieved through promotional emails.

10. Excellent Review Management

Finally, better reviews are likely to result in improved conversion rates. Meanwhile, guests are also usually willing to spend more on rooms in hotels with positive reviews, because they can have greater confidence in their choice. Indeed, when two hotels offer a similar product, the one with superior reviews will often be chosen by customers.

For this reason, to maximize revenue, it is important to have a comprehensive review management strategy in place. This will likely mean striving to deliver an excellent customer experience, encouraging guests to leave reviews, and responding swiftly and competently to reviews and feedback posted on social media sites.

Maximizing revenue in the hotel industry relies on the implementation of the right pricing strategies, which is an important part of your revenue management strategy. Typically, this requires the use of forecasting to understand and anticipate demand, as well as a willingness to adjust room rates strategically, make use of cross selling and upselling techniques, and manage online customer feedback.

7.4.3 Value-Based Pricing Strategy

The two basic ways of pricing goods and services are cost-plus pricing and value-based pricing. Cost-plus sets the price at the cost of production plus a profit. In value-based pricing, the price is based on what customers are willing to pay. The more value your product or service has to your customers, the higher the price you can charge. Value-based pricing strategies therefore are based on the value of the product to individual customers.

- **Identification**

To arrive at the optimum price, determine how highly your customers value your product or service. Examine factors such as whether your customers will save money or time by using your product or service; whether your product or service is unique; whether your product or service will help customers gain a competitive advantage; and what the competition charges. The answers to these questions will help you determine what customers are willing to pay for your product or service.

- **Effects**

When you are offering a product or service that is not unique and in a market where prices are well established, you may have to adopt the strategy of setting your price at the same level as your competitors. This may help you to enter the market, but you will need to lower your costs to raise your profit levels above your competitors, to gain a competitive advantage.

- **Expert Insight**

For some products and services, it may make sense to set your prices according to how much you will save your customers. Craig Stedman, writing in Computerworld, describes how software vendors set their license fees for individual customers based on the amount of internal savings customers can expect to achieve by using their product. Another company, selling gaskets that prevent chemical leaks and spills, charges customers based on the cleanup costs they will avoid by using the product.

- **Considerations**

For certain products or services, it may make sense to charge a higher amount relative to your costs. You can do this if your product is unique, if you are positioning your product as a high-status item or if it will save your customers money. For example, many luxury items, such as designer handbags, are priced at hundreds of times their production cost, but customers are paying for the prestige of owning the brand. Drug companies may price their products high and justify this by arguing their drug can save the patient an even more expensive medical procedure.

- **Potential**

Another type of value-based pricing strategy is to offer some customers a discount. This may be based on the amount they buy or on how often they use your service. Airlines, trains and hotels use a related strategy of pricing seats or rooms differently depending on when customers buy the tickets. When there are seats left to fill very close to the departure date, the airline is willing to sell these at a discount in order to fill the plane. This helps to maintain profitability.

7.4.4 Unethical Marketing Practices by Hotel Booking Websites

During the dot com boom, online travel agencies had taken the entire world by storm! Travel websites which offered customers the convenience of being able to compare and book hotels from the comfort of their home became bug business. Companies like Travelocity and Expedia have business interests all across the world.

However, about twenty years later, these travel websites find themselves in the middle of a storm. Hoteliers and travel agents in many countries are alleging that these online agencies work in unethical and probably even illegal ways. As a result, these agencies are facing the wrath of regulators in many countries. In 2017, the Turkish regulator temporarily banned Booking.com because it was alleged that the company was breaking the local competition law. Similarly, these websites have been under investigation by the United Kingdom regulator as well. In India, the action was not taken by the regulators. Instead, it is the hotel lobby that has decided to come together and cancel the bookings made from online travel websites. Many hotels are insisting that customers cancel the bookings made from this website. They are willing to provide the same price for an offline booking but are insisting on the cancellation.

In short, online travel agencies are facing the wrath of many stakeholders. This has been blamed on the possibility that they may be using unethical marketing practices. Some of the unethical practices have been listed below.

- **Restrictive Contracts**

Online travel agencies like booking.com guarantee lowest prices to their customers. They provide this guarantee because they sign contracts with hotels that prevent them from selling their hotel rooms at a lower price. Up until now, the hoteliers have been signing these contracts because the travel websites provide a steady flow of guests to them. However, of late, many hoteliers and offline travel agents have started protesting that such contracts are anticompetitive in nature. By blocking the hotel's ability to drop prices, the hotel websites are virtually creating a monopoly. The common belief is that hoteliers should have the ability to price their hotel rooms independently and hence the contracts written by these agencies need to be modified.

- **Subtle Manipulation**

Online travel agencies have also been accused of subtle manipulation by many consumer advocacy groups. It has been observed that the order is which hotels are listed on this website has a huge impact on their sales. Hence, travel websites charge a commission to list certain hotels at a higher level.

This is unfair to the customer since they believe that the order of ranking is based on the relevance of the search that they have conducted. The reality is that travel websites sell special packages to the hotel. As a part of these packages, the hotels are required to pay a higher commission if they want a better placement.

The end result is that online travel agencies are under pressure from consumer advocacy groups to segregate their organic searches from their paid promotions as Google does!

- **Fake Pressure**

Online travel agencies are also known to create fake pressure on the customers to make a purchase. This is often done by claiming that a certain number of prospective buyers are viewing the hotel property concurrently or that certain property has only a few rooms left for certain dates. There would ideally be no problem if the numbers provided by the website were accurate. However, in many cases, it has been observed that travel agencies create fake pressure on the consumers by claiming that a certain price is only valid for a certain time and that rooms will sell out shortly.

In reality, this is not often the case. The facts are often distorted by travel websites in order to pressure the customers into making a purchase.

- **False Discounts**

Online travel agencies sometimes promise steep discounts on the inventory that they are selling. In reality, this is not really the case. These agencies first mark up the price to take it unnecessarily higher. These prices are often weekend prices in the peak season. Then travel agencies claim that they are giving 30% to 40% discount. In reality, they are selling at off-season prices which the users would anyways get directly at the hotel.

Once again, this is unethical marketing. Practices like these are the reason that online travel agencies are facing resistance from consumer groups.

- **Deceptive Pricing**

Lastly, online websites are also known for publishing different prices as compared to the ones that they charge. Till the last instance of the decision-making process, they show a different price. Later when the consumer is about to book the hotel, these websites suddenly add convenience fees and travel insurance. Sometimes, users are not even aware of the fact that they are buying insurance or any other add on service! It is clear that the online travel website is hoping the consumers will not notice the change in prices and will continue to pay. This is obviously unethical.

To sum it up, the deceptive marketing practices by online travel agencies have now been exposed. These agencies desperately need to revamp their marketing failing which they are definitely going to run into trouble with regulators and consumer advocacy groups.

7.5 SUMMARY

Effective inventory management is vital for the success and profitability of hotels, integrating aspects of revenue management and yield management to maximize returns from the property's real estate through optimal room rentals. In the hospitality industry, inventory primarily refers to the available hotel rooms per night, making the management of this inventory crucial for revenue and yield optimization. Hotels utilize inventory management systems to mitigate losses and prevent theft, enabling them to accurately gauge product ordering needs from various vendors. These systems furnish detailed reports on vendor performance, accountability, and order management, aiding in the meticulous control of stock levels and ensuring compliance with vendor agreements and accounting practices.

The concept of distressed inventory highlights the challenge of rooms unlikely to be sold at full price, often due to last-minute cancellations. To combat this, hotels are adopting a pooled inventory model, allowing for the sale of all rooms across multiple channels simultaneously, enhancing room occupancy rates and revenue. Moreover, the advent of cloud-based mobile Property Management Systems (PMS) and online inventory management software has revolutionized hotel inventory management. These technologies offer real-time visibility into hotel operations and performance, facilitating timely and informed decision-making even when managers are off-site.

Inventory management in hotels is not one-size-fits-all; it must be tailored to each hotel's specific needs, taking into account the size and diversity of the inventory, occupancy rates, and business objectives. The ultimate aim is to align inventory management strategies with guest expectations and business goals to optimize profitability. Additionally, managing inventory carrying costs effectively—by keeping inventory levels neither too high nor too low—is essential for financial health, underscoring the importance of precision in inventory management practices. By striking a balance between maintaining adequate stock levels to meet demand and minimizing inventory costs, hotels can significantly enhance their operational efficiency and revenue generation capabilities.

7.6 REFERENCES

- Bragg, S. M. 2005. Inventory Accounting: A Comprehensive Guide (Wiley Best Practices). Wiley.
- Chadda, R.S. – Inventory Management in India, Allied Publishers, Chennai, 2004.

- Gujarathi, M. R. and M. Kohlbeck. 2007. Reliance Corporation: Inventory write-downs and reversals. Issues in Accounting Education (August): 503- 514.
- Hadley, S. W. 2004. A modern view of inventory. Strategic Finance (July): 30-35.
- Hadley, S. W. 2004. Safety inventory analysis: Why and how? Strategic Finance (September): 26-33.
- Jain, P.K. and Khan M.Y. – Financial Management, Tata McGraw Hill, New Delhi, 2003.
- Leitch, R. A. 2001. Effect of stochasticity, capacity and lead time cost drivers on WIP and throughput in a pull production environment. Management Accounting Research (June): 167-196.
- Mardak, D. 2002. The world of barter. Strategic Finance (July): 44-47. (Bartering unused capacity and inventory through barter exchanges).
- Olsson, P. 2008. Discussion of "inventory policy, accruals quality and information risk". Review of Accounting Studies 13(2-3): 411-417.
- Piasecki, D. J. 2003. Inventory Accuracy: People, Processes, & Technology. Inventory Operations Consultants.

CHAPTER 8

Capital Expenditure and Investment Decisions in Hospitality Business

INTRODUCTION

Capital expenditure (CapEx) and investment decisions represent pivotal elements within the broader scope of financial management in businesses, underpinning the strategic allocation of financial resources toward the acquisition, enhancement, or maintenance of long-term assets. These assets are integral to the company's operational infrastructure, including but not limited to plants, land, machinery, technology, and buildings. Such expenditures not only signify substantial financial commitments but also have enduring effects on the company's trajectory, influencing its growth, operational efficiency, and market competitiveness.

Capital expenditure encompasses the total financial investment directed towards securing, improving, and managing physical assets. This financial outlay is crucial not only at the inception of the business but also at critical junctures such as the launch of new projects, expansion into new markets, or significant upgrades to existing facilities. The decisions surrounding capital expenditures are characterized by their strategic nature, often requiring thorough analysis and planning to ensure that investments align with long-term organizational goals and yield a substantial return on investment (ROI).

Investment decisions, meanwhile, entail the strategic deployment of the firm's resources to achieve the highest possible returns for investors. These decisions are bifurcated into long-term and short-term investments, each category bearing its unique considerations, risks, and rewards. Long-term investments may include acquiring new assets or entering new markets, while short-term investments might focus on liquidity management or short-term yield opportunities.

The discipline of financial management is tasked with orchestrating the company's financial activities, ensuring a harmonious balance between the acquisition of funds and their effective utilization. Within this framework, financial management is fundamentally concerned with three primary decision areas: investment decisions, financing decisions (determining the best mix of debt and equity for financing the organization's activities), and dividend decisions (determining the portion of profits to be distributed to shareholders versus reinvested in the company). Together, these decisions form the cornerstone of a firm's financial strategy, influencing its capacity to fund operations, invest in growth opportunities, and generate shareholder value over the long term.

Therefore, capital expenditure and investment decisions are essential components of strategic financial management, requiring careful deliberation and foresight. These decisions not only determine the firm's ability to sustain and expand its operational capabilities but also directly impact its financial health and the value it creates for its stakeholders.

8.1 UNDERSTANDING CAPITAL EXPENDITURE

Capital Expenditure, commonly referred to as Capex, is a critical aspect of financial management for businesses. In simple terms, CapEx is the fund used by a company to acquire, upgrade, and maintain its physical assets like buildings, vehicles, machinery, technology, plants, and more.

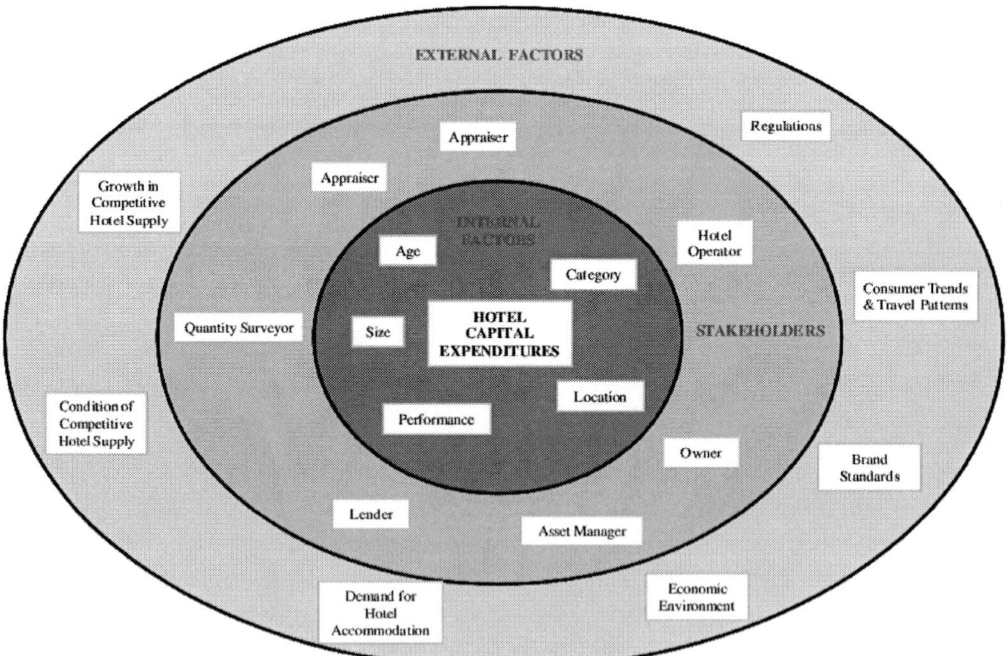

Figure 8.1: *The Consideration of Capital Expenditures in Hotel Valuations.* ***Source:*** *https://www.semanticscholar.org/*

An example of capital expenditure on fixed assets is repairing a roof (if it extends its useful life), purchasing equipment, or building a new factory. The purpose of this type of expenditure is to expand the scope of a company's operations or to add some future economic benefit.

However, in contrast to CapEX, there are other day-to-day short-term expenses called Operating Expenses (OpEx). Now that we know what capital expenditures are, let us look at how to calculate capital expenditure.

8.1.1 CapEx Formula

The Capital Expenditure formula for calculating the capital expenditure of a company is as follows:

CapEx = ΔPP&E + Current Depreciation

Where,

CapEx=Capital expenditures

ΔPP&E=Change in property, plant, and equipment

8.1.2 Alternative CapEx Formula

When a company's free cash flow to equity or FCFE, Debt Ratio, Depreciation, and Earnings Per Share(EPS) are known then use this alternative CapEx formula:

FCFE = Earnings per Share-(CapEx-Depreciation) x (1- Debt Ratio) – ΔNet capital x (1- Debt Ratio)

Example Demonstrating CapEx Formula

A manufacturing company in India invested in upgrading its machinery and facilities. The initial value of property, plant, and equipment (PP&E) was ₹10,00,000. After the upgrades, the new value of PP&E was ₹12,00,000. Additionally, the company's current depreciation expense was ₹50,000.

To calculate the capital expenditures (CapEx), use the formula:

CapEx = ΔPP&E + Current Depreciation

(12,00,000 – 10,00,000) + 50,000

2,00,000 + 50,000

CapEx = 2,50,000

So, the company's capital expenditures for the upgrades were 2,50,000 INR.

8.1.3 Characteristics of Capital Expenditure

The following are some of the characteristics of CapEx:

Depreciation

It's crucial to note that the value of a fixed asset decreases over time due to depreciation. This decline in value persists throughout the asset's lifespan, resulting in an annual reduction in its worth.

Measurement Challenges

Determining, computing, and accounting for capital expenses and their depreciation value can pose difficulties.

Long-Term Commitments

Capital Spending associated with fixed assets represent long-term investments, with their advantages and costs spread out over multiple years.

8.1.4 How to Calculate CapEx Using the Formula?

To calculate Capital Expenditure (CAPEX) using the formula, you can follow these steps:

- ***Determine the Initial Cost of the Asset or Project***: This includes the purchase price or the cost of acquiring the asset. For example, if you are purchasing machinery for 10,00,000, this would be the initial cost (PPE).
- ***Identify any additional capital expenses (AC):*** These are costs incurred beyond the initial purchase price that are directly related to the acquisition or improvement of the asset. Examples include installation costs, legal fees, transportation fees, or any other expenses directly associated with the purchase. Add up all these additional costs.
- ***Estimate the Salvage Value (SC):*** Salvage value is the estimated residual value of the asset at the end of its useful life. It represents the value the asset will hold after depreciation or obsolescence. Estimate the salvage value as accurately as possible.
- ***Plug the Values into the CAPEX Formula:*** Use the formula CAPEX = PPE + AC – SC. Substitute the values of the initial cost (PPE), additional capital expenses (AC), and salvage value (SC) into the formula.
- ***Calculate the Result:*** Add the initial cost and additional capital expenses, then subtract the salvage value. The resulting value will be your calculated Capital Expenditure (CAPEX).

8.1.5 Capital Expenditure in Accounting

Capital expenditure is recorded on a company's balance sheet as fixed assets generally have a depreciated factor. Meaning that every year their value reduces. This depreciation cost is then recorded on the income statement as an expense and reduces the overall profit of the year. Unlike CapEx, RevEx, or revenue expenditure, is immediately expensed and reflected on the income statement.

For example, Let's assume a company called XYZ Ltd. is planning to invest in new manufacturing equipment for its factory. The cost of the equipment is 10,00,000. Since the new equipment is a fixed asset, its depreciated value is 10,00,000.

Capital expenses do affect the income statement of the company. In any case, it does not happen during their purchase year, but rather in the following years according to their depreciation value.

8.1.6 Capital Expenditure Budgeting

Capital expenditure budgeting is the art of deciding how to spend your company's money wisely. Basically, it is the process of evaluating potential long-term investment opportunities to determine which ones will generate the most profit for a business.

When creating a budget, organizations typically distinguish between operating expenses and capital expenditures. Operating expenses (OpEx) include day-to-day costs such as salaries, utilities, and maintenance, while CapEx investment is specifically designated for capital assets.

However, some of the well-known techniques and methods for capital budgeting are internal rate of return (IRR), net asset value (NAV), payback period, profitability index (PI), capital rationing, and more.

8.1.7 Influence of Capital Expenditures on Free Cash Flow and Valuation

Free Cash Flow holds a pivotal role in corporate finance, with analysts frequently assessing a company's cash generation capacity, deeming it a primary means of enhancing shareholder value.

One straightforward approach to compute Free Cash Flow (FCF) is as follows:

FCF = Cash Generated from Operations – Capital Expenditures

In financial modeling and valuation, analysts employ Free Cash Flow calculations within a Discounted Cash Flow (DCF) model to ascertain the business's net present value (NPV). This aids in evaluating the company's overall financial health and investment potential.

If a company buys a set of computer systems for its employees, the cost of the computers will be recorded under the balance sheet. These computers will have a certain depreciation value. Let's say, their total depreciation amount is 10,000 INR per year. For the years that follow the purchase of computers, the income statement will report a depreciation expense of 10,000 rupees.

8.1.8 Types of Capital Expenditure

In a broader sense, there are five major types of capital expenditure. Including buildings, land, property, vehicles, computer hardware, buying new machinery or adding new technology, and software infrastructure.

Let's discuss a few types of capital expenditures in detail.

1. Buildings, land, and property

The cost of buying a building, property, or any piece of real estate is a capital expense since these assets are relevant to the business for many years. Maintaining and repairing these buildings are also capital expenses. These are long-term assets and require a high level of commitment and investment.

2. Upgrades to machinery

The machinery and equipment used to develop products are unavoidable expenses for businesses. This equipment and its needs evolve with time and the

Figure 8.2: Types of Capital Expenditure

changes in technology. Any upgrades made to existing machinery are capital expenditures.

3. Software Infrastructure

Nowadays, it has become impossible for many businesses to function without certain software. Whether it is management software or a cyber security infrastructure, digital solutions form the backbone of many administrative processes, especially for large businesses. The cost of purchase, installation, maintenance, and upgradation of this software is a capital expenditure.

4. Computer hardware

The cost incurred from buying computer hardware like desktops, laptops, servers, etc. is also classified as a capital expense.

5. Vehicles

Certain companies need to own multiple vehicles to carry out their operations. For example, delivery and shipping companies heavily depend on vehicles for transportation. The cost of these vehicles then becomes a capital expense.

Example of Capital Expenditure (CapEx)

According to our previous discussion, capital expenditure reported under on the Cash Flow statement.

Therefore, take a look at this example of a company, XYZ Ltd to gain a better idea about the treatment of CAPEX in a firm's cash flow statement.

Cash Flow Category	Amount
Cash Flow from Operating Activities	1,00,000
Cash Flow from Investing Activities	(50,000)
Capital Expenditure	(40,000)
Proceeds from the Sale of Property, Plant, and Equipment	10,000
Cash Flow from Financing Activities	20,000
Net Increase in Cash and Cash Equivalents	30,000

Now that we have observed examples of Capital Expenditure, let us check out differences between CapEx vs OpEx.

8.1.9 CapEx vs. Operating Expenses (OpEx)

Capital Expenditure should not be confused with Operating Expenses(OpEx). However, to simplify these terms, let's have a look at this table.

Feature	Capital Expenditure (CapEx)	Operating Expense (OpEx)
Definition	Purchases that a business makes as an investment	Expenses that a business incurs as a result of performing its normal business operations
Examples	Land, buildings, equipment, machinery, vehicles, software, intellectual property	Employee salaries, rent, utilities, marketing, insurance, repairs, and maintenance
Useful life	Long-term (typically more than one year)	Short-term (typically one year or less)
Tax treatment	Non-deductable from income	Deductible from income
Impact on cash flow	Reduces cash flow immediately	Reduces cash flow gradually
Impact on financial statements	Reported on the balance sheet	Reported on the income statement
Percentage of CapEx	Typically 10-20%	Typically 80-90%

8.1.10 Effective Capital Expenditure Budgeting Strategies

Managing large-scale capital projects with significant capital expenditures demands effective handling to prevent costly overruns. With careful planning, suitable tools, and adept project management, organizations can ensure efficient capital expenditure budgeting. Discover key strategies below.

Establish a Strong Foundation

Before initiating capital expenditure budgets, comprehensive preparation is imperative to avoid budgetary excesses. Begin by delineating the project's scope, setting realistic timelines, and obtaining approval. Determine the internal resources required, encompassing manpower, materials, finances, and services. Detailed planning at this stage enhances **budget accuracy**.

Embrace Long-Term Thinking

At the project's outset, decide whether to finance the capital asset through debt or existing funds. Funding allocation influences the acquisition timeline. Saving implies delayed asset acquisition, while borrowing increases debt and potential future borrowing constraints. The choice varies based on project specifics.

Implement Robust Budgeting Software

Select reliable and practical budgeting software from project inception. The software choice depends on project scale, program speed, and error risk, aligning with project requirements.

Collect Precise Data

Accurate data collection is paramount for efficient capital project management. Reliable information underpins realistic budget creation and valuable report generation.

Optimal Detail Levels

Balancing detail levels is vital. Excessive detail can lead to prolonged information gathering, rendering budgets obsolete. Conversely, inadequate detail results in vague budgets. Striking the right balance is key.

Establish Clear Policies

Given the multifaceted nature of managing capital total expenditures in large organizations, clarity is essential. Instituting clear policies ensures adherence, fostering budget adherence across departments, teams, and regions.

8.1.11 CapEx Interpretation: Negative vs Positive CapEx

Here's a concise table summarizing the differences between Positive and Negative CapEx

Aspects of Difference	Positive CapEx	Negative CapEx
Definition	Expenditures expected to generate	Expenditures that do

	future cash flows or increase asset value.	not generate future cash flows or asset value.
Purpose	Aims for long-term benefits like increased capacity, efficiency, or competitiveness.	Mainly for asset maintenance or regulatory compliance.
Examples	Investing in technology, facility expansion, new product development.	Repairs, maintenance, environmental compliance investments.
Accounting Treatment	Recorded on the balance sheet as a long-term asset, depreciated over its useful life.	Treated as an expense on the income statement in the year incurred, impacting short-term profitability.

8.1.12 Challenges of Capital Expenditure

Capital expenditure (CapEx) is a significant investment for businesses, and there are a number of challenges that can arise when making these decisions. Some of the most common challenges include:

- ***Uncertainty***: When businesses make a CapEx decision, they're essentially taking a gamble on the future. However, it's challenging to predict how a particular investment will perform due to the inherent uncertainty.
- ***Long-Term Nature***: CapEx projects often require a long-term commitment, as they can last for many years. This can be a challenge, especially if the business's needs or the market changes in the meantime.
- ***High Cost***: CapEx projects can be quite expensive, and businesses must ensure they have the financial resources to support the investment. A lack of cash can force a business to take on debt, which can increase the project's cost.
- ***Complexity***: CapEx projects can be intricate, requiring a deep understanding of the process to ensure success. It involves coordination among various departments, making it difficult to synchronize everyone's efforts.

8.2 CAPITAL EXPENDITURE DECISIONS

Capital expenditure decisions are just the opposite of operating expenditure decisions. It is the planning, evaluation and selection of capital expenditure proposals, the benefits of which are expected to accrue over more than one accounting year.

The capital expenditure decisions have the following features:

i. They involve large amounts of funds.
ii. They involve greater amount of risk.
iii. Capital expenditure decisions are irreversible.

iv. Cash outflows and inflows occur at different points of time.

8.2.1 Meaning of Capital Expenditure Decisions

The capital expenditure decision is the process of making decisions regarding investments in fixed assets which are not meant for sale such as land, building, plant & machinery, etc. Thus it refers to long-term planning for proposed capital expenditures and includes raising of long-term funds and their utilization. The key function of the finance manager is selection of the most profitable project for investment. This task is very crucial because any action taken by the manager in this area affects the working and profitability of the firm for many years to come.

8.2.2 Nature of Capital Expenditure Decisions

Capital expenditure decisions involve acquisition of assets that have a long life span and which provide benefits spread over a long period of time.

The nature of capital expenditure decisions can be explained in brief as under:

i. Substantial Investments

Capital expenditure decisions involve large amounts of funds. Such decisions have its effect over a long span of time.

ii. Irreversible Decision

Capital expenditure decisions once approved represent long term investments that cannot be reversed or withdrawn any time. Withdrawal or reversal of such decisions may lead to considerable financial losses to the firm.

iii. Estimation of Future Cash Inflows

Preparation of capital expenditure budget involves forecasting of cash inflows over several years for evaluating the profitability of projects.

iv. Maximization of Shareholder's Wealth

It helps protect the interest of the shareholders as well as of the firm because it avoids over-investment and under-investment in fixed assets.

8.2.3 Purpose of Capital Expenditure Decisions

The capital expenditure decision or capital budgeting is a process that plans to ascertain the long-term investments of the firm. The main purpose of capital budgeting is to recognize as well as prioritize capital investments on the basis of maximum returns to the business. It is also considered as a managerial tool required for efficient management of collected capital of the firm.

8.2.4 Objectives of Capital Expenditure Decisions

Financing decisions are one of the most crucial and critical decisions of a firm as they have a significant impact on the profitability of the firm.

There are number of objectives of capital expenditure decisions, some of which are:

i. Increasing Output

Output may be increased by utilizing existing facility or through expansion by installing new plant and machinery.

ii. Cost Reduction

The existence of a firm depends on profitability, which in turn depends on the production of goods or services at a reasonable price. This is possible if over/under-investment in fixed assets is avoided.

iii. Providing Contemporary Goods

Consumer tastes change every day. To satisfy the new demands from customers, either proper utilization of existing facility or installation of the latest machinery is necessary—which is not possible without proper capital expenditure decision.

8.2.5 Rules and Items for Determining Capital Expenditure

Capital Expenditure is that expenditure which results in the acquisition of permanent asset or fixed asset which is used continuously in the business for the purpose of earning revenue any amount spent on the asset which will result in increasing the production or reducing the cost of production may also be treated as Capital Expenditure.

1. Expenditure incurred for acquiring Land, Building, Machinery, Investments, Patents or Furniture etc. are permanent or fixed assets. The fixed asset is used in the business for earning profit and not for resale, is called a Capital Expenditure. For instance, when we purchase furniture it is a capital expenditure and at the same time to the Furniture Shop, who is engaged in buying and selling of furniture, it is not capital expenditure.
2. Expenditure incurred for putting an old asset in working condition or for putting a new asset to use, is capital expenditure. For instance, an old machine is purchased for Rs. 10,000 and Rs 2,000 is spent for its repairs and installation and the total expenditures are capita, expenditure.
3. Expenditure incurred on an existing asset which results in the improvement or extension of the business by increasing the earning capacity of the asset or by reducing the cost of production is also called capital expenditure. For instance, installations of machine or additions to buildings or plant etc. are capital expenditure.
4. When benefit of expenditure is not fully consumed in one period but spread over several periods, is called capita, expenditure. For instance, expenditure met for massive advertisements.
5. Expenditure which increases the earning capacity in any way of a fixed asset can be called capital expenditure. For instance, amount spent on cinema theatre for air conditioning.
6. Expenditure spent on raising the capital required for earning profit is called capital expenditure. For instance, underwriting commission, brokerage etc.

Items of Capital Expenditure

1. Cost of Land, Building, Plant and Machinery.
2. Cost of lease hold Land and Building.
3. Cost of manufacture or purchase of furniture and fixtures.
4. Cost of office Cars, Vans, Lorries or Vehicles.
5. Cost of installation of lights, fans etc.
6. Cost of erection of Plant and Machinery.
7. Cost of Trade Mark, Patents, Copy rights, Patterns and Designs.
8. Preliminary Expenses.
9. Cost of Goodwill.
10. Cost of addition to and extension of existing fixed assets.
11. Cost of development in case of Mines and Plantations.
12. Cost of invention.
13. Cost of increasing capacity of fixed asset.
14. Cost of administration in industrial enterprises incurred during the period of construction.

8.2.6 Capital Expenditure Decision Process

The capital expenditure decision is derived from and is closely associated with strategic planning which is an effort by an organization to define its mission and goals and the policies and strategies it will follow to attain them.

8.2.7 Quantitative Estimates

Reliable estimates and forecasts are vital to the capital investment decision. A sophisticated process of analyzing financial information and managing the decision related to a project is of little value if a casual approach is taken to development of these estimates. The foundations for good capital planning are reliable forecasts of marketing opportunities, competitive technology, likely actions by competitors and governments, sales volumes, selling prices, operating costs, changes in working capital, taxes payable and capital costs of equipment. Effective management of capital expenditure decisions, therefore, requires that controls be designed and operated to ensure that projections are realistic at the time decisions are made.

The estimate of the costs and benefits of a capital project should show the difference that results from making the investment. The important information is the change in cash flows as a result of undertaking the project, i.e., the differential principle.

The degree of precision necessary for the estimates related to the capital expenditure decision depends on:

a. the stage of evaluation of the project (i.e., in early stages less precision is needed),
b. the sensitivity of the project's economics to the level of accuracy and timing of each of the elements within the estimates, and
c. the similarity of the project to others already undertaken.

Fixed Investment Estimates

Fixed investments consist of all the costs necessary to bring the project to full operation. These include the equipment costs, installation, training, commissioning, initial spoilage, spare parts inventory, etc. The capital investment in a project can usually be estimated with greater precision than the other factors required for the capital expenditure decision, primarily because capital investments occur in the near future whereas operating costs and revenues are incurred over the life of the project.

The simplest means of estimating capital costs is to adjust the known investment ofaproject of similar nature. The most complex means of estimation requires a detailed project plan from which the costs of individual items and other costs are developed. In between, various yardsticks may provide adequate approximations of investment required. For example, the cost of a building may be approximated by the estimated cost per square foot to construct the building times the estimated square footage of the building.

In lieu of firm bids from manufacturers and suppliers, quick estimates can often be obtained without involving a great deal of their time as published information is often available.

If the project will result in the replacement of existing equipment, the net cash inflows or outflows from the removal and disposal of that equipment, including the tax implications, should be taken into account.

Working Capital Estimates

The analysis includes estimates of all investments required for a project. The project may require increases (or decreases) in cash, accounts receivable, accounts payable, or inventory. These changes in working capital should be included in the calculation as should the changes to these at the end of the economic life of the project.

The Planning Horizon-Economic Life

It is often difficult to estimate the life of a project (i.e., its planning horizon). The criterion is the continued ability to generate satisfactory cash flows or other intangible benefits. The economic life of a project is the lesser of its physical life, technological life or product-market life.

Physical Life

Physical life represents the time taken for an asset to become physically worn out so that it can no longer be efficiently maintained and must be replaced. However, equipment will often be disposed of before its physical life has expired.

Technological Life

Technological life is the period of time that elapses before an even newer machine or process becomes available which would make the proposed machine or process obsolete. Improvements will almost certainly be made sometime in all machines or processes now in existence, but questions of which machines or processes will be improved, and how soon they will be on the market are most difficult to answer. To ignore a process' or machine's technological life is to imply that the technological life is the same as the physical life.

Although a machine may be in excellent physical condition, and although there may be no better machine on the market, its economic life has ended for the organization as soon as it ceases to market the product. The product-market life of the machine may end because the particular operation performed by the machine is made unnecessary by a change in style or because the market for the product itself has disappeared.

The projected economic life on the return on investment is particularly important if the project lasts for a relatively short period, say ten years or less, and is less important for longer projects. It is therefore particularly important that special consideration be given to estimates of economic life if there is a high probability that the economic life may be short.

Because of the inherent uncertainties of making estimates in distant years, especially estimates related to sales volumes, some organizations set an arbitrary limit on the planning horizon to be used in the analysis. This planning horizon can be shorter than the estimated economic life of the project; in some organizations, it is ten years. In some organizations, cash flows beyond this planning horizon are disregarded in the interest of conservatism or if not significant to the project. Other organizations apply an arbitrary estimate of value for the benefits beyond the planning horizon.

Market Estimates

Some methods of developing market estimates are discussed in the following paragraphs.

Market Study

A market study forecasts sales revenue through the life of a project. It should describe fully all aspects of the company's position in the market and estimate the degree of marketing risk associated with the venture. It provides information on demand, supply and price trends in the overall market, and specific forecasts of market share, sales volume, net returns and selling costs, as well as what competitors are or may be doing in the market place.

Usually, this forecast proceeds from stated assumptions regarding the economic environment and general business conditions, to estimates of total market, subdivided by end-use, region, and major customer, and then concludes with estimates of specific sales potential available within that market.

When developing sales forecasts, consideration should be given to the possible obsolescence of products or services. Such items have a life of only a few years, so that organizations must compete, not necessarily on the basis of being the low-cost producer, but by being product innovators. The demand forecast must, therefore, consider: frequent introduction of new products, timely delivery, and flexibility in the production process to adapt to customer preferences. Such considerations must also be factors in the selection process for capital equipment.

Significant relationships between an organization's sales and economic indicators for the market as a whole, or other industry statistics, may be determined by using correlation analysis.

An alternative way of projecting sales is to use internal sources of data, such as information supplied through sales-men's call reports, supplementary information developed through interviews of market researchers, credit statistics, and general knowledge of the customer and his or her competitive situation.

Either method may produce a set of possible outcomes to which a probability figure could be developed. The appropriate figure to use is a weighted average of the possible outcomes. It is known as the expected value. However, in many projects such a probability distribution is either not feasible or not worthwhile.

Competitive Factors

The demand forecast should indicate the competitors and their market share. The productive capacity in existence and potentially available would then be assessed in relation to the forecasted demand to show the volume and timing of expansion needs. Competitors' expansion possibilities and economics should also be considered along with their product and technology life cycles.

Price Estimation

The estimation of price trends is frequently the most difficult area of market forecasting. However, analysis of the supply/demand balance and estimation of competitors' economics can provide a guide. The elasticity of demand in relation to the price may also be considered. A careful study of the product life cycle is often needed since, in the early development stages of a new product, the price is often high; it falls as demand levels off at maturity, and then declines further as new substitutes appear on the market.

The Organization's Position in the Market

The analyses of supply, demand and price are consolidated into specific forecasts of market share, sales volume and annual cash inflow through the project's expected life. In addition, it is important to state the major assumptions, the reliability of the market data and, if worthwhile, attach confidence limits to the forecasts. By doing so, the degree of marketing risk associated with the project is conveyed, and the sensitivity of the project to inaccuracies in the marketing appraisal can be evaluated.

Operating Cost Estimates

When estimating operating costs for capital expenditures, the following should be kept in mind:

a. Only cash costs after the payment of tax on income are relevant; non-cash expenses such as depreciation are excluded except to the extent they affect taxable income.
b. Only future costs are relevant. Historical costs may be useful in terms of providing a basis for prediction, but they do not represent what future costs will be.

c. Only differential costs are relevant. This means that only the difference in cash operating costs between implementing or not implementing a proposal need be considered.

Labor - Associated Payments, etc

- Labor costs should include, in addition to the direct wage rate, overtime and all associated payments and benefits.

Labor - Savings from Reducing lime Required of Individuals

- Labor savings often result from the saving of part of several individuals' time.
- Over the long run, it would normally be expected that the time set free for these individuals could be productively utilized elsewhere or that the aggregate saving in time will cause reduction in the number of employees.

Efficiency Improvement

Cost reduction projects often include improvements in efficiency which either reduce material consumption or increase output. The additional output should be valued at the probable profit which can be realized.

Services

The differential cost of services, (e.g., utilities, transport, computer services) often present problems. An investment proposal may result in the consumption of fewer services due to efficiency improvements. In such a case, the effect on a project's differential cost depends upon what can be done with the unused service. If any cash costs associated with keeping the service at the level prior to the investment can be eliminated, then the amount involved can be treated as a cash cost saving (negative cost). If the freed-up service can be used elsewhere and would have to be bought for this other use, then the amount saved by not having to buy for this other purpose would be a cost saving of the investment. If the freed-up service cannot be used elsewhere and must still be paid for, then there would be no incremental cost saving for the investment (the cost would continue whether or not the investment was made).

Maintenance

Maintenance costs should normally be the cost expected to be incurred in each year of the life of a project. Sometimes the use of an average may be justified. An average will sometimes be a greater amount than the maintenance cost in the initial years. Provision should also be made, as appropriate, for periodic overhauls. Estimates should also be made of the incremental costs for maintenance material and operating supplies.

Depreciation

No amount for depreciation should be included in calculating the cash flow since this is an allocation of the investment cost required to match expenses against revenues over the life of the investment. It does not require a cash outflow each year. In capital budgeting, the cost of the investment is taken into account when cash outlays or their equivalent take place. If depreciation were counted in determining cash flows, the investment cost would be inappropriately double counted. However, in the determination of taxes on income allowances for depreciation should be considered.

Property-Related Costs

Certain insurances and taxes are related to investment costs and should be estimated accordingly.

Plant Administration, Service Departments, etc.

If an organization is expanding, plant administration and service departments also expand, but such expansion may not be directly attributed to individual capital investment projects. Nevertheless some allowance for the cost of expansion is needed. It is suggested that general ratios may be applicable to most appropriations being prepared at a time. Periodic revision of these ratios is necessary.

Estimating Terminal Values (Salvage, Trade-in or Disposal Values)

The terminal value of a capital asset at the end of its useful life should include disposal values less the dismantling and/or site restoration costs plus the release of any associated working capital.

Estimating the Effects of Inflation

The effect of inflation on a capital project is to reduce the purchasing power of net cash flows over time.

Several techniques for recognizing the effect of inflation are used in practice. They include:

a. use of a discount rate that is high enough to incorporate inflation
b. adjusting all cash flows by a single percentage that allows for inflation, or
c. adjusting individual cash flows by rates that include the effect of inflation on each of them.

The first technique is perhaps the most common. Care must be taken to insure that the effect of inflation is not double counted, which can happen if two of the above methods are used together.

Risk exists in capital budgeting when more than one outcome may occur. A quantitative evaluation of a capital expenditure proposal requires that several predictions be made, often far into the future. As a general rule, the risk associated with achieving an expected cash inflow or outflow in a given year increases as one moves further into the future as there are more factors in the long term which cannot be foreseen but which will affect cash flows.

Most organizations do not make a specific allowance for risk. Some, however, provide the following information:

a. the range of accuracy for the estimate stated as a plus or minus percentage,

b. the expected value of the estimate based on a weighted average of all possible outcomes, and
c. the effect on the appraisal results using the widest range of error. Of particular interest is the amount by which a key variable can be varied before the project fails to meet its decision criterion, all other things being held constant.

8.2.8 Decision Models

Evaluation Techniques

Several techniques are available to arrive at a financial decision regarding a capital expenditure project. These include:

- the net present value method. This method discounts all cash flows to the present using a predetermined minimum acceptable rate of return as the discount rate. If the net present value is positive, the financial return on the project is greater than this minimum acceptable rate and indicates the project is economically acceptable. If the net present value is negative, the project is not acceptable on economic grounds.
- the internal rate of return method. The internal rate of return is defined as the discount rate that makes the net present value of a project equal to zero. It is the highest rate of interest that a company could incur to obtain funds without losing money on the project.
- the equivalent annual cost method. When considering alternative proposals, it may be that only costs are involved. In such situations, a choice of alternatives can be made by determining which has the lowest equivalent annual cost. Under this method, capital expenditures are converted to their "equivalent annual cost" and added to the annual "operating" costs. Equivalent annual cost is the annual amount that would repay the capital over the life of the project at a specified discount rate. It is similar to an annual, level repayment schedule for a mortgage. The alternative with the lowest total cost would be the most attractive (ignoring intangibles).
- the payback method. This method estimates the time taken to recover the original investment outlay. The estimated net cash flows from a proposal for each year are added until they total the original investment. The time required to recoup the investment is called the payback period. Projects with a shorter payback period are preferred to those with longer periods.
- the discounted payback method. The discounted payback period is the number of years fur which cash inflows are required to (a) recover the amount of the investment and also (b) earn the required rate of return on the investment during that period. In this method, each year's cash inflow is discounted at the required rate of return, and these present values are cumulated by year until, their sum equals, the amount invested. Projects with a shorter discounted payback period are preferable to those with longer periods.

- the accounting rate of return method. The accounting rate of return is a measure of the average annual income after tax over the life of a project divided by the initial investment or the average investment required to generate the income. It is important to note that this method assesses net income and not cash flows which are used in the other methods.

The internal rate of return, net present value and equivalent annual cost methods use discounted cash flows (D.C.F). The D.C.F concept considers the time value of money in making investment decisions, whereas the other methods do not.

The payback method (or discounted payback method) is useful where:

a. preliminary screening of many proposals is necessary;
b. a weak cash position has an important bearing on the selection of projects;
c. the proposed project is extremely risky; or
d. projects, such as routine replacement projects, have similar economic lives.

When the payback method is used, the required payback period should be consistent with that developed by applying the required rate of return on projects with similar characteristics.

The accounting rate of return method is useful when management is especially concerned with the effect of a large capital investment on reported financial results.

Ranking of Capital Expenditure Projects

Many organizations have several proposed capital projects which are economically acceptable, but they have only limited financial resources. Thus the entity must rank the projects and select those that promise the higher returns.

At any given time, management is likely to be considering several projects at various stages of refinement. At each stage in the evaluation process, proposals are assessed and accepted into the next stage, referred back to the sponsor for further work or rejected. A ranking procedure should be used at each stage. Ranking projects on the basis of quantitative criteria may be established by specifying a minimum desired rate of return on a project. This minimum rate is called the required rate of return (also the discount rate or the hurdle rate). This rate is used to calculate the net present value of each project and to rank them accordingly.

The internal rate of return and net present value methods are also used to resolve the capital rationing problem. If the internal rate of return method is used, the higher the rate of return, the better the project. If the net present value is used, it is necessary to first divide the present value of the cash inflows by the amount of the investment. The higher the resulting number, called the profitability index, the better the project.

In selecting the required rate of return to evaluate capital expenditure proposals, two approaches are widely used: calculating a cost of capital, or use of a number generally accepted by the industry.

In theory, the required rate of return on a project of average risk should be at least as high as the organization's cost of capital.

Non-Quantitative Evaluation Considerations

Qualitative or policy considerations may override quantitative criteria in the ranking or acceptance of projects. Some examples of qualitative considerations are:

a. relationship to business strategy;
b. product line or location and its significance to the enterprise;
c. timing of fund flows from the project versus the timing of fund flows required;
d. management, technical engineering and marketing capacities or constraints; and
e. balance desired in spending by product classification.

Projects may be worthy of approval on such non-financial grounds as protection of company property, employee health and welfare or to comply with government regulations in such areas as pollution.

Government and Nonprofit Organizations

The capital expenditure process for government and nonprofit organizations is conceptually similar to that in for profit organizations, and although the method of estimating costs and benefits is also similar, there are important differences in measuring benefits.

If feasible, government and nonprofit organizations attempt to measure both financial and social benefits. Social benefits can be difficult to quantify but include:

- direct benefits that accrue to the taxpayer or member, and
- indirect benefits that accrue to individuals or groups that may or may not be taxpayers or members.

The required rate of return on government or nonprofit funds is the return on alternative uses of these funds

8.2.9 Administration of the Capital Expenditure Decision

Figure 1 depicts, in general terms, the process which an organization may use in making the capital expenditure decision. This Practice describes only the decision making process (i.e. up to the "final approval" decision).

Each proposed capital expenditure competes for and should justify its share of the limited resources available. Formal procedures and rules should be established to assure that all proposals are reviewed fairly and consistently. Managers and supervisors who make proposals need to know what the organization expects the proposals to contain, and on what basis their proposed projects will be judged. Those managers who have the authority to approve specific projects need to exercise that responsibility in the context of an overall organizational capital expenditure policy [as approved by the Board of Directors or senior managers where appropriate].

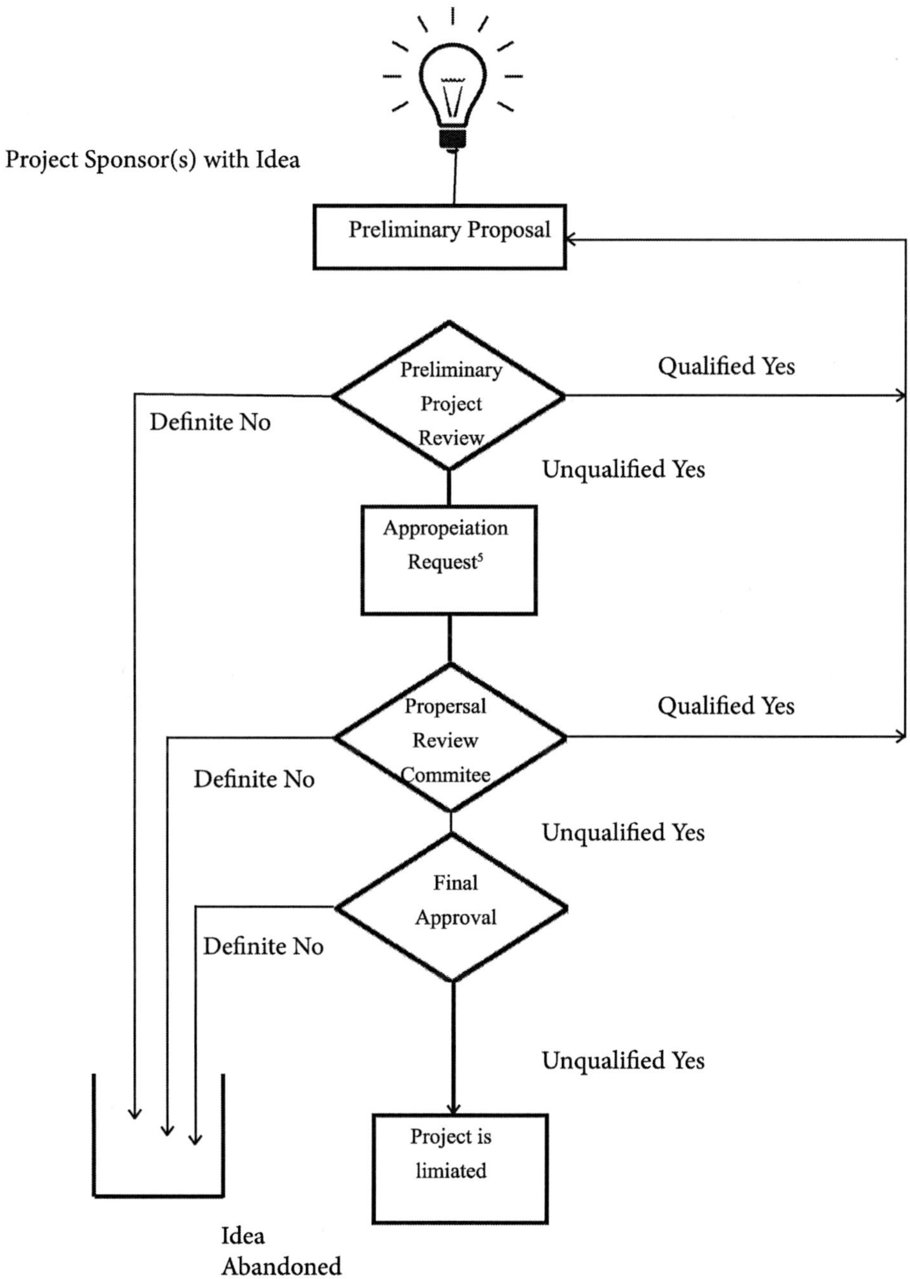

Figure 8.3. *Capital Expenditure Decision*

The management accounting function, which has the task of developing the internal controls in an enterprise, also has the responsibility for coordinating the input of the various functional groups and obtaining approval of this policy manual.

The policy manual should include specifications for

- an annually updated forecast of capital expenditures. This project by project forecast should cover a period of three to five years and should include: previous expenditures for approved projects, expenditures for the current budget year, a forecast of the capital expenditures required for the following two to four years, and the supply (both internal and external) of funds in the ensuing year.
- the appropriation steps. These should be sufficiently detailed to ensure that the proposal and approval procedures are identified in a consistent and orderly manner. The procedure for a revision to a previously approved capital expenditure application should also be specified.
- the appraisal method(s) to be used to evaluate proposals.
- the minimum acceptable rate(s) of return on projects of various risk. Normally, this provides guidelines rather than an absolute requirement, because not all projects are evaluated solely in terms of financial benefits.
- the limits of authority. Here the specification of the appropriate managers attesting to the desirability of the project in relation to the responsibility of these managers should be required as the basis for their accountability.
- the control of capital expenditures. The manual should indicate who is responsible for controlling capital expenditures once the project is approved and authorizing capital expenditures against authorized amounts.
- the procedure to be followed when accepted projects will be subject to an actual performance review after implementation. As a minimum, the policy manual should specify the expenditure limit above which a review will be required; the time it will commence after completion of the project; and by whom it will be undertaken.

The first formal step in the capital expenditure decision is a preliminary project review. This assessment is often needed

a. to give early consideration of and guidance to a project which could result in an appropriation request and to provide an early screen for ideas not worthy of pursuit,
b. to minimize the lead time to implement a promising project, and
c. to coordinate activities associated with a project.

An appropriate project sponsor should be identified who should ensure that all required documentation contains the information needed to reach a decision on the preliminary proposal. The organization's policy regarding the preparation of estimates for capital expenditure proposals should encourage managers to seek out and use the expertise of others who can help in the derivation of cash flows.

8.3 INVESTMENT DECISION

Investment decision refers to financial resource allocation. Investors opt for the most suitable assets or investment opportunities based on risk profiles, investment objectives, and return expectations.

Firms have limited financial resources; therefore, the top-level management undertakes capital budgeting and fund allocation into long-term assets. Managers overseeing business operations opt for short-term investments to ensure liquidity and working capital. Investment decisions are also influenced by the frequency of returns, associated risks, maturity periods, tax benefits, volatility, and inflation rates.

Investment decisions are made to reap maximum returns by allocating the right financial resource to the right opportunity. These decisions are taken considering two important financial management parameters—risks and returns.

Investors and managers dedicate a lot of time to investment planning—these decisions involve massive funds and can be irreversible—impact on the investors and business is long-term.

Also, individuals and corporate investors have to decide between various options—assets, securities, bonds, debentures, gold, real estate, etc. For businesses, investments could be in the form of new ventures, projects, mergers, or acquisitions as well.

Investment decisions are further classified into short-term and long-term. For example, the final decision may involve a capital expenditure on assets that pay off in the long run or an investment in inventory that converts into sales within a short period. A company might attempt expansion by taking up new projects; a business might increase the capacity of an existing facility. Capital investment is required for replacing an obsolete asset as well. In business, decision-making is everywhere.

Investment Decision is a part of Financial Management which deals with the allocation of the company's valuable funds into investment projects or potential assets.

It involves identifying such projects or assets to invest in and generate returns from them. Besides, these decisions significantly affect the profitability and stability of the firm.

Some essential investment decisions that organizations make are:

- Setting up new business
- Expansion of existing one
- Modernization of existing one

The selection of the assets is a critical task as the risk and return profiles vary.

There exists a direct relationship between risk and return. The more the risk, the higher will be the return and reverse. Thus, the top-level management must take strategic investment decisions with calculated risks.

For firms, investment decision plays an integral part in achieving their long-term goals. Usually, the amount invested is huge, and so is the associated risk. Along with value creation, it generates revenue and eases the firm's survival.

Firms take investment decisions for both the long and short term.

In finance terminology, long-term decisions are termed Capital Budgeting Decisions. Similarly, short-term decisions are termed Working Capital Decisions.

The funds invested in the fixed assets remain blocked for a substantial period of time. In contrast, the investments in current assets are generally for one year or less.

8.3.1 Investment Process

An investment process is a set of guidelines that govern the behavior of investors in a way which allows them to remain faithful to the tenets of their investment strategy, that is the key principles which they hope to facilitate out-performance. An Investment Process is a structured and systematic procedure used by investors to identify, evaluate, and manage an investment portfolio in order to achieve financial objectives.

There are 5 investing process steps that help you in selecting and investing in the best asset class according to your needs and preferences. Read here in details every steps of investing process.

Step 1- Understanding the Client

The first and the foremost step of investing process is to understand the client or the investor his/her needs, his risk taking capacity and his tax status. After getting an insight of the goals and restraints of the client, it is important to set a benchmark for the client's portfolio management process which will help in evaluating the performance and check whether the client's objectives are achieved.

Step 2- Asset Allocation Decision

This step involves decision on how to allocate the investment across different asset classes, i.e. fixed income securities, equity, real estate etc. It also involves decision of whether to invest in domestic assets or in foreign assets. The investor will make this decision after considering the macroeconomic conditions and overall market status.

Step 3- Portfolio Strategy Selection

Third step in the investment process is to select the proper strategy of portfolio creation. Choosing the right strategy for portfolio creation is very important as it forms the basis of selecting the assets that will be added in the portfolio management process. The strategy that conforms to the investment policies and investment objectives should be selected.

There are two types of portfolio strategy.

1. Active Management Process
2. Passive Management Process

Active Portfolio: Active management process refers to a strategy where the objective of investing is to outperform the market return compared to a specific benchmark by either buying securities that are undervalued or by short selling securities that are overvalued. In this strategy, risk and return both are high. This strategy is a proactive strategy it requires close attention by the investor or the fund manager.

Passive Portfolio: Passive management process refers to the strategy where the purpose is to generate returns equal to that of the market. It is a reactive strategy as the fund manager or the investor reacts after the market has responded.

Step 4- Asset Selection Decision

The investor needs to select the assets to be placed in the portfolio management process in the fourth step. Within each asset class, there are different sub asset-classes. For example, in equity, which stocks should be chosen? Within the fixed income securities class, which bonds should be chosen?

Also, the investment objectives should conform to the investment policies because otherwise the main purpose of investment management process would become meaningless.

Step 5- Evaluating Portfolio Performance

This is the final step in the investment process which evaluates the portfolio management performance. This is an important investing process step as it measures the performance of the investment with respect to a benchmark, in both absolute and relative terms. The investor would determine whether his objectives are being achieved or not.

Investing in an asset, security, or project requires a lot of patience; ideally, the decision-making process should be analytical. Following is a five-step process decision-making process that guides investors:

1. ***Analyze Financial Position***: For financial management, one has to understand the company or individual's current financial condition.
2. ***Define Investment Objective***: Then, investors must set up an investment objective—whether to invest short-term or long-term. They should also be aware of their risk appetite (level of risk they desire to take).
3. ***Asset Allocation***: Based on the objective, investors must allocate assets into stocks, debentures, bonds, real estate, options, and commodities.
4. ***Select Investment Products***: After narrowing down on a particular asset class, investors must further select a particular asset or security. Alternatively, this could be a basket of assets that fit the requirements.
5. ***Monitor and Due Diligence***: Portfolio managers keep an eye on the performance of each investment and monitor the returns. In case of poor performance, they must take prompt action.

8.3.2 Investment Decision

The investment process decision is finance terminology related to a decision made by the investors concerning the amount of funds to be invested in the various investment vehicles.

An investment process is a set of guidelines required to create the portfolio and sequence of actions involved, from defining the risk parameters to asset allocations. It gives a structure to the investor who helps him implement the strategy customized as per his goals, objectives, risk tolerance, and values that seek to manage the risk. All in all, it is the investing process that makes an investor a confident investor that can make decisions effortlessly without any self-doubt. If you are a newbie investor and want satisfactory investment returns, then you should incorporate an investment process in your investment strategies.

Simply, select the types of assets in which the investor as the investment decision invests the fund. There are two types of assets.

1. **Long-term assets**
2. **Short-term assets**

The investment process decision of investing in long-term assets is also called capital budgeting. Thus, the capital budgeting is the process of selecting the assets that will give you return over a long period of time. For example, investing in mutual funds, stocks, bonds, and real for more than a year comes under a long-term financial decision.

The first step involved in capital-budgeting is to choose the asset. The return of the investment depends on the type of asset you choose. The higher you take risk, the better return you will get. So, while making an investment decision, always consider your risk appetite.

The investment made in current assets or short assets is known as working capital management. In which an investor tries to balance between profitability and liquidity. The process of investment decision involves both long-term assets and short-term assets. If you have a good knowledge of the market, and know the investment process very well, then we advise you to choose capital budgeting over current assets.

8.3.3 Nature of Investment Processing Decision

The investment decision is a crucial decision for every investor as it determines profitability. It is advisable to do a proper study of risk and return before making any investing decisions. Let's look at the nature of investment decisions and understand why it is important in finance.

- ***Requires Huge Funds***

An Investment process decision requires a huge fund to be invested by a firm to gain profit. This decision is very crucial because firms have limited funds and demands for funds are very high. Every firm should necessarily design the investing process and control its expenditures.

- ***High Degree of Risk***

The investing process decision involves a high amount of risk if they are taken based on the estimated returns. Large funds invested in the current assets are totally at risk. The market patterns fluctuate, which will show an adverse effect on the investment decision.

- ***Long Term Effect***

Process of Investment decisions have a long-lasting effect on future profitability and firm stability. Your investment decision determines the growth of the firm and future. In case, if you make any wrong investment process decision, it may ruin your personal and professional growth. Whereas, the right investment decision brings a good return of the investment, and your company's growth to the next level.

- ***Long-Term Commitment of Funds***

Funds are invested for a longer-term by an investor through this investing process decisions. He deployed a large amount of capital for a long period permanently—a financial risk in investment decisions increases due to the long-term commitment of funds. An investor should properly plan and monitor all of his capitals.

- ***Complexity***

Investing process decisions are uncertain because they are taken on the basis of future events. Future cash flow and return of the investment cannot be predicted accurately as they are influenced by the market conditions, economic, social, political, and technology factors.

8.3.4 Scope of Investment Process Decisions

Scope of Investment Decisions Identify Degree of Risk. Here are those decisions help in identifying the level of risk associated with an investment opportunity.

1. Selection of Right Assets

An investment decision is the important aspect of the investing process as it helps investors to choose the right assets. Each available opportunity is properly analyzed by an investor while taking a financial decision. This way, every aspect of asset available for investment is considered, which leads to building a strong portfolio.

2. Identify Degree of Risk

This financial decision helps you to identify the level of risk associated with the investment. Your investing process decisions are taken on the basis of the return and risk required for earning such a return. With the help of asset tools you can properly manage your risk, and make your portfolio strong and risk-free.

3. Determines Profitability

Investing decisions regarding investment plans determines the future profit-earning potential of the firm. If you make the right financial decision, it brings a large amount of funds to your company. Whereas, any wrong investment decision may cause a huge loss.

4. Enhance Financial Understanding

Investing decisions impart a vast knowledge about finance to the individuals making these decisions. When making investing process decisions, investors take the help of a wide variety of tools and techniques to analyze the right assets and make sure their financial decision is right.

8.3.5 Factors Affecting Investment Decision

An investment is a planned decision, and some of the factors that are responsible for these decisions are as follows:

- ***Investment Objective***: The purpose behind an investment determines the short-term or long-term fund allocation. It is the starting point of the decision-making process.
- ***Return on Investment***: Managers prioritize positive returns—they try to employ limited funds in a profitable asset or security.
- ***Return Frequency***: The number of periodic returns an investment offer is crucial. Financial management is based on financial needs; investors choose between investments that yield monthly, quarterly, semi-annual, or annual returns.
- ***Risk Involved***: An investment may possess high, medium, or low risk, and the risk appetite of every investor and company is different. Therefore, every investment requires a risk analysis.
- ***Maturity Period or Investment Tenure***: Investments pay off when funds are blocked for a certain period. Thus, investor decisions are influenced by the maturity period and payback period.

- ***Tax Benefit*:** Tax liability associated with a particular asset or security is another crucial deciding factor. Investors tend to avoid investment opportunities that are taxed heavily.
- ***Safety*:** An asset or security offered by a company that adheres to regulatory frameworks and has a transparent financial disclosure is considered safe. Government-backed assets are considered the most secure.
- ***Volatility*:** Market fluctuations significantly affect investment returns and, therefore, cannot be overlooked.
- ***Liquidity*:** Investors are often worried about their emergency funds—the provision to withdraw money before maturity. Hence, investors look at the degree of liquidity offered by a particular asset or security; they specifically consider withdrawal restrictions and penalties.
- ***Inflation Rate*:** In financial management, investors look for investment opportunities where returns surpass the nation's inflation rate.

8.4 TYPES OF CAPITAL INVESTMENT DECISIONS

There are many ways to classify the capital budgeting decision. Generally capital investment decisions are classified in two ways. One way is to classify them on the basis of firm's existence. Another way is to classify them on the basis of decision situation.

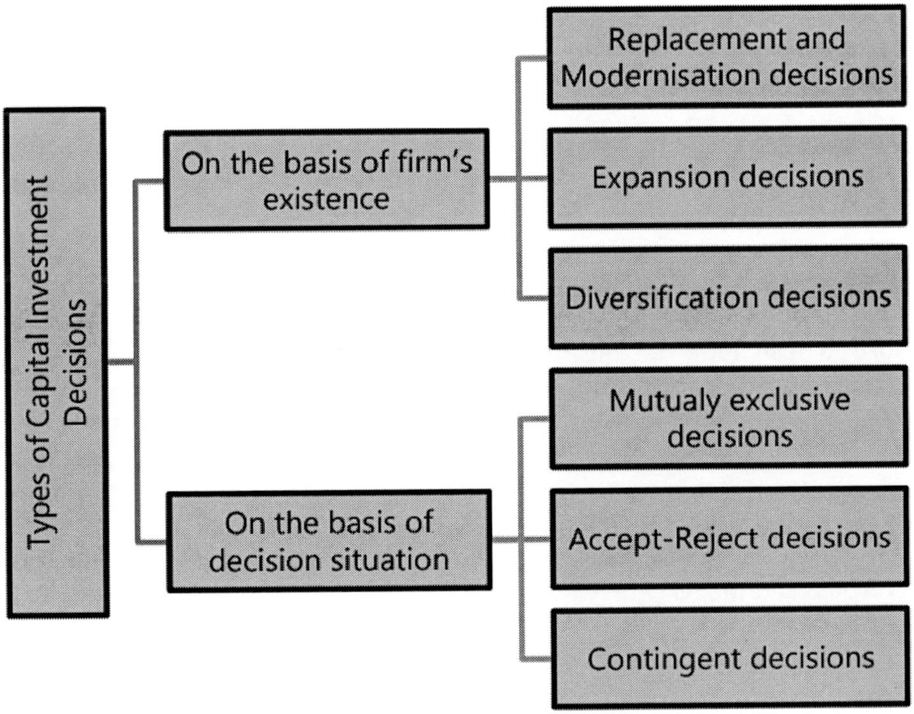

Figure 8.4: *Types of capital budgeting decisions.*

8.4.1 On the Basis of Firm's Existence

The capital budgeting decisions are taken by both newly incorporated firms as well as by existing firms. The new firms may require taking decision in respect of selection of a plant to be installed. The existing firm may require taking decisions to meet the requirement of new environment or to face the challenges of competition. These decisions may be classified as follows:

(i) Replacement and Modernisation decisions: The replacement and modernisation decisions aim at to improve operating efficiency and to reduce cost. Generally, all types of plant and machinery require replacement either because of the economic life of the plant or machinery is over or because it has become technologically outdated. The former decision is known as replacement decisions and latter is known as modernisation decisions. Both replacement and modernisation decisions are called cost reduction decisions.

(ii) Expansion decisions: Existing successful firms may experience growth in demand of their product line. If such firms experience shortage or delay in the delivery of their products due to inadequate production facilities, they may consider proposal to add capacity to existing product line.

(iii) Diversification decisions: These decisions require evaluation of proposals to diversify into new product lines, new markets etc. for reducing the risk of failure by dealing in different products or by operating in several markets.

Both expansion and diversification decisions are called revenue expansion decisions.

8.4.2 On the Basis of Decision Situation

The capital budgeting decisions on the basis of decision situation are classified as follows:

(i) Mutually exclusive decisions: The decisions are said to be mutually exclusive if two or more alternative proposals are such that the acceptance of one proposal will exclude the acceptance of the other alternative proposals. For instance, a firm may be considering proposal to install a semi-automatic or highly automatic machine. If the firm installs a semi-automatic machine it excludes the acceptance of proposal to install highly automatic machine.

(ii) Accept-reject decisions: The accept-reject decisions occur when proposals are independent and do not compete with each other. The firm may accept or reject a proposal on the basis of a minimum return on the required investment. All those proposals which give a higher return than certain desired rate of return are accepted and the rest are rejected.

(iii) Contingent decisions: The contingent decisions are dependable proposals. The investment in one proposal requires investment in one or more other proposals. For example, if a company accepts a proposal to set up a factory in remote area it may have to invest in infrastructure also e.g. building of roads, houses for employees etc.

8.5 DECISION-MAKING PROCESS FOR INVESTMENTS

An investment decision-making process helps you decide how much to invest in equity, bonds, real estate, gold, etc. It provides a customised strategy for asset allocation, diversification, risk and portfolio management.

For an effective investment process, you must assess:

- Your investment goals
- How much do you need to invest to reach the goals?
- The degree of risk tolerance
- Diversification of portfolio
- Choosing the right assets
- Investment returns
- Tax* provisions

8.5.1 The 5 Important Investment Management Process Steps

- ***Evaluation of investment goals***

Evaluation of investment goals is the first crucial step of the investment process. The purpose of your investment can be wealth creation, income generation or safety. Also, your goals may vary according to age and income.

Usually, young people invest with the aim of accumulating wealth and have a risky appetite. But income generation and retirement planning are the purposes of investment when you reach midlife and later midlife. So, chalking out your investment goals help you hit the right investment asset to generate adequate returns.

- ***Evaluation of the present financial situation***

You cannot implement an effective investment decision process without disciplined savings. So, after evaluating your long and short-term financial goals, it is necessary to know about your current financial situation. It helps you decide how much to save according to the time horizon of your investment goal. So, before picking an asset, assess your monthly expenses, assets, liabilities, risk-taking ability, etc.

- ***Asset allocation***

After an analysis of goals and financial situation, the next step is asset allocation. You can choose between equity, bonds, money market instruments, gold, real estate, etc according to your risk appetite and needs.

Diversification of assets is also an essential step to minimise risks. Asset allocation usually depends on your present financial condition. But you can change it according to your risk appetite and needs which might change with income and age. Also, ensure to include liquid and fixed income assets in your portfolio. This helps to meet your urgent financial needs and long-term goals.

Depending on your needs and risk tolerance, you can choose between the following portfolios:

- Aggressive: The portfolio consists of riskier assets that generate apt returns.

- Defensive: The portfolio has assets that are less sensitive to market movements.
- Income: Income Portfolio helps provide regular profit distributions and dividends for the investor.
- Hybrid: The portfolio has several assets including equity, bonds, real estate, etc.

- ***Choose the right investment strategy***

An appropriate investment strategy is another crucial step for better and stable returns. The strategies of investment are as follows:

- **Short term**: A short-term investment strategy offers returns in a short duration. It may include short-term bonds, cash funds, money market instruments, etc.
- **Long term**: This strategy includes investments in stocks, mutual funds, real estate, gold, etc. Long-term investments generate returns over many years and usually offer lesser risk and more returns. While investing in long-term assets remember that the capital is locked in for a longer duration.
- **Active**: An active investment strategy involves the active participation of the investor in fund management.
- **Passive**: Passive investment strategy doesn't need day-to-day involvement. It allows the investor to sit back while their investment generates returns.

- ***Track and manage your portfolio***

After following the above investment process steps, it is time to track and manage your portfolio. This step involves reviewing the performance of assets at regular intervals. It ensures that your investments are in line with your financial goals and needs. Apart from this, it is important to change your fund allocation according to performance, market volatility and risk tolerance. You must know when to sell and buy specific assets to generate more returns or avoid losses.

8.5.2 Investment Appraisal Techniques

Investment appraisal techniques are also known as capital budgeting techniques. Capital budgeting helps an entity decide whether or not a project would offer the expected returns in the long term. Also, it helps a company to choose the best project when it faces a choice between two or more products. These techniques are payback period, internal rate of return, net present value, accounting rate of return, and profitability index. They are primarily meant to appraise the performance of a new project. Before beginning any new project, the first question that comes to our mind is, "Whether it is viable or profitable? These techniques answer this question very well. Each technique evaluates the project from a different angle and provides a different insight. Let us understand these techniques in brief.

These techniques are classified into two parts that are, discounted cash flow techniques and non-discounted cash flow techniques.

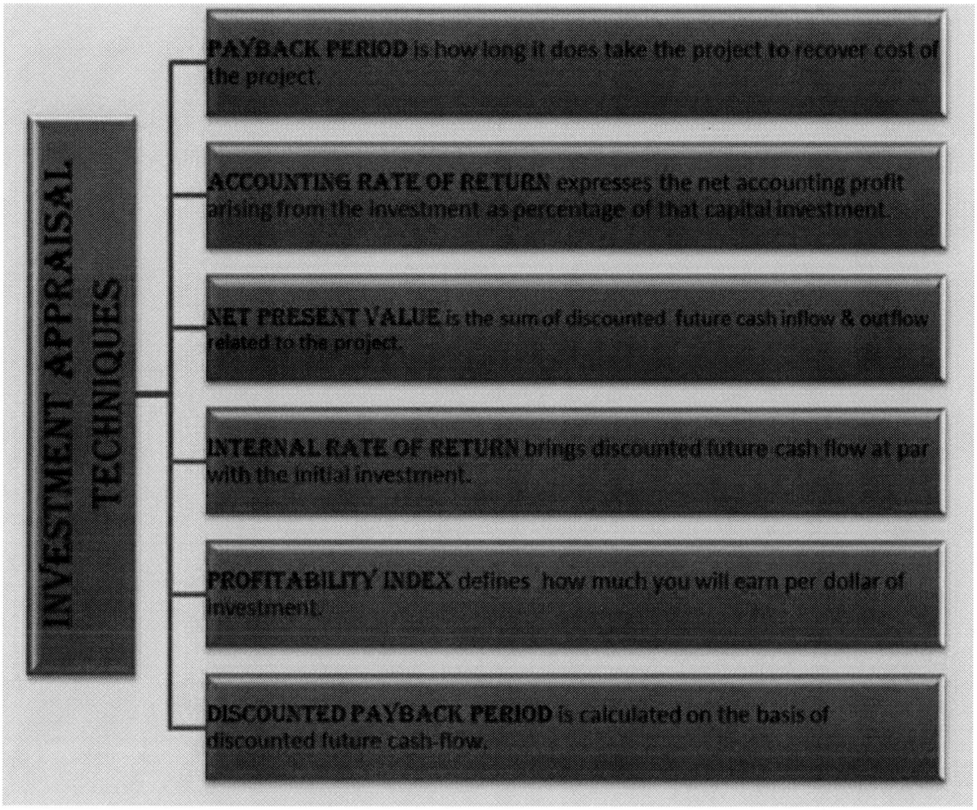

Figure 8.5: Capital budgeting techniques.

8.5.3 Non-Discounted Cash Flow Techniques

Under non-discounted cash flow techniques, future cash flows are not discounted to arrive at their present value. The following two techniques are classified under the head of non-discounted cash flow techniques:

1. Payback period
2. Accounting rate of return

Payback Period

One of the simplest investment appraisal techniques is the payback period. The payback technique states how long it takes for the project to generate sufficient cash flow to cover the project's initial cost.

For Example,

XYZ Inc. is considering buying a machine costing $100,000. There are two options Machine A and Machine B. Machine A will generate revenue of $ 50,000, $ 50,000 & $ 20,000 in year 1, year 2 & year 3 respectively while Machine B will generate revenue of $ 30,000, $ 40,000 & $ 60,000 in year 1, year 2 & year 3 respectively.

Machine A:

Year	Revenue	Cumulative Revenues
1	50,000	50,000
2	50,000	100,000
3	20,000	120,000

Machine B:

Year	Revenues	Cumulative Revenues
1	30,000	30,000
2	40,000	70,000
3	60,000	130,000

As per the above example, the payback period is 2 years & 2.5 years for machine A & machine B, respectively. According to the payback period method, machine A will be given preference.

The advantage of payback is that it is very easy to calculate & understand. Even people not from a finance background can easily understand it. But the disadvantage is that it ignores the time value of money & anything that happens after a payback point.

Accounting Rate of Return Method

Accounting rate of return is an accounting technique to measure the profit expected from an investment. It expresses the net accounting profit arising from the investment as a percentage of that capital investment. It is also known as return on investment or return on capital.

The formula of ARR is as follows:

ARR=(Average annual profit after tax / Initial investment) X 100

For Example

XYZ Inc. is looking to invest in some machinery to replace its current malfunctioning one. The new machine, which costs $ 420,000, would increase annual revenue by $ 200,000 and annual expense by $ 50,000. The machine is estimated to have a useful life of 12 years.

- Depreciation expense per year = $ 420,000/ 12 = $ 35,000
- Increase in average annual profit = $ 200,000 – ($ 50,000 + $ 35,000) = $ 115,000
- Initial investment = $ 420,000
- ARR = ($ 115,000 / $ 420,000) * 100 = 27.38%

Discounted Cash Flow Techniques

Discounted cash flow (DCF) techniques calculate the present value of cash flows to be received in the future. The following are classified under discounted cash flow techniques:

1. Net present value
2. Internal rate of return

3. Profitability index
4. Discounted payback period

Net Present Value

It is the most popular method of investment appraisal. Net present value is the sum of discounted future cash inflows & outflows related to the project. This method lays importance on the time value of money and is in line with the company's objective to maximize shareholders' wealth. Generally, the weighted average cost of capital (WACC) is the discounting factor for future cash flows in the net present value method.

In essence, this method sums up the discounted net cash flows from the investment by the minimum required rate of return & deducts the initial investment to give the 'net present value.' The company should accept the project if the NPV is positive.

The formula of NPV ={ + + …….. } – Initial Investment

Where,

CFi = Cash-flow of first period

CFii = Cash-flow of second period

CFiii = Cash-flow of third period

CFn = Cash-flow of nth period

n = No. of Periods

i = Discounting rate

For Example,

XYZ Inc. is starting the project at the cost of $ 100,000. The project will generate cash-flow of $ 40,000 , $ 50,000 & $ 50,000 in year 1, year 2 & year 3 respectively. The company's WACC is 10%. Find out NPV.

Formula of NPV = [$40,000/($1+0.1)^1$] + [$ 50,000 / $(1+0.1)^2$] +[$ 50,000/ $(1+0.1)^3$] – 100,000

Net present value = $ 36,363.63 + $ 41,322.31 +$ 37,565.74 – $ 100,000

= $ 115,251.68 – $ 100,000

The net present value of the project is $ 15,251.68.

Here, the net present value of the project is positive & therefore, the project should be accepted.

Internal Rate of Return Method

An internal rate of return is the discounting rate, which brings discounted future cash flows at par with the initial investment. In other words, it is the discounting rate at which the company will neither make a loss nor make a profit. We can also call this rate the yield on investment and the marginal efficiency of capital.

It is obtained by the trial & error method. We can also state that IRR is the rate at which the NPV of the project will be zero. i.e., Present value of cash inflow – Present value of cash outflow = zero.

The management approves an investment or a project if its IRR (internal rate of return) is higher than the cost of capital or the required rate of return.

Profitability Index

The profitability index defines how much you will earn per dollar of investment. The present value of an anticipated future cash flow divided by initial outflow gives the profitability index (PI) of the project. It is also one of the easy investment appraisal techniques.

Suppose the present value of anticipated future cash flow is $ 120,000 & the initial outflow is $ 100,000. Then the profitability index is 1.2. i.e. $ 120,000 / $ 100,000. This means each invested dollar is generating a revenue of 1.2 dollars. If the profitability index is more than 1, the project should be accepted & if it is less than 1, it should be rejected.

If we reduce complications, it is nothing but a different presentation of NPV.

Discounted Payback Period Method

Discounted payback period method is the same as the payback period method. The only difference in discounting payback method is that the payback period is calculated on the basis of discounted future cash flows. In contrast, the payback method is calculated on the basis of future cash flows.

8.6 DIVIDEND DECISIONS

Dividend decisions refer to the choices made by a company's management regarding the distribution of profits to its shareholders in the form of dividends. These decisions are crucial as they impact the financial health of the company and influence investor perceptions. Here's an overview of the key aspects related to dividend decisions:

Once a company makes a profit, it must decide on what to do with those profits. They could continue to retain the profits within the company, or they could pay out the profits to the owners of the firm in the form of dividends. The dividend policy decision involves two questions:

1) What fraction of earnings should be paid out, on average, over time? And,
2) What type of dividend policy should the firm follow? I.e. issues such as whether it should maintain steady dividend policy or a policy increasing dividend growth rate etc.

8.6.1 Dividend

"The term dividend refers to that portion of profit (after tax) which is distributed among the owners / shareholders of the firm".

In other words, dividend is that part of the net earnings of a corporation that is distributed to its stockholders. It is a payment made to the equity shareholders for their investment in the company.

Dividend is a reward to equity shareholders for their investment in the company. It is a basic right of equity shareholders to get dividend from the earnings of a company.

8.6.2 Dividend Policy

"Dividend policy determines the ultimate distribution of the firm's earnings between retention (that is reinvestment) and cash dividend payments of shareholders."

"Dividend policy means the practice that management follows in making dividend payout decisions, or in other words, the size and pattern of cash distributions over the time to shareholders."

In other words, dividend policy is the firm's plan of action to be followed when dividend decisions are made. It is the decision about how much of earnings to pay out as dividends versus retaining and reinvesting earnings in the firm.

Dividend policy must be evaluated in light of the objective of the firm namely, to choose a policy that will maximize the value of the firm to its shareholders. The dividend policy of a company reflects how prudent its financial management is. The future prospects, expansion, diversification mergers are effected by dividing policies and for a healthy and buoyant capital market, both dividends and retained earnings are important factors.

As we know in corporation, owners are shareholders but management is done through Board of directors. It is the Board of Directors to decide whether to pay dividend or retain earnings for future projects. It is a matter of conflict between shareholders and directors. Shareholders expect a quick return on their capital. On the other hand, directors have to consider a number of factors in determining divided policy.

Most of the company follows some kind of dividend policy. The usual policy of a company is to retain a position of net earnings and distribute the remaining amount to the shareholders. Many factors have to be evaluated before forming a long term dividend policy.

8.6.3 Types of Dividends

Classifications of dividends are based on the form in which they are paid. Following given below are the different types of dividends:

i. Cash dividend
ii. Bonus Shares referred to as stock dividend
iii. Property dividend interim dividend, annual dividend.
iv. Special- dividend, extra dividend etc.
v. Regular Cash dividend
vi. Scrip dividend
vii. Liquidating dividend
viii. Property dividend

Cash dividend

Companies mostly pay dividends in cash. A Company should have enough cash in its bank account when cash dividends are declared. If it does not have enough bank balance, arrangement should be made to borrow funds. When the Company follows a stable dividend policy, it should prepare a cash budget for the coming period to indicate the necessary funds, which would be needed to meet the regular dividend payments of the company. It is relatively difficult to make cash planning in anticipation of dividend needs when an unstable policy is followed.

The cash account and the reserve account of a company will be reduced when the cash dividend is paid. Thus, both the total assets and net worth of the company are reduced when the cash dividend is distributed. The market price of the share drops in most cases by the amount of the cash dividend distributed.

Bonus Shares

An issue of bonus share is the distribution of shares free of cost to the existing shareholders, In India, bonus shares are issued in addition to the cash dividend and not in lieu of cash dividend. Hence, Companies in India may supplement cash dividend by bonus issues. Issuing bonus shares increases the number of outstanding shares of the company. The bonus shares are distributed proportionately to the existing shareholder. Hence there is no dilution of ownership. The declaration of the bonus shares will increase the paid-up Share Capital and reduce the reserves and surplus retained earnings) of the company. The total net-worth (paid up capital plus reserves and surplus) is not affected by the bonus issue. Infact, a bonus issue represents a recapitalization of reserves and surplus. It is merely an accounting transfer from reserves and surplus to paid up capital.

The following are advantages of the bonus shares to shareholders:

1) *Tax benefit:* One of the advantages to shareholders in the receipt of bonus shares is the beneficial treatment of such dividends with regard to income taxes.
2) *Indication of higher future profits:* The issue of bonus shares is normally interpreted by shareholders as an indication of higher profitability.
3) *Future dividends may increase:* if a Company has been following a policy of paying a fixed amount of dividend per share and continues it after the declaration of the bonus issue, the total cash dividend of the shareholders will increase in the future.
4) *Psychological Value:* The declaration of the bonus issue may have a favorable psychological effect on shareholders. The receipt of bonus shares gives them a chance sell the shares to make capital gains without impairing their principal investment. They also associate it with the prosperity of the company.

Special dividend: In special circumstances Company declares Special dividends. Generally company declares special dividend in case of abnormal profits.

Extra- dividend: An extra dividend is an additional non-recurring dividend paid over and above the regular dividends by the company. Companies with fluctuating earnings payout additional dividends when their earnings warrant it, rather than fighting to keep a higher quantity of regular dividends.

Annual dividend: When annually company declares and pay dividend is defined as annual dividend.

Interim dividend: During the year any time company declares a dividend, it is defined as Interim dividend.

Regular cash dividends: They may be paid quarterly, monthly, semiannually or annually.

Scrip dividends: These are promises to make the payment of dividend at a future date: Instead of paying the dividend now, the firm elects to pay it at some later date. The 'scrip' issued to stockholders is merely a special form of promissory note or notes payable.

Liquidating dividends: These dividends are those which reduce paid-in capital: It is a prorata distribution of cash or property to stockholders as part of the dissolution of a business.

Property dividends: These dividends are payable in assets of the corporation other than cash. For example, a firm may distribute samples of its own product or shares in another company it owns to its stockholders.

8.6.4 Who makes dividend decision?

The company's Board of Directors makes dividend decisions. They are faced with the decision to pay out dividends or to reinvest the cash into new projects.

The tradeoff between paying dividends and retaining profits within the company:

The dividend policy decision is a trade-off between retaining earnings v/s paying out cash dividends.

Dividend policies must always consider two basic objectives:

1. Maximizing owners' wealth
2. Providing sufficient financing

While determining a firm's dividend policy, management must find a balance between current income for stockholders (dividends) and future growth of the company (retained earnings).

In applying a rational framework for dividend policy, a firm must consider the following two issues:

1. How much cash is available for paying dividends to equity investors, after meeting all needs-debt payments, capital expenditures and working capital (i.e. Free Cash Flow to Equity - FCFE)
2. To what extent are good projects available to the firm (i.e. Return on equity - ROE > Required Return)

Dividend Decision Matrix

Factors	FCFE> Dividends	FCFE<Dividends
ROE> Cost of Equity	Good Projects Cash flow surplus No Change	Good Projects Decrease Dividends Invest in Projects
ROE< Cost of Equity	Poor Projects Cash flow surplus Increase Dividends Reduce Investment	Poor Projects Cash flow Deficit Decrease Dividends Reduce Investment

Where, ROE: Return on Equity and FCFE: Free Cash Flow to Equity.

8.6.5 Types of Dividend Policy

In a classic study, Lintner surveyed a number of managers in the 1950's and asked how they set their dividend policy. Most of the respondents said that there were a target proportion of earnings that determined their policy. One firm's policy might be to pay out 40 % of earnings as dividends whereas another company might have a target of 50 %.

On the basis of interviews with corporate executives, Lintner concluded that firms select target payout ratios to which they gradually adjust actual dividend payments over time. This would suggest that dividends change with earnings.

However, dividend policies may vary between various firms as every firm sets its own policy for dividend distribution.

Firms may pursue any one of the following dividend policies:

1. ***Generous or liberal dividend policy***: Firms that follow this policy reward shareholders generously by stepping up dividend over the time.
2. ***Stable dividend policy***: Firms may follow the policy of: Stable dividend payout ratio: According to this policy, the percentage of earnings paid out of dividends remains constant. The dividends will fluctuate with the earnings of the company. Stable rupee (inflation adjusted) dividend policy: As per this policy the rupee level of dividends remains stable.
3. ***Low regular dividend plus extra dividend policy***: As per this policy, a low, regular dividend is maintained and when times are good an extra dividend is paid. Extra dividend is the additional dividend optionally paid by the firm if earnings are higher than normal in a given period. Although the regular portion will be predictable, the total dividend will be unpredictable.
4. ***Residual dividend policy***: Under this policy, dividends are paid out of earnings not needed to finance new acceptable capital projects. The dividends will fluctuate depending on investment opportunities available to the company.

5. ***Multiple dividend increase policy***: Some firms follow the policy of very frequent and small dividend increases. The objective is to give shareholders an illusion of movement and growth.
6. ***Uniform cash dividend plus bonus policy***: Under this policy, the minimum rate of dividend per share is paid in cash plus bonus shares are issued out of accumulated reserves. However, bonus shares are not given compulsorily on an annual basis. They may be given over a period of a certain number of years, for example 3-5 years depending on the accumulated reserves of the company that can be utilized for the purpose of issuing bonus.

8.7 SUMMARY

Capital expenditure (CapEx) and investment decisions are foundational to the financial management and strategic growth of a company. CapEx encompasses the total funds a company allocates to acquire, upgrade, manage, repair, or sustain its physical assets, such as plants, land, machinery, technology, or buildings. These expenditures are crucial for maintaining the operational capacity and efficiency of the company, and they are recorded on the company's balance sheet as fixed assets, subject to depreciation over time.

The process of making capital expenditure decisions involves evaluating potential investments in fixed assets that are not intended for sale, including significant infrastructure like land, buildings, and machinery. These decisions are pivotal because they involve substantial, often irreversible, allocations of financial resources and have a long-term impact on the company's operational scope and its ability to generate future revenue.

Investment decisions, meanwhile, focus on allocating the firm's resources across various asset classes (such as equity, bonds, real estate, and gold) to achieve the highest possible returns for investors. This process is intricate, requiring comprehensive planning and analysis due to the massive funds involved and the high stakes of these decisions. Firms face the challenge of limited available funds and competing demands for these resources, making the efficiency of investment decisions crucial for maximizing profitability and ensuring long-term sustainability.

Financing decisions, which determine the optimal mix of debt and equity financing, are equally critical. They directly influence the firm's profitability and risk profile, impacting the overall value provided to shareholders. Given the significant and long-lasting effects of these decisions on the company’s financial health and strategic direction, investors and managers devote considerable time and effort to investment and financing planning, underscoring the importance of meticulous analysis and strategic foresight in the financial management process.

8.8 REFERENCES

- Amat, O.; Campa, F. Contabilidad, Control de Gestion y Finanzas de Hotels; Profit: Barcelona, Spain, 2011.

- Atkinson, H.; Brown, J. Rethinking performance measures: Assessing progress in UK hotels. Int. J. Contemp. Hosp. Manag. 2001, 13, 128–135.
- Borges, A.; Macedo, J.; Moreira, A.; Isidro, H. Práticas de Contabilidade Financeira; Áreas: Lisbon, Portugal, 1998.
- Brealey, R. A., Myers, S. C., & Allen, F. (2017). "Principles of Corporate Finance." McGraw-Hill Education.
- Chand, M.; Sharma, K. Understanding the importance of management accounting practices in Indian hotel industry. Int. J. Hosp. Tour. Syst. 2020, 13, 29–36.
- Chenhall, R.H. Management control systems design within its organizational context: Findings from contingency-based research and directions for the future. Account. Organ. Soc. 2003, 28, 127–168.
- Copeland, T. E., Koller, T., & Murrin, J. (2000). "Valuation: Measuring and Managing the Value of Companies." John Wiley & Sons.
- Damodaran, A. (2012). "Investment Valuation: Tools and Techniques for Determining the Value of Any Asset." John Wiley & Sons.
- Faria, A. Management Accounting Systems in the Algarve Hotel Sector: Plan or Improvise? Ph.D. Thesis, University of Algarve, Faro, Portugal, 2012.
- Gitman, L. J., & Zutter, C. J. (2015). "Principles of Managerial Finance." Pearson.
- Graham, J. R., Smart, S. B., & Megginson, W. L. (2011). "Corporate Finance: Linking Theory to What Companies Do." Cengage Learning.
- Lamelas, J.P. Sistema Uniforme de Contabilidade Analítica de Gestão Hoteleira um Estudo de Caso, 1st ed.; Vislis Editores: Lisbon, Portugal, 2004.
- Lima Santos, L.; Gomes, C.; Arroteia, N. Management accounting practices in the Portuguese lodging industry. J. Mod. Account. Audit. 2012, 8, 1–14.
- Lima Santos, L.; Gomes, C.; Faria, A.R.; Lunkes, R.J.; Malheiros, C.; Silva da Rosa, F.; Nunes, C. Contabilidade de Gestão Hoteleira, 1st ed.; ATF—Edições Técnicas: Cacém, Portugal, 2016.
- Moyer, R. C., McGuigan, J. R., & Kretlow, W. J. (2011). "Contemporary Financial Management." South-Western Cengage Learning.
- Oliveira, H. The dismissal of information technology opportunities in the management accounting of small medium-sized tourism enterprise: A research note. Smart Innov. Syst. Technol. 2021, 209, 351–359.
- Pajrok, A. Application of target costing method in the hospitality industry. J. Educ. Cult. Soc. 2014, 5, 154–165.
- Pike, R., Neale, B., & Linsley, P. (2009). "Corporate Finance and Investment: Decisions & Strategies." FT Prentice Hall.
- Ross, S. A., Westerfield, R. W., & Jaffe, J. F. (2017). "Corporate Finance." McGraw-Hill Education.
- Shapiro, A. C. (2012). "Capital Budgeting and Investment Analysis." Pearson.
- Trigeorgis, L. (1996). "Real Options: Managerial Flexibility and Strategy in Resource Allocation." MIT Press.

INDEX